The Unnumbered

Also by Sam North

The Automatic Man
Chapel Street
The Gifting Programme
By Desire
The Lie of the Land

THE UNNUMBERED

SAM NORTH

First published in Great Britain by Scribner, 2004
An imprint of Simon & Schuster UK Ltd
A Viacom Company

1 3 5 7 9 10 8 6 4 2

Simon & Schuster UK Ltd
Africa House
64–78 Kingsway
London WC2B 6AH

www.simonsays.co.uk

Hardback ISBN 0-7432-4850-3
Trade Paperback ISBN 0-7432-4851-1

A CIP catalogue record for this book
is available from the British Library

Typeset by M Rules
Printed and bound in Great Britain by
Mackays of Chatham plc, Chatham, Kent

THE
UNNUMBERED

ONE

Nio Niopolous was planted on the pedestrian bridge spanning the A406 North Circular Road, looking over the handrail on to the traffic below. Hundreds of vehicles hammered along, nose to tail, thousands of people per hour covering millions of miles. He could see the odd pair of hands on a steering wheel, a lap, a pair of knees, as they flashed past. He wondered where everyone was going, what they all did for a living, how so many of them could all fit . . . He squinted until the Orions, the Astras, the BMWs and the Nissans all blurred together; and if the streams of traffic were a bead curtain then he wanted to claw it apart and allow this one person to step through, into his life; it would be some journey they'd have.

He felt giddy, staring down. Underneath the speeding cars the tarmac was pearly grey, written with its code of white lines, seamed with repairs, and beneath the road was raw earth, he could see it in his mind's eye, brown like dark sugar, fruitless, waiting. Only a hundred yards ahead, on the left, it rose stumbling to the surface to grow the tangled profusion of the old St Pancras Cemetery with its crowded lines of the dead. Would her grave be next to his, share the same surname, describe them as beloved? Perhaps they'd be old, with a family of their own. Worst of all would be if his death and hers were separated by decades – empty time and space – Nio couldn't bear that thought.

There were further patches of open ground around St Pancras Cemetery – it was bordered by Coldfall Wood and the playing fields on two sides, and the allotments were tacked on the back. The area was well trampled by dog-walkers, runners, gardeners, young lovers, the bereaved, footballers and sportsmen, council workmen, loners and perverts, tearaway youths – but, like no one else's, it was Nio's domain. He'd covered every inch, knew it backwards. His migrations would scribble over pages 15, 28 and 29 of London's A–Z map, except the North Circular Road would be a clear band, unmarked; he couldn't drive – not yet – so never had joined this river of people flowing under the bridge, all of them curious, headlong in pursuit of life and love and . . .

Then his reverie was interrupted.

At first he thought it was a bird – a jay or a magpie – but the cry lasted too long. He glanced left. It was a woman in trouble – the sound of, anyway – and he was going to try to help, or leave well alone, depending on the dispute. A dozen steps carried him back over the bridge towards Muswell Hill. From here he could see down the slip road which funnelled traffic on to the A406 westbound carriageway; and parked tight into the edge, camouflaged by the vast, broken skeleton of wrecked cars piled on the lot of ground beyond, was a dilapidated caravan. Its door hung open; the woman was leaning out and again loosed a stream of cries, her voice rising and falling sharply in volume, in pitch. She was a bright patch of colour and movement, of human life, in this bleak, closed off place where everyone else was safe in their cars. Nio felt a lurch of anger, mixed with fear. She was either being pushed out or prevented from leaving, he couldn't tell which – the infrastructure of the bridge interrupted his view. He ambled closer, his stomach heavy with a sudden block of nerves. Exhaust fumes caught in his throat. The smell was as familiar as that of the hot tarmac and the takeaway food and the parched, dry foliage in these summer months. The sun was harsh on his forehead, he wiped the back of his wrist against the dark hair which curled across his crown and took away a lick of sweat. Beside him, waiting, stood the line of cars, exhaling quietly. A number of their occupants were glancing towards the fraças through open side windows but they couldn't help, they had to stay in their vehicles, they were queueing at a red light which might change at any moment and they'd be required to move off.

As Nio walked down the slip road the woman – girl – escaped, she came running towards him; uphill and against the flow of traffic her arms flailed as if for all these twenty yards she was saving herself from falling. His instinct was to hold out his hands and catch her like you would an escaped animal but it might frighten her so he stood aside. As she passed by he shouted, 'D'you need help?!' but she didn't respond, her run was headlong, she pawed her way to the main road, a twist of printed fabric blown past, her hair and breath a cloud mixed around her face – he saw she was of Asian descent. Then he was left standing on the edge of the slip road, cars passing by, their drivers offering incurious looks. It felt like a spring cocked in him, the desire to help, but he couldn't know what was for the best. Her breath – harsh, urgent, quick – stuck in his memory. She had been frightened and it had infected him; he wanted to run, also. Yet, what was the right thing to do, now that she'd fled?

Downhill from his position, a figure was standing at the doorway of the caravan, watching. For a moment both men registered the encounter, then the other man walked towards Nio. His movement was odd, punctuated by sudden jerks of his limbs as if there were too much electricity in his nervous system.

Nio looked back up the slope; the girl had disappeared. Since he was guarding her escape it was important to be here – so he was stuck. He guessed it had been a domestic dispute and he was about to be told to mind his own business. Thankfully, the man stopped a few yards away, so maybe Nio wouldn't be physically attacked. The other man's hands were on his hips. He wore a lightweight, glossy leather jacket and white jeans. One cuff of his blue shirt was frayed and a twist of thread hung from his wrist like jewellery. He was thin, with a prominent nose structure which seemed to take in part of his forehead and mouth as well. His skin colour was grey more than white and his eyes held Nio's accusingly.

'All right?' asked Nio. He was ready to agree it was none of his business. His smile was broad, engaging. He would always be the peacemaker, smooth away trouble, make everyone happy. Now, he just needed to allow her enough time to get away.

'I called the police.' The man's tone was unpleasant. He tapped at the mobile phone which hung at his belt, as if it were a gun.

'What?' Nio was confused.

'I've called the police,' he repeated, 'so your game's up, mate.'

For several long moments there was silence. 'Whatever you've done,' the man continued, 'I've clocked you, I can put the finger on you', and he pointed heavily, Nio was made sure of that finger, and so he was wrong-footed now. This stranger obviously thought that *he*, in some way . . . He explained, 'I was just walking over the footbridge and I heard a woman call out, so I came back—'

The man's knee wagged nervously, then stopped. 'I was phoning the police, she was sitting quietly in my caravan drying her eyes, when she looks through the window, sees you coming and runs for it, hell for leather.'

A complete picture appeared in front of him, Nio suddenly understood. 'So *you* don't know her?!'

'*I* don't know her from Adam.' The man stepped closer, lowered his voice. 'There was a banging on my door, all sorts of commotion, and she tells me she's been attacked, some man—' He shrugged, glanced here and there, 'She's all over the place, so I sit her down and call the police.'

Moments passed. Both men stood by the side of the slip road. Cars came steadily forth from an inexhaustible supply; the occupants showed their faces in a flash of white, they must have wondered what on earth kept these two, motionless, in such an exhaust-blasted, unwholesome place.

'Well—' Nio stirred, broke the silence. 'OK then, I guess the police will catch up with her.' He prepared to move off, his mind turning to his original destination: the Friern Barnet Mental Hospital. He should be on his way. The incident had emptied of alarm, it had soothed itself. There was no need for him after all. Featureless minutes stretched ahead here; he didn't want to get involved in any explanation if there was no need.

Then, the other man was holding his elbow. 'Hold on a minute.'

What was happening? Nio found this difficult to process. He was taken with a sense of disbelief. He wanted to withdraw his elbow from this stranger's grip. He knew his own arm was the stronger, he was taller and his chest was deeper, his neck thicker, but even so, the aggression bled out of Nio, because it was only a misunderstanding.

'Just for a bit,' added the man.

'What?'

'Till the police come.'

'I don't think—'

'Look at it from my point of view,' the man interrupted, doggedly. 'How'm I to know you're telling the truth? You say you don't have anything to do with it, but all I see is that when she spots you coming over, she takes off as if you—' He shrugged. 'Eh?'

'I've never seen her before.'

'All the same, she said she'd been attacked. What does that mean, what did you do to her?'

Nio considered a moment. 'I don't mind waiting for the police. But I didn't do anything. Or see anyone.'

'Let's wait inside the caravan, then, OK?' The man tilted him firmly. 'Citizen's arrest, all right?'

'Inside this caravan here?'

'Yes.'

Nio was head-shakingly astonished but he agreed. As they walked down the slope, he admired this man's sense of justice, he compared it to his own, they were obviously alike on that score, but if he himself were being arrested, it seemed unfair – he'd intended to help but potentially had ended up in trouble himself. Yet, he'd nothing to fear. The police would deal quickly with the situation and if his evidence was needed, then he'd give it.

They approached the caravan. It was small, hump-backed, with an oblong window at the back, and practically in the ground with disrepair, it hardly stood out from the wrecker's yard immediately behind. It had the word 'Cherokee' written across the back in slanted writing. The bodywork was a discoloured cream, mottled with road dirt. No passer by would be able to see in through the windows, they'd been covered up from the inside. The wheel looked tired, with a crescent of debris lodged against the uphill side. The alloy trim was corroded. Nio found himself stepping through the door from which the girl had escaped not a few minutes ago. He ducked his head, felt the sudden implosion of space – mild claustrophobia – and the panic of having a thin, uncertain, hollow-sounding floor beneath his size eleven boots and walls made of cardboard within touching distance on every side. Behind him came the grating sound of the door being pulled shut, and the unwanted intimacy of the other man sharing this confined space. It was a rat's nest of litter – there were scores of newspapers, food wrappings and empty cans on every surface. The narrow foam seating constructed in an H shape was slashed, vandalized. There was a miniature kitchen unit in one corner, but it was piled with junk – multiple copies of some magazine or other were strewn in the sink and on the draining board. The fold-down bed lurched, broken footed. There was a curtain track which was set in the ceiling – presumably to partition off a sleeping area, but it dangled uselessly. The table was in pieces, leaning against one wall awaiting repair. Nio allowed himself to be guided, then he sat on the bed, while the other man perched on the bunk seat. Everything was too close. He could if he wanted reach out and touch either wall, the ceiling, this stranger's knee, all at once. On the floor, he noticed, were hundreds of those miniature envelopes you'd use if you were sending someone flowers.

For a while, nothing was said. The man occupied himself with the business of rolling a cigarette and wiping his nose on the back of his hand. Nio continued to look around. He could see where the fittings had been removed and the infrastructure left to hang; this place was about to collapse. A fire had once been set in the corner and had scorched the wall and cracked the panes of glass on that side. A slight movement caught his eye and he realized he was looking at a pigeon, blinking nervously but otherwise unmoving, settled in the lip of the skylight.

They waited. The traffic lights squaring off this side of the bridge must have changed again – in sequence with the colours green and red, each new set of cars released down the slip road added to the background concussion of the A406 fifty yards away and this was the only noise, apart from the almost inaudible sound of an engine rising and falling earnestly in tone as the electromagnet lifted the wrecked vehicles, nearby.

Nio examined the windows which – he could see now – had been pasted over with newspaper and the light was therefore diffused, giving a yellowish glow to the cluttered oblong of space.

'Police here in a moment,' murmured the stranger, tamping his cigarette with the end of a match.

'Yup, OK.'

Nio listened for a siren, but apparently they were slow in responding.

It was odd: to be here in this caravan which, yes, he'd noticed before, but he'd always thought it was part of the scrapyard.

Presumably it belonged to this weird guy opposite him. Yet it didn't fit. How come he was dressed so smartly if he lived here? The caravan had been stuck in this spot for months – the debris caught by the wheel had told him that. 'You . . . er—' He had to break the silence. '. . . live here or—?' he asked.

The man blinked. 'Been here a while,' he answered, 'and before that, the next roadworks along. Kind of becomes like home, you know?'

'Roadworks?' Nio sensed the answer coming at him.

'Under contract to the Highways Commission and Haringey Council. Provide the free recovery.'

'Oh, right.'

'See?' asked the man, standing up now with his roll-up cigarette on his lip. He nodded at the ceiling above Nio's head. Nio turned and saw the small television monitor bolted to a bracket. As he watched, the picture jumped and settled for a minute on a stretch of the A406 which Nio recognized as only a short distance westward from here, where cars were funnelled through a single lane restriction while a new bridge was built. That explained it, the works had been going on for more than a year. On the television screen each vehicle was a ghostly image, moving silently in an orderly fashion; it was difficult to imagine that inside were people, innocent families.

'They say free recovery but of course I'm paid,' the man tapped the wall with his knuckle, 'nothing's for free is it, but they sit in their cars, nervous often, especially the women, wondering how it's done, how someone knows to come out. It's a public service, though, I'm the guardian angel, you know? Usually, have my rig here, parked up or whatever, but . . .' he sniffed, '. . . in for a service myself. Trusting there's no litter for a couple hours.'

This man was working, it was his paid job to be here, he had that over Nio, no wonder his confidence. Nio liked people's work, what they put their hands to. Yet this man didn't look like a mechanic, maybe he wasn't actually working at the moment. He wore a shiny leather jacket, not overalls. His hands were clean. His trousers looked brand new. Maybe it was his day off.

They fell silent again. The police failed to arrive. Nio wondered if there was an emergency somewhere else in the borough, that they couldn't get here faster. Ten minutes! She might as well have been torn limb from limb for all the good the emergency call would have done.

Another minute ticked by.

The man patrolled the caravan, checking the windows, the light tinting his face as he leaned over – like a blush of jaundice, suddenly.

Nio waited.

'Guess what?' the other man began.

'What?'

'Well, here we are, you and me, a pair of guys who weren't going to let this go, we wanted to help that girl and we took action, unlike, you might think, the police, obviously they don't rate it enough to come and check it out.' Then he added emphatically, 'It's like we're the police. Or better. Eh? It's like we're brothers in arms.'

A sense of pride stole over Nio; it expanded quickly in the golden light of the caravan to cover also his introduction to this stranger. Yes, they'd both decided to try to help the woman, they hadn't taken the easy path out of the situation. Nio was struck by the absurdity of it just happening, out of the blue like this – he'd thought he was making his usual trip to the disused mental hospital, but instead, he was a volunteer in the fight against violence against women! 'I suppose,' he admitted.

'Definitely. *We're* the heroes, *we* were the ones who took action,' said the man, 'it was only us, wasn't it, who were ready to put ourselves out?' He stared at Nio, then went on, 'All those pricks in their cars, all the people running this way and that, *but*, it was only you and me that bothered. We're meant to call for help aren't we, all good citizens eh, but what happened when we did?' He strode to the door of the caravan and pulled it open, letting in the breath of the cars and the outside noise, calling back, 'Where were you going, anyhow?'

Nio rose to his feet, it was dawning on him that he was no longer a prisoner, even a voluntary one, the map of events had changed without him noticing, he was being let go. He answered, 'To Friern Barnet. To the old mental hospital? You know it? I work in the grounds there.'

'You've wasted your time, haven't you.' The other man made it sound like his own complaint. 'Still. Let me have your address anyway? In case the police want to know. Yeh?'

His address – it was a sticky question. Nio didn't want to admit to a stranger that over the last three years he'd been slowly building a shack in a hidden corner of St Pancras Cemetery, using old doors and timbers recovered from skips. It was weathertight now, and had a pot-bellied stove and a chimney, it even boasted two storeys. This construction had to be kept secret otherwise it'd be torn down by the local council, he was sure of that. So he replied that he still lived at home, at his parents' dilapidated house in Muswell Hill, the same trick as when he signed on, and when he was arrested on the graffiti charge, for decorating a bus stop with psychedelic, mind-boggling patterns. 'Curzon Road.'

'Yeh, OK,' said the other man, 'so what's the actual number?'

'Seventeen. It's the one with the ice-cream vans outside,' he added. His mum and dad were the first generation immigrants, they'd sold ice-cream from the pair of Bedford vans for the whole of their working lives and still barely spoke English.

He noticed again how the other man's forehead was raked sharply back from the centre which gave the impression that his face had once been squashed, or slammed in a door. 'Right, I know where you are now,' he said. 'We can say goodbye.'

'OK, bye!' said Nio, smiling in wonder. 'Thank you.' He stepped out of the caravan and turned to give the stranger a handshake. He felt the brief clasp, and then, once it was done with, the other man actually pushed Nio's hand away, as if lightly batting aside a ball thrown to him.

Nio blinked in the late afternoon sunlight. The world seemed like a different place. Yet there it all was, same as before: bridge, North Circular, Tesco superstore, skate park, waste ground, carbreaker's yard. He started walking.

It took a hundred yards for him to start slipping back into his own skin. That was weird. What kind of man was that? He wasn't sure what had happened back there.

He lifted his T-shirt to his face, wiped his nose, but he must stop that habit, they were building site manners, she wouldn't like it.

Where had he been, in his head, before this interruption?

Oh yes, Mila, beautiful as anything, never far from his thoughts, always cast in her best light, the unruly blonde hair held in clips or tied with rags and beads, the streetwise clothes, what a smile as well, thick eyebrows widely spaced over dark eyes . . . he found her at each turn, she inhabited him. His imagining of her was visceral, he conjured her presence and felt its effect, how it opened his heart and there he followed. He sent a wish – vehement, wilful – for her to be let in . . .

The sweetshop boy was at his station behind the ranks of confectionery when this girl came into the shop, at first he thought definitely OK, but then a couple of glances later, it was like being whacked across the side of the head. Christ. He tried to appear busy, swayed from side to side, looking for whatever, he wished there were something brilliant he could be doing – but what? Truly, she was like something out of a magazine. Better. He stared, couldn't stop himself. She had olive green combat trousers on, with a sparkly boob tube. Her stomach was flat as a plank from one hip to the other. Her face – it was a fight not to look at it, or he'd only look too much, for the rest of his life he could drink in that face. It spoke to him – what did it say, the clear brow, the eyebrows wide apart and sloping down, such a perfect shape, the eyes grazing the sweets in front of her? All that her face was asking, surely, was for him, himself, to be *enough*, fucking *man* enough . . . He felt his whole spirit rise to the challenge, he could slay a dragon now, *had* to, minimum. She picked up bubble gum, a mint Aero and the Sweethearts, and showed them to him, laid out in the palm of her hand. His heart sank because wasn't it like, the pits, that all he could do was take money off her? Was that all he amounted to? He couldn't do it – and so he wouldn't. No. He waved at her, rolled his eyes towards his dad, signalled that he was *giving* her the sweets, quick though before he noticed. His reward was her suddenly arrested expression, then her amused stare, she'd noticed him and now she drew a breath, probably she was about to thank him but she glanced around, smiled and mouthed the words instead.

Then it was a joke, that the lights blinked brightly and blew the fuse just as she was walking out. He almost laughed. His dad was on the ladder anyway, sorting the top shelf of the fridge, so he only had to move it to climb to the fuse box and push back the trip switch. Meanwhile, he himself went to the doorway and pretended to fiddle with the rack of papers just so he could watch her going down the street. Twenty out of ten. Thirty out of ten. That boy alongside her must be her younger brother, maybe? A filling came loose from his molar and fell on his tongue, it seemed – again – pretty logical that she was responsible for that as well. He mouthed the particles to the front and spat them out. He put the tip of his tongue to work, finding the hole.

When he lost sight of her he turned back indoors and the shop was the same as ever, the lights were back on, but he couldn't keep still, there was a mad energy suddenly in his frame, he wanted to follow her, find out her name, put himself up for going out with her. He squeezed through to the back, via the storeroom, to stand in front of the mirror in the toilet and check he was there, at all. Maybe she'd come in tomorrow. He wrapped an arm in front of his neck, pushing his elbow until that hand could slip under his shirt and reach between his shoulder blades, where he found his crop of boils. He squeezed them all, hard as he could.

Mila trotted down to the bottom of Sydney Road. She was riding on stacked heels which slowed her up. Her little brother ran in front sometimes, then behind, up on the bank to one side, or he stopped to look inside cars. She was more interested in the houses. Any of these places, she'd die for. When she saw one that was boarded up she had to stop herself from turning into the pathway and checking around the edges of the chipboard because if she found a gap only an inch wide, they'd be in there, she and her whole family, if no one else wanted it. She tried to imagine what it would be like to live behind such a door, with a number on it, an address, a home.

She ducked into the newsagent's to load up with sweets: Hubba Bubba Seriously Strawberry, Mint Aero, the fizzy tablets called Sweethearts which had love messages written on them like 'you're mine' or 'kiss me'. She kept one eye on her brother, to make sure he wasn't stealing anything. There was the usual reaction in here, like anywhere she went – the boy behind the counter, quite a groovy kid with spiky hair, hung open his mouth, stared. His dad it was maybe practically fell off the stepladder trying to look down her top, and the boy wouldn't take any money for the sweets. She sort of had to go along with it, take it as more of the same good luck she always got, because she looked OK. She grabbed her little brother's collar to pull him away from the magazines. They walked out.

Mila chewed hard on the strawberry Hubba Bubba. She had the address in her head, number 262. She wound down the hill, closer to the North Circular, the Edwardian houses disappeared and instead there were blocks of flats built five storeys high, set back from the road with patches of grass between them. There were fewer cars, all cheaper, older, slumped at the kerbside. She stared at the entrance to one of the blocks, she could see a plaque mounted next to it, marked 121–137. She kept going.

It was the fourth block, close to the end of the road, where the eight-foot-high wooden partition screened the North Circular from view. She went into the stairwell and climbed to the third highest walkway. Here an arrow pointed her along the balcony which fronted flats 260–265. Little Vlad went ahead, running his fingers along the top of the parapet and looking at the view. She found it, the door was painted blue and had a square of reinforced glass in the middle. Before she pushed the bell she tugged at her top and practised English greetings. She knew all the words but didn't always put them in the right order and she didn't like her own accent. Of course, she had her smile ready. She checked to see that her brother was out of the way. He was leaning against the parapet and looking over the golf course, beyond the rough ground to the retail park in the middle distance. He was held by the open space. Little Vlad, who was so sharp and quick, who hardly paused, didn't stop hunting stuff down for himself, not for anyone, was suddenly motionless, there was just the slight twist of his toe against the concrete. She thought she might remember him like that for ever.

The buzzer was under her finger; she pressed. Immediately from inside the flat there was the sound of a dog barking and a girl's voice called, 'Hold on.' Mila popped the gum from her mouth, stuck it back in the wrapper. The dog was just the other side of the door. There came the scratch of its nails on the woodwork. A thump. The girl's voice came again, 'Hold on.'

Eventually, the door clicked and stood open a fraction of an inch.

'It's open,' called the voice cheerily. 'Come in.'

Mila pushed – the dog was there, wagging its tail, smiling. She bent to pet it and looked down the dim corridor. 'Hullo?' she called.

'Yeh, I'm here.'

She could see the girl framed by the lounge doorway at the other end of the corridor, sitting with a plump arm on the side rest of a chair; in her hand stood the black stick of the television remote control. 'It was him who opened the door for you,' called the girl.

'He open the door?' exclaimed Mila.

'Always does, you let people in, don't you Sandy?'

Mila walked into the lounge. She thought it was best to go on petting the dog, but she took in the TV, the table pushed against the wall, and the sports trophies, someone had won a lot of identical little silver cups, very small, with the figure of a man running on top of them. Then she dared to look at the girl again to read her face, see that she was big, with a frank, open gaze. Her legs, encased in black leggings, were open carelessly wide, like a man's. She asked, 'So you're Mila, right?'

'Yes, and you Donna?'

'Donna Owen, you like the name OK?'

'Is fine, yes . . .'

For a moment they both looked at the television. On the screen a girl was lying on her side, dressed in a skimpy one-piece nightdress. Curled around her was the figure of a man dressed only in boxer shorts.

'What this programme?' asked Mila politely.

'*Baby Club*. Showing how to have sex when you're pregnant.'

An elegantly dressed middle-aged woman took the models and arranged them in a different position. The models' faces were downcast, solemn as they crossed limbs and adopted a static embrace. 'But this way,' the woman explained, 'she can control the angle of penetration . . .'

'So it's Tesco's if I remember?' asked Donna.

'I so hope, yes, if that's all OK?'

'Should be. I've never worked there before. Go on to that table look.'

Mila moved obligingly to the sidetable.

'That bit of paper, see?'

'This?' Mila picked up a folded square closely printed with information.

'Bring it over. You ever seen one before?'

Mila shook her head.

'Bring it me then. Doesn't matter you haven't. But look. Pee forty-five, up in the corner. It's the name of the form, that's what they'll ask you for, where's your pee forty-five. There's your name. Donna G. Owen you are. The G stands for Gabriella. Here – your National Insurance, NI they call it for short. OG 01 03 52 B. This is your birthday, right, you're twenty, OK?'

Mila wondered, 'Can I look twenty?'

Donna frowned for a moment. 'Yehhh – go on, course you can. Just about. They're not going to bother anyway.'

'Better learn the birthday, know it, so I can say to them.'

'Don't worry about it. Just hand it over if you get past the interview. They won't give a shit. Y'know, if I were you I'd use your real name as well, tell them it's a nickname, it's what your family call you. Otherwise they'll be, like, shouting "Donna!!" over and over and you won't notice. Bit suspicious.'

'What about my accent, they notice my accent.'

'Tell 'em you were brought up somewhere else. Like France. France is all right. And say your dad's English, that'll do. They're so desperate for people, they're not going to try and catch you out, you know. Not really.

'Thank you. And – how do I pay? What is the system?'

'First off, go and make us a cup of tea. Kitchen's through there.'

Mila smiled. 'OK.' She went through and found a kettle. A small corner had been torn out of the box of teabags, as if a mouse had poked its nose through. She washed a cup, ready. Next door, she could hear the smooth voice of the television, 'No, that's a common misunderstanding, you can have sex right up to the last moment, there's no reason why not, unless either of you feel . . .' Mila waited. This was weird – other people's lives. Here was Donna's kitchen, she was sat in the lounge, there was the dog. She looked up to see her brother pass by the window, he was wandering up and down the walkway outside. She looked for a bottle of milk, but could only find some little individual cartons taken from a café. The empties were littering the place so they must be what she used. Mila peeled back the foil and poured one into the tea, stirred it and took out the teabag, then walked it through.

'Cheers,' said Donna. She planted the cup on the arm of her chair. 'So what will happen, right, is if you get the job, you pay me the first week's wages and then ten per cent of everything after that, so if you earn a hundred a week you give me ten, OK?'

Mila frowned. 'Is enough? I mean, how can you . . . I mean—'

'Don't worry about me,' replied Donna airily, 'I've got more than one job you know.'

'Oh,' replied Mila, chastened.

'Tell me how it goes. And bring me back the P45 if you don't get it? They're expensive, they are.'

'Of course. Yes.'

'Or else I might have to kill you!' Then Donna added, 'Joke.'

They watched TV for a while. Donna asked her, 'How long you been here then?'

'Three years,' replied Mila.

'Hmmm. And you've got, like, family here?'

'Yes.' Mila nodded vigorously. 'Some of my family is here.'

'They working?'

'Sometimes bits and pieces. We were picking vegetables . . . and now—' She trailed off. 'My mother and little sister on a cleaning gang. In the West End. I was, too. My dad—' She shrugged.

'Hmmm. Well, you know, if you want passports, driving licences, all that stuff, here's the place, we don't keep anything here, of course, but just come over and put in an order.'

'Thanks.'

Mila didn't know how to say goodbye. This was it, over and done with, but it was strange how the girl didn't get up. Eventually she just stood herself.

'All righty,' said Donna, 'you know where I am and I know where you are, so we should get on all right.' She nodded along the corridor. 'Sandy will see you out.'

Mila was escorted back by the dog, who looked up at her anxiously when she was outside. 'Goodbye!' she called back. She heard Donna's reply, 'Cheers, good luck!' while the door moved across between them. The dog was panting. Then came Donna's low command, 'Close the door Sandy. Close the door. Go on, close the door.' Mila thought it was her duty to wait while the door bounced on the latch once or twice, then there was a click and it was shut.

She unpacked the Hubba Bubba and popped it back in, gathered up her little brother, headed off.

Later that afternoon her heart was in her mouth as she slid the P45 across the desk and gave the unfamiliar name. She was sure the thick way it sounded coming from her mouth must betray her, but it went off all right, and she did, she landed the job, they didn't question the fake document, she was in.

Anjali stopped running when she reached Greenham Road. Somewhere, she'd lost her glasses. Sweat dampened her brow and stung her eyes. Her legs were empty of strength. Breath sawed harshly back and forth in her chest.

Everything was perfectly all right. Nothing had happened. She'd escaped. She'd been lucky. She wanted to go home, tell everyone about it. Laugh even. She'd been in a scrape. Maybe inform the police. After all, if she hadn't struggled, if she hadn't run, then . . .

Yet, the idea of her family or the police – or anyone – knowing how stupid she'd been . . . She relived the incident continually as she walked, over and over. She'd trusted him – really liked him! – and how wrong she'd been, he'd turned out to be someone utterly, completely different. More than anything she wanted to lock it inside herself, it shouldn't ever be known, felt by anyone else . . .

Although she'd slowed to a walk her heart knocked against her chest still. Questions ran at her, one after another: where should she go – to the police, home, her sister's? She told herself to brush it off, it wasn't too bad, things like that happened all the time, by next week she would have forgotten about it.

On each side houses walked by. They contained families: these streets were a breeding ground. She felt the density of human life, its fertile growth, its self-confidence, exclude her. The attack on her was a travesty of the common sexual act that within the walls of *this* house and *this* one fuelled desire, inspired daily urges of love and satisfaction and grew families . . .

Ahead of her, builders ran to and fro pushing wheelbarrows; she crossed to the other side. She decided to go home, tell her mother.

Then she was running again. The houses slid past more quickly: fence, hedge, window, garage, wall. She weaved through passers-by – their curiosity she could deal with, they'd think she was hurrying for a late music lesson or from a row with her parents or boyfriend. Let them look, and guess, they'd none of them know; whereas the truth was like a thread, each step entangled her in more complicated knots. She wanted to turn the clock back, not to have listened to him, not to have liked him for one moment, not to have suffered that failure. She wanted to be someone else.

Now she could see the slatted grey wooden fence held by white-painted concrete posts that marked out the front of her family home. It brought a surge of energy and relief. She ran for all she was worth and alongside her – so it seemed – ran the 5-year-old girl she'd once been, coming home from school. The echo of the smaller footsteps was haunting because at that age running had been triggered usually by happiness and she'd actually lived in this house, whereas now . . .

She slowed to a walk, suddenly concerned not to bring shame on her house, this was the worst crime. To mark the whole family with distress, misfortune – in families like hers – wasn't allowed, *ever*. She slowed her breathing, blinked away tears. As long as she herself was fine, if her family saw that she was confident – and she could tell them she'd fought him off after all – then everything would be all right, they could be proud of her. She pushed at the little gate and felt its familiar rub against the path and its signature squeak, which everyone inside would have noticed. She could hear the shouting of her younger brothers and the trample of footsteps over the wooden floors – the accelerated pulse of a house in which young people lived.

Her glasses were lost – yet, somehow, she still had her bag. She searched in it, but couldn't find the keys. She went for the bell push, then drew back. The news she had to tell was a stone she'd throw, knocking out the fun and games, dispelling the human warmth, drawing the household to a stop, so it could examine her shame. She couldn't carry it off, not straightaway. She wasn't strong enough yet. A flood of guilt bore her away, back down the path.

Then she stopped – and faced up to the door again. For a moment she thought it would open without her knocking: a shadow passed behind the coloured glass panels set in the door.

Her mother, she could tell. She held her breath, waiting, but the door remained closed.

A thought ran at her in the same moment: she really should tell the police, that would stop him, because it might happen to someone else and next time maybe that other person wouldn't fight him off – so he must be reported. But she couldn't deal with it, she wasn't that far along yet, she had to look after herself first, wait just for a bit, until she was stronger. Two seconds later she told herself she'd never be able to go to the police and tell them that she – of all people – had put a lonely hearts ad in the local paper. It was too shameful.

She began to chip away at an idea: don't tell anyone, ever. Just mend herself quietly and carry on with her life. Or, maybe tell only her mother, then her father and brothers – the men – needn't know, the impact wouldn't hit, together the women would be able to contain it. She turned away for the second time and passed through the gate, handling it carefully to minimize the noise; and after a moment's hesitation she really did leave, she began to walk up the road to the bus stop. Already her next move was clear: she'd go back to her room in the hall of residence and catch her breath, fight her way back, recover. Then maybe she'd call her mother, arrange to meet her in private. She summoned in her mind's eye the occasion: she and her mum, sitting on the bed in the All Saints site of Middlesex University, holding hands and walking the crisis forward, calmly and in private. 'Mum, I met this guy, he seemed nice, but then suddenly . . .'

Her mum would heal her.

She was swept up by the throng of people pushing forwards to board the 102 bus. As she stumbled up the steps to pay, the incident was an ache in her bones – *unfair.*

Nio strolled into the superstore and before he'd finished enjoying the importance of having these automatic doors *swish* open to welcome him, the second set of doors *swished* open and he was enclosed in the jangling, family embrace of Tesco.

He paused at one end of the row of checkout desks and sought her out. He grazed them all but couldn't find her; the backs of the tellers were towards him and many were obscured by threads of customers passing through. He took a step or two forwards and noticed that one of the queues was longer; this would lead to her position, he was willing to bet. She'd been working there for only three weeks and already people favoured her.

Nio headed down to the second avenue so he could make his way to the end without breaking through lines of people. He came back up through Wines and Spirits, and joined her queue. There she was, checkout number sixteen.

She had this unruly blonde hair, caught up in clips and rubber bands and wound with bits of coloured rags. Her skin was glossy enough to look as if water wouldn't wet it. Her face, really, was a smile, the whole assembly tended towards that design, everyone basked in the sudden warmth but men particularly. This smile encouraged everyone to try for her.

He picked up a can of dogfood, idly, as the queue hitched upwards. After a while she glanced in his direction; he was hoping she'd latch on to him but not a flicker crossed her face and she was giving others smile after smile as they passed through.

It came to his turn. 'Have you got a Tesco Clubcard, sir?'

'No.'

She swept the can of dogfood past the scanner.

He said, 'My name is Nio, what time do you get off work?'

She stopped in amazement. 'I beg your pardon?' From such a blonde, light and young person, her accent was dark and throaty, these foreign words jumbled uncomfortably together on her tongue. Her toughness was in her voice.

He repeated, 'Can we meet up, you know?' He smiled.

'I don't know abou' that, we not to be with the customers, is a rule.'

'Go on, though,' suggested Nio.

'I might to call for s'curity if you go on talk to me.' She frowned.

As he paid for the can of dogfood, he asked, 'Shall I come back and meet you in half an hour?'

She paused, gave him a blank stare; then from behind it came a smile. Nio felt the admiration of the rest of the queue, like applause, there was a ringing in his ears with the warmth of this achievement, and the smiles she'd given to other people held only a trace of the long, continual smile she had for him now. 'OK. My name is Mila.'

Then, 'Hey,' she called after him. 'This is yours!' She pointed at the can of Pedigree Chum which had rolled to the bottom of the counter; he'd left it behind.

'That's for you,' replied Nio.

She looked at it, then frowned, pointed at herself. 'Like I'm a dog?'

'No, not for you, for Nisha.'

She melted, a sudden gratefulness softened her; and the spell was broken, everyone could see there was private knowledge between them, they knew each other.

Ahmed stood at the automatic doors of his furniture warehouse, irritated as usual at the sight of the gypsies or whatever they were. What were they doing here, smelly so-and-sos? It was not allowed, they were in everyone's way, very bad for business, no one wanted them here. This was not some piece of waste ground, it was a newly built development of warehouse retailers – 500 square feet of floorspace, every one. Comet, Homebase, Computer World, a McDonald's, a sports store called Fitness Warehouse and his own premises stood shoulder to shoulder around three sides of a 300-vehicle car park. The caravans were a pile of rubbish, as far as he was concerned, over at the far side where unbroken land feathered the edge of the tarmac with dust-blown grasses.

Yet somehow this pretty girl was among them: God knows how she popped out from among that lot. He watched from here every day as she threaded between the rows of parked vehicles to the gypsy camp. She was still wearing the Tesco uniform, so she could hold down a job, that was a surprise. Today she was accompanied by a young man whose lolloping stride seemed to beat once for every other step of hers. The top half of his body was skewed, he dangled over her. Ahmed was jealous. He could use the gypsy girl himself. An older man such as he would know what to do with her. Better than that idiot anyway. Ahmed wouldn't hold back. Use her thoroughly, he would. Drive her and her family away . . .

He watched the pair traipse across the empty space which always surrounded the caravans – because shoppers were scared of parking too near – until they disappeared into the biggest one which had outside it piles of God knows what, covered in plastic sheeting held down with bricks, what a mess. A moment later the girl reappeared and levered out some dogfood into a tin bowl for the sinister looking mutt that sloped around the place.

With nothing more to see, Ahmed turned back into the furniture warehouse. Almost time to close up; the staff had gone home. He checked his jacket pockets for cigarettes. Nothing except a toffee. He threw it back in the bowl of sweets positioned on a low coffee table near the entrance. The idea was that children might help themselves while he loitered nearby to engage the parents. This gesture – the free sweets – was to celebrate their first anniversary of trading. Bona fide retail psychology was at work: if he was nice to a child, its parents would feel an obligation, and the only way to fulfil that would be to buy something. So far so good. Except, the gypsy children came in without any parents at all, and just grabbed handfuls of sweets and then ran off. Everyone became annoyed. The gypsies' shabby lives and their cheating and thieving were a cloud over the whole place. Get them out of here. How many times had he called Haringey Council? Every day for months. He made it a point of honour, to keep up the campaign. He cheerfully said, told them straight, he'd pick them up and throw them in the back of the dustcart himself.

He patted his chest, still looking for the Camel Lights, but they weren't in the inside pocket either. How many cigarettes had been left, enough for tonight? He thought so. But where were they? He'd left them lying around some place. He scanned the tables around him. Nothing. Buy a new packet then.

Seven p.m. Ahmed unhooked the keys from his belt, switched off the electronic sensor which controlled the doors and locked them shut, top and bottom.

He meandered through, heading for the office at the back but making various detours to neaten the closely packed furniture. Each item was presented as part of a stage set: these were possible lifestyles. All tastes catered for. Yet the stock stayed here for so long that he was having to clean it. That should be their job, the people who bought the stuff. He'd know he was making money when he didn't have to pay the cleaner to hoover these sofas and chairs, dust the tables. He wanted to clap his hands and shoo the furniture out of here. Go on! Go! He smoothed back the remains of his black, slightly crinkled hair. The oil slicked his fingers. He was fighting off an attack of rage.

Then he caught sight of a shoe, and as he took a further step, a leg attached to the shoe; one step more and the rumpled trousers, then the complete picture: a child was lying in the tunnel between the two back-to-back sofas.

Ahmed's heart jumped once, then he could tell the kid wasn't dead but just asleep or hiding. He was swept by anger and stooped to grab the boy's ankle. Unmistakably, it was one of *them*. He prepared to shout, 'Hey, fucking gypsy, wake up—' but the instant he held on to the leg, it tore from his hand; it was like disturbing a wild animal. The body twisted, buried deeper into the furniture, looked for a moment to be stuck, then after a vigorous struggle it was gone.

Already out of breath, Ahmed stood up. He could hear scuffling and caught flashes of the boy – a mop of hair, an elbow, his back bent low as he ran – and he could also see items move, so from these signals he could tell he was making his way towards the front. No way out, my son. Ahmed walked smartly around Art Deco, cut through Victorian and turned down the next alley; he could trap the boy at the locked exit. He shouted, 'Hey, hey!' He was flushed with adrenalin, he hated these kids, they were like rats, there were so many of them.

There was a bump and a crash as a standard lamp tilted and fell; then the boy ran across open space, headed for the door. Ahmed ranted, but stopped short at the sight of him running full tilt into the glass, he must have thought the doors were stood open; he bounced off and dropped to the floor loose as a rag doll.

His tie held flat against his stomach, Ahmed trotted over. He was anxious; his first action on arriving at the scene was to unlock and open the doors. He would lift the boy outside. Pretend to have found him there – might have been a car that had knocked him down. Because, if there was a serious injury, he didn't want any kind of compensation claim to be made against him. It would be a white lie, to say it had happened out there, and wouldn't affect the boy's medical treatment. Already he was decanting the mobile from his jacket pocket, his finger too large, swamping the 9 digit, pressing three times.

The phone was still connecting with its network when the boy got to his feet, turned in a complete circle and ran straight out, across the car park – a Beamer nearly had him, next door's manager's Astra swerved. Then he was gone.

Ahmed stopped the call, pocketed the phone. He stared after him. Thank God. Crisis over. The shop had been closed, no one had seen. And the child was all right, he'd run off, must be OK. He relocked the doors, walked back and slumped in the office. He poured himself a plastic beaker of vodka and rested it on the surface next to him. He wanted a smoke to go with his drink, but he'd have to do without. He knocked back a first hit.

It was satisfying – that kid had been scared! Now Ahmed knew he wasn't hurt, he felt the desire to hurt him return. So many customers had been put off coming here. Thousands of cars had driven in to see what was on offer but they'd clocked the gypsies, swung around and headed straight for the exit. Gone. They'd wanted nothing to do with the place – not just his store but others as well. All over Muswell Hill – credit or cash – money was walking out of people's pockets, but the retail park was left out. They were failing. Strangely, its very newness, the way it had been so quickly cut out of the site, gave it a derelict atmosphere right from the off. And now the gypsies made it worse. They were like a disease. They had no right . . . Figures tumbled in his head, he'd like to know the turnover he must have lost since the place had opened. He'd even gone back to the old scam, printing the Searsons invoices with a false VAT number so he could keep the tax himself when he supplied the south coast outlets. Again he felt the same urge, to wave his hands, shout at the furniture. He sipped from his drink.

Ten minutes later it was time to walk the boundaries, mark his territory. He tilted his vodka down his throat and then pushed the beaker away delicately, rose to his feet and strolled into the warehouse itself. It was eerily poised in its low wattage night-light. Ahead of him ran the central alley which divided it in two, ending at the exit doors. This square of glass was now a panel of grey; dusk was settling. In the morning, it was a blaze of gold when sunlight struck.

As he walked up to it, a shadowy reflection came to greet him – how much heavier he became, step by step. He dabbled with his tie, patted his stomach, felt again the seams of his jacket pockets. When he was close enough to see through the glass, he gazed over at the caravans. Lights of different colours stood in their windows. The curtains had been drawn. Stuff was piled around the doorways. That dog they'd got hold of from somewhere slunk up and down on its chain. They had a rusty car, an old Ford Cortina, with the bonnet up, a wire trailing from its battery in through the window of the largest caravan, which must be for the fridge and TV and so on. As he watched, the door opened and the lad, the one he'd chased off, came out with a bag slung over his shoulder. Might as well have 'swag' written on it, thought Ahmed.

In the descending dusk, it looked like a scene from hell. Shadows moved across the curtained windows. How disgusting it must be, inside those shabby, poverty-stricken vehicles, the gypsies packed in like sardines.

Little Vlad ran out of the furniture warehouse and across the car park – chest bursting – but his feet were loose in his shoes, they were a couple of sizes too big. On the back of his neck he could feel the stare of the fat guy who owned the shop. His brow and the back of his hand throbbed from the collision with the glass door. He was nearly run over, twice. He held the oversize trousers close against his hip to prevent them from falling down, he mustn't lose pace, had to keep going.

When he reached Social Services Nisha came at him, oversize ears pricked, her back end slower, as if the rear quarters of an older dog had been grafted on to the front of a young one. She barked twice, ears alternately flattening and rising, her tail fanning the ground. Little Vlad hardly paused, just dropped a hand to her, a brief touch of bone and fur and saliva as he ran. She tried to follow him but her chain ran out and she was brought up short.

Nisha could cover a broad cut of territory and the tether made a sinister rattling sound; no one strayed near.

Little Vlad yanked at the door and threw himself into the tobacco smoke and exhaled human breath of Social Services. Immediately, his younger brother and sister were at his pockets, his sister as tall as a giant suddenly in the pair of adjustable red and yellow rollerskates she'd got from somewhere which clunked gaudily at the ends of her feet. He tore himself free, showing them nothing but empty wrappers, the brightly coloured twists of paper littering the floor, his brother squatting to examine each one, his sister insisting on checking his pockets for herself. Around him was the comfort of his native language, it was like a song; he was home. He wasn't going to cry, he wasn't. He headed straight for Mila, who was sitting next to a stranger – another guy after her, this one looked all right. He arrived with a bump at her knee, unwrapping the last toffee, and he pulled back his hair to show her where it hurt, he showed her the cigarettes he'd got as well. She never wanted him to smoke so it was always a dig at her, everyone, he was grown up, he could do what he liked. There was most of a packet of Camel Lights.

Then Mila spoke in English. It caused a hole of silence to open and the spell was broken; the language struck fear in him. Immediately, he knew the tousle-haired, big-booted man who was sitting squeezed between Mila and his cousin must be *englezeste* . . . 'Fish and chips?' he asked. Everyone laughed. 'Yes, Mila's going to eat him,' someone replied. She was saying, this was someone, introducing them to each other. She lifted Little Vlad's lip, showing his pointy teeth, so he knew she was explaining his name to the stranger.

Little Vlad allowed his gaze to meet Nio's, and he saw there a bottomless affection waiting for him which made Little Vlad the easy winner over this man. At one leap he assumed a superior rank, he could be condescending and pitying towards any and all fish and chips. Every word he uttered was safe, the stranger couldn't understand.

He said to Mila, 'Doesn't look like a stupid English.'

'Greek before English.'

Little Vlad nodded – that was good enough. He dawdled for a half-hour, made sure of his money and the new cigarettes, then he picked up his bag and was gone. He hated any kind of trespass on his home ground.

As he walked, the bag slung on his shoulder, he added up bits of money, worked out where, how he could get it. These streets carried so much, there were acres of it; some of it must be his, he could turn it into his own pockets somehow. He would . . . He took out the Camel Lights and counted them . . . *doua, trei* . . .

There were sixteen. He pegged one in his mouth, fired it up. Strong brand, but the low tar version – shame.

At Bounds Green tube station he was among a thousand pieces of humanity pouring down the city's escalators, it was a continual flow, water down a drain. The barriers – the automatic policemen of the London Underground – thumped back and forth like a child's mechanical toy. Only a few people leaped over them, lawbreakers fighting for their own cash flow, but one such, now, was Little Vlad, no more than a flash, like a trout rising from a smoothly moving stream, a glimpse of unruly black hair, a clumsy bag dragged behind him.

If it was a hundred people pouring into the tube, then it was thirty or so taking the escalator down to platform 3, the Piccadilly line southbound – thirty sets of pockets filled with coins, notes. Little Vlad shared looks with those on the opposing stairway, searching for eye contact. He took in the advertisements for West End shows, department stores and bestsellers, standing quietly, his cloth bag – it looked like a laundry bag – on the step above him.

Then as the train pushed its column of air on to this particular platform, it was twice that number waiting there, their eyes streaming from the grit and clothes suddenly agitated, a brief flurry of energy before everyone settled into the carriages – so maybe twenty handbags, a handful of personal stereos, a hundred credit cards.

The light switched to green and the train slid down the rails. Little Vlad breached the doors between carriages, nonchalantly stepped over the metal jaws which threatened to chew off his foot if he strayed too near the join, dragging his cloth bag. He slammed the door shut with his foot, shot an arm in the air to bring his hand through the end of the oversize sleeve, then crouched over to untie the drawstring and reveal the Hohner Student II squeeze-box. He pulled the bag from underneath and draped it around his neck and flipped the leather strap over the top. He stood, slipped his left hand underneath the wrist brace to feel for the buttons while his right hand found the hook for his thumb and settled on the keys. He moved with perfect economy like someone working on a production line – it wasn't a stunt but the dreary everyday. He switched on a brilliant smile while his gaze sought out those most likely to reward him – women and children. He opened the valve, sucked air into the bellows, but didn't bother with any tune, his country's music was wasted on these people. Instead he drew out several long notes which sounded all right together, and talked his song in a language no one would understand, 'Give me all your money because I need it more than you—'

He edged along the carriage, nodding and smiling, his black hair like a helmet, the dark eyes as if they'd been plucked from his father's head, they were so akin, his oversize clothes uncoordinated and colourless. He paused frequently to hold out his hand and collect coins. He was a twelve-year-old boy far from home, but he was bigger and better than any of this crowd – for all their money and jobs and their comfort in their own language, they were one poor lump while he was the brightest star, the true individual, separate from the rest, better than anyone, the centre of the universe. They were there for him to manipulate; the only question was, what did he want to do with them?

Stop after stop rattled by; he was on his way to scoring a third carriage when he heard the click and sudden echoing silence of the tannoy, and sure enough came the announcement which he knew off by heart. 'Ladies and Gentlemen we'd like to inform you that buskers on the Underground are part of organized gangs, often operating in concert with pickpockets. We'd respectfully ask you—'

Little Vlad was already unhooking the squeeze-box from his neck, clawing open the bag and dumping it in before pulling the drawstring tight. He mumbled, 'fucking bastards, *la revedere*'. When the train came into the next station, he trampled on the heels of those in front in his rush to escape. He burrowed through the crowd, adrenalin surging in his system. He jumped the escalator steps two at a time, the bag knocking against those he passed by. At the top, he lifted the bag on his head and pushed hard against the back of a middle-aged woman to squeeze into the same chunk of space given her by the barrier, so he wouldn't be seen jumping over. When he emerged on to the street he was twenty foot tall, each footstep he took had three times the reach of anyone else and his secret language, his tongue, was more fluent and beautiful to the ear – and not to be shared with the masses or polluted by the advertising billboards. Everyone else was small, troubled, not as brave.

He'd escaped.

Leicester Square. He headed northwards, walked quickly. When he reached Oxford Street he stopped and planted the bag on the ground, smiled and waved at the blank eye of the first CCTV camera, jerked his hips forward lewdly, threw half a dozen V-signs and then carried on.

*

Nio sat wedged tight with Mila on one side and a quiet youth of around eighteen on the other side, the toddler stood at his knee. The elbow of the man watching TV was only a couple of inches away, it was tight but there was room for everyone. Nio was awed by the incomprehensible chatter. What were they saying? The words seemed to be made in the back of the throat, not in the mouth. The woman was in charge, it was good to have someone giving orders. The girl clumping around on roller skates had stopped crying now, her father or whoever it was hadn't smacked her very hard. Nio sat tight, amazed to be here. Every few seconds Mila was checking him, making sure he was all right, he smiled back, OK.

There was a fringe of white lace running across the top of the miniature television – he liked that.

Suddenly there was a bang and the door flew open, a boy stumbled in, out of breath, something had happened, he was nearly crying. The younger children squirmed towards him, they were at his pockets, he threw them off. Mila called to the new arrival, he could tell from her tone of voice she was asking what was wrong, what had happened. The boy was now tearing free of the other kids, taking their hands out of his pockets, his sleeves were dangling, longer than the arms inside. With two steps he'd arrived with a thump at Mila's knees, talking all the while, separating out the silver layer from a toffee paper but sparing a moment to swipe back his hair and show her a bump on his forehead. His voice was broken and then unbroken so maybe he was eleven or twelve, but small for his age. She wrapped his face in her hands, looked at the damage. She kissed it, spoke some more in soothing tones. The boy took out a packet of Camel Light cigarettes, showed them to her. Her tone changed – *fumatol!* – she didn't want him to smoke. She appealed to the older man – her father, must be – who shrugged; he was smoking himself. She made a lunge for the packet but the boy was too quick, held them close to his chest and taunted her, catching Nio's eyes. Mila broke into English to say,

'This is Nio, he's my boyfriend. Nio, this is my little brother, we call him, something like you say, Little Vlad.'

Nio held out his hand, calloused with work. 'Hiya.'

Mila continued in English, telling everyone, 'Nio is not his real name, he's really called Aristotle because he was so clever but they start to call him Nio at school because his surname was Niopolous.' Then she grabbed hold of her little brother's shoulder, shook it, turned to Nio, 'And Little Vlad is called Little Vlad,' she explained, 'because it's like how you would call Dracula, look at his pointy teeth—' and she lifted the boy's lip to show the incisors, neat and pointed at each side. 'He is our hero. He is also very bad. Like the devil. And as well he is the child of a dragon. He fights our enemies for us.'

With this burst of English for his benefit, silence descended. No one looked at Nio. The proverbial angel flew overhead. The man squinted at the TV, the smoke from his cigarette trailing idly. The lad sitting next to him leaned back, cocked his leg on his knee. The toddler was repeating a word over and over, it sounded like a question but Nio couldn't answer.

Then Little Vlad made a comment in his own language and laughed. Mila frowned and answered back. Little Vlad shouted something to his sister and moved away without having spoken to Nio. A while later, he picked up a garish bag with a drawstring top which looked like it had a giant log in it. He slung it over his shoulder and left.

Their language was an impenetrable code but Nio felt like he understood – he sort of soaked it up. It sounded something like Italian and French mixed together. He took in the stained fingers of the man in the tunic, the hair sprouting from the ears and cheekbones, watching TV – Mila's dad. The oscillation of the stout woman's hips as she worked at the miniature sink unit at the other end – her mum. The press of the young man on his other side, he was a cousin maybe. The constant traffic of the children was by turns good humoured and the next moment they were at war. All this was a vivid impression, a strange novelty continually repeated. He was in a foreign land; he was himself different. On top of that, Mila was at his side and that cast a spell, also. Her phone bleeped, sang.

As she talked to some friend or other, Nio mused on this strange, foreign family of hers. He wanted to know their story, every detail. How had they got here, what had happened? Where had they got these trailers and how come they'd ended up in this car park? He wanted to join in, to contribute. They'd nicknamed the caravans 'Social Services', 'The Home Office' and 'The Kingdom of God', they hadn't lost their sense of humour despite being poor. And he'd picked up there was some kind of struggle going on with immigration, employment, but what they'd run from, or even from whereabouts in Romania they came, he hadn't been told yet. He was teeming with desire for Mila, he wanted to be part of her family, her life.

For now, though, with this strange language excluding him and Mila on the phone, he was left with the toddler, who regularly pressed through the obstacle course of people's legs and arrived at his knee, staring. He had a big dome of a forehead and not much hair, which made him look solemn, brainy. He wore a scrap of T-shirt and a nappy. His feet and hands and face were ingrained with dirt. Nio took a coin from his pocket and held it in the palm of his hand, then closed it in his fist. The infant clawed at him to see the coin again. When Nio allowed his fist to be opened the coin was no longer there. The child held its breath in surprise. Nio opened his other hand and there was the coin, instead. The toddler breathed out a note of satisfaction, delighted with the trick and to have the coin. Nio smiled. Now he'd have to do it again.

He became aware that everyone was looking at him. Someone had said something. The little magic trick had entertained them, also.

Then, incomprehensibly, Mila's father shouted, 'House of Lords!' He continued shouting in Romanian. It occurred to Nio it might be the name of another caravan, but he couldn't bring himself to interrupt Mila and he was frightened of that silence coming back, didn't want to slow them all down.

Instead, he did more tricks for the toddler, he conjured the coin from the child's ear, then he tore two scraps of cigarette paper and glued them to the tips of both forefingers, held them up, but as the child reached out to touch the white squares he made them disappear. He enjoyed the kid's hand on his knee, its delight and trust in him. Social Services was a warm, accommodating place. Everyone, even this small boy who could so easily have been shy, was accepting him on his own terms. This family, with their history of persecution, of flight, could teach everyone a thing or two about tolerance, about accepting people for what they were rather than judging them according to which racial group they belonged. Nio felt in here the triumph of the human spirit over adversity. Soon he'd pick up a few words of Romanian; Mila would set him tests, like in school. Then he'd understand. He'd help them, yes, find a new place to go, if the council were going to move them from here. He'd write to Haringey, himself. Housing associations – get them on the housing lists. Except, they weren't residents. He'd write to the European Union – they must have some way of helping displaced persons, economic migrants. The United Nations, even. Yes, Nio would do that, he'd got to, soon as he could. It was important, it was urgent . . .

When it was time to go home Mila escorted him. They opened the lightweight aluminium door and negotiated the two breeze block steps down to the tarmac – and it was like culture shock: suddenly he was back in his world, the place he knew, where people spoke English. The deserted car park was bleak and cheerless and dark compared to the crowd of voices, the struggle, the agitation within. The warehouses stood silently on two sides of the square, the stage sets in their front windows immobile, lifeless. Along the bottom edge, the McDonald's fed people, an eating machine. He and Mila held hands; it was electrifying, they were happy, he thought, and he enjoyed the sudden wave of responsibility, he wanted to build on that, keep it going, make it work, keep it utterly safe. Then she tugged at him, stopped, they swung close, embraced. Her mouth was on his and her hand was in his hair, pulling him closer, he was falling into her mouth, it was like that, a kind of vertigo gripped his stomach, almost like sickness.

They kissed for ages. It became odd, they were stuck together so long, he had to take her face in his hands and hold her off, before it was impossible. She looked glazed, as if she were about to fall asleep or had just woken up. His heart broke with feeling for her.

For some minutes they borrowed an outside table from McDonald's and sat and talked. They went through what would happen next, and what had happened already. She taught him how to roll his 'r's. They said goodbye, their fingertips reluctant to break contact.

As he walked home his thoughts were full of how to help with this immediate crisis – their eviction. He dreaded her family disappearing without a trace, it seemed like it might happen this instant. He'd turn up and find them gone, no sign, where they'd lived just occupied with ranks of parked cars. He himself had somewhere to live, of sorts, but it wasn't anywhere he could invite the whole family. No access, for a start. He could ask her, Mila, alone, of course, and he would – God that was like a dream – but he wanted to finish building it first, he was nervous of inviting her. It would be impressive enough, surely, if he could just finish the bedroom? He was wary of going too fast with her, pushing his luck. It felt too important. He knew she dreamed of a proper home. It was as if he was holding something delicate in his hands, he could easily break it.

So – where could the Rosapepe family go, if things were that desperate? Somewhere nearby . . . he thought of his parents' home in Curzon Road, they'd had the two ice cream vans parked out the front for the past thirty years and there was a mains cable fixed to the tree which looped into the vans to keep the refrigeration units boosted. Maybe he could ask them if the Rosapepe caravans could park in their road and use that cable as well? But in the same moment, he knew they'd be dismayed, the neighbours wouldn't like it either, they'd refuse and he'd be hurt. No good.

His way took him due west for a hundred yards along the North Circular and then up the broad, two lane exit to Muswell Hill; and as he breasted the rise it faced him – on the other side, on the slip road which descended again to the North Circular, there was the caravan, the one which he'd sat in, three weeks ago. The Highways Agency – he remembered the TV monitor, that strange man with the pointed face, immaculately dressed in the middle of all that mess . . . Nonetheless, it seemed like a sign. It was a caravan, after all. Odd . . . He wandered down, to have a look. There were no lights showing. The modest shape – a little bump of a thing, compared to the trailer he'd just been in – squatted there just the same, except it was silent now, shrouded in darkness. He remembered the name 'Cherokee' written on its rump. He walked around it once, and the idea lodged in his head that this was a piece of waste ground of sorts – the edge of the slip road gave way to twenty yards of scrub before the boundary of the breaker's yard. He walked further down. This strip of land, because it was alongside the road, couldn't trouble anyone else. In his mind's eye he put the Rosapepe trailers here – would it work?

No. There was hardly enough room, the slope was bad, the little Cherokee wasn't any too level and the slope was worse further down. He went back, stood at the door. He remembered the handshake between himself and that strange guy . . . the way his hand had been pushed away . . .

Should he come back tomorrow and knock? Probably not – it wasn't a good place.

He walked home in the dark of this summer night with Mila's kiss still expanding in him like a pool of happiness. He knew he'd do it, he'd help them all, he'd pick up their circumstances and – bit by bit – change them, make everything all right.

Mila didn't like the way her dad's teeth were black. When he shouted, you could see the damage, it was why his breath smelled of sick. On top of this, now she didn't like his joke about the coin. It didn't matter to her that Nio didn't have money, but now she found herself lying to her family, she had to make him a good idea in their eyes. She told them, 'He is rich. He has a job, a good one, his own company. He is building his own house. He pays for *everything*.'

There was some jeering from her cousin.

Her father – he'd been watching television – then threw his arms in the air and said, 'House of Lords!' He turned to them all and pointed at the TV. 'You see?' he asked, dropping back into Romanian, 'they are in the fucking HOUSE OF LORDS.'

Mama pressed her hands against her ears; her knuckles were heavy and gnarled from work, her dark hair a cowl around her face and neck. She scolded her husband, 'The Glasgow families, shut up about the Glasgow families!'

'They are in the system,' called her husband back, 'see what they get, in the system.'

'You go in then, and see what it gets us, we would all be off to that new place, that new prison. The Glasgow families – they were in the old system, they didn't have the special, the quick prison, then . . .'

Mila interrupted, 'Dad . . .'

He rounded on her, 'You with your Englishman who pays for you and your job and your English language.' The tufts of hair bristled on the heavy cheekbones, his black eyes were older, fiercer, more disappointed than Little Vlad's. 'You are . . . young and could go anywhere or do anything. But don't tell me, don't tell me' – he thumbed his own chest – 'that I can live like this! Godless, the Glasgow families are, yet look at their reward, they're talked about in the House of Lords!'

Mila slumped back, she knew this mood, she couldn't argue. Her father wasn't Orthodox any more, his faith couldn't hold up, he accused everyone else better off than he was. She suddenly remembered him floating down the Danube, in the middle of this great expanse of swiftly moving water, holding a cross aloft in both hands – on New Year's Day. It was freezing cold and he was smiling, buoyed in the water and carried downstream, his dark hair slicked back, the cross symbolic of a journey. He could do difficult and dangerous things, couldn't he? There was something about that memory – how much space there'd been around his tiny, bobbing head, he'd been a dot in the expanse of water, wearing his smile. Along the banks was just a scattering of people from the village to watch. Here, in London, he was hemmed in. Whether he was outside or inside there were people at his elbow, under his feet, looking down on him, driving past, all of them in their houses, with jobs, in cars . . . and he'd lost all his spunk, he expected to be looked after. He would only mend if he was taken somewhere else, away from here, where he could get back into his head. But what could she do? She loved and hated her dad. Most of all she wanted to shave those tufts growing out of his cheekbones and cut the hair growing out of his nose and ears. She'd pay for him to have that done. She wanted to buy rollerskates the right size for her little sister, and loads more ghost books. She wanted to upgrade Nio, have him earning money. She wanted her mum not to have to get up at 4 a.m. to wait for the minibus into work, and for her not to wear jeans, she never did before. She wanted . . .

It was getting dark, she leaped to her feet, struck a match to light the gas mantles. As she carried the flame from point to point, she made a list of what she wanted: to build a whole pile of happiness, carve herself the right space, the right people, leave home, a place of her own, a job . . .

She'd made a start on all those things – look, here was Nio, a really lush guy, she'd chosen him, true love – so she was pointing the right way. She told herself to keep going.

Lucas Tooth awoke with a jerk, his left eyelid fluttered. It was 10 p.m. and he felt his interest quicken; it was important, this urge to leave the caravan immediately, in time for the pub.

He scuffed through the litter to see if there were any notes he'd dropped – he was careless with money. He stared at the video monitor, watching the mute cars slide through, then stood in front of the cracked square of mirror for a moment, touched the collar, the cuffs of his shirt, it was important to be clean, sleek.

Now he could leave.

Outside the caravan he turned right, headed up the slip road. For a while he stood on the bridge, deciding which way to go – Palmers Green or Muswell Hill? He was poised. It was a rare moment of stillness. To cut him in half down the middle would reveal, from the top, a mind that lived for the next half-hour, mostly, which guaranteed constant good health. Any event, however strenuous, was cast off, unimportant once it was past. The here and now lived in him – what he could put his hand to, exactly. His thoughts were emptied out every few minutes, the space refilled by a handful of common desires, constantly visited in the emotional and physical sense: food, drink and other recreational drugs, clothes, cars, the mothers and the sisters. He had a good brain in perfect working order except for those pulses of energy which went to his throat or fingertips or knees, causing the continual swallowing, the fussy rub of his fingers, the knee wagging.

On first waking, his heart beat with irregular bursts as if at any moment it would give up, sprint to the finish. This electrical malfunction was the cause of Lucas' supernatural wakefulness. If he fell below the shallowest level of sleep his heart would stop and he'd die. Doctors had brought him back from the dead three times in his childhood before they'd diagnosed his condition. Their only prescription had been to plug him into an expensive alarm system to wake him every two hours, unfailingly. Eventually he'd learned to dispense with the alarm, instead he woke at the first instant of the plunge into the abyss which signalled heart failure and the adrenalin kicked his system into action. In effect, his body had learned to alarm itself. It meant he never slept for long.

There was a girl's hair stuck in his teeth, glossy and mouse-like in colour; his tongue constantly sought the spot, worked to remove it.

He decided – Muswell Hill. Soon he was on the move; when he reached Colney Hatch Lane he swung uphill, towards the Broadway, stopped at the all-night petrol station to buy a copy of the *Haringey Times* and then veered left, finding the narrow alleyway, his shoulders barely squeezing between the two garden fences. His white shirt and black trousers were immaculate. He was careful to avoid dogshit; his shoes gleamed with health under the yellow sodium streetlights. He shook the paper open and folded it back to scan the personal ads. He held the paper close; the light was poor and the words were shadowy, unreal, they floated in and out of focus. As he gained the pavement at the top of the alley, the few people passing around him might be those who'd advertised in this paper, its circulation was that local. He knew what he was looking for in the lonely hearts: only sadness, or innocence. He could smell these two things. No good to him were straightforward, untroubled souls who were having difficulties finding a mate. He might get a meeting out of it, but never a hold on them, not without those two ingredients, the sadness, innocence.

His feet moved automatically up the rough path that separated the golf club from the backs of these people's gardens. He found one possibility – so then he stopped under a street light, knelt, and with care he tore out and folded a neat square which he put in the breast pocket of his brilliant shirt, almost phosphorescent in the summery darkness. As he walked on, the bulk of the paper slipped from his fingers and landed on the path, like a bird shot down.

His strange axe-like face moved between gardens and through the hidden yards and past the garages which this wealthy suburb of London gave rise to. As he ducked through a broken fence and crossed the bottom of someone's garden his white shirt caught the light thrown from the French windows and an old lady, resident for thirty years, her grandchildren safely asleep upstairs, clutched at her chest; it was like seeing a ghost, by the time she'd reached the phone to dial for the police the apparition had disappeared, Lucas had crossed three more gardens, vaulted the wood-panelled fence at the other end and was on his way to the Broadway. As if by magic, his white shirt was unmarked.

When he arrived at the Brewers' Yeast he immediately searched for any good-enough sisters in this church that had been converted to a pub. Employing on weekend nights two bouncers in full dress uniform, boisterous youth went here to be seriously overtaken by drink. It was a vast temple to hedonism; adulterous, fornicating, drunken sinners had taken over in numbers that would shame the count of the last congregation, eight years previously. He queued at the bar to score a slim, clear drink and squeezed through the herd, still looking. The pressure built in him like white noise; it maddened him. He was like a diver rising to the top for air, he was determined to have someone, that's what it was like, it would keep him alive. He pushed through to the food area and found what he was looking for – two sisters, sitting alone.

A waiter had just finished taking an order, and had moved away. Lucas knelt in front of them. 'Hi, I'm Luke,' he began affectionately. He might have used one of a number of names.

They stopped talking and looked at him suspiciously.

He prattled on, 'God, it's horrible when someone just comes up and chats away like he knows you, but I've got to find fifteen girls to have a free haircut, d'you know the Vidal Sassoon hair clinic in, like, Mayfair? Well, we all kind of work there, and we're trying to find people who want a free makeover, maybe, for going on a TV show we're doing, girls who are like you, you know, not absolute stunners but, you know, good looking, it's like part of a festival of style, and we're doing this whole music thing . . .'

His pointed face aimed at first one then the other – he was democratic, fair to both. His shirt was clean and as he waved his arms it danced, a curtain of light, hypnotic.

When the girls' food arrived, Lucas stood; he held himself extra straight, beamed. His smile reached so far either side of the narrow ridge of his face, you might think if he laughed the top of his head would flip back, open his throat. 'I'll leave you to it,' he said, in a tone of cheerful regret.

By now the sisters were his friends. He imagined they were judging him as not conventionally good-looking but 'there was something about him'. They waved at him to sit, he must stay. For a moment Lucas protested, he enjoyed their persistence. He caved in and agreed, stalled the waiter from leaving to give his order, too. 'But only if you let me treat you,' he insisted, in his turn.

Saliva flushed his mouth. They offered him pickings of their food to keep them company until his meat arrived.

As he ate, inch by inch his mood changed. He slowed down, the rush of the first mouthfuls turned to a solid march through the steak. He felt the food clot at the top of his stomach and a calm orderliness set in. The electrical surges in his body came less frequently. At the same time the faces of the two girls blurred, their speech became indistinct. Whereas at first he'd interrupted them, eager to top their comments with his own and roll the conversation forwards, now it was difficult to get a word out of him.

When he'd finished, but before the bill arrived, he excused himself to visit the gents' and didn't come back. He was gone. Among the throng of youngsters he ran, his sharp face carving a path; he magically appeared at one place then another as if underground tunnels linked nightspots, pubs and off-licences; always his shirt was immaculate. Alcohol sang in his veins, yet he was never drunk. One-thirty p.m. saw him in the garden of a mother in Birchwood Avenue, she let him in through the back door and he harassed her for an hour, making sure she was unwavering and he still had power over her. When she was ready, tears coursing down her face and one shoulder out of her dress, he lost interest; as he idly twisted the latch on the front door he slid a twenty out from under the coins piled on the hall table, it fluttered between his fingers as he left.

His last amusement was to remember the address of the two sisters who'd fed him and turn up at their door. A hundred residents of Coniston Road lay fearful in their beds in flats squeezed three at a time into Edwardian family houses because he was out in the street, throwing chips of stone at the girls' windows, shouting their names. The sisters appeared, excited, white faced. A window opened.

Lucas called, 'I got beaten up, I was in the bogs and got beaten up.'

The sisters hurried downstairs, let him in. They listened to his story and felt awe that anyone could think Lucas was *gay*, and attack him for *that*, when he so obviously *wasn't*.

He gave them the twenty for his meal, told them he'd gone back to his place especially to get it because his attackers had taken all his money when they beat him up. The girls tried to give it back to him, the least they could do was to have bought him the meal, after what had happened. Lucas refused. No – he didn't need their charity. Instead – strictly as a loan, because they'd taken all his credit cards and he didn't have any way of taking out money – he took a fifty.

It was clear which of the two sisters was his because the good-looking one had a boy in her room, waiting. The other one, the one with a pin in her nose, had that light switched on for him which told Lucas she could be taken. It crossed his mind to put out some cocaine, but it didn't feel safe.

He was tender, uncharacteristically slow. He touched her beneath her neck, and drew a line across her chest, catching on the way the strap of her slip, until the same shoulder was bared as on the mother only two hours earlier just over a mile away; this time the scent was stronger, he drew her to him and turned her to the floor; she yielded immediately. Things became more interesting when he was about to do this sister. On the very point of it, she stopped him. 'Wait . . .' She caught her breath.

He murmured, 'What, what . . .' Her resistance excited him, this was what he wanted, the hand on his chest, the pressure against him.

'I haven't . . .' she began.

'Haven't what?'

'Are you wearing a condom?' she blurted.

'No,' he confessed and sunk his head on her shoulder. 'Sorry.'

'We can't, then,' she said, 'we mustn't.'

'No,' he agreed. He let his weight relax on her. 'We can't,' he echoed.

'I'm sorry,' she whispered, 'so, so sorry—'

'That's OK.' He kissed her neck. Then a moment later he suggested, 'I can be inside you . . . and not spill, and then . . . let go on the outside.'

'It's not safe, is it?' Her voice was urgent.

'It's safe. I want to move inside you, I want to . . .'

'We can, when we have the condom.'

'Now, I want to go inside you now. I won't come, I'll take myself out.'

'But it's not . . .'

He interrupted, 'You can watch me, it's safe, I promise.' He began to go for her.

'It's not safe,' she moaned, pushing him away.

He pushed back harder. 'I'll make it safe.'

'Is not safe sex.'

'*I'm* safe,' he murmured, kissing her neck. 'Promise you—'

He drove through the pressure of her hands on his hips and pressed into her; he was home. For six minutes he was chewing the mass of dark curls near her ear. He emptied inside her without a change to his stroke nor a sound from his throat – she didn't notice. He kept going, worked out the last residue of feeling.

When he began to go soft, he stopped, full in her, and lied: 'I've got to pull out now, but you can watch, you can see me.' Her mouth was open, quick breaths moved her chest, her chin was turned sideways, but now she lifted her face towards him. Her eyes were a deep liquid, in the dark. 'Watch me,' he said and withdrew, held himself, performed! He stroked himself wildly then slumped over her. She made it exciting for him, she pushed her chest out, the whiteness of her breasts phosphorescent in the gloom, she stared at where he was working in astonishment and when he fell on her, she pulled him tight, soothing him. 'There it is, see?' he said. 'Safe, you're safe, it's all here, in my hand.' He wiped his dry palm on a twist of sheet. She caught it, held his fingers, bravely licked them; for a moment he thought he'd be found out, but she went into a frenzy, he wanted to laugh, she chewed at his fingers like a starving animal.

Afterwards, he didn't sleep. For a while he watched her. That couldn't be a diamond stud in her nose, it looked like glass. He imagined unhooking it and taking it with him to be tested. He removed her arm from his chest, inhaled the gust of warm odour as he lifted the bedclothes, then he dressed, followed his nose and was gone. This was his night in Muzzers – carelessly, he'd added one more.

Mila chewed on a Cool Cola while she waited. She was stationed to one side of the entrance; customers streamed from their cars towards the Tesco superstore. From among the incoming tide she looked for Nio, the wanting was enough to make her drop, she was dying to see him, everyone else she batted aside. She hung on to the memory of when she'd last seen him and tried to bring the picture to life in this huge expanse – where was he?

She caught sight of him, then.

God, he was so charged up, his face was white, he looked frightened with love as he walked towards her. They were, like, glued to each other with this stare, it was loaded. She just stood there, struck dumb, and wanted him – he was so different from everyone else, taller, and other people had their noses buried in their shopping trolleys or in the boots of their cars whereas he cruised along, way higher than that. Only she could reach him. His stride was longer, slow. None of the selfish worries which demeaned everyone else were attached to him. He was lush, he was something else. She felt the smile crawl across her face and his expression answered, she loved that, how he slow-burned his way through life, engaged with each and every thought properly, it was a sort of freedom, it was so, so romantic. If only he had loads of money.

Then his hands were on her – at each shoulder – and the happiness was intense, she walked into his embrace, held him tight, the wanting was answered a bit now, he was here, perfect – dead cool. His arms were heavy around her, she couldn't escape. For a long while they stayed like that. His fingers were in her hair, cradled the back of her neck. He was murmuring something but she couldn't understand what, often this happened but she let him go on, she caught the drift of his tone of voice and that was enough, the vibration was what moved her, she didn't want to interrupt, make him explain.

They headed off towards the petrol station, holding hands, cutting through the forecourt and out the other side; a dozen strides later they broke all the rules and walked along the A406 North Circular, headed westwards against the traffic, well tucked into the edge but there was no hard shoulder so it was dangerous on this road with its heavy freight of traffic. He protected her, walking on the outside. The points at which they touched – fingers, hands, arms, hips, thighs – they both kept up. She glimpsed the passing drivers, surprised, angry, curious, framed by the car windscreens, as they appeared and disappeared in an instant of travel, one after the other, two or three every heartbeat. His old boots, she could see, ate up the road in that particular steady way. How she loved his rough clothes, the way they lived on him, they liked him, that's what it was, his clothes really wanted to hang out with him, they stayed on, really did, for as long as they could. It was her turn to talk – she felt the English coming out not too badly, she was beginning to sound like she lived here. She went through all the stuff about work, the gossip, it was all rubbish wasn't it, why couldn't she tell him what she really wanted to – that she'd got Social Services, she'd swung it, they had the place to themselves for later, this was it? She couldn't tell him, no, because it was too fierce, wasn't it, for the girl to arrange the where and when, to go to such trouble? Over the past few weeks she'd asked to see where he lived enough times, but he hadn't taken the hint, she'd become fed up with waiting, he kept on putting her off. It was embarrassing, but she'd actually called a motel, she'd wanted to book a room at the Travelodge down the road before she'd found out how much it cost.

Half a mile later they were on the next slip road; they gained the safety of a pavement at the top. Mila answered her phone three more times, it was Jayne from work begging her to come out, and then Petru who wasn't going back home after all, he was sending money back but his 14-year-old wife was still divorcing him, and then Vasiluc rang on a borrowed phone to describe his mother dressing up as a Western businesswoman.

They turned right, headed for the Warner Village, and went into the building on the southernmost edge of the entertainment complex. In the queue to pay for entry Nio stood behind her and wrapped her up. She leaned back into him as they waited. It was dreamy. She held his hands closed tight across her stomach. She wanted to break, run somewhere. She wanted privacy, like, how much? Yet, if they went back now, they'd have hours to wait and she didn't want him to have to sit and watch her family. Want, want – everything in her life was the wanting . . . waiting . . . Seven o'clock – it wasn't long – this was what she had to hang on for, that was the time, it would happen. She felt goosebumps, chilled but excited at the same time.

At the desk she took out her pay packet and did the business. She was proud of her money, she loved the way Nio was crowing about it too, his eyes popped, he said it was amazing, it made her feel good.

They changed shoes and went to their bowling station. There were a few groups with kids, it was a time for families. She showed Nio how to put his name up on the screen, how the scoring worked. She plugged her fingers in a medium-sized ball, hoisted it up and went to the line. She felt her own body poised – and knew it looked good. She bowled in three fluent steps, and liked how the ball skidded at first on the polished wood, then started to roll. She watched it strike out four skittles.

She couldn't stop talking, now, it made the time pass quicker, happier, she so wanted to fast forwards. 'And you know,' she was saying, 'I'm called Donna, to the supervisor? She call me, Hey

Donna. I have to remember, kick myself. Of course, is me, I'm Donna, I live in Sydney Road. And I have to behave as if I'm twenty years old, not fifteen.'

'Fifteen?' asked Nio. He was pushing his fingers into a ball, holding it to his chest, cupped in the other hand, smiling at her.

'You can guess I'm twenty, though?'

'I didn't even think about it.' Nio frowned.

'But, is what all men dream about, fifteen, that age, true?' She smiled. 'On the Internet?' Then her face fell. 'What's the matter?'

He was trying to pull his fingers out of the bowling ball. 'Stuck,' he exclaimed. She watched as he locked the heavy ball with his left arm and pulled harder, this time his middle finger popped free. 'Christ—' He waved his hand.

A silence opened between them. He had gone quiet, and the blood had drained from his face. All because of this finger being stuck in the ball? Did it hurt that much? She carried on talking, 'My supervisor, she don' believe it either, I know she don' believe who I say I am, is why she calls me Donna, she always says, like, with really a heavy voice "Donna", she know something was wrong—'

She chatted, they played the game, but Mila felt like she was carrying the whole thing suddenly, she was dragging Nio along whereas before they'd been running together. What had happened?

When they walked back along the North Circular afterwards, everything had changed, she had to pick up his hand and wind their fingers together, she had to lift his arm and walk under it, hold it across her shoulders. She was worried. What had gone wrong? She wanted – God, there it was again, how her whole life was made up of wanting – to reach the other side of this, it was so stupid, what was going on, what had she said that had put him off? She began to panic.

By the time they arrived back at Social Services, she was in a frenzy. Even before her watch showed 7 p.m. she started ranting at her family, 'It's past seven, come on, you said, you agreed.' She waved the money at her mother and father, they tried to take it off her but she was going to keep hold of it until they'd all actually left, for certain, she didn't trust them an inch. She had the confidence of a breadwinner, carving some space for herself. Was Dad giving Mama money every week and not only that but bringing home loads of out of date food? No, he wasn't.

There were cries of dissent. Her father turned on her. 'But! It's not yet seven. When it's seven, it's seven.' His skin was even more deeply corrugated now – he'd been forty when Mila was born. His eyes were dark chips of glass in an otherwise unhealthily matt, grey surface as he looked at her money, right under his nose. The tufts growing from his cheeks had turned grey, even. This weather had closed him down. How much better he'd looked, remembered Mila, in the sunshine. He turned on her now, 'And what's wrong with *his* house? Why don't you go there?'

'I told you, it's still not ready, it's not finished. He's building it himself.'

'Hmmphhh.'

The teasing of her family didn't let up. Her cousin was droning in a voice like in a horror movie, 'Seven o'clock, and then it starts to get dark . . .'

Mila rolled her eyes.

'Time to light candles, to breathe soft words of love.'

'Shut up.'

'With a stupid fish and chips.'

'He's not English, he's Greek!'

'Ahh-ha, he *was* Greek.'

Little Vlad wanted more money, he said it wasn't enough, he was going to stay unless he got his own amount separate from everyone else.

Mila shouted him down and then turned to Nio and broke into

English. 'I'm going to get changed.' She tugged at the dark blue fabric of her Tesco uniform. 'Hold on.'

She left Social Services and trotted over to the Home Office where she and her sister, mother and girl cousin slept. She clawed through masses of clothing to find what she wanted. At the little plastic sink she stood and stripped, poured a bit of cold water, wiped the flannel under her armpits and around her neck. She was miffed not to have had a bath, the best she'd done was to have showered that morning at a co-worker's flat, but she'd worked a full shift since then, she had to top up her hygiene so she went for the deodorant. She was going to get up close and personal with Nio. She begged, please, please God don't let tonight be spoiled, she wanted it to be cool, fresh, she wanted it to be the sparkliest, ever. They were going to do it. Solid mayhem. She so, so wanted Nio. Her changing into these clothes was the same action as climbing out of here, away from her family, to freedom. She leaned close to the mirror to catch what light there was, to make up her face – and these colours were to light him up, turn him on. Whatever had happened, gone wrong, she'd push him beyond it, no trouble, but what should she wear?

Nio waited for Mila. It was worth it – she was wearing a sleeveless jersey halter crop top showing off her midriff under a baby lambswool jacket cut to the hip and blue jeans decorated with sequins along the belt, tight to the knee and then flaring out to where embroidered dragons chased around her ankles. Clips held swatches of hair back from her face. She still had the money in her hand. He couldn't get over the shock of what he'd just learned – she was only fifteen years old.

As soon as she came in there was a shout, it was the same row as before. Nio listened to the sudden anger coming from the man with tufts growing in his ears and cheekbones – Mila's father – and now he understood. Of course he was angry, his daughter was only fifteen and here she was hanging out with him, Nio, twenty-three years old. It must be that. He watched as Mila's face grew hurt, tears glistened in her eyes. While the argument went on, everyone else fell silent except the children who buzzed around. The toddler at his knee turned to check the tone of voice, but then forgot and looked to Nio again for entertainment.

Mila was holding out the money, with her other hand she occasionally picked at the clothes she wore, explaining something vigorously. Her father had one word which he kept repeating. Nio imagined the word must mean 'fifteen'. Mila pushed through to come and stand next to Nio, still holding back tears. At Nio's eye level, a gold stud winked in her navel, before she turned and shouted something, loud, as if to a crowd.

Then, oddly, the entire population of Social Services left, one by one. There was some muttering and smiling between Mila and her relatives and a sour look from her father, then everyone was gone. Mila followed them to the door and when she came back, the money had disappeared from her hand. There was some sort of family outing which she'd agreed to pay for? Mila was that generous.

He watched as she locked the door, turned off the TV, lit candles. He drew breath – he couldn't think of words beautiful enough to describe her.

The sweethearts were alone. Mila was pleased with the candles, but wanted more of them, she liked it when they were crowded on every surface. Nio poured compliments on her – how she looked, what she was wearing – she was incredible. He had been about to ask where her family was going, but something stopped him. He kept quiet.

The silence inched along.

Mila touched on things here and there, straightened the clutter. She sat next to him and picked up his hand; it was becoming a habit. She held a forefinger, squeezed it as if testing for ripeness, and turned it over. She kissed it. Then she put his finger in her mouth. The sudden warmth and liquid softness made him jump. He got to his feet and walked a pace away, then came back. She was leaning forward now, holding out a hand for him. 'I want you.'

Nio waited, nonplussed. What could he say to her . . .

'We are all alone,' she said. 'Come here, over here and lie down with me, please?' She lay back on her elbows, tugged down the top she was wearing. 'Come on,' she smiled, 'let's have some boy behaviour.'

He stammered, felt unconfident – if they started down that road it would be difficult to stop. And he knew what was right, what was wrong. She was too young. It was a criminal offence.

'Mila,' he began.

Her smile fell away; instead, she grew a frown. What was he about to say?

'We can't, not yet,' he explained.

This was the oddest thing ever. Mila sat up slowly. 'No? Why no?'

'We shouldn't . . . you're not old enough . . .'

Not old enough? Was that for real?! 'I don' believe it—'

'It's illegal, Mila. It's not right to . . . to take away something precious like that, in a wrong way—'

'Is that a problem, I'm not old enough? Fifteen?' Her smile grew, she wanted to laugh, this was incredible.

'It's illegal,' repeated Nio. 'And it's wrong, also.'

She scooted to the edge of the bunk, she didn't think this could be happening for real. 'What does it matter, it must be a really good thing, that I am young. Is it?'

'A lovely thing, but . . .'

Suddenly, she was insanely angry. She wasn't a child, she knew everything, more than any grown up, about people, and life . . .

more than him even! 'You know what?' she asked, 'look, all the people here in London, how many walk from the Black Sea, or hike-hitched, losing from their family in Braşov, how many waited in the old school, three months we waited in that broken down old school, in the yard, how many go and made the journeys with no ticket, or no money? Our family split up two times! I had different shoes, you know, for months, not a pair, but different, and I wanted them, for dear life. Two hours in the middle of the road, next to the metal thing, too scared to move, two whole hours, like this, next to . . . and Mama carrying his spectacles, all that time, when there was only one glass, only one side was in, the other gone, empty. In the petrol service station area, when we are in this country, our whole family, with nowhere to go. No police escort because there are too many of us and it's a Sunday. And every man . . . every one . . . especially the what is it, junior housing officer, here in Haringey, he offered me . . . well . . . to run away from the housing officer, with nowhere to go . . . And you know what, Vlad took a photo of me, he was asked to do it by this man in France, he was given a camera to take a picture, given it for free, and you know what happened to that picture, it went all around London, and back in France I get men who have seen the photograph, they send other men with money, and they offer to pay me everything to come here, hundreds of pounds they will pay me, but I have to say no because I know about the traps, the houses here in London where girls are prisoners. OK? Anyone in this whole country who did that, who's that happened to them, any girl who's twenty years old! Or fifty years old? How about, is all right?!'

'I only meant,' began Nio.

'Don' mean, though. Just don'. I am old enough for *anything*.'

Even when she was in a bad temper like now, Nio thought she was an angel. Her knees were wide apart, as she sat on the bed glowering. The candlelight heated her complexion, cast her in gold, lit small versions of itself in her pupils. A tuft of hair sprung from above her frown, clipped by a miniature purple butterfly made out of plastic infused with glitter.

Perhaps he was one of the few men on this earth whose gaze wouldn't stray down her neck to the inside pocket of her cleavage, but it was true, he ought to hold her eye if he possibly could. 'Mila, you know, it would feel like . . . a theft. You're the best person, I think about you all the time, you are . . . ah! . . . in my head, it's not . . . I'm not. . . it's just I don't want it to be like . . . stealing from you.'

'What does it matter, I'm nearly, so—'

'Nearly, yes. Exactly. So we can wait. It will be fun, to wait.'

She threw herself back on the seat. 'Oh,' she said, as if addressing the ceiling of the caravan. 'Great fun. Fantastic.'

Nio struggled on. 'It's just that I believe . . . you should hold yourself . . . you know, count yourself as a valuable thing, not give yourself when you can't be ready, when we've known each other such a short time.'

With one quick movement she crossed her arms, pulled the sleeveless jersey crop top over her head and threw it at his feet. 'In a few weeks I am sixteen.' This bra was brand new – Tesco's finest. To Nio's eyes, her shape was breathtaking, it was perfection. Her breasts were so . . . there. He blinked, stared. His voice was smaller, plaintive, when he repeated, 'No.' Then he added, 'Your father would agree with me.'

She exclaimed, 'My father sells me if you offer him money!'

He didn't believe that. 'No, I'm sure you—'

'No, no,' she interrupted, 'wait, he sells my kidney first, then he sells me later.'

'No—' he protested.

'Yes. In our countries, they are *married* at twelve, only. What is this sixteen, so what sixteen?' She wanted to scream. Punch him. Drag him into her arms.

'Maybe,' suggested Nio, 'if I was fifteen as well, it wouldn't matter, then it wouldn't be me, aged twenty-three, you know, too old for you, taking advantage.'

'How is it to be, advantage, if I want to, even more than you, as well?'

'Because,' began Nio, then he stopped.

'Because of the illegal, the police, you worry. Maybe I called the police, sometimes afterwards, and say I am—' She came to a halt.

They waited, for a while. Nio was unashamed, his staring was continuous, this girl in front of him, with her incandescent youth, the strange accent, the beautiful shape of her, was a rich thing to have happened, to have her intimacy, her store of human goodwill, offered him . . . he picked up her top, gave it back. She pulled it on. He tried to think of a new subject, something to talk about, but couldn't.

A minute later she said, 'You know, I hear the other day, I don' know, on the radio or TV or something, and they were saying, for a teacher to have sex with a miner, this was very wrong, to have sex with a miner, and I was all the time thinking, what's wrong for a teacher to have sex with a miner, strong man, very fit, hard working, good job, why shouldn't anyone have sex with a miner, no one should go to prison for that thing, because of the job the boyfriend has . . . then someone told me it was minor, meant only young, like I am very young, the minor—' Then she added, 'Maybe you listened to that radio, too.'

For the next hour, he tried to keep up with her. She paced the caravan like a wild animal, plugging the minidisc through the speakers to play her CDs, dragged him into a dance, then squealed into her phone, always her phone was nearby, a constant stream of pips came from it, either voice messages, texts or calls, she leaped at each one, ignored him, and then she'd come off the phone to tell him about people and things he knew nothing about, Mariuca being charged 800 for a visa to France, plum brandy made in the village still, the mafia, and then she'd veer back to them, their relationship, as if there'd been no break, their time together stitched around these interruptions, perfectly seamless.

Then, she was sad. Nio grew closer; it was safe to embrace her. She made no play to turn it to anything else. They lay next to each other. She asked him, 'If you won't do it, then tell me, say what it will be like in words. Please. Go on. Start with, I am sixteen, like it is today . . .'

'When is your birthday?' asked Nio.

'November.'

'November what?'

'November one. First.'

'OK,' began Nio, 'let's say it's the day before. I will bring you a present, a really good gift, something you want, but you are not allowed to unwrap it until midnight, when it's actually your birthday. Then, when you've unwrapped your present, we will be somewhere alone—'

'Where you live?'

Nio hesitated. 'Maybe, yes . . . but whatever, we are somewhere nice, really comfortable, and I will look at your body, I know it'll be amazing, the most perfect thing I've ever seen. I'll just look at you for ages. We'll be lying next to each other, until we are both warm, until we fit together, you know, as if we'd been lovers already for a long time. Maybe . . . you know, maybe even it's morning by now—'

Mila jumped up, screamed, and swung at him with both fists.

'And we'll make love!' Nio held her off. 'We'll make love like crazy!!' and then suddenly she was next to him again, her head leaning against his chest, she was hugging him tight.

'I want it as well,' he continued, 'I do, but without anything in the way, without your parents, or the police, or my own head, saying I ought not to. We can wait for a short while can't we? November the first, it's not very long, for it to be like . . . what is it, six weeks . . . It's only six weeks, that's nothing!'

She pushed him away. 'Not long!?? Go! Fucking go!' Then she pulled him close, kissed him as if she was going to eat him. She wanted to make him rich. 'Stay here, stay with me,' she breathed. Nio stared for a long time, sick with love. Then she turned him around and gave him a shove in the back. 'Get out! You are a child, not me!'

Nio took a step towards the door, then turned around, ready to enjoy the joke, but instead he saw tears in her eyes. This wasn't funny. Suddenly, she'd moved on, she was thinking of something else. He asked, 'What's wrong?'

'You boys,' she began, 'you want it all the time so perfect, us to be so perfect, but you make it as well bad, you pull us down—' She was crying openly.

'Mila, Mila, what's the matter, what is it?'

She shouted as if calling across a distance, 'Fucking boys!'

A sudden banging on the window answered her, making both of them start. Mila clasped her heart in shock. She cursed in her own language. Nisha was barking furiously and running up against the end of her tether. Without a thought Mila tore at the curtain, pressed her nose to the glass to see into the dark outside. 'It's the man from the furniture shop,' she called back to him, 'he hates us.'

This was her toughness, she was so brave, Nio thought.

Then for an unbroken minute they stared at each other. Everything waited. He stared back, until they fell through and beyond each other, it was magic, they tumbled in love, it was really something else. There was a hush; even the noise of the traffic died away.

TWO

Mrs Elinor Ginsberg tilted the bed back to the prone position, touched Julia's forehead, recognizing a normal level of fear – it was, after all, scary to have the bottom half of your body anaesthetized, rendered incapable and unfeeling. She arranged the tent in front of the pregnant mound of stomach so Julia wouldn't see what was going on. 'Soon be over,' she reminded her.

She didn't often work in hospital, but as a senior midwife in Haringey's Home Birth Team Mrs Ginsberg had the principal relationship with the mother and had agreed to attend the elective Caesarean.

The husband came in and took up position next to his wife – and she stared deep into her own husband's eyes and asked him, 'Can my husband come in?'

Her husband answered, 'Darling it's me, I'm here.'

Mrs Ginsberg felt Julia's hand squeeze her arm, suddenly. 'Everything's OK—' she soothed.

Julia's eyes were starting out of her head as she turned to Mrs Ginsberg and asked, 'Can my husband be with me?'

'That is your husband.' Mrs Ginsberg nodded at the gowned, capped and masked figure standing the other side of the operating table.

'It's not,' said Julia, 'that's not my husband.'

Unmistakably, that was John Edwards. Mrs Ginsberg smiled, 'It is your husband, it's just that he's wearing a funny costume and a mask and a hat, but he has to, if he's to be in here. Barrier against infection.'

She felt Julia's fingernails cut into her arm. 'He's not my husband.'

Out of the corner of her eye Mrs Ginsberg saw the quick, certain swipe of the knife below the mound of Julia's belly. No one should tell Julia this was the surgeon's first Caesarean. But it would all happen quickly now. She smiled at John Edwards, 'Just drop your mask for a moment so she can see it's you.'

John lifted his hand to his mouth, took a pinch of the mask and pulled it down so his nose and mouth were uncovered. With the puff of cloth now sitting on his chin and his face even rounder in the tight-fitting cap and a tense, wild expression in his eyes, he did look funny. 'It's all right darling, it's me.'

Julia screamed and hung on to Mrs Ginsberg's arm for dear life. 'Get him out of here, for God's sake, he's going to steal the baby.'

Mrs Ginsberg looked down into the frightened face of her patient.

'Get him out of here,' hissed Julia.

'Darling, Julia, it's me—' John Edwards looked bewildered.

The surgeon now had his hand inside Julia's stomach; he'd be checking for the umbilical cord and grabbing the baby's legs. The stricken husband was repeating, 'Julia, it's me—' Julia herself was trying to sit up. Mrs Ginsberg held her down with both hands. She broke all the rules, told the husband, 'Take your cap off, just for a mo.'

'Whatever you do,' Julia begged her, 'don't let them start the operation, not until they get him out of here—'

John Edwards had been told not to remove his cap so he hesitated, at the same time he saw the baby swinging from the surgeon's hand, covered in creamy white vernix, the lips a healthy liverish colour. 'Girl, breathing,' reported the surgeon quietly. John Edwards' firstborn was dangling in the air and she noticed the rush of excitement and pride in his face, they were signalling it was his chance to cut the cord and he was heading down there. Mrs Ginsberg could understand the problem from Julia's point of view, all she saw was the intruder declining to remove his disguise and about to interfere – and so Julia shrieked in alarm, 'Stop him!'

'Julia, that *was* your husband. I promise you.'

'Don't let them start the operation.' Julia looked into her face, beseeched her.

At that moment there was frantic cleaning up going on, the surgeon was in there hand over fist, the placenta had pulled away from the wall of the uterus and he soaked up swabfuls of blood and threw them on the floor like he was trying to stem the Niagara Falls.

'Don't let them do it,' begged Julia, just as the other midwife brought the baby and lay it on Julia's chest, and it cried for the first time, right under her nose. 'It's a girl, she's perfect, well done.'

'Nnnnhhhuh!' shouted Julia.

'This is your daughter, it's all over, it's done with, finished, this is your daughter,' repeated Mrs Ginsberg.

'They've . . . it's happened, already?' Julia was shocked, desperate.

'All done, they're stitching you up now.' Julia's expression was that of an animal's desperate love and fear for its young as she scoured every inch of her daughter's face, and burst into tears. 'Is it . . . is she—?'

'It's a girl, your daughter, she's yours, it's finished, done.'

'Oh my love,' cried Julia, 'you've *arrived*—'

John Edwards stood over her, they could only stare at their daughter, touch her, incredulous. Julia held her husband's hand, 'Darling, I'm sorry, I thought you were someone else.'

'Doesn't matter, not a bit, look at her, she's here, she's

perfect—' The new baby was somewhere in the middle of their embrace.

Elinor Ginsberg had liked the way the surgeon had just said that so plainly, 'Girl, breathing.' Yes – exactly.

Another child had been delivered – a girl. She called all the children she delivered 'her beloveds', in her own head. The infant would be taken back to the Edwards' slightly neurotic, cheerful house in Muswell Hill, which was itself like a pregnant mound sticking out of North London, growing whole families who fed off its good state schools, its flats and houses with gardens, its cleaner air. Anyone who wanted these things – a family, a house with a garden that only cost a small fortune, a high standard of council-run education from nursery through to secondary, some greenery around them, a sense of airy superiority over the lowlands – such people could scour the whole of London and not find a place so fit. Parents clamoured to live here, they beat at the door to be let in, it was an intense and crowded breeding ground which Elinor helped daily to fill beyond bursting point, yet she loved all of them; in every street she could find her families, the ones she'd helped. There was always room for one more beloved.

Mila walked hand in hand with Nio. Although it was past the middle of September the day was so hot she could feel the warmth of the paving stones coming through the soles of her sandals and it was a relief to step on to earth and then the cool grass. The leaves of the trees were coated in dust in this entrance way because it was a building site, no one was allowed in, but Nio led her to a gap in the enclosure where all the construction vehicles were parked. The property development company had put up signs warning people off, illustrated by the black silhouettes of fierce dogs, but Nio ignored them, he told her they'd be perfectly safe, the grounds of the Friern Barnet Mental Hospital were deserted at the weekend. He held her hand as they squeezed around the end of the six-foot high chain link fence. She liked the way he wasn't nervous, it was like stuff was there for him, he could use this place and so could she, because she was with him.

She followed her boyfriend into dense undergrowth. They were a few hundred yards away from the torn shell of the enormous building, but he was right, it was a Sunday, there weren't any workmen. She'd begged him all morning to tell her what this was about. In her excitement she talked constantly, she fought to straighten out what she was saying into English.

They moved deeper into the woodland; here the branches closed overhead and the daylight that came through the feathery pines had a grey somnolent quality, as if it had a separate existence independent from the sun's rise and set. It would always be the same, she felt. The undergrowth cleared, there wasn't enough light, instead underfoot was a sponge, her feet sank in, it felt like walking on someone's bed. The dry pine needles scattered over the surface made it slippery and they pricked her feet through the gaps in her sandals. Only the sound of the traffic on all sides stopped her thinking she was in the forest, back home. She'd thought maybe she was going to see where he lived, he'd told her it was in a wood and that he was building it himself, in secret, but he'd insisted no, it wasn't that. So what could it be? She imagined some beautiful spot, or a ruined mansion where they used to chain up the mad people, or a tree which they could climb, to sit in its branches and look into each other's eyes. Maybe a swing he'd made?

At last he stopped and pointed. 'My latest work,' he said.

In the gloom stood a horse, it really was a horse, she almost thought it was alive. She walked closer. It looked like a hologram, constructed out of thick pencil lines scribbled like mad in thin air. In fact, as she drew closer, she saw it was woven out of thin, pliable bits of young trees, and the outermost skin was made out of creeper of some kind because coming out all over the place were these curly sprigs which looked like a crazy hair style, but she knew they were the tendrils that plants sent out to catch hold of things and climb. It made the horse look like it had been electrocuted.

'Wow.' She looked at him, and there was the smile she recognized, the one that was always waiting on her. 'So cool, to have this animal . . . just here . . . incredible.' She allowed her jaw to drop and went closer, walked around it. There was a tail made out of the tendrils of some ground creeper or other, she scooped it up and let it fall through her fingers, that was clever, how he'd tied them in at the top with a neat coil of rope which looked like a bandage. Underneath the weave which shaped the horse's rump she could make out thick pieces of wood bolted together to make the structure. She reached out and touched, checking back with him to make sure he was watching her, she wanted him to see how much she was taken with it, she loved his eyes on her, so needed him to keep looking. She completed her circuit of the mute animal, brushing her hand lightly over its flank and looking into its eye – was that a lump of coal? Yes. She stood at the front and stared. The black eyes gave the horse this dark power, a sinister quality. She repeated, 'Wow. Is fantastic.' She looked at Nio steadily, earnestly. She stopped chewing for a moment because it was important to say, really seriously, 'I love this horse.' She held his gaze for a moment and then smiled, blew a bubble, it snapped on her lips. 'It's cool.'

She could tell he was happy at her reaction because he began to talk in that way he had, sort of an important tone, serious. She wouldn't understand everything, but he was explaining how it worked. 'All the . . . growing . . . old hedge,' he strode around the horse, touching, 'took hours . . . carried bolts of . . . over here last winter . . . stems were dormant.' He dropped to his knees, poked about in the horse's legs. She found herself looking at his hands, how they worked, moved. Like tools, a real boy thing. She knew his arms were hard as iron, she liked that. His serious face turned back, she listened hard but most of it went over her head, '. . . struts . . . random weave . . . the willow . . . honeysuckle I pulled off . . . fallen over there, and ivy . . . dogwood, old man's beard here . . . make a fine mesh, on the surface—'

He was an important artist, she told him, really he was, but he said no, he used this phrase, he was only 'small potatoes' and she liked that, when he explained it meant not very important at all. She disagreed, 'You are big potatoes.'

For two hours she watched him work. He fetched and carried, he took a machete down from its hiding place in a tree and now it dangled from a cord at his wrist; then he knelt at the horse's hindquarters to thicken its rump and add more strands to the back legs. Was it only because of his chest that she loved him? His shirt was open and two perfect mounds of strength burst out. Was this like how men stared at girls' breasts? She wanted to kiss him, touch. She was mad to get to the inside of him. Crazy, how he was holding back, she could scream. But then, look at him, the scoop of flesh under his cheekbone, the way his dark brown eyes were always alive, more alive than anyone's she'd seen, the springiness of the dark hair curled on his brow. He wasn't great looking, he was too odd for that, his nose too big and his mouth was fleshy, but that's what she liked best, how she could look at him and be a bit freaked out. She told him she'd like to ride his horse, it was magic, it could take her through the woodland and maybe they'd find the trees went on for ever and ever, they'd find an empty castle, they could live there and keep goats and chickens, she would change her style completely, grow long hair and wear dresses all day, other artists would come from far and wide to visit, there would be music and dancing, her family all played instruments at home, in the old days when she was a child.

God – so much magic, she wanted to protect their love, any small threat to it she fought with, strangled. She wanted to get him rich and famous as an artist, she'd grow him into one massive potato . . .

Then she remembered why she was feeling so mad – he'd refused to sleep with her because she was too young, and she ticked him off again, stamped her foot at this stupid waiting for her birthday thing – what did it matter? She should have told him it was her birthday tomorrow, not 1 November. She wanted to beat him along, hurry him up. Otherwise, she warned him now, out loud, 'I'm going to find someone else, don' hang around you know, yes, I will!' He looked at her, hurt. She pressed on, 'There is loads of handsome boys around, really. I can fall in love with someone else, *easy*, you know?' She clicked her fingers. He murmured something in reply, God knows what it was. But he smiled as well. Maybe she would run after someone else for a bit, make him worried. He could do with being more worried about everything, all round.

After a while she was happy to talk less, instead she unpeeled the strawberry, blackcurrant and orange Starbursts and ate the lot, enjoying the heat in a small patch of sunlight which speared through from the canopy above. From this spot she watched her man. It was great. Odd place, but cool. She didn't need to say anything when he was there. The silence wasn't any kind of bad thing. She could daydream. He was doing his thing. She was happy.

Except – she got to her feet, kicked her way around the trees – she was so itchy to get on with it, six weeks was too long, what did he think he was doing, she had to push him on a bit . . . shove him, give him a kick, it was impossible to wait six weeks . . . *really* was . . .

Anjali so needed her mother's smile – its warmth, the maternal love, brought her everything she needed, the honour and goodness in it brought her close to tears when she was struggling with betrayal and feeling so stupid, but she managed to return it; thankfully then all she had to do was listen as they climbed the two flights of stairs in the halls of residence. Her mother was talking in Urdu, but Anjali replied in English, conscious of anyone who might be listening and wanting to be less foreign. She let them into her room – halfway along the corridor and conveniently placed for the annexe which contained the kitchen and the bathrooms. Her mother was excited at coming back to the university for a second time within a month. Anjali cleared the stuff from the bed so her mother could sit down. Trailing from her fingers was the woollen bag, knitted in many coloured stripes and decorated with tassles and bells, which she'd made herself. She let it dangle, then dropped it on the floor, making a space. Her mother sat on the bed and bounced once, exclaiming, 'I am still green, at my daughter, with a place of her own, to study what she likes! What more is going on? Are there more meetings and societies you have joined, what happened to the psychologist's group?' Her smile swam in Anjali's eyes.

She nodded. 'I joined it, it's called the Psychological Society. We meet once every two weeks.'

'Good!' Her mother clapped her hands.

No, not good, psychology was already disappointing; its emphasis on statistical theories and sociological modelling drew Anjali too far from where her interest was – the inside of an individual. She'd begun to blank off during the lectures and seminars after the attack, growing inwards, exploring the hurt which now had taken up more of her internal landscape. Her chosen subject was being used in a way she couldn't have predicted – on herself. She was only interested in criminal psychology.

Then her mother handed over the usual tupperware packages containing food which might easily be reheated. As Anjali piled them up – she knew she'd never eat them – she listened with cold dread as her mother told her approvingly, 'You know, we had a visitor, a friend of yours, a young man, he knocked and I answered, he was very courteous and he apologized and he gave his name, you know, Luke, and he said you had given him your home address and he wanted to know if you were in?' She clapped a hand on Anjali's knee and went on in a teasing voice, 'I said no, you weren't in, what a shame, but then we joked, he and I, you know, that there were many young men who might want to visit you, he was very kind and not at all . . . pushy. He didn't ask for your phone number or your address here at the university, he only made sure that I should tell you he called, and that you might call him back if you felt like it. He was very insistent,' she added proudly, 'he really made it clear, he wanted to be sure that you'd know he had called by. He was very well dressed, quite thin, with dark hair and dark eyes. He looked respectable, what we would call well to do, you know, although of course he wore the latest fashions —' She nudged her daughter.

Anjali couldn't bear it, how the shame speared her, she'd have to blurt it out . . . she felt the inevitability of her bad news, how stupid she'd been, how nothing less than her faith in human nature and in her own judgement had been destroyed, how this piece of bad news, this personal crisis, existed defiantly, as solid as the chair or the bed, like an unexploded bomb in this very room which she herself knew about, she could hear it ticking, but her mother didn't see it yet. She stacked the containers neatly in her lap, one by one, as she listened to her mother's chatter about women today, the menu girls could pick from, choices which hadn't been available in her own youth, how you could go out with young men and choose the one you liked best . . . Her enthusiasm was mounting, rising in step with the boxes piled in Anjali's lap, and in turn Anjali felt the moment inexorably arriving when she would either suddenly interrupt, or burst into tears.

In the event she couldn't find the courage to interrupt and tears were streaming already when she tried to swallow the first sob. Her mother immediately stopped talking. Anjali didn't look, but knew that her mother's jaw had dropped open, she could sense her shock and concern. She felt the familiar hand arrive on her shoulder. 'Anjali?' she heard. 'Anjali?'

'I'm sorry,' Anjali leaned closer to her mother. 'Sorry.'

'What is it?' There was panic in her voice and Anjali felt an urge to look after her, protect her. 'Nothing really.'

'It must be.'

'I didn't want to tell you, because Dad and the boys' – she was smearing the tears from her face – 'Dad and the boys,' she repeated, 'I don't want them to know.'

'What? *What??*'

Now Anjali could look at her and it was like seeing a reflection of herself in a mirror but with years piled on: the grey hair a soft curve around the top of her mother's head, the deeply browned face scored with worry lines, the anxiety a prick of light in her eyes with their yellowing corneas, corresponding to the weariness she felt in herself right now. She held her mother's hand. 'D'you promise not to tell Dad, nor the boys?'

Her mother measured the seriousness of this. 'I promise. Until you want me to, I won't say a word.'

For a while the two women were silent. Anjali was halfway there, it had been a struggle but finally she'd arrived at this point – telling her – and this was a woman who had soothed everyone in their family. Yet Anjali was faced with a last hurdle – to share her bad news was also to deliver its burden, it was in some ways a selfish act. This added to the guilt she already felt, the sense of blame attaching to the victim being a celebrated tenet of criminal psychology and here it was, alive in her.

'What is it?'

Anjali couldn't answer. She waited. A picture came to her mind of her mother's return to the house. She'd be unhappy and disappointed at the thought of her daughter having been desperate enough to have advertised for a boyfriend, and then stupid enough to have believed in Luke. The men would be waiting – her father would be out in the garden or chatting to neighbours over the fence; perhaps he would be taking his twice daily stroll down to the end of the road to keep the smoke from his cigars out of the house, while her brothers would be back and forth on the rat run between the bedrooms, building up a head of steam on the band or the home-made promotional video, or they would be languishing in front of the TV, covering all the chairs with oddly jointed limbs, burning up testosterone. Her sweet mother, the only oestrogen in the house, would be weighed down with her secret, the one Anjali was about to deliver, and the sadness and distraction couldn't help but read on her face. What chance would she have, with everyone asking her what was wrong?

'What is it, Anjali?'

'I've been—' began Anjali.

'You must tell me, whatever it is, I will help you, I won't be angry, I'll be on your side.'

She blurted out, 'I've been . . . in debt. I am in debt. I'm sorry.'

While Anjali cried bitterly, her mother visibly relaxed; Anjali knew she could enjoy this old chestnut. Anjali was kept afloat by an allowance because her father didn't approve of student loans, but he hadn't set up a standing order, nor any steady arrangement. He treated it instead as a hike in the pocket money he'd given her every so often from the age of fourteen. In dribs and drabs he handed over hundreds of pounds in cash if and when she asked for it. He didn't make it comfortable, either. He had this theory about the children of other accountants, somehow they were all on grants, they'd managed to fiddle their incomes to look like they were on the downhill side of the means test. He, who was an honourable accountant and paid his dues and didn't create tax havens for himself in the ex-colonies, was being penalized. It infuriated him – and she was the one who had to hear about it most often.

'Anjali,' said her mother firmly, squeezing her shoulders, 'I'm going to sit down with you and go through your expenses. Then I am personally going to be setting up a standing order, for the same amount every month. None of this is your fault!' she exclaimed. 'It's silly nonsense, this way your father has of coming here, in his car, himself, with money in his pocket, which he gives you any old how. You are a young independent woman, I'm proud of you, I am going to do it properly, even if he refuses.' She repeated this; it was her own claim to independence, 'Even if he refuses!'

Anjali broke through her tears to gallop on, 'I don't know how it happened, we had to buy some books because they weren't available in the library, and everyone else was buying them, so I felt I had to. Then the rent for here came, and I didn't want to ask Dad about the books –'

Her mother was convincing her, 'Anjali, this is dealt with, OK?'

'OK.'

'There's nothing else wrong, is there?'

Anjali smiled and shook her head. 'No—'

'Good, I know you'd tell me—' Her mother patted her hand.

It was the first time Anjali had directly lied and she felt a knife cut the join between them. None of it was untrue, but it wasn't the truth that she'd invited her mother here for, so by omission it was a lie; and her father was taking the blame for something which otherwise she'd have coped with in a very different way, by taking the job in the student bar.

A sense of isolation swept over her. It added to the picture of herself as the criminal. Her own voice was like an echo: sounding the same, but a hollow replica to deceive people as to where she truly stood.

Later, as they walked back down the stairs to the entrance

lobby, her mother was talking quickly, enjoying the euphoria of such a close relationship with her daughter. 'You know, it is an odd thing, but as I get older, the more it is that inside me is the same child as was always there at the beginning. Exactly the same concerns, you know. To be loved by my family. To be admired by someone outside the family! To be looked after and to be needed. To look after others. To have food to put down in front of us. To grow. Maybe to grow is the most important thing, to become bigger, yet this is so difficult, because, perhaps, one is always becoming smaller. Yet, to give is the secret. If one gives, one becomes bigger – it is food for the soul. And you are a giving person, you don't like to take your father's money. That is difficult to you. But it is our pleasure to give, you must realize, seeing you here at the university, and to be able to help you do well, and buy the books that everyone else buys, that you young people need to make your way in the world, this is a good thing—'

Anjali listened to the slap of her mother's sandals on the concrete steps of the hall of residence and fought back tears. She accompanied her as far as the bus stop on White Hart Lane, kissed her goodbye and then walked back; the weakness in her legs made her think she might fall.

Nio was warmed through by his encounter with Mila. A whole afternoon and an evening – and they hadn't run out of feeling. The pavement beneath his feet was a magical path into the future, the night sky with its bowl of orange light over London was incandescent, the reach of foliage over the railing as he skirted the cemetery was like the hailing of an ecstatic crowd. He was blessed; Mila was a vision. She was worth waiting for. He trudged steadily; as he passed under each street light, it switched on his lopsided smile – in the darkness between posts it was still there, but invisible.

He turned down a track between the cemetery and Coldfall

Wood. This path was frequented by dog-owners in daylight and at night by drug takers and thieves. Nio was unafraid; it wasn't in his nature to think any wrong might befall him. As he loped along, his pupils widened, accommodating the depth of night into which he moved. The scent of nettles and dogs was a powerful mix.

Coldfall Wood was patrolled by an eight-foot-high spiked alloy fence – after one too many attacks on schoolgirls – but here, in this far corner where the woodland was joined both with the cemetery and the five acres of allotments, there was one rail he'd neatly hacksawed through, fixed in place top and bottom with a catch of wire so as not to alert anyone. He'd coached a screen of beech across to disguise the entrance and was careful to lift any damaged vegetation which might betray his passing back and forth. Darkness was a common ally.

Nio stooped to flip the wire at the bottom and squeezed through sideways. It was his front gate.

A dozen yards on was what he'd come to call the Clamp. This construction had started – before the advent of the alloy fence – as a secret place under the boughs of a conifer where he'd stored woodland finds until he could later retrieve them. Then he'd left a chair here permanently, it was a good spot to sit and think about the next thing. The graves in this corner dated from the seventeenth century, they were long forgotten, but they prompted a philosophical turn of mind – thoughts of life and death. He'd come to know some of the inscriptions off by heart, and he'd grown confident that not a soul ever found their way here except him. A roof followed, just to keep the rain off, the first one was a canvas flysheet strung between the boughs. Next he'd put up one side wall because he'd found some old doors in a skip, then came a floor made out of roofing boards – he liked the upside down logic of that. The front was constructed out of french windows of differing specifications screwed together to form a glazed screen, which gave it a thirties look. A proper roof followed, made out of floorboards and bits and pieces of felt and plastic, painted over with tar. He'd started building the extension only last year, it wasn't finished yet, but nearly. Soon, when it was done, he'd invite her.

Tonight, with its single globe of yellow light a beacon through the fogged glass, Nio felt pride at the Clamp stirring the already impossible excitement of Mila and he wondered if he'd ever be happier. Yes, on her birthday, then he'd be a million times more happy, if that were possible.

He pulled at the nail which served as a door handle and stepped across the threshold.

'Yo!' heard Nio.

'Hi?' he called back.

Charmer steeped through from the extension. The spirit lamp on the floor threw up a sinister relief map of his milky white face, sulking aggressively. He shrugged into the room, his oversize clothing like sails around his legs and torso. 'Where you been? I'm starving.'

'I've been with Mila.' Nio unhooked his bag from his shoulder.

'D'you bone her?'

'Nearly,' Nio admitted. 'But . . . no, I didn't.'

'Why not?'

'Because she's only fifteen. It's against the law.'

'*What*?' Charmer was incredulous. 'She's only fifteen?'

'Nearly sixteen.'

'How long 'til?'

'About six weeks.'

'And you're going to *wait*? She'll be gone. Long gone. She'll have found someone else.'

'I don't think so.'

'She'll have found some bloke with a sports car. And a bigger *wad* in his pocket.'

Nio shook his head. 'We're in love.' That brought Charmer up short, maybe he had to chew on that, work out his reaction. For a while, both of them ate the chips that Nio had brought home. 'Vinegar?' suggested Charmer, holding out the foil slip. His voice was flat. He was softly built, big for his age, brown hair like a rug on his head, slanting over his eyes and cheekbones. He wore this sad expression, as if at any moment he'd be found out. Nio liked this interlude, the silence, stillness, but he could see it begin to work on Charmer, within two minutes it was intolerable for him, he couldn't let it happen, he had to stand up, walk around, say something. 'So – on her *birthday*, you're going to do what, give her the usual romantic nonsense, and then bring her back here and do her, it that it, am I right?'

'Yes.' Nio chewed on, smiled.

'Does she know you live like a stray dog in a hedge next to a cemetary? No washing machine, no kitchen, no toilet even? No cooker? No car to take her home in? No flat for her to move into? No jewellery, no furs?'

'She doesn't have a flat or a car herself,' Nio explained. 'She won't be worried about anything . . . like that. We have each other.'

'Except that it's those types, the lookers who don't have anything, who want stuff – *the most*. You're the older man, you're meant to help her escape from the grotty caravan scenario and the skanky mum and dad. She'll want to climb the ladder, not jump off it.'

'It's not a grotty caravan,' argued Nio, 'there are three proper trailers, one of them is quite new.'

'Have you told her about me being here yet? Have you?'

Nio didn't answer. He was worried, did Charmer think he lived here now, permanently? He was the only person who'd discovered this place to Nio's knowledge, and this time round he'd stayed for weeks, so maybe he felt threatened by Mila? Nio couldn't know the answer, the younger man was wrapped up in so much bluff, it was difficult to guess what he really thought.

Charmer mooched back and forth, eating his chips. 'You're a bit thick in the head, you are,' he said, pulling at the duck's tail of hair sticking from the back of Nio's neck. 'All girls want, right, is to have some inches, a successful bottle, more richer bottle than their friends, come along and take them away to luxury.' On his next turn round, he dabbed at Nio again. 'Someone to buzz round, fetch and carry for them, and the top job making you rich and all that, it's you giving them everything, basically . . . especially the babbies!' He knuckled the top of Nio's head twice, as if he were knocking in a fence post. 'They're always after the babbies in the end, but it's the throttle they go for, maximum throttle, innit, they don't want some tramp who doesn't eat his greens, they want the bloke who can fuck them up,' – and now he pushed Nio's chips onto the floor –'take them off somewhere decent, Sound Machine and all that, not bring them back to a hole in the ground like here.'

Nio calmly rescued his chips. Everything that Charmer said was true, but also untrue, girls wanted the same as boys; and more than *anything* that *anyone* ever wanted was – to fall in love. He and Mila had the best thing going. Once he'd finished the new upstairs bit, he'd invite her . . . but it was no use explaining to Charmer. Instead Nio continued to eat steadily, watched the performance, gave his applause. It was what was required of him, he'd learned. He'd often thought Charmer should go and study drama somewhere, but he was allergic to the word school.

Later, Nio was lying in the upstairs bedroom that he'd so nearly finished, hands behind his head. The covers were a motley collection of orange and brown blankets, rough against his skin, and he lifted a knee and lowered it again to try and settle the bedclothes more comfortably. This drew in and expelled a breath of air from the bed as if it were alive, filling and emptying its lungs, but in the pitch black Nio realized the smell just drawn over him was strong. He reached down, peeled off his socks, cast them aside. The smell was worse. Horrible. It was the opposite of the scent behind Mila's ear; and he remembered her immaculate jersey top, the brightness of her blue jeans with the sequinned belt and the dragons chasing around her ankles. How would she keep her clothes clean, if she came to stay with him, here? He sat upright, suddenly, a bolt of love sent through him. She would cope. Charmer was wrong, Mila would be happy to live in the Clamp, so what if it was a bit of a trudge to the launderette, it was no less than what she was doing now. As for bathing – Nio himself either went to his Mum and Dad's or borrowed people's bathrooms, it was part of his social life to turn up at friends' places and use their facilities – and she was the same. She'd fit in easily.

Hope clutched his heart, it was a physical sensation, deep and searing. He and Mila would live together. Total happiness might be only weeks away.

He spent an hour formulating plans for self-improvement, then tiredness overtook him and he fell asleep.

The following morning, an autumn mist lingered among the unkempt grasses of the graveyard; the riot of greenery was given a grey cast by the moisture and a special delicacy attended the air as if all this had grown overnight and today was its first awakening. Nio unbuckled his trousers and squatted over a hole in the ground he'd dug a moment earlier between two tumble-down gravestones. The granite tablets were lines of respectable soldiers in the battle of life knocked awry by nature and vandalism. Charmer's words came back to him, 'a hole in the fucking ground like here'.

But – Nio frowned as he pushed hard – these toilet arrangements were much *better* than those she was used to; having to blag the McDonald's toilets was a trial, she had to pretend to buy fries or hang around and wait until the manager had disappeared before sneaking in – nightmare. Much easier – nicer! – to take a spade out in the early morning, dig a foot square of turf, do the business – just like this . . . He finished up, replaced the sod on this morning's spot and trod it down, thinking yes, Mila would count it, as he did, a sublime communion with nature which put him at one with the other creatures who chose to live in this unvisited, neglected quarter of St Pancras Cemetery. Especially on a morning so beautiful, with the graves a respectful audience. Even when it was for longer than a week or two, after the novelty wore off, and the weather had turned bad, and she'd been disturbed a few times, Nio was confident Mila would still be held by the enchantment of it. He himself preferred this kind of toilet, day after day, yes, even in winter. He trudged back to the Clamp, the spade over his shoulder, the roll of bog paper carried on his thumb.

Later that evening, there was a third occasion when he could triumphantly answer Charmer's list of complaints. Nio returned to the Clamp; daylight still glazed the motley line of french windows. He'd braced himself for Charmer, but this evening he was alone. He unpacked from his bag a packet of Abbey Crunch and a salami; and as his penknife scored the biscuits' brittle plastic wrapping, the thought came to him of Mila's mother, her broad hips oscillating at the miniature plastic sink in Social Services as she scoured pans after another cabbage stew had been fed to the family. There was no cooker in the Clamp. Nio and Charmer ate from packets and paper bags, without knives and forks. So – would Mila be happy with endless chips and cold meat, biscuits and hunks of bread? Probably not, she would want cooked food. But there was a simple answer – he'd buy a Camping Gaz stove.

There was nothing between himself and Mila, except a short delay.

The evening wore on; Nio was disturbed only by the crows and those still at work in the allotments not far away. This rural quiet was subtly underscored by the continual, exhaling sigh of the traffic on the North Circular, the other side of the cemetery.

Suddenly, for no reason, he lost confidence, he felt panic –

where was Mila, what was she doing, who was she with? That phone of hers was always chirping.

Lucas Tooth walked up the street, marking every mother and sister. His hunger tightened – he should kick off someone new, maybe. He had the advert in his pocket, he could tweak the phone from its clip on his belt, or . . .

He decided on the plump, heavily made-up girl working in Charli's, the upmarket clothes shop for the rich of Muswell Hill. She'd vaguely smiled at him when he'd walked past the window last week and she was OK, good enough.

He retraced his steps and went in.

Idly he leafed through the racks of clothes, glancing at her occasionally. She was twisting her fingers and looking around the place as if she didn't know what she was doing – Lucas might guess this was her first job. How old was she, eighteen? Any young sister who wore that amount of make-up was insecure and that worked for him, he could get them to listen and to move closer, but then he could still hope for what he most wanted – resistance, the hand on his chest, the refusal, the fight back. Excitement.

The sister rubbed a toe on the blond Swedish flooring, looked at the ceiling, the window, the walls, as if something must happen. She picked up a tablet of paper on the sales desk.

Lucas called out, 'Excuse me?'

Her face brightened, she slunk over to him. 'I wonder if you can help me?' Lucas smiled ruefully. 'Because to tell the truth, I saw you, I thought how pretty you were, so I came in. No other reason.'

Her jaw dropped, literally. 'Oh,' she repeated, and he could watch the blood rush to her neck and jaw in patches.

Lucas laughed. 'Now you're even prettier.'

She stared at the ceiling, the window, the floor.

Lucas ducked forwards and kissed her on the cheek as if they'd been friends for years.

Then he walked out.

As he left, he turned, walking backwards and pointing at her, 'I hope your boyfriend appreciates you!' His voice was loud and confident in the hushed, self-conscious shop. She had her hand in front of her mouth, he could tell what she was thinking, she was excited at the same time as relieved he was going, she wanted him to come back and tell her more – because the fact that he'd left without her asking him to, meant he was so obviously *safe* . . .

Outside, as he walked past the window again, Lucas stuck out his tongue and waggled his fingers in his ears.

Mila jumped up and waved at Nio, signalled him over . . . yes, like always, she loved how he walked as he threaded between everyone in the packed bar, it was like he nodded along, each step was deliberate, he had this unstoppable stride, would just keep coming. She waited until he'd reached her and then wrapped her arms around his neck and kissed him. She was so looking forward to this, couldn't wait. She turned back to the plump red sofa which she'd bagged for the three of them and pointed to the lad who was sitting there nervously, holding his fingers, his hair all gelled up and wound into points, like he was sprouting thorns. 'This is . . . what's your name?' She'd had a couple of tries at remembering it.

The lad stood up now and went to shake Nio's hand. 'Tony.'

'I call him Sweetshop Boy,' said Mila, 'because he works in his dad's sweetshop and he always gives me free stuff.' She watched Nio gleefully. 'Is that OK, if is here with us for a bit?'

'Sure,' said Nio. He looked freaked suddenly – good, so he should be. She asked him, 'What d'you like to drink because you know I'm eighteen years old so I will go to buy the drinks at the bar?'

Nio rubbed his chest self-consciously, he was getting the message big time, she could tell. He replied, 'Oh . . . I'll have a pint of Carlsberg.'

'Watch this,' she said darkly and walked straight up to the counter, she was already a bit drunk and of course the barman came straight over and served her again. She could feel Nio's eyes on her back. Let him see how old she was! She was in here, in Ruby In The Dust up on the Broadway, with its cool sofas and low tables and banging sounds and everyone in here over eighteen and she could walk in and be one of them, easily. She put down her own money, which she'd earned, paying for him aged twenty-three for real, with no money.

She brought back the drinks in one clutch and plonked them down. She stepped over Nio's legs so she could sit between the two boys. She felt the triumph as she plugged in again to the three much older guys who were already hitting on her from various points in the room, they were all there, still hers. She turned to Nio. 'Look what he brought for me!' She leaned forward and fingered all the sweets on the table. 'Space Poppers, so great. And – And – Look, these is new.' She tore at the packet, took out the coil of paper with the strip of fruit gum down the middle of it. 'You just roll it in your tongue like this . . .' She nibbled on the first inch of the roll, pulling more off and chewing, pushing it into her mouth to stop it looping down her chin and out of control. 'Isn't it great?' she mumbled, finally biting it off and holding the roll out for Nio. 'Want to try?'

'No thanks.'

'Don' you like his hair?' She took Sweetshop Boy by the shoulders and skewed him around so they could all see. 'He put gel in, so then his big sister come along and smunches it all and these points are made over his head and then the gel is hard. Is it cool?'

'Looks OK,' replied Nio.

'You should do that!' exclaimed Mila and mussed Nio's hair,

trying to make his curls stand up. Then she patted them down again and combed with her fingers, pulling out the curls on his brow. She leaned close to him and whispered, 'Hope you don' mind I bring Sweetshop Boy because he was sad and I thought why not go out with him even though he's only sixteen, imagine that.' She gave her biggest smile, but didn't get one back. Good – the more these two boys were uncomfortable and a bit hurt on this sofa the more she felt like showing off. She wanted to fly, she was a bit drunk and everyone was looking at her, it was enough to make her head buzz loudly, she was excited. 'Only sixteen,' she hissed again and shook her head in pity. Then she turned quickly, 'Sweetshop, tell us what your life is like, what time do you get up for the papers?' She watched the lad stir uncomfortably and start the tale of his daily routine. She interrupted often, goaded him to say things about his family. She teased him, made him blush. How many other girls did he give sweets to, she wanted to know? She kept him going, wouldn't let him stop. He had to shout louder and louder over the noise of the place. She was aware of Nio at her shoulder, politely listening but more and more left out. Very good! Let him be left out! See how he liked it.

For two hours she showed off, while the talk in Ruby In The Dust became thicker in the air around them and everyone's eyes brightened, the girls were leaning more into the boys, everyone was drunk. No one was doing better than she was, she had a boy on each side plus the older, cooler guys trying to catch her eye. Those kind of looks were coming at her thick and fast and she could feel Nio slowly boiling with jealousy and guilt as well because she'd bought both rounds of drinks – she wouldn't let him go up to the bar – and because she was dragging Sweetshop Boy deliberately into a dream world. Look at all the gifts he had brought her. Where were Nio's gifts? It was driving him mad, it must be, because he stood up and said maybe it was time they moved on, it was obvious he expected her to come with him. She looked at his solemn face, all hurt and worried, and this evil plan crossed her mind, she had to do it. 'Yes, I agree.' She stood, swayed, and announced to Nio, 'I have to take Sweetshop Boy back to his home, I said I would, sorry about that, but can you find somewhere a phone and call me tomorrow?' She reached behind her and pulled the exhausted, hoarse Sweetshop to his feet, reached for her jacket. She deliberately didn't kiss Nio goodbye, she just gave him an insane smile and told him, 'He's very young, he needs looking after.' Then she left, towing the youth behind her, plus she gathered a last few lingering looks from the older guys in this smoke-filled, blasted, happening room.

Outside she tucked her arm in Sweetshop Boy's and started to walk him back down Colney Hatch Lane, talking too much, she was drunk, what was happening? The fresh air, and the sudden absence of music, and the cruel London night with its heartless chasing around of humanity, all this changed her mood, second by second she felt more stupid, what had she done? Yes, the drink had carried her away, with each sip she'd gone a further distance from her real self. She missed Nio, plus she was being cruel to Sweetshop Boy.

She stopped, tugged her arm free. 'I have to go,' she said urgently, 'can you find your own road?' She kissed him on both cheeks. 'Thank you.' Then she turned and hurried back, her stride unsteady, tears in her eyes; that was the trouble with alcopops, you were always more drunk than you thought. She had to catch Nio, tell him it was all right – she broke into a run now.

She caught sight of Nio, then, walking from Ruby In The Dust down to the fish and chip shop, she guessed. He had his hands in his pockets, a mournful figure, his shoulders sloped with disappointment, she'd hurt him. 'Stupid man,' she muttered under her breath. She broke into a run and caught him up, lifted his arm and walked under it. 'Joke over,' she said. He left his arm over her shoulders but didn't say a word, so yes, if he was wooden like this, and quiet, then maybe she'd gone too far. But he deserved it! She elbowed him. 'Cheer up.'

After he'd bought them chips, they strolled back, spearing their food with the wooden forks. Close to the roundabout she looked up and saw – surprise – Sweetshop Boy, he hadn't gone home after all, he'd followed her, and he was the mournful figure now, kicking his heels outside Ruby In The Dust, and when he saw them he swung away, pretending he hadn't noticed. She felt a thrill of triumph and a pang of guilt at the same time and wondered, maybe it was all right, Nio was jealous, so it had worked.

Halfway down Colney Hatch Lane there was a litter bin and they threw their chip papers away. Come on Nio, she thought, hurry up . . . she couldn't wait, she wanted to kick him, slap him! Life was too short to hang about and not have what you wanted . . . why wouldn't he take her home, so what if the bedroom wasn't finished? She took the palm of his hand, clapped it against her bum, held it there. Then she took it off, threaded it round her neck and moulded it around her breast. No reaction, it was crazy. What did she have to do?

Two days later, Nio was helping her family move from the Retail Park, hours before Haringey Council were due to throw them out. He was signalling that he needed help, while she ignored him. Anyone else and she'd have stepped up for it but she was still in the mood to punish him because he wouldn't break his own rule, he'd turned her down for another two whole days. She watched him lifting the bricks off the plastic sheeting and making a neat pile of them, then he drew off the sheet; it floated to the ground, a giant apron of black – She loved him, though, for helping, look at her cousin who did nothing, expected things to happen by themselves, and her brother . . . and her dad . . .they were dotted around, trying to pretend this wasn't happening. Social Services, The Home Office and The Kingdom of God all had their doors open and they were in and out, mournful, useless.

Nio waved at her again, he wanted her to help him fold it. She waved back cheerfully and didn't move an inch. Did he know how lucky he was? Look how she had men crawling after her, begging her for what every man wanted? They tried to buy her at Sangatte, and the Haringey housing officer had wanted to move her into his own home, and there was the Adventist religious guy, plus the men at Ruby In The Dust . . . She wandered into The Kingdom of God, the most cheaply built of the trailers, the home of the men – her dad, her cousin and her brother – and looked out at Nio through the window. Maybe she only wanted him so much because he refused to give in.

Her father stood beside her, he moved the pages of a newspaper, licking his thumb in that way he had and grumbling, 'How does he know we can stay there?'

'He doesn't know, he just thinks we can.'

'Is it a friend of his?'

'No, someone he just met by accident, who works for the roads.'

'Have you met him?'

'No.'

'Maybe he will ask us to pay.'

'He can't ask for money, it's not his place, he just works there.'

'How long can we—?'

'I don't know, Dad, how would anyone know that?' She watched as Little Vlad hauled the dog, Nisha, along on her chain.

'The land under our feet should belong to us, to—'

'Well, it won't.'

'Who owns the ground there, who actually can walk on that ground, where we're going, and say it is mine, right through to the middle of the earth, that inch of ground is mine, who is that, hmm?'

'Dad, how do I know, it's just the edge of the road, the road goes down and at the end—'

'Downhill?? What good is that?'

'It's not steep.'

'Why doesn't your boyfriend have us in his house if he likes you so much? Hmmm?'

'Ahh!' Mila stamped her foot. She wanted her dad to go away, she wanted just to watch Nio without being interrupted. He had folded the plastic sheet now and was carrying belongings over to Social Services. The ramp on the old Mazda pick-up was down; from the back a pair of hands appeared, and lit a cigarette.

'You have been to his home, I suppose?'

'They are still building it, when it's finished I will be invited.'

'Is it big, his house? He is very rich?'

She didn't answer – didn't want to say no, nor did she want to tell her father what kind of place Nio lived in. It would sound worse than their own lives. She'd lied to them, she'd said he had a job and so on and now it was too much like hard work to keep it up, she wanted to throw up her hands and admit everything, he had nothing, no money at all, not even a proper job like she had. Bad, bad news! But could she help it? She was beating Nio along, she really wanted to push him around, get him a job or have him make some things and sell them or . . . anything.

An hour later, because she was the lightest, Mila was in the driving seat of the Nissan they'd borrowed. The men pushed her around the car park. She dropped the clutch a few times and felt the engine, lumpy and weak, fail again and again. It caught, then stopped. And again! It was hot and everyone was tired and fed up.

From her position looking out of the side window of the car she noticed a figure coming across the car park. From his gait, how his feet in their loafer shoes pointed slightly outwards, and the way he held down his tie and smoothed his hair back with the flat of his palm, she recognized the guy from the furniture place. She felt the blood heat in her veins. As he drew near, several of her clan went to meet him and she thought for a moment there was going to be a fight – she'd join in. Without hesitation she pushed open the car door and stepped out, ready. She saw her cousin turn and point at her, so she put on her best sulky face and stroppy walk to go and give Furniture Guy an earful, see him off. He was the one – he'd admitted it – who'd called Haringey every day to get rid of them. And he'd banged on their window that night, for no good reason, probably he'd been drunk. The anger rose in her. He was smiling, holding out the palms of his hands, which made it worse. His face was red, swollen with embarrassment. 'I've come to ask if there is anything I can do to help,' he began.

'Yes. Give us a million pounds.'

'Seriously, if you need . . . I am very sorry to see you go.'

'It was your, you . . . you—' Mila's English ground to a halt. She slumped on one leg, glared at him.

'Listen, I just wanted to say no hard feelings, I hope? And I see you have trouble, I can put my own vehicle at your disposal. OK? That's all. Bygones are bygones.' He held out his hand but she didn't shake it. 'I have a big vehicle,' he went on, 'with a tow hitch and you have . . . your troubles . . . well, I am at your disposal. Really. At all times. OK?'

Mila squinted at him, didn't nod once or acknowledge what he was saying, she just stared him out, the creep. She watched him turn, walk away. Again came that distinctive gesture, how he caught hold of his tie, moved it to the middle, patted it home. He gave a half-turn, a half wave goodbye, but she didn't offer him anything in return. The loafer shoes, toes pointed outwards, carried him back to his shop. He had this other thing he did – he often felt at the hem of his jacket, as if he'd lost something in the lining. They'd got very used to seeing him, going in there for the sweets in that bowl.

She sensed Nio come alongside. He asked, 'What did he want?' and for a while she didn't reply. Then she found an answer, 'He wanted my phone number.' She smiled at Nio because – look! – a cloud of jealousy passed in front his eyes, it had jerked his chain, it was great to see that, so she rubbed it in, smiled at him some more and said, 'He says he has a very big . . . oh, he has a very big something, I didn't understand, but he said I can do what I want with it.' She watched him nodding and smiling ruefully. 'I see,' he replied. She was so, so going to get Nio. He'd never keep this up.

Of course, two seconds later, love for him just melted her. 'Not really,' she admitted and sighed heavily. She punched him in the chest. 'Don't look like that, go away!' she said. 'Because I go now to drag him out of his shop and go out with him.' She told everyone to wait and stalked over to the furniture warehouse, not even looking back to check Nio's reaction. She went in and trailed the aisles until she found – what was his name? Ahmed, she read on his lapel badge, in gleaming brass letters. She didn't know how to pronounce it so began her question, 'Arr-med.'

A couple of hours later, she was pushing Nio, along with the dog, into the back of the Mazda pick-up and lifting the tailgate on him, while she herself was the only passenger in Ahmed's brand new Shogun. It was unreal, the seat held her like she was a fighter pilot, the whole thing moved off with a dizzying rush and no engine noise, until they caught up with the lumbering back-end of The Kingdom of God. She was miles high, everything smelled so clean, the plastic fascia was so muscular, it was a rich, rich place. She watched the gold bracelet dangle on Ahmed's wrist, how it glowed against his dark skin, as he drove the few hundred yards to the next exit. He was explaining something but she didn't understand.

The half-mile journey was like a fairground ride. She hoped Nio was having his teeth broken, riding in that old Mazda which didn't have any suspension. Just wait till she told him that she wanted a Shogun car just like this, and he had to buy it for her or else, no questions asked. He had to get out there and work hard . . .

They took the next exit, but instead of turning left for Muswell Hill or right for Tesco's, they followed her dad straight over, as if they were going to rejoin the North Circular. There was the little caravan, tucked away on rough ground at the verge. The Cortina pulled in ahead of them, but her father's driving was rubbish, she held her hand to her mouth when she saw their trailer clip the caravan, it bucked sideways, he'd given it a good whack. As she drove past she spotted a bit of damage, they were in trouble right from the start. Ahmed hadn't seen, he talked on, God knows what about, she didn't stop him, she just waited while he drew in ahead of the Cortina and slowly reversed Social Services into line. She held her head in her hands, she didn't want trouble from this stupid accident.

She waited until the last possible moment before she pulled on the handle, let herself out of the Shogun. The door felt heavy, yet it seemed to spring open almost by itself. She climbed out and started to walk uphill and Nisha was there, right under her feet. Mila bent to pet her. She kept her gaze down, she didn't want to see her father having a row, maybe even a fight . . . but she had to look up, find out what was happening. When she did, the autumn sun crossed her, she lifted her hand to shield her eyes, couldn't see a thing.

Lucas was writing out names and addresses and filling the little envelopes, when he felt a jolt to the body of the caravan. Fear interrupted his heart's rhythm and it stopped, literally. For two seconds it rested, inert. Then adrenalin surged in his chest and it started again, with the first five or six beats coming as quick as a bird's wing. He was short of breath, as if at the top of a mountain. Everyone and everything disappeared, he was alone, there wasn't even firm ground beneath his feet, he only existed in this one thought – what was happening? He was on his feet immediately, he swayed, his instinct was to run, hide, but he waited for the impulse to pass, because if it had been the police they'd just have burst the door.

No, a car must have swerved, run into his caravan. In which case . . .

Self confidence clothed him, now. He pulled at the door; bright autumn sun bleached the scene outside, he shaded his eyes and stepped down into the road, annoyed, to see what had happened.

Downhill from him was a mobile home, a much bigger thing than his, a trailer, and the jolt had been caused by its swinging too close. As he stared, two of the same were slowly towed past him down the slip road, indicators merrily signalling.

It was a buckled Cortina which had sideswiped him. Now it was skewed at an angle and the driver's door was opening. A thickset man with a tuft of grey hair growing from each cheek-bone rolled out and stood upright. The other two caravans were pulling over in front; the whole convoy stretched far enough down the slip road almost to touch the traffic on the North Circular. The man with the coarse salt-and-pepper hair was coming towards him.

Lucas looked at the damage. A spray of fibreglass was torn from the white skin of his caravan. It looked like a piece of dried muscle. He couldn't tear his eyes from it; he was cold with anger. It had been a lucky find, this shell, the private carapace of his goings on: the two-hourly sleeps, the winning of the mothers and sisters, the trading in the magazine adverts, running the stash . . .

He felt the presence of the man nearby and curbed his instinct to fly at him. 'You can't stay here,' he turned and stated flatly, 'this is for the Highways.'

The man replied, but in an incomprehensible language. One word came in English, 'sorry'. Lucas stood, chewing his cuff, uncomfortably exposed – what was going on? 'You can't stay here,' he shouted. 'Go on, fuck off.' He felt a judder start from his spine and vibrate through his shoulders ending in a spasm, he shook like a dog throwing off water. This was dangerous, he ought to walk away.

The moaning of the other two cars' engines stopped; there was now, downhill from Lucas Tooth, what looked like a parade of holidaymakers: three caravans and three cars. The first one was backed close to Lucas', hitched to the Cortina skewed in the roadway. Next was a bigger one, delivered by an incongruously new Mitsubishi Shogun, its passenger door opening. Parked beyond, just coming to a halt, was a smaller unit delivered by an old Mazda two-door pick-up with a home-made top bolted on to provide cover. The aluminium tailgate was lowered; inside was packed with people. A dog, an old Alsatian, was the first to slope off the ramp.

Then Lucas saw the sister as she stepped out of the Shogun and dipped on one knee to pet the dog. She straightened, shielded her eyes against the bright autumn sun and walked uphill towards him. She was wearing a tight bra top with a shiny silver Puffa jacket and ripped jeans with the top button undone as if she'd casually forgotten it.

She was OK, she'd do.

He turned round. It was important she didn't see him like this, and not here. He stepped smartly into the caravan and slammed the door behind him, stood rooted to the spot. A sudden gravity pinned him down. He made plans – how to meet her. From what he'd seen this sister, yes, was worth something, if a bit young. He could picture her lying at his feet.

Ahmed roared up the entrance road with customary disregard for the speed bumps. There was a gathering around the spot where the caravans had once stood. The bailiffs and police were gone; these were the council's refuse and sanitation services who'd agreed to clear up in advance of tomorrow's trading. A type with an orange safety jacket was pushing an automated cleaning machine back and forth like a lawn mower. Others threw the last bits of debris into the maw of the rubbish truck. He parked outside the doors of Family Furniture, pegged the handbrake on its first click and sprung from the vehicle. Good news, now they could start making some money. The car park was back to normal except for an oil-stain. The rubbish truck's doors were slamming shut, its brakes hissing as it executed the turn.

Before he went into his warehouse, Ahmed walked around to Computer World. Once or twice he'd spoken to the manager and now he wanted to share the triumph of that girl riding in the front with him . . . and he knew her name as well – Mila . . . something. She'd sat right next to him. How about that? He looked through the glass frontage, but couldn't see anyone. When he turned, he was swept by a sense of the desolation of the after-hours Retail Park. There were only a few vehicles, and no one around except the idly moving population of the McDonald's restaurant in the bottom-most corner, which operated its own car park and drive-thru service. His eye was drawn back to the oil-stain left by the gypsies. This was the first mark against the newness of the place, and the perfection of his surroundings – so hard won, so expensive – was something Ahmed fought for. If they threw down sawdust and then burnt it off, the tarmac might be good as new. Might.

He strode back to the Shogun, his heels thudding uncomfortably hard. Putting on weight again. Must do better. Less bread. Young girlfriend like Mila, he needed to keep himself young. As he passed his gleaming new vehicle, he thought that even this strong and uncompromising piece of machinery, which had so impressed the girl, was beginning its descent into the realm of second-hand. A scratch nagged him constantly from its position on the vehicle's flank. He sought it out like an irritation on his own skin.

As he unlocked the sliding glass doors to Family Furniture he cursed himself for always alighting on what was wrong, however much circumstances should buoy him up. Just two years ago his complaint was with the family business in Holloway Road – a second-hand furniture shop crammed to the rafters with useless junk. He'd escaped by developing a business retailing reproduction stone and marble fireplaces. He'd done well, got out of that with a bit of money in hand, so now he owned and ran this immaculate warehouse dealing only in new product, plus within the financing package he'd found a corner to pay for the Shogun. Top of the range, long wheelbase, all the trimmings. He'd done that, come this far, and now, *now*, all he could do was worry about the scratch on the effing vehicle. He'd railed against the gypsies, yet, what was it, ten minutes later, his hands still grubby from unhitching their caravans no less, he was building up a head of steam against the little oil-stain they'd left behind . . .

He locked the doors behind him and felt a twinge of regret, though, at not having Mila close by any more. Shame. It was a regular date they'd had – his observing her return from work at the Tesco superstore. Dressed in the uniform, of course. Dark blue – rayon he'd guess. Electrifying. Then her reappearance, very different, in the girlish fashions she wore. Neither his own female staff, nor that of Computer World or Fitness Warehouse, held such fascination. His feelings towards her type – gypsies or refugees or whatever they were – aggravated his commercial instincts at exactly the same time as they stirred his libido, even so far as a pulse in his groin lifting his manhood in a delicate nod in her direction. Such a gentle, secret greeting! And one that was at odds with the cursing he gave them for losing him money. He could only imagine how the oil on the tarmac would correspond to a similar but different type of stain that would have settled on the back seat of the Shogun, following his tender lovemaking to her, which unaccountably she would need, enjoy. With Ahmed, here at last she'd be with someone who knew what he was doing. He rubbed his hands. And who was established in this country. Decent wheels, everything. Her eyes would have been opened to the world of real men, men who had a few miles on the clock, who carried a bit of weight, his belly would pin her down all right. She'd become dependent on him, hungry in a way that never before . . .

He blinked several times. It wasn't productive, this train of thought. He had to prepare himself now for an onslaught of customers, a vigorous trading climate would prevail tomorrow. He walked the aisles, heading for the office. Beyond the right product in the right place, what was mostly required in successful retailing was a kind of mental and physical fitness – that was the work.

Except, the girl's absence, the empty Shogun, felt like a mild grief.

Anjali paced her room this lunchtime, back and forth, often stopping to look out of the large window from which she could see the driveway leading into this All Saints site of Middlesex University. She could see her reflection also – the round face, the bob haircut, the pools of the eyes, all darkness and shadow – that was herself, no mistake, she had to live with it, no getting away . . .

When she saw her father's car drive in the gates she knew she wouldn't be able to contain her emotions. He was meant to be here to go through her living expenses and set up the standing order, but he was always on the lookout for the worst of her behaviour, he dug for any small shame that might lurk, all the time he did that, what chance would she have of keeping her secret under his critical gaze? And what was her secret? That she'd advertised for a boyfriend and hadn't managed to see what type of person he was – she, a student of psychology, had been blinded by the shine on his jacket. She scooped up her credit cards, her student ID and her weekly Travelcard and stuffed them in her purse, which she dropped in the striped woollen bag; she was quick enough and left just as the buzzer sounded in her room to announce him. She hurried down the stairs at the opposite end of the building and left via the side entrance, for pedestrians only. She didn't want to see him, couldn't.

Yet, it was likely he'd hang around and wait for her. She ought to go somewhere, hide . . . She hurried down the street, the striped woollen bag bumping her hip. Where could she go?

Then she found herself at the bus stop. She waited for a while, wondering what to do. All she knew was that she had to avoid him. It was no penalty either to escape from that claustrophobic, lonely room. A bus came, she followed the line of people, rooted in her bag for her bus pass and got on. It wouldn't cost any extra just to ride the bus there and back, whichever one it was.

Among the crowd, she understood that everyone was like her; she was like everyone else. The sounds of these bodies – the mingled whisper of their breathing, the rustle of clothing, the shuffle of footwear across the deck of the bus – were the disguise behind which everyone lived in silence, their interiors the same as hers, they were occupying together common ground, all troubled enough no doubt. She felt as cheap and ordinary as a newspaper. But, among this shifting pack of anonymous citizens, Anjali felt a purpose grow in her – to escape from this shame. And maybe the only way to kick free of it was to go back and confront him, now. After all, she had liked him when she'd first met him. She had so *liked* him. That must be worth something, she couldn't have been entirely wrong.

When the bus swerved into the kerb at Bounds Green tube station, she didn't move. The bus emptied, filled. She was pressed even closer by her own kind. She continued to Muzzers – so was this a decision, now?

The journey terminated here so everyone poured off the

bus – she was carried by the flow. She walked down Colney Hatch Lane, kept going past the turning that would have lead to her parents' cul-de-sac. Although her footsteps tried to turn in that direction, she kept going towards the North Circular. She would ask him why . . . what . . . it was like an itch.

Her own recklessness set her on edge. She tied back her hair with a scrunchy and pulled sunglasses from her bag although the sky was overcast. For a moment, next to the petrol station, she paused, almost turned back. She took another circuit of the aisles in the mini supermarket, and when she came out she found she had the courage to go on, yes, it felt like everything to do with raw courage, just to look at where it had happened. He'd apologize, it was drink, or something, he'd explain. She'd forgive him, and leave behind the ashamed, damaged side of her, the side of her which had been happier in the crush of people in the bus than among her own family, which if she didn't watch out would be her home now, the only place she could feel anonymous – where her shame was as secret as everyone else's, regardless of race or gender.

She walked onwards, hurrying, the signwork above the shops familiar from her childhood, flashes of colour in the window displays. Small details of her life had been played out on these pavements, but to conjure them now was to see them happening to someone else, not her.

A mile further on, the road swooped in a gently declining corner before rising to the intersection which would set vehicles either heading around the North Circular Road or straight on for Tesco superstore and the borough of Barnet. The pavement here was reduced to a foot wide; she had to step into the road to let a rare pedestrian pass. Her head was down, yet, through the line of greenery the wrecked cars winked, glinted, caught the eye through gaps between foliage and the hoarding advertising the coming skate-park. They rose like an apocalyptic vision, it seemed like they were still moving, strange metal fish plunging in a crowded tank caught in the flash of a camera, forever eloquent of a single moment of violence, their impact. They reflected the collision she herself had suffered . . . she was likewise still damaged, the shape of the impact was still printed on her mental frame. She felt a wave of sorrow – yet she was prepared to forgive him, she *wanted* to, so she could go back to being her old self.

Her utter carelessness, which felt like courage, carried her along quicker as she approached the intersection, breasted the top of the rise. The last time she'd been here she'd been running in the opposite direction, but now she grabbed hold of her fear with both hands, turned it round. Her heart was in her mouth; she felt sick, her knees were weak. She slowed, looking ahead, waiting for the green emblem to turn to red, so she'd have a reason to stop. It worked in her favour: as she reached the crossing the red figure lit up, she was exactly where she needed to be. She glanced left down the slip road to see the caravan – just the same – tucked into the fence, except like a bad joke now there were *four* caravans in a row. She was shocked – in one moment her courage deserted her and she wanted to run. It was as if his vehicle had been breeding, there were four men like him now. It left her feeling stupid and small and . . . she wanted to go, immediately. Cars filtered left, preventing her from crossing, so she looked again, and her pulse beat wildly when she imagined that the doors of all four caravans might swing open and out step four men like him – relatives, brothers – who . . . a blot of cloud obscured her imagination, she shook her head. She needed to get away.

Across the road, the red emblem disappeared; beneath it the figure in green switched on, signalling she might cross; her feet stumbled as she ran. Get real, she told herself. She blinked back tears.

She remembered the sequence of events: first the idiotic

placing of the advert in the lonely hearts, it was so unlike her to have done something like that but she'd got fed up with waiting . . . didn't matter, it was water under the bridge. His phone message in response. The first meeting in the pub up at the Broadway. He'd worked in a prison, he'd said, running a drugs rehab programme. He'd borrowed money from her . . . it was all lies, she should never have believed in him for one minute. More like, he'd been in prison himself. That was why he could talk about it so authoritatively. He hadn't run the programme, he'd attended it. The money he'd borrowed and never returned . . . she was so naïve, she'd believed him and . . . Get real, she told herself again, she'd been fooled and betrayed utterly and she should report him to the police to prevent the same thing happening to someone else.

Beyond the Tesco superstore the pavement emptied of people and the cars became fewer; she felt uncomfortably exposed with the tears running down her face. People looked at her; she needed the anonymity of a crowd. She crossed the road and waited at a bus stop. She boarded a 134 and headed into town.

At each stop, people climbed on; for every new soul she measured a decrease in her own anxiety. When the bus was sufficiently crowded that someone had to sit next to her, it was a comfort. These unusual sensations, opposite to what she would normally have felt, she observed in herself critically as if they were happening to someone else. She measured their vibration, analysed their causes. She was an experiment, a laboratory rat, disposable. She looked carefully at the legs of the man next to her: brown jeans, much washed, neatly encasing his thin legs. From this, she tried to guess what he might look like. She glanced at his face – wrong.

At Tottenham Court Road the bus came to a halt and the engine juddered and fell silent; this was the end of the journey. Along with everyone else she trooped off. It was by now around four-thirty in the afternoon. She took a few steps, found herself staring at an empty stretch of tarmac underneath the Centrepoint building and so blindly turned back to join the general flow towards Oxford Street. She found her rhythm, allowing others to carry her along, never forcing a path but waiting to be taken wherever the crowd willed. The crowd was enormous, closely pressed, she was lost in the unstructured warmth of humanity. Such numbers, moving with such care, enclosing her. It was like a ridiculous wealth.

An hour later, her legs and feet had grown tired; her shoes were hurting. Perhaps she should buy a new pair? And she was looking for somewhere to rest. So, for a while, she sat in the shoe department of Selfridges. The shop assistants asked her twice if she needed any help, they were sympathetic; she left before she outstayed her welcome.

She was hungry now, and managed to find a stool in the window of a Starbucks Coffee Shop which was packed with people. Again she was faced with her reflection in the glass. It was automatic, to tell herself her face was too round, she wasn't pretty enough, but the dark eyes were large, soulful . . . She sipped her coffee and ate a doughnut.

As she sat there, a wave of sadness broke over her. The striped woollen bag slipped from her shoulder, snagged her arm, trailed from her fingers; she let it go on purpose, mentally said goodbye.

After a while, she didn't think it was right to take up a seat when there were others having to stand who'd bought refreshments. The moment she shifted from her seat, someone had their hand on it. She smiled, moved on.

The pace and meaning of the city had changed. People who worked here during the day were going home; now it was Friday evening and revellers were drifting in to enjoy themselves. Many of the big stores were closed. There was louder talking on the streets. The cars gunned their engines more fiercely and music was broadcast from open windows.

She sat on a bench just off Bond Street in an upmarket pedestrian street which she'd never visited before – the shops were too expensive. A group of young people colonized the bench next to hers; she politely moved on to allow their greater number to spill over and use her bench as well. They were much younger than she was – in their early teens – yet were dressed in rich clothes and carried shopping bags printed with the names of the shops on either side.

Hunger opened wider in her middle but she wasn't concerned to find food; more important was a place to stop where she wouldn't feel the pressure to move on. It was a nice autumn evening; she wanted a pleasant spot. She walked some distance, for at least an hour, and settled finally in Trafalgar Square, with the towering authority of Nelson's Column taking her eye to the starless London sky, and the grand weight of the lions implacable, with the fourth plinth playfully holding an inverted replica of itself, a reflection cast in transparent resin by a leading modern artist.

She sat and thought what a wonderful city London was, drawn such a long way through history that it was overwritten a million times; it was like the proverbial schooldesk occupied by so many generations of children that their signatures carved one on top of the other have become indecipherable. She hoped London would cling for ever to its grandeur and never be torn down by war or poverty or misuse, she felt a great love for her city, and it was odd to have this thought just when she had nowhere to call home, but she silently begged the planners and architects and the mayor's office to please have respect, good judgement, and yet a sense of innovation and adventure.

The character of the city changed further. Alcohol seeped into the population like groundwater rising, to float people's behaviour to this level of excess, whether of happiness or aggression. By tomorrow morning it would have subsided. She picked herself up, stretched her legs by taking a turn around the lions. If people looked at her, she smiled back. When she came round to the same spot, she felt comfortable enough to sit down again. It crossed her mind to go home, but her Travelcard had been in her bag, which had contained everything she'd needed to cope with everyday life – her credit cards, student card, railcard, phone book, driving licence. No matter, because in any case she didn't want any of it, nor did she want to return home – instead she wanted to sink lower, yes, if she was falling, if that was the direction she was going, she'd grit her teeth and go with it, fall faster, swim deeper.

She felt tearful, yet strong, at the sudden charge in her.

Lucas Tooth lingered on the pedestrian bridge spanning the A406 North Circular Road. He stood as straight as a post, immobile, hands on the rail, watching the five sisters who worked in the Tesco superstore cross the bridge. He liked the idea of them as a pack, wearing their uniforms, and from the labels pinned to their breasts he knew their names. Led here by the best looking one, he'd become entranced by these uniformed girls. He'd watched them for hours this past week – taking in how they worked at such a lick, how they sat in rows at the checkouts, their backs swaying as they reached for items and passed them over the supermarket's infallible electronic eyes. There was a table in the café area from which he could view them in comfort. He couldn't be sure, even, that he was the only one taking an unhealthy interest in them. Jayne, Donna, Maria, Lynne, Emma – yes – he wanted all of them together now as he spied on them walking jauntily across, showing off to each other. One was smoking. On the other side of the bridge Donna turned down the slip road as he'd expected, past the caravan which he'd abandoned now. It was a dead haunt, he'd taken his stash, folded the sheaf of E's into his inside pocket, slipped the twelve grams of coke into a belt purse, and moved camp to Birchwood Avenue. He didn't like having to look at the mother there quite so often, but it was clean. He'd always managed to look immaculate himself; even in the detritus of the abandoned caravan he'd kept sleek. The inch or two around his person, what he touched against, he was fastidious about, nothing else mattered, but where he was parked now, the mother ironed his shirts the same night.

He watched as Donna greeted the dog, and then pulled open – it took some effort, two or three tugs – the door to the third caravan in the row. She stepped up. She had good legs, good everything. Then she disappeared; a moment later her hand reappeared, slammed the door behind her. He wasn't concerned to lose her, he knew the best-looking sisters were often the most disappointing: either they wouldn't listen, no connection would be made, or if they did listen then often they just folded, gave way completely and would do anything, which was less good for him.

As he watched, the ragamuffin brother or whatever sauntered down the slip road and gave the same two or three tugs at the door, disappeared inside as well, carrying something. Lucas Tooth imagined following the boy into the caravan. She'd be changing her clothes. The uniform would come off, a cheap fabric like that would leave her body hardly without touching. There was a wintery chill in the air today; she'd be shivering in bra and knickers. She'd scrabble for stuff to put on. All this he could see in his head.

He crossed the bridge himself now, enjoying the small betrayal of Donna disappearing from sight. It felt God-like, on this bridge, looking down on the fragile trailer the sister lived in. It was as if he might cast a spell, say she was his, he'd have her.

He followed the others up Colney Hatch Lane. Leaving Donna aside, there were four left to play with.

The sweethearts walked in a circle, just to make sure no one could see them. The trees stood slim and straight on all sides, threaded with scores of paths made by dogs and their walkers. There wasn't time to notice the trees' slow, invisible growth – the cutting of the paths by human feet was the virulent life force in Coldfall Wood.

Mila took a call; it was Hilly or someone like that, Jayne's flatmate, leaving their address in Barnard Hill where Mila could stay the night whenever she wanted. Mila stamped, leaned into her phone. Nio shepherded her.

When they came around again to the topmost corner, Nio checked in all directions. He took a while; there was no hurry. Sometimes the kids climbed the trees – he scanned every corner of the woods, he wanted to make perfectly sure there was no one in sight. Then he guided her to the part of the fence which he'd cut, slipped the wire catch and they ducked through. A minute later they were out of sight in this ancient, neglected quarter of St Pancras Cemetery.

'Close your eyes,' said Nio.

'OK.' She grinned, popped the gum from one side of her mouth to the other. He took her elbow and guided her forward.

'I hope you don't mind walking on people's graves.'

'No, long as they are really dead and don't pretend.'

He guided her carefully for a dozen paces along the path, then at first sight of the Clamp he stopped her. 'OK, open.'

She did – and saw how the path ran like in a fairy story through the graves to the door of a crooked house. It was an erratic construction of doors piled on one another, at least half made of glass and all of them painted different colours – red, green, black and white. Some of them were laid on their sides, some upright. Yet it all fitted tightly and at one end, just like he'd told her, there was a bedroom above. She was about to say, 'Wow', as she stood and faced Nio's home that he'd built for himself here, because she loved it and she knew his gaze was on her as she looked over every inch, and yes she was amazed; this was, like, another really cool thing to have done, but she didn't want to say 'Wow' again like before, so instead she went the other way, to tease him, she shrugged and said, 'It's OK.'

Nio's heart leaped, she was clever to tease him; just when it meant a lot, she'd put him on the end of a skewer, he fell in love with her again.

'Surprise it took so long, though,' she said.

Pride rushed to Nio's breast, and a storm of appreciation, at the way she was handling his stupid attachment to this place. They stepped forwards together – picking their way over the jumbled, hidden graves. Nio stopped her, 'I like this one. "Anna Tannen, died aged 56, 1874. Don't weep for me, you who pass me by, as you are now, so once was I, as I am now, soon you will be, prepare for death and follow me." Isn't that sad?'

'Really sad,' agreed Mila. She didn't have a clue what he was talking about.

Closer to the Clamp itself, she could see part of the front wall was made of a bookcase, it had shelves on which stood ornaments he must have found in the graveyard, broken bits of stonework.

Mila felt an attack of nerves, this place had in an instant doubled up the love she already had for Nio as an artist, she could say he was good with his hands all right, she so could say that, feel that . . . and she had plenty she could give him back, she had her job and her good looks and she could sing really well and . . .

He tugged on the nail to open the glass doors and she walked through ahead of him. He put his hand on her hip and he loved it when she dragged it around to the flat of her stomach so they walked in together; it made him topple against her. The loose button at the top of her jeans was a thrill; what an invitation that was, he felt it, and it was dangerous, he had to wrestle with all his might to keep his mind on the straight and narrow, to be honourable, he must treat her decently.

She, on her part, couldn't believe he wasn't going to deal with her now he'd brought her here. Anyone else would have, long ago. 'Is *fantastic*,' she said, looking around inside. There was a little stove and it must be alight, the place was warm. She felt him break from her and he strode over to the back wall – so maybe he wouldn't want to cling to her for every second. His voice was a vibration, it was one of those times she could only understand odd words. '. . . are just doors,' he was saying, '. . . throw them out . . . all the time you know . . . And wherever I had a . . .' he tapped a plane of glass, '. . . in a window. I've got my own . . . fit it . . . shape . . . so that's why . . . are so odd.'

She liked the tools hanging around, the saws and chisels and hammers, all these boys' toys, she wanted him to have everything he wanted, to build, play, be an artist, whatever, her guy should be who he wanted to be.

He pointed out three windows dotted about, one only six inches square in size. 'This one here,' said Nio, peering through the green circle of light, 'is just a wine bottle cemented into the hole.'

'I want more of those,' exclaimed Mila, peering into the tiny windows. She frowned. 'And I want them now. Because the colour.' She turned, gazing at the ceiling, taking in every inch.

He pointed. 'The roof is made out of floorboards', and then he stamped his foot, 'and the floor's made out of roofing slats. Wrong way up, this house. And the chair I was telling you about,' he announced, dropping a hand to the dusty pink arm-chair which had been here the longest, it was the original thing he'd found and put under the tree, the whole place built around it.

'But you don' want to live? Here? With me?'

Nio hesitated. He knew she wanted to leave home, he had to give her somewhere, but could it be here? He wasn't sure; like Charmer had said, it might not be right, in the long term, it was

OK for a while, but . . . Charmer's warnings about 'lookers' came back to him, she'd want the normal things. He covered himself, 'I am living here at the moment, while I get a job.' He could see her excitement at that – yes, she wanted him to have a job, he knew that now for sure. 'And then I can afford a proper flat.'

'A proper flat?' Mila didn't want to wait for some 'proper flat', mostly she didn't want to hear one more word about the cousin her family had lined up for her. She wanted to be Western, not Eastern European. She wanted to be with Nio. While he got the job and the flat, she could live here with him, surely? After the birthday? Wouldn't he invite her? He must, had to.

'We need a flat really, if we can afford it.' He smiled. 'And we have to buy you a big car, of course.' He smiled.

She clapped loudly, stalked the room with her coltish gait. 'At last. Yes please. I will have that Shogun. Brand new. Sunroof and electric windows.' She bumped up against him, it was like she was on a piece of elastic. She picked up and turned his hand and examined its mechanics, tested how far the fingers separated, curling and unfolding them; its weight and strength compared to her own almost scared her. It felt heavy and inert, like a mechanical tool. 'I still have Ahmed's number, you know.' She smiled at him, couldn't stop.

Her smile fed his in return – but even as a joke, Nio couldn't bear the idea of Mila anywhere near Ahmed and the Shogun, nor anyone else for that matter. His stomach was a pit of nerves.

He asked, 'D'you want to see upstairs?'

She blinked. 'Upstairs?'

'The bedroom.'

Mila thought, this must be it. She took a serious, serious kiss from him, snuck a finger into the belt-loop of his jeans and tugged. 'Proper bedroom,' she said, very, very softly, and leaned against his shoulder. She could make it happen now, she'd worn him down. She pushed against him. She'd wind him up so much, the sex would be cool; she'd release him really fast, she knew she'd be able to deal with guys so, so well. 'Show me.'

Nio took her hand. 'I finished it yesterday.'

He went through to the extension and stood at the foot of the stairs while she climbed. As she moved higher he stood to one side and held out his arms. 'But no banisters still,' he explained, 'so I'll have to catch you.'

She smiled down at him. 'I'm no' going to fall.' She was filled with a sense of fate as she climbed higher. This was where it would go off; it was going to happen . . . right now. She poked her head up through to the floor above. She gave an exclamation of surprise. 'This is like a boat.' She climbed forwards on hands and knees because there wasn't room enough to stand; and the whole of the floor was a mattress made up neatly with orange and brown blankets. But the most lush thing was the stained-glass window, she went and kneeled close by, she touched the pattern of colours – there were greens, blues, orange, blood red . . . all divided by a tracing of lead. What was the picture? A figure – a man with a beard. And a woman, her face downcast, hair tied at the nape of the neck. Her gown was a patch of bright blue. Behind them, a green hill. For a moment, Mila lost track of time, a bell tolled in her heart. She waited, the euphoria lasted for two or three moments . . . She turned and watched Nio climb up to join her. 'You don' need a new flat, you have this beautiful place—'

He loved winning her smile, to see it spread at something he'd said or done, it was the richest reward, made him want to say more, do more, win different, other smiles.

'Is amazing and beautiful, your new bedroom,' she said.

'Can't stand up, though.' They were both on hands and knees. 'Which is a pity, but if I'd gone any higher they'd have been able to see us from the allotments. And – it will be cold in winter.'

'No heating?'

'The chimney from the stove goes through,' he pointed out, 'but I don't think that's going to be enough, not even this small a space.'

They sat on the bed and held hands, looking into the window as if it were itself a blazing fire. For a long time they said nothing – and the whole world was all right.

Then, inexplicably, the silence grew deeper, it became uncomfortable. Mila had to break it. 'This window, where you get it?'

'Found it,' said Nio, 'at Friern Barnet, same place where I'm doing the horse. I was wandering through and I nearly stepped on it, there were weeds and stuff growing over it. Bits of the frame were rotten but I rebuilt it.'

'Is like a cabin in an old, old ship,' she said.

They took off their coats and lay down; she rested on his chest, gazed at the coloured light. After a while, she heard his breath quicken. She started up, looked into his eyes and he stared back; it was mesmerizing, it became like a tunnel connected from his soul to hers, they both felt so in love, full of honour and promise. The importance, the gravity of the situation grew.

She asked herself, was it going to be here? Was it now?

He told himself, it mustn't be here, now – really mustn't.

They fitted together perfectly. She felt a stirring of nerves in the pit of her stomach, a mix of fear and hunger. She looked down the length of his clothed body. The window's colours were projected on the rumpled slope of Nio's shirt, the length of his legs, his working boots neatly crossed. She picked up his hand. She wanted to lie back in this cool place, lift her hips to allow him to slide down her knickers; she wanted to feel his breath on her thighs and belly and to reach for him, hold his face in her hands and stare into his eyes to see close up the exact moment he went into her and such pleasure she'd give him that he'd come inside her on that first stroke – and she'd have captured him.

For a long while they stayed like that, not speaking. She

watched his groin. Yes, for sure, she loved this guy really, really a lot.

He cleared his throat.

After a while, their mouths were locked together; they lay side by side, she pressed hard against him, trying to cover every inch. She moved his hand to her breast, she so wanted this to go off, she needed his hand to move. Her eyes were closed; in the gathering darkness, she was sealed against this man whom she wanted.

Stubbornly, Nio told himself don't, it would be wrong, and he unlocked their mouths, yet immediately he moved to kiss her neck, and he put his hand on that undone top button of her jeans. He really must stop soon, he thought.

She monitored his hand on the top button of her jeans. It stayed there placidly, its strength not put to any use but she could feel its warmth; she so wanted him to rip her pants off. The friction of his mouth at her neck as she leaned over him made her want to scream, or laugh. Instead, she sat up vigorously and rode astride him. She noticed with satisfaction how in the half-dark his eyes were glazed, sugary, and his mouth hung open – how easy had been the work, to get themselves to this state!

Nio began to worry that he might lose control if this went on much longer. What should he say, or do, to stop? She was a post growing from his middle; he could make out how her face dropped as she leaned over him, her hair skewed outwards, as always with stuff tied in it. He wanted to loosen the clips, have her unadorned . . . he was in trouble . . . He started to undo the miniature buttons of her shirt but as fast as he undid them she did them up again, joking, 'No, when you have made the kitchen. After you buy me the car.'

Then Mila pinned down his arms and stooped to kiss his chest in the V thrown open at the neck of his shirt. She heard him breathe her name several times. When she looked into his face it was to hear something like a cry for help, from him – 'Not long to go.' She smiled, unbuttoned the front of her shirt herself and drew it from her shoulders. She loved the look on his face.

'Two weeks, Mila—' Nio would be true to his word, she had to know that he meant what he said, every word he uttered should be true, he wanted to offer her that certainty. 'We shouldn't.'

Abruptly she stopped, pointed. 'Just behind you is the policeman.'

'We mustn't,' he added. 'It's no joke.'

Then she was angry, 'But you said—'

'I know,' interrupted Nio, 'but . . . it's not long. Two weeks, that's nothing!'

'So why not, then, if is nothing?' argued Mila.

'It would be like stealing.'

'Steal from me, then!'

'I would!' said Nio, 'but—'

'I want you to, now—' Mila pulled the straps of her bra from her shoulders and leaned close to him, rolled him over. She felt a wave of surrender and a sudden gust of pleasure at his full weight lying between her legs, because it was his turn to pin her down; she felt like a caught animal. Surely . . . but Nio took her bra straps and hoiked them back on to her shoulders; she couldn't believe it, he was trying to cover her up, and now it was his turn to fasten the buttons of her shirt; she watched in disbelief as her cleavage disappeared.

The desire in Mila was floating, for a while she couldn't come down to earth, she'd have carried on by herself, almost.

Nio was determined – the buttons were small and numerous and the nerves in his fingers weren't working properly, but he persisted, each button was a piece of work; he told himself less speed more haste, how difficult they were, tiny, it was taking ages.

She so, so couldn't believe it . . . She watched as he fiddled, closed all her buttons in the wrong order, for God's sake, the stupid man; her heart melted, she really loved him, this was his thing wasn't it, wanting to do right? But God, it made her so, so *mad* . . . She belted him on the chest, he caught her arm, she struggled and bucked, he pushed her sideways, pinned her down. She stared at him . . . moaned, 'Why not? *Why* won't you?'

'Because I *love* you,' urged Nio.

Feeling shot through her, then, and quickly took her to another place – it was because he *loved* her . . . a heaviness invaded her limbs, her mind soared, somewhere faraway yet closer to him, still. The wanting lessened. She was so wrapped in him, it was everything, all her heart . . . he loved her? She'd be heartbroken if she couldn't have him.

For a while they slept. It was a perfect escape: a journey towards intimacy, she felt safe, wanted, and he had been successful, honourable.

Their dozing was interrupted by the scrape of the door downstairs. Both woke suddenly, then froze.

'It's Charmer,' whispered Nio.

Mila groaned in disappointment. That spoiled everything.

They listened as Charmer moved below them. There were footsteps, a sniff.

Nio called out, 'Charmer?'

The call came back, 'Yoh?'

'I'm up here.'

'Boom Shakah!'

'Mila's up here as well.'

Silence. A while later, Charmer's line drifted up, 'I don't care *who's* fucking up *where*—' Then there was more silence.

'We're not doing anything though. Just thought you should know,' added Nio.

Nio descended the ladder first, Mila followed, utterly depressed that the whole mood had been blown apart. Charmer would be shy with her; most boys were. She'd have to wait ages to be his friend, it would be hard work. Then after a while she'd be like his younger sister. She'd encourage him back to school. He'd turn out to be a doctor, lawyer or architect, they'd have a life-long friendship. He'd always say that if it weren't for Mila . . .

But Charmer had disappeared. Soundlessly, he'd left the Clamp. The door stood open.

Mila thought – this boy was jealous of her?

The sudden emptiness affected them both, Charmer's disapproval left their love affair temporarily disconnected. For a few minutes they were as blank, as faraway, as drivers alongside each other on a motorway.

THREE

Nio knew that, for him, the only way to get a job would be like this: to tramp the streets, knock on doors, happen on good luck. As he went from house to house he daydreamed, mapping out a future – he'd start off being a gardener, just by himself, and then he'd hire a couple of people to help, a year or two later he'd buy his first van. He conjured up the name he'd paint on the side, 'Paradise Landscape Gardeners'. Encouraged by Mila and spurred on by the birth of their two children, he'd own a fleet of vans. A workforce would answer to him . . .

First things first.

He turned into Grosvenor Road – these were some of the bigger houses, owned by people rich enough to employ him. Here properties crowded on to the golf course; their gardens were large and well tended, hours of work for someone, why not him? He stopped without exception at each door; when there was no reply he wrote down the number of the house on the back of his hand so he'd know to come back.

He loped slowly along, never concerned at the rejection, it was fair enough people didn't want him, maybe they already had someone helping out. Occasionally they didn't even let him finish asking the question, they interrupted, denied him and closed the door. He guessed they'd been harassed by door-to-door salesmen and he always tried to squeeze in an apology, 'Sorry to have bothered you', before the door clicked shut.

In fits and starts he made his way along the street. While

hanging around waiting for doors to be opened he made other plans: to have a bath or a shower himself every day, to buy some socks, to rig up a water supply in the Clamp – perhaps he could poach it off the tank that served the allotments? Take Mila bowling – he couldn't expect *her* to pay all the time. It crossed his mind more than once that he really did want to buy her the Shogun – it was ridiculous, but yes he wanted to, even though he knew she was only teasing. Further up the scale, the one-bedroomed flat, a fringe of keys in his hand, passing them to her . . . that was more serious. Charmer had been right, the Clamp was OK for now – but she needed a proper address in the borough of Haringey, her own door number and postcode, because she wanted to start trying to get into college, and in order to get a grant, and a student loan, and study, and get a proper job . . .

He wanted central heating, just to turn a radiator on. A bath of their own, lit by candles. Loads of candles. It might be a bigger place shared with others, it might be . . . whatever, they needed somewhere. Step by step he added to his fleet of vans, Paradise Landscape Gardeners grew in size, so did her job, more qualifications built on the end of her name, they'd have a better place, loads of children . . .'Loads of' – that was her phrase. She was beginning to take him over. Mila's determination was infectious, now he was filled with it too. He shook a fist at his immediate foe – money! He wanted to take up arms and find it, earn some. The most urgent thing was to buy her a birthday present.

The next house – no. They already had a gardener. It was noisy with children; he imagined himself and Mila occupying just such a property, with their own children running through it, Mila carrying the baby on her hip, the next oldest dragging on her hand, she was smiling at him in the doorway . . .

Another house – an old man answered the door, his wife a fleeting presence behind him. Given half a chance he and Mila would live that long, run like mad all the way to old age, Mila still graceful and alert, himself a bit older, more sleepy, she'd indulge him . . .

By lunchtime he was no better off. No, no, no. It seemed like everyone except him had a job, all these countless people thronging the Broadway were in work, must be, although he knew that couldn't be true.

It was tiring, beating down doors, fighting against circumstance; he stopped for a rest at the café at the top of Muswell Road. He'd have to break into his last note, a tenner. He cautioned himself not to buy food and noticed the disappointed look of the café owner.

While stirring his tea and leafing aimlessly through a newspaper left there, Nio changed his mind about rich people, they weren't the best hope. They were already well organized and more to the point even if they did want to try out a new gardener they'd never invite someone in off the street. So, when he left the café, he wandered the smaller, more densely populated streets of Muswell Hill. Most of the houses had been divided into flats. Often the gardens were shared between the ground and first floors. All these families, he thought – each took their few square yards, the land was spoken for to the last inch, densely inhabited, thickly spread with people and cars, where could he find room for himself and Mila?

Common sense told him that finding a casual gardening job was a numbers game, a question of chance – he had to shake hands with the right person at the right time. He moved along briskly, and there were several near misses. 'If only you'd turned up yesterday' and 'come back in three weeks' time'. There was more sympathy for him, these people were closer to having to do this themselves. They weren't frightened of him. He kept hammering, took the knock-backs, carried on.

Now he found himself in Cranley Gardens; Dennis Nielson had murdered an unknown number of homeless young men here in the 1980s and had then dismembered and cooked them before flushing their remains down the toilet. Nio had been raised in this borough, he remembered the dole-supervisor's crimes from his childhood. He sensed the awful plummet in value which might be placed on human life according to anyone's whim. He was hungry, he'd been walking all day and had seen more than his fair share of humankind; and with not one offer of work forthcoming Nio felt tears flush quickly, he gasped at the sudden pessimism which assaulted him as he walked past the murderer's house. He felt as if he were walking shoulder to shoulder with the still unnamed young men who'd died at Nielson's hand behind that door . . . their last steps had been on this stretch of pavement which he himself now trod. He felt the connection snap tight between himself – alive – and them, long dead. All those years ago it was people like Charmer and himself who might have been only two short steps – this one and that! – from such a fate. Nio let the downhill pull him along faster, to leave the house behind . . . he made a resolution never to come via Cranley Gardens again if he could help it.

He searched and searched, restless because it was only ten days before Mila's birthday. He put his name down with an agency, but it was a drawback that he couldn't be contacted by phone. He said he'd call them, and every day he did just that. There was nothing. He wouldn't give up, though.

Mila and her family still had to lean against a bit of a slope, even with the aluminium legs at one end of the trailers folded up completely and the legs at the other end fully extended and bricks pushed underneath. It gave Mila a pain in her hip – it was like a kind of torture, having an uphill and a downhill in your own home, even if it was slight. Plus – cars zooming past only just the other side of the wall, night and day? Her whole family was complaining about the new situation on the slip road. The dog wasn't safe. The TV reception wasn't as good as in the Retail Park, her dad was forever waving the aerial and cursing. The police had visited twice already. Her 18-year-old cousin had left, gone without a word. It wasn't reckoned by anyone they'd be here for longer than a week. Everyone was unhappy. Mila wanted to escape more than ever.

She went through the gear brought home by Little Vlad after his latest dipping expedition. There was a Robbie Williams CD, a card wallet, a Filofax and a striped woollen bag with little silver bells stitched around the top. She shook it – no tinkling, the bells were silent. She flipped through the card wallet, examining each one. 'Bleeding storecards,' she murmured.

'That's OK.'

'To be a thief is *not* OK Little Vlad.'

'You can take the cards and buy things for me.'

'I don't want anything to do with them,' Mila complained. 'I don't want to become a thief like you.'

'OK then. If you don't do that for me . . .'

'What?'

'I'll tell your fish and chips'

Mila grabbed his hair and twisted hard. 'You won't.'

'All right—'

'Promise.'

'I promise! Ow!'

'You better not. God, I won't tell you *anything, ever again*.'

Little Vlad picked up the storecards from where they'd fallen. 'I'll give them to Maria then,' he said disconsolately.

Mila waved at the stuff jumbled on the bed. 'How come Maria didn't take them to begin with?'

'This was after,' said Little Vlad, 'I took this after we'd done our thing together, by myself.'

'How many times were you stopped?'

'Twice. Both times it was Robin Hood.' They called this one

officer Robin Hood because he always took the dippers' cigarettes off them if they were under sixteen and gave them to the homeless.

Mila warned him, 'Don't keep this stuff, it's handling stolen goods. Take it away. *We* can be done for this, let alone you.'

Little Vlad scraped it off the bed.

'Except this,' added Mila, and she took the striped woollen bag. 'This is cool.' She hooked the multicoloured cord handle around her neck, stood up and swung the bag at her side. She bumped it with her hip. 'Neat!' She liked the little bells stitched around the top.

'Now you're a thief as well.'

She handed it straight back. 'No I'm not.'

'You can have it for ten quid.'

'No way, not if you stole it.'

'Didn't steal it. I found it. Promise.'

'You stole it, I'm not buying that.'

'I found it, honest. So you can have it. Ten quid.'

Mila thought for a while. Then she said, 'Ok, I will buy it off you. But only as long as you don't tell him the truth.'

'Deal, OK.'

'Promise?'

'Promise.'

'And only five quid. I'll pay you later.'

'Six quid if you pay me later.'

'No – four quid.'

'All right! Five. Deal.'

'Hand it over then.'

For a couple of days, Mila carried the bag on her shoulder. But it made her feel guilty, it was someone else's, she shouldn't have it. Yet she so wanted it. She could die of bleeding wanting, sometimes. 'Bleeding' – that's what Jayne always said.

After a while, she stored up a massive dose of courage and

went to the police station in Muswell Hill. She liked the British police, they were proper, they didn't carry guns, and they liked her back, they were always kinder than they should be – she'd twice been given lifts home in squad cars just for fun.

In the police station she watched as two sets of people filled in forms ahead of her. One of them said this cool word in English, 'mind-numbing'. It sounded good, she stored it to use later.

When they signalled it was her turn she jumped up and placed the bag on the counter. She explained – it was lost by someone. Her little brother had found it in a Starbucks on Oxford Street, trampled on the floor. He'd picked it up and brought it home. Had someone reported it missing?

The duty officer explained to her that technically it would have to be stored for a period of six weeks and, if no one claimed it by then, she had the right to come back and get it. 'Treasure trove,' he explained, with a smile.

'What?'

'That's the name of the law, it's the term they use concerning found objects. In six weeks the bag will become treasure trove and it will be your right, as the person who handed it in, to keep it. Finders keepers.'

Mila brightened. 'Great!'

'But you know what? Something of no value like this? Don't bother. Never in a month of Sundays will we get a call about it. Take it with you right now, save us all the bother.' He smiled at her and winked. 'Go on, take it.'

'Now? But someone might have reported it.'

'No – I promise you they haven't. Never do with things like this. It's yours.'

She smiled, thanked him.

'You weren't here, right, we didn't have this conversation.'

With gusto she left the dreary, stained cabin of the front office. The police station had double doors opening on to three steps leading down to street level – one of these doors was bolted shut, the other open. Briefly Mila clipped her fingers on each side and leaned out over the steps, the bag on her hip, looking both ways to gain a sense of direction; a cloud scudded past and for a moment the sun's strength dialled upwards dramatically as if at her appearance. Mila herself felt the suspense, the held breaths of passers-by. The policeman had given her the bag. Everyone was giving her what she wanted. Even Nio, soon. She could have any job she wanted. She could become a policewoman, easily. The world was at her feet.

Lucas Tooth had to jump, hang on to the plastic guttering but quickly grab the roof bracket, it was stronger, so he could pull himself up. It was worth the tear in his jacket, the scuff marks on the toes of his shoes, the dirt on the front of his shirt – all that would be quickly mended by the mother in Birchwood Avenue. He crept across the flat roof to the small, innocuous window which beckoned, a lighted oblong in the dark. As he did so, he looked around, behind him. This side of the Tesco superstore was backed into Coppetts Wood. He couldn't be seen from the loading bay or from the road.

He had a feral stillness, then, as he waited – as long as it took. His mind emptied. He thought of food – a steak and kidney pie. He counted the envelopes – how much money would come to him today, tomorrow.

His view was obscured by a net curtain hung on a plastic covered wire on the inside of the glass, but when someone came in, he made out the movements below, the tilt of the girl as she bent to pull down her knickers from under the uniform, sit on the staff toilet. He couldn't be sure which girl it was, but it didn't matter. He watched closely, took in every movement.

The toilet emptied, became silent. He didn't move. The roofing felt was abrasive, but he felt nothing, only watched . . . this was good, the exhilaration, the dry hunger scooped in his belly, the fear a taste in his mouth as he stalked the girls from the checkouts. From the labels pinned to their breasts, he imagined their names – Jayne, Donna, Maria, Lynne, Emma – and he felt life itself, tingling at the ends of his nerves. They were somewhere in there, all of them would come to this room at some time or other, and they'd all undress, partially . . . He had a set of pictures of them now, and he ran through them as if looking through holiday snaps, ticked them off, crossed them.

Someone else came in – the blurred shape moved in the panel of light. He inched closer. Which one was it? The tip of his nose touched the glass.

Anjali dreamed that she ran effortlessly down the pathway from her family home, past the tree standing in their tangled and forgotten garden, past the slats of the fence like grey, wooden soldiers lined up; there was the sense of airiness in her running out of the gate and down the road, a giddy exhilaration as she fled, left the house far behind . . . she gathered speed until her feet pedalled thin air, lifted off the ground because she was going so fast, it was dangerous to be this high up, she'd fall . . .

With a jerk, she awoke. She was aware of the soreness in her hips, shoulders and neck. She was hungry.

She half-drifted back to sleep, her eyes were closed, but when she felt the gentle tug at her foot she woke again and sat up. Squatting on his haunches next to her was a police officer. His helmet was on his knee. His hair stood in an unlikely quiff.

'Hiya,' he said. 'Morning call.'

Anjali smiled, but hoped he would go away. She noticed – as if from a distance – that no words came out, she still wasn't talking.

'You're new,' remarked the officer cheerfully. 'What's your name?'

Still she didn't answer. He waited patiently, but when his next two questions weren't answered, he tried something else: he took out a nearly full pack of Camel Light cigarettes and offered her one. 'Smoke?'

She mouthed, 'Thank you' and it was really to avoid having to say anything, and allow him to leave, that Anjali took a cigarette and held it as she'd seen people do. Now he was going to light it for her.

As he cupped the match in his hand he asked again, 'Can you tell me your name?'

Maybe if she lit the cigarette, he'd think his job was over. She smiled politely and dipped the tip of the cigarette into the flame. Could she manage not to inhale, she wondered? She took a sip of the dry uncomfortable smoke and held it in her mouth. She knew what to do in theory – breathe in so the nicotine could enter her bloodstream – but it seemed an impossible plunge to take, like drowning yourself.

'Don't mind you not saying,' shrugged the police officer, 'I'm not trying to interfere. It's only if you want help, you should know you can get it. I've never seen a homeless Asian woman, ever. Loads of men, most of them white, and quite a few girls or women of other races, but not yours.' He smiled. 'See, I can talk enough for both of us.' Then he asked, 'You, like from India or Taiwan or somewhere?'

She looked at him steadily, because this was a policeman, and she had something to tell him, she wanted to. He could prevent it from happening to someone else; all she had to do was speak, tell him everything. Yet if she spoke, she'd hear her own middle class voice, it would connect her to that house with her brothers and parents as surely as a rope thrown to her; she'd be up in front of her entire family, she'd . . . It was no reflection on him or the police in general; she could see he was a good listener, he was doing well. Yet there was nothing between this man and herself except a blanket of air and moisture, and the cigarette smoke now as she blew it untidily from her mouth. The truth of what had happened remained locked inside her.

'I'm from Reading,' he offered. 'Working-class family, dad a bricklayer, mum a teacher at the infants.'

Anjali nodded.

'What about you, got a family?'

She didn't answer.

He unclicked a biro and wrote something on the cigarette packet. He said, 'Anyway, if you want to chat, ever, I'm going to write down my name and number at West End Central.' He finished and handed her the packet. 'There you go. Don't have to call for a reason, just, you know, to ask for another fag's OK.'

Again, Anjali nodded, mute.

'I've also written down the telephone number of a charity called Missing. If you call them, you can get a message back to your folks that you're OK, stop them worrying.'

It was a good idea, she'd do that. She didn't want them to come and look for her. She smiled at him gratefully.

'Cheerio for now,' he added.

She watched as he made his way down the underpass. When he came to the next figure some twenty yards away, he stopped, just as he had done with her, kneeled, no doubt to go through the same routine.

Between her fingers the cigarette burned, a cheerful glow at its tip, the hypnotic column of smoke drifting upwards. She lifted the filter to her lips and took a mouthful . . . why not try? She breathed in – and it felt like a block of wood had been tossed into her lungs; she fought against the impulse to cough, but lost.

After a while her breathing settled. Pain lodged deep in her chest. A minute later, she took a further mouthful and inhaled again. There was the same seizure in her lungs, but it didn't last as long. There didn't seem to be any pleasure involved, except for the achievement of controlling the smoke and to see it come out in a stylish, orderly column, like the breath of a dragon, the same as when you breathe out on a cold morning, instead of in a ragged cloud.

She sat quietly and experimented with different techniques, holding it between her thumb and forefinger, then returned to the traditional grip. She tapped ash on to the concrete beside her, and watched the brown circle of nicotine grow denser on the end of the butt. When the cigarette was halfway down, she felt a powerful loss of control, a giddiness combined with nausea. She stirred, thinking she should get to her feet, but this accelerated the rush and she couldn't manage anything other than to wait on all fours. She dipped her head lower, hoping not to faint. As she waited, she cursed. What was that? She felt out of breath. Pain banged in her head. She rocked back and forth.

Then she heard a voice reverberate in the tunnel, 'Walk into the snow, man, walk into the snow.' The next person along, the young man floating in a blue sleeping bag, was looking at her. 'You OK?' he asked. 'D'you need any help, there?' He had a beard and rumpled blond hair.

Anjali shook her head and he turned away. She moved carefully back to a sitting position. That was her first hit – yes, that was the right word, hit. Incredible, the way it had lifted the top of her head off. She looked at the burning stick of tobacco with new respect – that was what the fuss was about. Even so, there hadn't been a pleasurable thing about it. Yet for what she wanted, which was to sink, to nudge at the undersides of consciousness until she knew well enough the very lowest she could fall . . . it was useful. She wanted to disappear, lose utterly her sense of being an individual, rub out the distinguishing marks between herself and others. It was a dull ache, like anaesthesia. The formal licensing of her existence – credit cards, driving licence, and so on – had gone when she'd let her bag slip from her fingers. She was in the gutter but it wasn't low enough. She wanted to be no different from the cardboard, the concrete beneath, or the earth beneath that, the very earth that was but a fragment . . . and *what was* consciousness, after all . . .

That was enough nicotine. She stubbed out the cigarette on the concrete next to her. Idly she counted how many were left: fourteen.

The first few people were beginning to appear now that the steel gates had slid back and the Underground station had opened for business. The earliest workers were the office cleaners, most of them of foreign birth and with the careworn expressions of the low paid. Later, towards 7.30 a.m., came the labourers and tradesmen making their way to building sites and those who owned or worked in breakfast cafés in the area. An hour later a flight of secretaries hurried past. After 9.30 came the media lot and then it turned into a jumbled mix of characters, including tourists.

Anjali observed the procession of the gainfully employed pass in front of her – at this end of the working day from left to right mostly – and wanted nothing from them. Others of the homeless colonizing this subway put out hands or begging cards, but she merely watched. She was struck with the magic of such a multitude's existence – how could all these people walking past be clever enough to survive, to find their individual habitat as it were – jobs, friends, hobbies, a place to live? It seemed an impossibly romantic achievement. It sponsored humility in her breast, a sense of wonder.

That cigarette – the hit she'd taken off it – had pushed her, in her mental journey, further along. As she gazed at the crumpled butt on the concrete next to her, with the tunnel now resounding to the tread of a hundred feet, she made a decision: yes, she'd smoke another one sometime. Harmless. She looked at the packet: in biro was written the name and telephone number of the police officer. She'd keep it safe and she'd call him, she would, when she was ready, because she didn't want what had happened to her, or worse, to happen to anyone else.

Nio winced at the sudden noise – a torrent of anger poured from Mila's dad. He banged the flimsy wall, the top of the TV. The tufts of hair sprouting from his cheekbones were standing up with anger. And the finger was pointing at him, Nio, he was the trouble; Mila was only fifteen and hanging out with him, that's what it must be. The sound of the rain on the roof, and the tilt of the vehicle, how it moved with each footstep, and the proximity of everyone, how everyone was within inches of each other, made it seem as if this fight were happening on board a little boat in the middle of the Atlantic Ocean. He wished he understood the language.

Mila shouted back at her father, who then picked up a magazine and waved it at her. Nio watched as her brow twisted out of shape and she stamped her foot and waved, her voice carried by the same dialect, guttural and angry. She clicked her fingers three times and smacked an open palm against her temple, a brief dumb show before the shouting continued. Mila's father dropped the magazine and caught that hand, the one that had just given the performance, and squeezed it, hard. Mila cried out, 'Ahhh—' She had to lean sideways, her father was exerting pressure. More voices joined in, her mother barked, Little Vlad picked up the magazine, rolled it up and used it to whack his father's backside.

A head of steam was building in Nio. If that man carried on hurting her for one more second . . . He saw pain crease Mila's expression. Her father was crushing her hand. Tears sprang from her eyes and now she was talking quickly in a low, pleading voice. Then she was crying openly. Nio stood up, the blaze of anger in Social Services was alight in him as well and he stumbled towards Mila's father and wrapped an arm around his neck as if taking hold of a rugby ball. He tightened his grip and walked Mila's father sideways one step, treading on his foot clumsily, but now that he'd got the man's head he didn't know what to do with it, all he could do was push him down until he was lying on the floor, a stream of language emptying from him. From the corner of his eye Nio caught the flash of a lime-green platform shoe as Mila kicked her father – twice. The storm in Nio's breast died immediately; he unstuck his grip and stood back, flushed with guilt, anxious that no one should be hurt. Mila's father was muttering and rubbing his neck. Nio stood and looked around Social Services. Everyone was staring. Had he done that? He'd always been afraid of this man who was now an uncomfortable heap on the floor of the caravan, the roll of flesh around his middle squeezed tight under the grey sweat shirt, his slacks scuffed, one shoe lying abandoned nearby.

'Sorry—' Nio scanned the others again. He swapped looks with Mila's mother and Little Vlad and Mila herself, the sister . . .

'Don' say sorry!' Mila hung on his arm. 'Is not your fault!' Then she unleashed a stream of curses at her father. She looked as if she might kick him again. Her father was sitting up, blinking angrily. He tipped forward on his knees and with difficulty planted his feet and stood, unevenly because he was wearing only one shoe. 'Sorry,' repeated Nio. He didn't want Mila to be kept from him, or the family to move to a different country . . .

Then Mila's father hit him. Nio accepted the blow against the side of his head, he didn't even put up his hands because to defend himself might turn it into more of a fight. Little Vlad started clapping, which he thought was unfair. Mila kicked her father again and shouted at Little Vlad. Nio continued, 'I am really sorry—' Another blow came; he remained upright, received it dutifully. This man with the hairy cheekbones should just carry on, if it meant that Nio got to keep Mila. 'I thought you were going to hurt her,' explained Nio, tasting blood. Would he understand English? This caravan was too small to enclose so much violence and movement. Everyone was pushed around, but only by an inch or two. Nio weathered another blow – he lowered his head an inch, took it on the forehead, then it was his jaw and the side of his head, all the while he explained that he'd only been protecting Mila from harm. He saw Mila turn and take three strides to the downhill end of the caravan, shouting at the top of her voice, reaching for various objects and discarding them before pushing her mother aside and returning with a saucepan to bring it down on her father's head. The inch or two of stew left in the bottom splattered over all of them, and the concussion dropped her father to his knees. He repeated the same grunt several times, leaning over on all fours, his breath ragged, practically on Nio's boots. Mila clawed at the mess on her arms and returned to the other end of the caravan to engage her mother in a furious exchange and clean herself up.

Nio watched as she swept her hair up into more clips and then came back; he was collected like the coat and bag she wore and then they were outside the caravan, away from that cramped, violent space and into the pouring rain and driving wind, the weather just as much chaos as in there. Nio took off his greatcoat and held it over their heads. They sailed past the abandoned Highways Agency caravan, up the slip road, then, towards the bridge. They were OK, they were together, Nio felt relief. She wiped him down, examined his face, two minutes later she was laughing about it. The wind caught his coat, they flapped along. 'Where shall we go?' called Nio.

'Anywhere!' cried Mila. She took his hand and they headed uphill, towards the Broadway, weaving through other people trying to dodge the rain. She ranted against her father. He heard her out, until she nudged him and finished, 'You are fantastic, you are mind-numbing.' She squeezed his hand. 'You rescued me!'

'Why was he so angry?' asked Nio.

'It was . . . nothing.'

'Was it because of me?'

'Only sort of—'

'About your being too young?'

'He's worried for himself, that is all he worries.'

They pushed through the doors into Ruby In The Dust. She bought them both hot chocolate, and looked at his lip, touched the bruise on the side of his face. They pored over the story of their relationship, revisited when they'd first seen each other, their first words, a certain smile that had stuck in his memory as being like a switch turned on, going to the cinema together for the first time, the guy who had followed, shouting at them, late at night, and Nio had talked him out of it, trying to lift the horse and move it closer to the exit in the grounds of the Friern Barnet Mental Hospital. They tracked their friendship right up to the very point of *now* . . . and guessed what would happen next. She'd go to college and be qualified as a clothes designer, he'd be a famous big potato artist – it was perfect.

Nio still hurt from having taken a beating but the way they'd looked after each other, come through it together, meant they were a real couple, weren't they? Although she was still only fifteen, she was at least as old as he was; the way she'd shrugged off the violent scene, and moved on, laughing minutes later outside the caravan, spoke of how much life she'd packed in compared to him. Maybe she would always be older, feel more worldly.

She was poised opposite him, the lime-green blocks she wore kicked off to one side of their table. With her coat off, men's stares were glued to her tight top and women stared enviously at the flat plain of her loins. He wanted her badly. Each time they were together was like a notch cut in a stick – when there were enough of them, they'd reach her birthday. Just six days now. He'd chop away at this length of time . . . Yet, he didn't want to shorten her life; he valued Mila's youth and strength as priceless bounty. The idea of her birthday present gnawed at him. He wanted money.

Mila's father ranted at her, he stood like a bull, head down, and let off. He'd found out she'd lied to him. He pointed at Nio and shouted, 'He's poor he hasn't got a job he has nothing—'

'*Da* – but so what? Neither have you.' Mila stamped her foot.

'You told us he had money, that he paid for you, but that's not the truth, you pay for him! You pay for him before your own family!?'

'I pay for you as well!' shouted Mila. She turned and cursed Little Vlad, what did the bleeding squit think he was doing, telling Dad? Then she went back to her dad, 'Me, and Mama, and the cleaning, we all bring your food, I—'

'And he's frightened of women!' Her father rampaged around the caravan until he found the magazine, it was called *HomoActiv*; they'd had it at work to laugh at, and somehow it had ended up back here, so that now he could wave it at her. 'Hides behind his dirty magazines! What kind of girl is it that takes up with a Godless pervert? And a poor one?! My daughter!'

She couldn't believe it. 'That's not *his* magazine. That was the magazine that was given to me at work as a joke . . . oh forget it!!'

Her father caught her hand, then. 'You're marrying Arnod. Next year.'

'No!'

'You are.' He squeezed her hand tighter, it hurt.

'NO!'

'You are.' He was crushing her fingers, she was crying with pain. Then Nio walked over and just carried her father off, wrapped his head in a big embrace and pulled him down on the floor. Mila felt so hurt and angry she kicked her father as he lay there, twice. And she didn't want Nio to apologize. He was so brave, when her father started to hit Nio he just stood there and took it, he was so strong and kind and brave and . . . she couldn't believe this fight was happening, Nio would be hurt. She hated her father so much then and, with Little Vlad clapping and jeering, anger enveloped her and she stormed over to fetch a saucepan and she clunked him one. It was satisfying, how he dropped. She cursed Little Vlad and told him she'd never tell him anything ever again.

Then they were out of there, she was so glad, she never wanted to go back, never wanted to talk to her little brother again, she'd fly, escape, it was bliss, the pouring rain and the wind were like, perfect . . . she was so, so happy, Nio at her side lifting his coat like a great wing above them, they could take off.

Ahmed was stuck in traffic. The empty seat next to him was haunted by the ghost of that girl – it's where she'd sat, close as anything. The ride had turned her on. He should cruise past her caravan, dangle the gleaming Shogun in front of her again, she'd beg for more. Or, when he next shopped at Tesco's, he'd bump into her, ask her if she wanted a better job . . . that would only be the start of everything. As he sat there immobile in the queue for the lights, he gave his stomach a two-handed pat. When he had her working for him, maybe he'd invite her to the back office, after hours? Why not? He pictured it – simply asking her. She'd say yes. Comment on what a nice room it was. He'd pour them a drink. There'd be a little smile, a look between them. She'd know all right, so would he. They'd both want the same thing. Together they'd go out and fetch a nice blood red Belvedere sofa bed. He'd push, she'd pull. It would be a laugh. Steer it through the office door, manouevre it into position. Open it out, the Belvedere was amazingly quick. Then, a longer look between them, a serious one. Move towards each other. She was so young, he'd tell her what to do. Every single inch of the way, he'd coach her. Then, wash in the little sink where they made the coffee. And do all of that more than once, maybe all the time. A bit of a legend around the Retail Park, would be Ahmed and Mila.

Then he saw himself from a further distance. A middle-aged man tinkering with a young member of staff? What about that? They'd laugh at him probably. The Belvedere dented and second-hand. Should he or shouldn't he? He told himself not to be stupid, he was pretending to have the choice when he didn't.

Lucas followed two of the Tesco girls – Jayne and Donna.

He walked at their exact pace up Colney Hatch Lane, but fifty yards behind, anonymous among the flow of other pedestrians, giving them their marks out of ten. Jayne was bulkier, pigeon-toed, whereas Donna's legs were straight and fitted neatly into the plate of her hips. Donna's hands were thrust into the pockets of the coat crimped at her waist. Her walk was coltish, fluid, quite fast, the top half of her body pushed into leaning forward against the hill by the stacked shoes. Jayne worked harder, her gait was slower, but at each step her rear swayed from side to side and that was hypnotizing, it answered him. Worth it. But what mattered most would be something else – how it played out. The sense of resistance, combined with the invitation to try it. Desire and denial. All that, plus sadness and innocence in the mix as well. He needed a girl to reel him in yet at the same time turn him down, say yes and no. He only really wanted what should be his, but was denied him.

From time to time the Tesco girls paused and glanced behind them. Lucas didn't falter, he just stayed far enough back to remain unnoticed. Their behaviour – this looking back – told him they must be about to catch a bus, maybe. In which case . . .

Yet, now they were separating – Donna was waving, heading off in a new direction, whereas Jayne kept going along the main shopping thoroughfare. Which one was his? Eenie, meenie, miny, mo – Jayne.

He dived after her, but already she was lost, that indecision had cost him, where was she? He waded deep into the madness of the crowd; it was busy now, so it was like joining a beast, suddenly he was a small, insignificant part of a huge, kicking, insane animal – the mass of population – and it didn't suit him. He made a swimming action with his hands. The river of people had to divide around him, give him space.

Then he saw her again. Everything slowed down. If he kept his gaze fixed on her, blotted everything else out, then he could make it as if the crowd had disappeared, he was surrounded by cotton wool, peace and safety came to him, it was like after a big meal, the feeling of contentment, there was no one else in the world apart from himself and Jayne, they alone were of any importance, they were going to . . . He lost her again; the crowd flooded back. For ten minutes he fought against it, hoping for luck to bring him back on to her trail.

He stopped, then, and cleared his face of all disappointment and turned into the newsagent's doorway, because a dozen yards in front of him was the other one, Donna.

She was carrying a bag of some sort, it bumped against her hip. As he followed, he marked the looks she won from every man, the way she lit a fuse in all of them. The women looked at her, but with a different idea – they were beaten in the competition.

He followed her all the way down Dukes Avenue, through Alexandra Palace, down to the railway station. He watched her from a position out of sight in the ticket hall, as she waited on the platform. He boarded the same train – bound for King's Cross – but in a separate carriage. He rehearsed, briefly. He had a sudden feeling of righteousness – he loved these Tesco girls. An idea was to have two or three of them at once. It was something to do with the uniforms that allowed him to think he might.

When the train stopped at the next station he left the train and re-entered her carriage. He strolled directly to her section and waited until a seat became available opposite her. He briefly glanced at her; then he looked out of the window. For a long time words failed him, they were on the tip of his tongue, but the others sitting around them, standing in the gangway, didn't help. He could feel a burning sensation in his forehead. He wasn't getting what he wanted. It sharpened his hunger; anything was more desired if it was difficult to reach.

He pulled the phone off the clip at his belt and switched it off. Then he pretended to dial a number and held it to his ear. He adopted an inward look, concentrated on the silence, listened intently. Then he kicked off the play. 'Hi. It's me. OK . . . Good . . . We can go with that, that's good money. How many more do we have to find? Give me a precise number. Three. OK. Three more girls.' With the first glance from her, he knew it was the right track. 'Can't be that impossible,' he carried on. 'Let's just go through the books again and see if we can find them. Sure. The money's there to pay them after all. Young enough, pretty enough, same old story.' He glanced at her again now, incurious. She was staring, her mouth open, before she quickly looked away. 'Well, let's put a timetable on it,' he continued. 'By the end of the week. Hair and make-up, Vidal Sassoon, I would recommend. Yup, and they get to keep the clothes, of course. Only the best girls'll do. The tyre hits the road at the start of next week.' He listened to his empty, dead phone. Then he put in, 'We have other gigs being offered to us, after all.' He paused for longer and it was easy to manufacture some impatience, it was close enough to how he felt, how much he wanted to take her. Then he wound up the charade. 'Listen, you can call me throughout the rest of today and into the evening. On this number. I'll leave the phone on. Let's try and wrap it up by the end of the working day. Good. OK. Bye for now.' He took the phone from his ear and dropped it in the inside pocket of his leather jacket.

He met the girl's eye, then, and gave a tight smile. 'Sorry.'

'Is OK.' She smiled back. Her voice was inflected, it had an accent. An easy lift to it. He relaxed.

'Mobile phones are horrible,' he said. 'Just had to take that call.'

'Sound important.' Her eyes popped.

He shrugged ruefully. 'Sometimes the bore of carrying a phone all the time is worth it, but mostly I hate them. Especially when other people are droning away on trains, disturbing the peace.'

She smiled – it was a door opening. He wondered which name to call himself. Should he drag out that old chestnut, Jon Rawle? Chris Noakes? He wouldn't use Lucas Tooth. The name was important, it should put him up there, in her eyes, not undermine him. It only took one small thing to go wrong and the play would fail, he'd lose.

As he began his grazing of her, he could feel her squirm with interest. He looked away enough to catch her looking at him. Then he swung it the other way. He allowed her to discover him looking at her with greater curiosity. They swapped names. She said she was called Mila – not Donna at all. He had to assume she was giving him a false name, so it was with some satisfaction that he gave his as Jon Rawle. She was going to visit a friend at King's Cross who had started to work there in a clothes shop. He was going into work. An office in the West End. Yes, his own company. A management company. Models, actresses, singers, that kind of thing. He told her a bit more about the day's work. They were trying to find three more girls. It was a party for a Formula One boss and the television companies wanted to buy in a bit of glamour. But she refused to give him her phone number – that felt good. He gave her his instead. He could always find her again, after all. This was promising.

By the time they left the train at King's Cross, they were walking together, in step.

*

Nio squatted on the floor with his sellotape and wrapping paper; he could feel the cold through the thin planking, whereas Charmer had the chair, the original dusty pink armchair, next to the fire. He paused in his wrapping of Mila's birthday present and stared at Charmer for a minute, the latter had his head thrown back, his legs splayed. On his feet were a brand new pair of trainers. They were like giant white boats on the end of Charmer's feet – dazzling – you almost had to lift a hand, fend off the glare. Nio found himself insulted by them. He had to bite his tongue, go on with the wrapping of the present. He'd made it himself – hadn't been able to find anything good enough for Mila, given his lack of money. Instead, he'd carved a miniature set of three arrows and decorated them with flights of coloured feathers, and out of old shoe leather he'd stitched together a little quiver to hold them. She'd been telling him, before, about the little wooden Cupid carved into the altar frieze in the church outside her home town.

Charmer wagged his trainers back and forth. How come Charmer could afford such blinding footware? He must have sold something, a scooter. Nio knew it wasn't worth asking for any of the small sums of money he'd lent Charmer, nor for any reckoning on the food he'd shared with him. Two or three times he'd suggested to him that he might go out and collect wood for the stove – it hadn't happened. Nio told himself, either put up with Charmer, like him for what was good about him, or don't. Instead, tell him to go.

Charmer's head popped upright. Nio told himself, now or never. Gingerly, he made his request. 'Errr . . . I wanted to talk to you about Friday?'

'Talk about Friday?'

Nio cleared his throat. He didn't want to make it sound like a pronouncement, or like he was asking for some big thing. 'I want to bring Mila here on Friday afternoon. It's her birthday the next day and—' He paused, because the sound of his own voice was wrong. Why should he be nervous? He shouldn't be asking at all, this was his place after all, he should be telling him . . . 'We'd like to spend the evening here, if that's all right.'

Charmer stood, stared at the floor, scratched his head. 'Her birthday, yes, course.'

'I'm going to pick her up around lunchtime,' went on Nio evenly, 'we'll come back here for a bit, then we might go out but we might not, we might stay here, but anyway, we will be spending the night here and the next day.'

'I see.'

'I thought I'd mention it because you're kind of spending every night here now, but—'

'Tell you what!!' said Charmer, as though this were his own idea. Nio could hear the anger in his voice, 'Why don't I piss off out of it, then the coast is clear, so you can wheel her in, give her the old birthday treat? How about that?'

Nio wanted to laugh because it was true. 'That's right,' he smiled, happiness churned in him. When the laugh broke, they shared it, it stretched for longer, kept going.

'Far and away the best idea.'

'Thank you.'

'I'll be quite happy wandering round the woods all night. If I'm the tiniest bit uncomfortable, I can always climb into an old . . . skip . . . and sleep on a mattress someone's thrown out.'

'Just for one night,' Nio begged. 'When have I ever asked for—'

Charmer stopped him, he flung out a hand and uttered in a fairy-tale voice, 'And behold, her luck changed.'

'What?'

'They made their little home her own. They made up a bed for her next to the fire, where it was cosy. They looked after her. They mended her clothes and brought her choice morsels to eat.

They washed and scrubbed and cleaned and cooked for her. Then they went to work, digging graves. And like their friends the animals—' He ranted on, walking here and there.

A minute later, the difficult silences returned. Charmer went back to his chair, sat and splayed his legs. 'I'm fed up with this place anyway, it's too cold.' He flung his head back. As if it had a life of its own, one of the spanking new white trainers lifted in the air and the heel was positioned on the toe of the other, where it began to wave back and forth like a metronome. No, the shoe was saying, no.

Mila held Little Vlad's hand as they weaved through the crowd walking the Broadway. These shops were so lush, even the price tags themselves looked expensive. She glanced at the top of Little Vlad's head and thought what a bleeding twat her younger brother was, but he had his uses sometimes. She tugged at his arm. 'Don't muck about, OK.' She'd noticed that her language had got worse since she'd started hanging out with Jayne and the other girls from work.

Little Vlad shrugged her off.

As she walked, she closed her eyes, opened them again. If everything went all right, she'd come out of this with a day's work that would pay her more than a whole week of slavery at Tesco's. She was dressed in her fake leopard-skin coat, fluffy gold wool jersey and tight black ski-pants; these clothes were old friends, they'd bring her luck, she'd altered and mended and cleaned them a million times, they owed her.

They were early; half an hour to go. She wanted a treat, maybe a hot chocolate with a double chocolate muffin. They wandered further along the Broadway and found the café. Mila warmed one hand on the plastic cup and used the other to dip the muffin. She plagued her little brother with, 'Do I look OK?' and so on.

Little Vlad shook his head.

She knew she did, but she made a dummy run to the toilets just the same. When she came back, Little Vlad was playing with the sugar like a 5-year-old, he didn't want to be here. He treated everyone, everything, equally badly.

'Time to go,' she said.

'OK.'

Outside the café she unzipped the striped wool bag and took out the slip of paper – she knew the number off by heart but wanted to make sure. Added to Jon's name and mobile phone number was his address, written in Mila's handwriting because she'd called him to arrange this meeting. She hadn't told any of her family, so it could all go wrong and it wouldn't matter, but she didn't know the guy, which was why she'd brought Little Vlad for protection. She was suspicious that this was just another guy like all the others, offering to help her just to talk to her, get to know her, try to take her out. It worked the other way as well, of course; she was guilty of using this stranger to get the day's work, but it was his business, she wasn't pretending it was anything else but for work. She'd said she was interested in the day at the Formula One party, and he'd invited her to meet him. If there was good news today, then she could tell everyone.

When they reached Queens Avenue, Mila took Little Vlad's arm. 'I'm going for it, OK? Don't get in my way.' He didn't take any notice. She smothered him in her coat. 'Pretend you're invisible, but stick around, because he might be a sicko.'

On either side of the street were the hugest mansions – they must all be millionaires, these people. It was cold, she was shivering a bit. One of these houses she'd be going into, soon. It would be warm. And it was awesome, how there was suddenly so much space, room to spread out.

When they reached number fifteen she recognized Jon Rawle sitting on the top step of this, like, palace, holding a mug of tea. Mila was impressed. To live here he must be really successful.

What did they put in houses like these? How did they fill them up?

As she approached, he stood up and came down the steps to shake hands.

'Hi.'

He looked different – older. The house was a mountain of bricks behind him. His angular face was clean-shaven. He wore an immaculate white T-shirt, leather jacket and jeans. He was taller than Nio – she suddenly pictured him sitting down, in the train seat opposite her.

She didn't try too hard. She was looking out for anything that would give him away as a creep. 'Thanks for whatever, you know—' She felt a mixture of insignificant, small in value, but very cool, also, to be handling this alone. 'So . . . is this your house, where you—'

'Don't worry about the house,' he interrupted, 'it's not important . . . it's just . . . appearances, yeah? Don't think about the house.'

Mila felt her nerves straighten out. He was so *not* lecherous. He seemed almost determined to disappoint her. She had to fight to keep her confidence.

'Who's this?' he asked.

For a while, Mila was disoriented enough not to remember her own brother's name. Then it came back to her and she hurriedly explained. 'Little Vlad. Because where I come from is Dracula, and Vlad was like the real Dracula for us . . . and he has the little pointy teeth at the corners.'

Jon Rawle shrugged. 'OK.'

She was worried that he was in a bad mood. Maybe he had big worries, there was a lot going on in his life, she was small potatoes.

'Hold on,' he said. He mounted the steps deftly and left the mug of tea on the top step and came back down. 'OK, let's go.'

He sort of ignored her, he had other stuff on his mind, probably loads of other models, he had to think of everything.

On the way they stopped off at a shop where he bought a Polaroid camera, just like that, it was nothing, walked in and walked out with it.

They went to the pub, which had been converted from a church, on Muswell Hill Broadway. It was mind-numbing, really good, and they were lucky to find seats. Little Vlad knocked about nearby. Mila sat while the camera whined and delivered the picture. Together they watched the image bleed in. Her spirits rose; she was being well treated, but he wasn't hitting on her. Drinks stood in front of them – hers was a Strawberry Teezer, Little Vlad's a glass of coke. Jon Rawle had a gin and tonic.

She took off her fake leopard-skin coat, removed a clip, mended her hair and positioned the clip again. She suddenly had a wrong thought – Nio's scruffy clothes and slow, innocent smile, in here, in the presence of this older and more sophisticated man, would suddenly look a bit goofy.

'How old you are?' asked Jon.

'Seventeen.' Mila waited for more trouble about her age. 'Is that OK, for the Formula One day?' she asked.

He reacted in a weird way, he twisted in his seat, his leg shot out, he looked in all directions. 'Don't—' he began. She waited. 'Don't get all hung up on the quick money thing. It doesn't matter about being a model, or what I do for a living or what you do for a living, just don't . . . you should just ignore everything . . . Don't get hooked on being a model, so many girls . . . you shouldn't give a fuck about being a model, it's rubbish, you know?'

He was incredible, so honest and, like, not spoiled by it all. Mila shifted on her chair. She still wanted the day's work, that's all, but she didn't know what to say. 'It's not really being a model, is it? Being at a party for the Formula One.'

In the silence that followed, Jon tapped his fingernail against the Polaroid photograph of Mila, which stood on the back of the seat. The little square was slightly crooked, miniature, informal. 'You're good looking enough to be a model,' he began, and for a while he just looked at her, and she could deal with that, before he continued, 'but it's all bullshit. Girls like you – few and far between, but being a model is nothing to do with happiness, is it.' His voice was coming as if from a long way off. 'I've known some girls who can handle it and win, and others who can't . . . who just . . . fail. You know?'

'I don't know what to say,' she replied. She put down her drink, to cover the puzzlement which threaded to the very tips of her fingers. 'You want to know what sort of character I have?'

Jon sniffed, and gave that twitch, then he asked, 'What d'you want to do when you leave school?'

She was wary, didn't want to tell him she wasn't at school, nor about Tesco's, that she'd borrowed someone's National Insurance number to get the job. There flashed across her mind the line of checkouts – and how pleased she was to have that job, let alone what he seemed to be talking about . . .

He prompted her, 'Any idea at all?'

'Don' know,' she began. She looked at Little Vlad, who had wandered off to the gaming machines.

'In a way,' continued Jon, 'it doesn't matter, I mean, what do I care?'

Mila laughed, her hand flew to her mouth, it was exciting, that he could be so offhand with her, it made him seem very truthful. She replied, 'Well, I want to do . . . something good.' It seemed like his whole face bored into her, she was pinned down by his look, the fix of his eyes was intent, it felt dangerous. He shrugged, 'Good can mean well paid or it can mean—'

'What?'

'Can you sing in tune?' he asked abruptly.

She nodded. 'I did sing, with my uncle, he had a . . . you

know . . . we played on this old boat and I sang with him, when I was a child, years ago.'

'D'you like clothes, fashion?'

Mila nodded vigorously. 'Yes, is more my scene, sometimes I make my own clothes or I buy clothes and change them around, I always like doing that.'

He asked, 'How tall are you?'

'Five feet seven inches.'

'And you're only seventeen, so you might grow taller.'

'Models are a lot taller.'

'Some models aren't.'

Inside, excitement stirred in her. 'So you think—'

'I know,' interrupted Jon Rawle, and she watched him intently, she could see him working out what – and how much – to say, 'I know for certain you shouldn't buy into to all this model crap, because that's what it is, just crap—'

'But is a way of making a living, earning money.'

This annoyed him. 'Yes and no, depends. I wouldn't recommend it.'

'But if I wanted to—?' She left the question hanging. As she waited for him to answer, she felt like at the outset of the journey to Great Britain, a hollow of fear scooped from her middle. But this time her fear was tinged with greater promise. Sky high.

Suddenly he was telling her what to do. 'First off, get some ten by eights done.'

'Ten what?'

'Photographs. Glamour shots. Start a book.'

'Oh.'

'We'll have them taken by a professional, OK? They'll know what to do. Then, once we've got the photographs, there's no question we can sell you. Get you loads of work. Make you very rich. No question. That's the easy part.' He leaned back, broke eye contact, added, 'But. Now's the time to think about happiness, blah blah blah. That's more difficult.' Then he drew a line in front of her neck with a finger and said, 'You should wear a necklace or a choker, though. Good neck, show it off. It would underline your face. It's not just about looks, though, is it? Something else as well. It's a light switched on inside, you know? Which glows. And then we're like moths to a flame, we come and look for you. Beat against the light. We don't know why but we do. Can't help it.'

God, he's talking about me, thought Mila. She frowned, waited. His knee was bouncing up and down. She exclaimed, 'I just never . . . I'm amazed to be here, this is amazing for me, someone like me.' She took a deep breath, and now she wanted to take over the conversation, however bad her English. She prattled on and told him everything. He'd been so honest with her, he'd told her it maybe wasn't such a good thing to be a model, and so now she returned the compliment, told the truth, she described how the caravans had been moved from the Retail Park to the slip road, and that now they were going to be moved again, probably to the site of a dismantled church hall in Camden. He had this way of listening, every word was important to him, often he stopped her and made her say things in two different ways until he understood. He asked more and more questions. It was important that she answered and that she told the truth, suddenly it had never been more important. She told him about the job at Tesco's and how she had to remember she was called 'Donna' by her supervisor . . . She told him all her saddest, funniest things . . . even something she hadn't told Nio yet, how she and her family had waited for months in this broken-down school, they were waiting for their turn, and they haunted this old school, that was what it felt like, they were ghosts, forgotten, rootless, they kicked through locked doors, used the furniture as firewood, played outside when it was sunny, she remembered the sprigs of green poking up more and more through the paving as spring wore into summer. Her older brother – her English was all over the place now but she carried on, throwing out enough words in the right order for him to understand, because she knew that he'd always drag her back to the start again if he didn't, so she was sure of him – yes, she went on, she had an older brother, he was the one for the clothes, really, how strange it was to her, that he was always smart and clean, he always looked handsome and interesting, he played cards a lot and was lazy, but he broke his ankle jumping off the wall in the schoolyard, so they had to leave him behind for two days while the rest of them walked to Pierroasa, to take their place in the queue, and when their father walked back to be with her brother, and wait until his ankle was better, he was gone, there was just a message scratched on the wall, the same wall as he'd jumped off, he'd written it with a piece of chalk from the schoolroom, all it said was, 'It's not your fault.' No one knew where he'd gone, still didn't know. They thought maybe he'd pretended to have broken his ankle so he didn't have to walk because, yes, he was lazy . . . they just didn't know. Their father had spent two months looking for him, but then had to start to make his way to England and join the rest of the family and work in the county of Kent. So – now she was nearly in tears – she had an elder brother whom she hadn't seen for nearly three years, he was really lovely, quiet and always kind to her, she'd go back and find him when she had the money, all she needed was to have a visa so she'd be let back in, and some money for the fare, and then she'd go back and find him . . .

Jon Rawle listened so hard, he nodded, stayed quiet.

'. . . and that's maybe also why I want to be a model and quickly earn some money,' she finished.

'What was . . . what is . . . his name?'

'Ilie. You know like the famous tennis player?'

'In a couple of years,' he said slowly and very quietly, 'you'll be sat in that same chair, maybe right there.' He touched her bag, the one with the bells stitched around the top. 'In your bag, your passport and visa, all sorted.' Then he pointed at her, from top to toe, 'Wearing, maybe, the Versace top and Gucci jeans. Moshino sandals. Hair and make-up styled by the photographer although maybe it's not how you'd have done it yourself, because you'll have just come back from your latest assignment in the Bahamas. You'll own your own house, plus maybe one for your family. Cars, as well. You'll be complaining to me about your new contract. No, no, that might be true, that'll be my job, to look after that side of things.' He waved at the door. 'Limo waiting for you outside.' Then he patted the empty seat which separated them. 'And – your brother Ilie will be sitting next to you.'

Her nose tingled, tears streamed from her eyes. 'D'you think?'

'I know . . . for sure. Give me your phone number.'

She wrote it down for him. He took great care to read it again, he made sure he had it right. She dried her eyes, felt suddenly, really brilliant.

On their way home, Mila ran full pelt, she swung Little Vlad around by the hood of his coat, she talked loads, she was ecstatic. She went a little crazy. Suddenly she knew her brother Ilie was alive, he must be. Jon Rawle was a really something-else guy, spot on, really emotional, truthful, this was so, so much of an overload, now it was happening for real, she had something to live for. A model?? What did he say? 'In a couple of years—' She was brand new, wasn't she? A top UK model?! She was leaving behind her old life so quickly. But she hoped as well she'd hang on to what she was, even with limos outside the front of the hotel, and really great food, she'd still want her family, she'd still watch her dad floating down the Danube, still want to go back home and find Ilie. She wanted the solid fun and games of success and fame but not the overload, so many of the sparkliest people crashed and burned, she'd have to watch out . . .

No, she could handle it. She was going to arrive soon; this was the promised land that she'd always known existed on the other side of thc adverts, where people had houses, cars, where they had jobs which weren't, like, slavery. This world was practically hers now, it was all around her on the trip home, she was part of it, it was happening, she was about to break down the door, fame and fortune on the other side. And Ilie would be at her side! However much she pulled herself back, told herself to remember that sometimes it didn't work out, she could only let it run, this was kicking off, now. The solid truth hit her, she was going to be so, so rich maybe, she'd be able to buy loads of stuff, she was going to buy things for everyone. Little Vlad – she could clean him up. Her whole family – she could buy them a house. Two houses. The pavement carried her closer to all this; it was paved with gold, the wind blew her along, she felt the pressure increase in her ears. 'Won't you be happy, though,' she crowed to Little Vlad, 'with a big sister who is rich?'

It seemed odd but the street was still there, the people were still there . . . Deliberately, with each step, she threw herself into this new world and it felt cool; she'd reach it OK, she'd be all right as long as she didn't allow it to take her away from what she was, what she knew to be true and good. Yes, it was to leap through to the other side of the TV screen, to walk into the poster, to be a picture herself – and to earn money quickly . . . it was what any other girl would die for, but she should remember her family, everyone she loved here . . .

Charmer and Nio stepped out of the Clamp just after 2 p.m. on Friday, 31 October. Charmer hadn't been outside for two days and the bright, cold sunlight blinded him. He saw Nio off down the path with a big finger pointed at him, a slouch, a dance from one foot to the other and, 'Go on Brother, bring back the woman and bone her, tonight's the night.' He watched as Nio weaved through the graves, disappearing down the path.

He had someone else's MZ 250 Trail lying on its side here

because there was no side stand. He heaved it upright, sat astride the saddle. He was off – yes. Nio had his underage teenage gypsy totty coming to stay, there was no room for Charmer tonight. He'd tried his hardest not to mind, but it was hopeless. Did that fathead Nio even realize that he was breaking up with Charmer, at this moment? No.

He twisted the ignition wires together and kick-started the bike, it was super-loud, no baffle in the silencer; the two-stroke engine ding-dinged and carried him across the graves. He'd go a different way, he couldn't fit through the gap in the fence. The MZ bucked and wobbled, tipped over once, but he wrestled it back on to the path. It was a bigger catch than normal, he tried to steal only scooters, easier to sell. This was one motherfucker of a trail bike . . . The task was to get it up in the hedge, along the bank . . . and away. He scrambled it up the narrow path OK, but then it fell, he couldn't command this chunk of metal in the same way as the febrile, plastic scooters. He tore his leg clear from underneath, heaved it upright and mounted again. 'Come on you fucker!' he cursed. He leaned forwards and kicked the engine over again; the engine caught and held. 'Buggery cheapo Russian junk!' He stabbed it into gear and tried again, this time making it to the top. The hedge disguised an earth bank, and on the other side, a short way along, the path dropped down to the playing fields. He'd skim across and escape from Nio for ever.

Little bites of the clutch, both feet close to the ground, kept the bike running on the path on the top of the bank. With a scooter, he could spit along here deftly, feet up, but this was different; even though it was a cross-country bike it was so much bigger. The front wheel slipped away from him, down into the hedge. He could only hang on, ride with it. The rear end followed inevitably and with a thump the engine stalled. He couldn't climb out because thick vegetation constricted him. The bank itself had scored his left side and everywhere he was scratched and bruised.

'Shitheap!' he cursed. His breath came in clouds, it was fucking cold. He began tearing off the twigs closest to his face, he punished the tank of the bike, he tried to kick his legs free. The winter sun was blinding.

When he heard a dog bark, he froze. Once before the police had sent dogs into the woods to find him; he'd known enough not to run, instead he'd played dead, the dogs had smelled him out but he'd been unhurt.

This wasn't a police dog. It was a red setter. Charmer peered through the thick hedge and glimpsed the dog drawing near. He watched its ears lift comically as it came to a halt, looking in his direction. It barked once, continued to stare. The owner followed and looked, and then Charmer could see her shock at finding a bike tangled in the hedge with a lad crouched over it. For some moments, both sides stared. Charmer could see the penny drop on the woman's face, it took a while, but this must be the boy who stole all the bikes and scrambled them around the woods and the playing fields, leaving the burned-out wrecks. She frowned, took a step towards him. Her dog barked copiously and darted forwards.

Charmer shoved the bike sideways, which had little effect because it was held in the many-tentacled grip of the hedgerow. He squirmed, pulled himself free to clamber up the bank, but it tore off one of his shoes, so he ran off missing a Reebok cross-trainer worth more than he would have got for the heap-o-rust MZ. So, it was a double loss, he cursed as he stumbled over the bank. The cold ground immediately attacked that right foot. Look at the state of him, freezing cold, like Peter Rabbit hobbling along, while Nio, no doubt, was cosying up to the girlfriend, strolling along in the sunshine. He cursed again, and again.

It was an automatic habit, to make for the cemetery. People gave up searching when they were among the graves, it was irreverent to chase a teenager in a graveyard. Added to that, it was a large and complicated acreage with many twists and turns, fraught with dangerous tablets of stone littering the undergrowth. He found his way, stopped to listen several times.

A half-hour later, when he was sure neither the dog nor its owner was following, Charmer limped around to the western edge of the allotments and came to Coldfall Wood from the other direction. He made his way through the fence, back home to the Clamp.

He approached warily, peered in through the windows. Had Nio brought her back already? The inside was deserted – probably not. Then he asked what difference would it make, there was nowhere else for him to go, his old shoes were here and . . .

He pulled on the nail, stumbled inside. He called out but there was no reply from upstairs; he was on his own. He tore open the hatch in the stove and chucked on more wood, opened the vent. He sat and pulled off his wet sock, examined the sole of his foot for bruising, thorns, frostbite, what a mess. Thaw it out. He took off his remaining Reebok and hefted it in his hand. They were the best shoes he'd ever had, custom-built for his kind of life – he could run, creep silently, or stamp the pedals on the scooters. And one shoe was worse than no shoes at all. Bad news. But then he thought, not all bad news, because, of course . . .

He rummaged among his stuff and found his old shoes, the only other pair he had, and he went to the door, pushed it open, took a few strides and threw them as far as he could into the undergrowth. Then he went back inside, hogged the stove. That was that. He was staying.

There was a bit of the room that stuck out, gave them a useful shelf. On it was the birthday cake, with a blue and white ruffled collar. Bought from somewhere. He went over and had a look. He counted the candles: sixteen. Charmer shook his head. He found a hacksaw blade, cut himself a slice and ate it.

Surely no one, especially not Nio, could chuck out a guy in this cold with only one shoe. He waited in, stuffed the fire some more. Sat close. Nio would complain that he'd brought no wood, done no work, made a mess of the place. Nio would expect him to be gone, whereas . . .

When Nio returned, sure enough he had his birdage with him. Charmer latched on to the sight of her and in one instant saw everything, measured her, judged her. Her eyes were pools of black make-up, the face white with a dribble of blood from the corner of her mouth. Of course, Hallowe'en. Long black coat, fake fur. Underneath, the T-shirt was cut up to look like a spider's web. A red T-shirt showing through. Big boots, blocky wooden heels. Her blonde hair was tied up in swatches, using what looked like coloured pipe-cleaners. She was wearing a choker of black velvet. Charmer's heart leaped to his mouth; he wasn't meant to be here. Shouldn't have seen this. Her skin was flawless, the eyes alive and glowing in the centre of the black make-up, although unhappy at the sight of him, of course. He was envious, he couldn't keep his eyes off her.

'Happy Birthday to you!' he sang. Silence. 'Sorry, couldn't be out of your way after all, 'cos I lost my shoe,' he explained, holding up his bare foot.

More silence. And he could swear, it wasn't only because he, Charmer, was here at all, stopping their fun, it was something in the air right from the off. Something had gone wrong between them. 'All right?' he asked, but they hardly answered, looked like they'd seen a ghost. No hand-holding to go on with. She'd been crying or was about to start up. 'Oh,' he said, 'so, not a happy birthday then.'

She didn't give him an inch.

Charmer eyed her. That strap around her neck was good. He knew it straightaway, she'd have been all right.

No, all was not sunny and bright between Nio and this girl. Which made him the biggest, fattest gooseberry, but somehow he still wanted to hang around. Get a life, he told himself. Yet it was cold outside, he only had one shoe, so he just sat there. After what seemed like an hour he asked Nio politely, 'Got a job yet?'

Nio began to pick up some fragments of wood. 'No.' He stooped to open the pot-bellied stove. 'D'you get any more sticks?'

'No.'

Minutes passed.

'Can I have some more of this cake then?' he asked, which didn't go down well. Nio blinked. Everyone was miserable in here.

A half-hour passed. They went upstairs for a bit, and he sang out of tune, played spoons on the paint cans, generally made his presence known. They got the message that he wasn't going to leave, and came back down. He watched Nio root around the place, drag out the old motorcycle cover, then he murmured something to her, she nodded and off they went. Charmer gave them a wave. Were they going to do it in the woods, on an old bit of canvas? 'That's all right,' he called after them, 'you can borrow it.'

As he watched them go, he knew it wasn't just him – something, or someone, had burst Nio's bubble. He felt bad though. Charmer the wrecker. But what could he do? He went and fetched the pair of old shoes that he'd thrown into the bushes, so he could leave if he sunk too far, too low. He turned back indoors, pegged the door shut, hunkered down next to the stove. Stay put for now, Charmer. Defrost your foot.

Little Vlad watched his sister getting dressed. Then she tore off everything, swore at herself in the mirror and changed again. Hallowe'en – she put on gothic make-up, a dribble of blood from her mouth. Then, as a final touch, she lifted a choker to her neck, black velvet with beads stitched on it. She dropped it, then lifted it again. Asked him to help put it on.

He offered her a cigarette and she replied that she didn't smoke, nor did she want to start smoking. He said he'd feed the dog for her tonight if she wasn't coming back but she took no notice. When he volunteered to go with her, keep her company, she said she didn't need him. He asked her to go trick-or-treating with him later on, but she said no, she was busy all afternoon, all night, all day tomorrow, the night after that, the rest of her life was booked up. He worried away at her until she helped him with his cloak, made out of plastic bin bags. She positioned the pair of horns on his head, switched them on to see if they worked. Yes – each horn flashed red, alternately. She spared him some of her make-up. Anything else, she asked.

Yes, it was simple, all he wanted was the five quid she owed him. She definitely had said she'd hand it over, for the striped woollen bag. She had the money OK.

And then he didn't like being taken by the shoulders and turned around and pushed out of the door. It felt stupid, he'd got changed too early. No one else was in Hallowe'en gear yet, it was still daylight.

God! – fierce cold hit him, the sky a sharp blue. The winter sun was hard, bright. If he stepped into its pattern, it burned his eyes. Cross the line into shadow and he was dead cold. He kicked his heels, shivered, hung around at the top of the slip road. This was some grief, from his big sister. No one liked being turned over. People didn't do that to him. No way. Not even for a fiver.

He could hear a motorbike skidding across the playing fields, it sounded like an insect half crazed. Then it went quiet. Dead.

When he saw Mila's fish and chips stumbling down the road, he didn't reply to the friendly greeting but instead loitered, gave him a look. He watched the guy head down and into The Home Office. It was worth Little Vlad's while to wait, see where they were going. If he tagged along, he might annoy his five quid out of her maybe. So when they came out, Little Vlad ducked through a gap in the railway sleepers, skirted the wrecker's yard, cut off a big corner, straight to Colney Hatch Lane. When they walked past he followed at a distance. His sister was glammed up for Hallowe'en, the fish and chips was the usual shambolic figure.

As he meandered after them, Little Vlad felt sore. Look how they were holding hands. Mila was still in a bad mood, he could tell, but the fish and chips was having a good time, he was smiling. He, Little Vlad, was the one who should be smiling; with the five quid he would be. She'd taken the bag that Little Vlad had found, she had the goods right now, look, there was the bag, he'd delivered his side of the bargain and she hadn't. Now she was going to get a whole load more stuff from her boyfriend and it wasn't even her birthday. Unfair.

Then they switched direction and headed across the playing fields. Here Little Vlad would be exposed, following them, but he didn't care. They swung their joined hands, surrounded by the chill green expanse of the wintry playing field. He was the figure tracking them. He felt like a killer or a detective on TV.

Of course she noticed him, out in the open. She stopped and broke with her fish and chips, came back. That expression of hers – disgust at his following them – it made up his mind. There was only so much unfair he could take. He walked straight past her and up to the fish and chips. His English was word perfect. The killer and his victim. 'The truth. You—' – he pointed at Nio – 'I tell you, her birthday, right. For real. I would like to inform you. NOT NOW. Not tomorrow. NO. The truth, is, right . . . *Treizeci Novembrie*. Her birthday is November thirty. For real.' Then he smiled, swayed from one foot to the other. 'Not tomorrow.'

It was like rocks tumbling from a cliff, how the smile fell right off the fish and chips' face.

*

The sweethearts strolled arm in arm up the slip road; Mila was dressed for Hallowe'en but Nio had forgotten. She didn't care, she could enjoy her own clothes without anyone else having to join in and, besides, she had more important things on her mind, she was a bit wiped out by the confusion of what today should mean, how her heart was torn in two suddenly, she felt a thrill of danger, this guy had popped up who had seriously turned her head. She hadn't told Nio about him yet, that was the dangerous bit, watch out, she wanted to say, for what I don't tell you . . . but she knew she had to tell him now; it was bursting in her and so she clasped a handful of hair at the back of his head, leaned up to kiss him, left a black mark on the side of his mouth, held him tight. She was excited, yes, but also guilty, because the good news might take her away from Nio, it was going to be big potatoes . . . and Nio had been looking so hard for a job and hadn't found one, her heart went out to him. So, with a mixture of anxiety and excitement she blew it out, stayed really solemn to contain it, make it smaller, 'Guess what.'

'What?'

'I might have a job.'

'No!!' It was like a knife going into Nio – he'd been trying so hard himself to find one and had failed, whereas she'd quickly succeeded, she was rising faster than him, maybe beyond him . . . He was gutted.

'Might, *might*.' Next she had to tell him what kind of job, and she knew he couldn't be happy about her being a model, besides, it didn't seem right to tell him, just when they were about to go off and do it, have sex, maybe in a few hours . . . She felt heavy-hearted, confused, happy and sad at the same time, torn in both directions. Maybe she didn't want to have sex after all. Perhaps she would tell him no. It was like the pressure on it was too much, it had become too big a thing, she wanted . . . or was she just frightened? Or did she just want to leave him, keep him as a brother? And maybe she didn't want to be a model at all, either.

'What is it?' he asked. 'The job?' He was sick with nerves.

'I met this guy on a train and he said, like, sorry he was on his phone, isn't the mobile phone horrible, and then he was talking about work, he say he wanted to meet me and maybe he can find work for me, like, as . . . a model.'

'A model?' Nio was immediately falling, this was awful, didn't she know . . . a guy on a train? He was . . . didn't she realize . . .

'Is nothing like that,' she said, rolling her eyes, 'I know what that is, you know, a *model*. I would not do all that, he wasn't that, he was—'

'He was a nice guy?'

'Really nice, so, so cool, you know, so *not* . . . he has like some agency; anyway, I went and met him just for a drink.'

'You went and met him?' She hadn't told him she was going to meet someone so he went cold with jealousy, suddenly he was in real trouble. This was meant to be the best day for them, but now, suddenly, it hurt. He remembered all his plans – the cake, the fire alight, the bedroom, the gifts. He so wanted today to be good . . .

She shrugged. 'Yes. I met him. And he said I could make it maybe. As a model.' She ran on, telling him everything. Nio bit hard on his disappointment, the only way out of the pain was to run right through it and out the other side, to get involved, to help her. The guy had said she'd need a dozen ten by eight pictures, they had to find someone – his photographer friend, Nick, could do it maybe?

'Is he professional?' asked Mila. They had to be right.

As they began to cross the playing fields, they discussed the details and how much it would cost. Nio tried hard. 'This man is right,' he said reasonably, 'you are different, there is something, a light on inside you which shows . . . you are beautiful. He's right after all.' They held hands. Anticipation of the near future sent a shiver down his spine, he wanted it too much but suddenly it was filled with difficulty, conflict.

Mila was worrying, too. Was she just scared because it had become this big event, they'd waited for too long? Maybe she should tell him she wasn't sixteen after all. Keep it straight between them and give herself a bit more time. She imagined Nio's face, it swam in front of her, then she swapped it for Jon Rawle's face. She pictured his house, then tore it down, put up Nio's house. One thing she promised: even if she became a top model she'd never desert her family, nor Nio, she'd take them along with her, or stay with them, however it worked out. Nio – she felt his placid strength next to her and clung to him – Nio was solid, the most solid of all; she mustn't lose him. He was there, next to her, it was love, it was. When she was up and down the rollercoaster of fame and fortune, meeting all sorts of lush guys, he'd keep her sane. She pushed away the idea that he moved a bit slowly, that he wasn't very sophisticated, that he wouldn't fit in with her new crowd. So what, that was exactly what was good about him. Today . . . look at him, he was so charged up, ready for it. Yet, she was thinking how to pull back, how to disappoint him.

'D'you want me to come with you to the photographer?' He was worried at how distracted she was, it wasn't normal, even her hand in his was inert, not as lively as normal. Something was wrong.

She could see the jealousy going into him like knives. 'Not you,' she replied, 'you might stand up and hit the photographer if he touches me, I know you would—'

'I wouldn't!'

'With your big strong arms, you'd hit him, but maybe I take someone from my family. I can know the rules, what is what.'

Nio hurt with love for her. She was so newly made. She was so nearly his. A few hours away!

Mila drank in his wounded look. This was for real. This was life, she had to choose what to do. Not some time in the future. Right now. It was today, the time and the place were rushing towards them, couldn't be stopped. Tell the truth or not, make love with him or not? They were crossing the playing fields, on the way to the Clamp, two figures hand in hand, threading through half a dozen teams playing football in different colours, and it was the last day in October. They were going to hang out for the afternoon, then go out tonight maybe. Or stay in. The other boy wouldn't be there. Nio had lit the stove, it would be warm. He said he'd bought a cake. At midnight, she would unwrap the gift, something he'd made for her with his own hands . . . Then . . . she was frightened, she just needed a bit of time. Should she turn him down, having made all that fuss? What could she tell him? There might be someone else she wanted? All she knew was, now it was she who wanted to wait, the world to stop turning. She leaned close to Nio, put her chin against his shoulder as they crossed the acres of playing fields.

He tugged her close, her under his arm, close as anything. They were among the dog-walkers and the schoolchildren playing football, black figures cutting across the green. Then he felt her stiffen, heard her mutter in her own language. Suddenly she broke free, headed back the way they'd come. When Nio turned to see why, he recognized Little Vlad under the make-up and Hallowe'en gear, who walked straight past his sister and up to him instead, poked him in the chest and without any greeting just started talking and his accent was strong, it took Nio a while to work out what he was saying. His horns flashed red. 'The truth. You . . . I tell you, her birthday, right. For real. I would like to inform you. NOT NOW. Not tomorrow. NO. The truth, is, right . . . *Treizeci Novembrie*. Her birthday is November thirty. For real.' Then he smiled, swayed from one foot to the other. 'Not tomorrow.'

They were tiny figures, a tableau in this expanse of cold winter sunlight. Everyone else on the playing fields was walking or running, these three were stationary, poised at the middle of something. The tightly packed graves on the other side of the fence were a silent audience, the dog-walkers and schoolchildren were unknowing passers-by, the pressure-cooker of Muswell Hill's breeding ground built imperceptibly around them.

It *wasn't* her birthday? Nio felt utter disbelief, yet one look at Mila's expression told him it was true. The disappointment was intense, crushing. She had lied to him, and suddenly her gothic make-up really was frightening, she held such power and with that mask on . . . Not her birthday? So it couldn't happen now, they had to wait for longer after all? It was a joke, he so wanted it not to be true . . . He asked her if . . .

Mila couldn't help laughing. And she shouted. OK! She stamped both feet. But for a fucking good reason she had lied to him! It was all mixed up in her, what an overdose, the anger, shame, but a real thrill as well at being found out . . . She was furious at Little Vlad – shouted after him that he'd better not show his face ever again. As for Nio – he looked so unhappy, defeated. She really had lied to him big time but for a good reason, she told him, and he ought to be proud! At the same time she couldn't get away from the weird feeling of happiness. Just when she'd needed a break, she'd been given one, she'd been let off the hook. She needn't go through with it. Give herself time to find out if Jon Rawle was going to change her life.

The look on Nio's face – heartbreaking – he was like a dog that had just had its bone taken away, the wounded look he was giving her, that frown, God she loved him, she was really broken with laughter, she couldn't stop, it was so, so embarrassing, total . . .

Little Vlad peeled off. His cloak flared behind him, the horns on his head switched off for now, but later they would flash in the dark. Little devil. Dracula. Son of Dragon. She thought, it was his night, tonight. Bleeding squit. Later on, he'd go trick-or-treating.

As they walked to the Clamp she paced in front and around Nio, seriously explaining why, how, she'd lied, it was only because she'd wanted happiness, she hadn't broken his trust, not really . . . and then . . .

He watched her, nodded, understood. Of course. He wanted her as soon as possible as well. It killed him now, though. Double killed him. He suffered long mournful silences as they made their way. If she'd lied about this, maybe she'd lied about other things.

Yet, after a while, she saw his smile break through, and he held her, squeezed her tight in his arms, she knew both their feelings were all boiled up together, couldn't really be separated. She slowed down. Their anger, laughter, frustration dissolved to a big, wide, open stretch of . . . yes it was love, really was. If she couldn't have him as part of her life she'd be . . . half what she was now.

Then, another conversation, and they both dissolved back into unhappiness again, and worse was to come because when they reached the Clamp Charmer was there, which killed them both, another small death to cope with. Immediately he asked for money for a new pair of trainers, said he couldn't leave because he only had one shoe. Nio argued with him. The whole afternoon had sunk, for him, into gloom. And Charmer had taken a slice out of the cake, it seemed part of the whole thing, Mila could use the cake to accuse Nio: look, make a big event of something and watch it fail.

Charmer hardly spoke to her, or looked at her. She didn't understand everything he said but she knew he was jealous of her. When they went upstairs he was singing and drumming with spoons down below. It added to the unhappy atmosphere between them. Their date, this special last night of October, Hallowe'en, couldn't be going worse. Up here, too, the gift in its brightly coloured paper accused her, it was evidence of her lying to Nio. He'd made her something, wrapped it, and now it was useless. She begged him to keep it for her, her birthday was soon. If he was still talking to her. She felt sad, lost. Another whole month – what would happen to her and Nio? She wanted them to love each other, simply and purely, whatever.

Nio thought about the immediate future – it was bitter, disappointing – and struggled to come to terms with the fact that there were another four weeks he'd have to strike his way through, day after endless day, until 30 November. He would just trudge across the desert, count himself forwards, look at it positively, he was going to stick to his word, carry on, it was like he'd just seen a mirage and had to ignore the illusion. They wouldn't be ordinary days, he'd remember them for ever: each one hitched their love higher towards the moral high ground, these passing weeks would – even more than before – measure the honour of his love for her.

Was that so? Really? Maybe he should stop fooling himself . . .

'We can't stay here,' said Mila. It was a sudden realization. Too much was wrong. She shivered.

'You want to go somewhere else?' he asked.

She nodded, yes. He could hear in her accent the language of her birth, it was like the shadow of a different person.

They dressed in two coats each against the cold and took an old motorcycle cover, then they went outside and lay in a square patch of the old graveyard. It was three p.m. and the bright winter sun still came in low to grace this conjunction of cemetery, woodland and allotments, it cut shadows from the brittle, denuded trees which gave their spot this delicate lace edging. The faint sound of the children on the playing fields brought a sense of distance, it was like their private island of graves. It was crowded, yes, but with the long dead. Nio lay, hands behind his head, and the sponge of wet earth underneath the motorcycle cover gave him a buoyancy, comfort, but his thoughts were racing, tumultuous. On his chest lay this pulled about, tied up mass of blonde hair: Mila. He could see her hand curled, fresh-looking. One finger moved unconsciously against the fabric of his coat, wearing away at a line an inch long, he felt a tiny vibration, he was sure that buried under layers of clothing his skin would be marked, it was the lightest touch but of such importance, like when she whispered, and the words – barely airborne – carried so much weight.

She didn't *have* to kiss him, Mila thought, just because she usually did; everything that had happened told her she was allowed to withdraw, give them both time to think . . . it was too much . . . she told herself not to worry, deal with it later. Take the time, it had been unlucky for them both today, she so wanted to go past this point, maybe sleep . . . Mind-numbing.

They lay folded together tightly to keep from the cold. Nio felt her leg arrive over his, her knee pointed over him, the clump of her boot rested on his shin. She pressed closer, then after a while her breath deepened, the automatic movements of her shoulders and ribs took over as she relaxed, was delivered to sleep. She'd stayed out late last night, with friends.

The weight of her boot increased. The wooden heel was cutting into the bone only a millimetre beneath the skin. He didn't move. The pain sharpened for a while and he closed his eyes, the cold, blue bowl of the sky disappeared and he searched the darkness behind his eyelids and found nothing, no picture of her, but he had her smell in his nostrils. The sound of the children playing was the only thing, it seemed, that tethered them here. He imagined moving inch by inch along the seam between himself and her; even through their bulky clothes, it was to him as if there were no distinction, they were the same flesh. Her ear was against his chest, his heartbeat would be sounding in her dream. Her hand lay still now, poised but inert. Her breast and stomach were edged into his side, her hips a maw that gripped him, the leg floated on him, he was possessed by that leg. The heel burned into his shin; now that she was asleep he turned his leg an inch and the pain subsided. He fell asleep, too.

When they awoke she was printed with the fabric of his coat and there was a circle of saliva on the cloth where her open mouth had rested against him. Her make-up had loosened on her face. She was groggy, disoriented, cold. 'I dreamed,' she said, surprised. She stood and hopped, smacked her arms around her sides.

'What about?' He climbed to his feet, too, and began to fold up the motorcycle cover.

'I was beating at something. It is coming towards me, and I was, you know, maybe with a stick, beating it off?'

'What was it?'

'Just, something . . . from below. Coming from the ground, like an animal, or . . . I couldn't see what it was. Then I had to climb, to escape—' She shivered; it was too cold to stay any longer. She released the clips and shook out her hair, scratched her scalp.

'Beating at something,' mused Nio, 'like an animal? Might be me?'

She smiled. 'Maybe.' She picked at the watch on her wrist, looked at him sadly. 'What shall we do?' She wasn't sure if he'd like her so much, now she'd lied to him. It made her uncomfortable, she wanted to go.

'Dunno—' said Nio. 'I—'

'What?'

'I said I didn't want to take . . . but you're not like . . . you *are* older than fifteen, I know that, really, but . . . the trouble is, if I say something, I want you to know that I mean it, that I stick by it—'

'Is OK,' said Mila, irritated, 'we can just let it go, we can have some days pass by, it doesn't matter, we have our whole lives, I don't want to worry about now, about what we were going to be doing—'

They stood and embraced. She hung off him, a deadweight. Normally they'd kiss, thought Nio, but they didn't. Not to worry. Failure – take it in, move on, won't be for ever. They'd reach for each other again, he knew for sure. They left their square of graves and walked the paths hand in hand. He steered them through the maze, otherwise she'd have been lost. It was getting dark already. They reached the playing fields, crossed the plain of grass and went through the housing estate on the other side. He left her at the mini-roundabout, so her family wouldn't see him. No one wanted any more fights.

Now they kissed – briefly, lips closed – nonetheless Nio felt an extra heartbeat, and as always when he was with Mila among the to-and-fro of other people he was blessed in the eyes of passers-by. Then they separated.

As he watched her walk away from him, Nio felt anxious at the change in Mila. It was dark now and her good looks seeded this cloud of danger around her, to which she herself was either oblivious or she ignored it. Her walk had a youthful kick to it and signalled all predators, look, fair game.

Mila walked away glad to have a break, she needed time to herself, sort out the mess her heart was in, her head spinning, these feelings were coming at her from all directions. She wanted it to be like last week, when all she knew was Nio and her designs on him, and the lie of her birthday had been just a funny trick. As she walked down the slip road to the caravans, their dog Nisha was pleased to see her; Mila welcomed the affection of the animal . . . if only life were that simple.

When she was inside her phone sang its tune, she scrabbled in the striped woollen bag to find it, she so liked this bag, it went everywhere with her now.

Jon Rawle's name was written on the phone's miniature screen. Nio didn't even have a mobile phone. Suddenly she didn't feel old at all, she was small and lost, not twenty for sure, only fifteen, she wanted everyone to leave her alone, she wasn't grown up . . . All these much older guys, these English fish and chips, coming at her. None of them knew what she was, who she was, what she'd gone through, not really . . .

Her thumb hovered between the cancel button, inscribed with a small red 'c', and the 'OK' button, which was green. If she pressed red to cancel, she'd lose Jon's call, it would be the same as sticking with Nio. If she pressed 'OK', she'd get Jon Rawle, she'd run with him, her life would take that path and she felt in her bones that it meant she might lose Nio. The two men, the two buttons – green for Jon, red for Nio – signalled insistently, sang their alarm, waved their different colours; she couldn't decide.

The phone called again – four times now she'd been asked to make her choice, and she only had two more chances before the voicemail took away the decision.

She held her breath, her thumb swapped from red to green, the buttons were plump, tactile.

A voice called from the other end of the caravan, 'Answer that fucking phone!' It was her 8-year-old sister, her face cloudy and sorrowful, almost invisible squashed into the gap where the little cooker had once been, it was where she liked to read her ghost stories, one after another. Mila stood open-mouthed, the phone singing in her hand, so uncertain, so confused, trapped like an animal in an enclosure, this was the human zoo and she was the insignificant, poor specimen. Yes, she felt small – but then again, the very next moment she swelled with pride, she was more important than ever, and braver because she stood on the brink of something really big, she had Jon Rawle who was going to take her away from here, he was going to accelerate her forwards, upwards – beyond the adverts – maybe to somewhere she didn't at all want to go . . . this string of thoughts wasn't composed in Mila as a logical sequence, one after the other, but rather they were condensed as a single, immediate sensation of excitement and danger mixed.

The fifth ring of her phone ended; her heart thudded. This was her last chance. She was so effing confused, everything was uncertain, it was like her life had narrowed to a point – *right here, now* – should she press OK, or not?

Her thumb moved just as the phone rang for the sixth time, she'd lose the call if she waited another second, and this exact moment lasted for ever, it was like a week-long vigil, she had time to notice the unmade bed, the old blanket a sea of corrugated green against the brown stripe of the converted seating, the inches deep litter of girls' clothes belonging to her sister and her mother and herself, the pile of underwear emptied out from the launderette bag waiting to be sorted, the photographs curling and dusty pinned in the little strip of wooden trim tacked to the side of the caravan wall, the broken-off head of a stone dog which Little Vlad had brought back from the cemetery, the phallic tube of Sure deodorant, and the green diode winking on the clock radio in the October dark – it was as if this flashing dot of green, what was it, something to do with the alarm function, were connected somehow to the calling of her phone, it was part of the conspiracy, go for green. The dot had an insistent rhythm, it was hypnotic, a sign . . .

She pressed the small green button on her phone marked 'OK'. Jon Rawle. 'Hello?'

'Where've you been?'

Jon never went through any of the hellos, the how-are-yous, he didn't even give his name, he just spoke as if they'd been in a conversation already for some minutes, it was a kind of trick but it gave him more confidence; maybe it was a good idea, she could use it herself, it would be cool just to drop everyone into the middle of what she wanted to say.

'Been around,' she replied.

'Had a booking for you earlier, but I had to be able to say yes or no, right then. That minute. So, I had to give it to someone else. Where were you?'

'I was—'

'Doesn't matter, plenty more where that came from.'

'What is the booking?'

'Just a little catalogue, as it happens, but it puts a few miles on you, gives you a bit of experience.'

She was excited, had to ask him more. What catalogue? How much work was it for?

'Oh – y'know. The usual.' There was a pause. All her hopes hung on his reply. She waited, and it was a while before he answered, 'Freemans. Hundred and twenty a day.'

It was her turn to say nothing because suddenly, with that pause, she had this ridiculous thought – it was probably because of everything that had happened, her own lie about her birthday in ruins at Nio's feet and so on – but the idea jumped into her head that it was all bullshit, it was a trick, there had been no booking, there was no model agency. It was mad, though – just because she herself hadn't told the truth didn't mean to say everyone else was lying as well.

'Doesn't matter,' he went on. 'My fault. Should have texted you but my brain was fried. So much going on. I don't want you doing crappy catalogue stuff anyway, you're too good for that.'

At a stroke she found her belief in him again. She knew he was all right.

There was another pause, she wanted to track his thoughts, were they the same as hers, that all of this mattered loads, because something important was going to happen. They'd met on that train, and now . . .

His voice came again, 'Listen, bad news for you, I know, but not for me. It's nothing, peanuts. When you see where you're going in the next year, OK, you'll be glad you never worked for a catalogue. Tell me where are you, right now?'

'Home.'

'You're coming for a drink with me. I'll straighten your head out a bit and then send you back happy. OK?'

Just at the sound of his voice, the way his words tumbled from him quickly, the thought of him, she wanted to agree with anything he said, like something had softened her bones, her heart felt quicker, her brain more clever, she straightaway said, 'OK.' Hope soared in her, that he'd suggest she come to his house, 15 Queens Avenue, because she wanted to see inside.

Instead, he asked her to choose a pub, anywhere on the Broadway. Another thought jumped in her mind – he must be married, not to want her to come to his home, but even if he was, she fought off the disappointment, it didn't matter, this was a professional relationship, she needn't worry about things like that. She replied without thinking, 'Ruby In The Dust?' and then cursed herself because that was where she and Nio went, she'd forgotten, it was a small betrayal but it didn't seem fair . . .

They made the time – in fifteen minutes.

Automatically she steered herself out into the cold, the car lights flaring, catching her as she stepped down and shut the door behind her, this *effing* door which was always so stiff, it took all her weight to close it. She kept to the edge, her ankle turned on the rough ground, she avoided looking into the cars as they swooped past, all of them preyed on her, she wished for Nio or Little Vlad, or Jon Rawle, to be with her. Once she gained Colney Hatch Lane she strode quickly, broke into a trot, then back to a quick walk when the hill grew too steep. It was the worst thing, loads of people in Hallowe'en gear clowning around; men zoomed in, like suddenly it was dark so it was illegal for her to be out on her own, on foot, she was fair game, all the daytime friendship of men was gone, there was only drunken craziness and crude hunger, which she had to walk through, every stride was like a kick, she fought her way up the hill, moving through clouds of her own breath. For about the millionth time she told herself to go to karate lessons, she could do with that, with being able to fight them off, for real.

She walked up there to meet him. From the bottom of her heart she wanted to blow air into this balloon, this possible new life, until it was so big that everyone could see her living it up, think she was great, she'd believe in herself like Nio did, then everything would turn out to be all right. She circled the round-about at the top of Muswell Hill and pushed her way into Ruby In The Dust.

The heat embraced her. She scanned the crowd and among the made-up faces, the blood dripping from the corners of mouths, the fangs and greased hair and kohled eyes, she found him almost immediately, he was sitting on the same plump red sofa where she'd last sat with Nio. He was right in the middle, the exact seat where she herself had been, and his arm was protecting the part of the seat where Nio had sat but instead there was now a folded coat. Their eyes met – she smiled and waved and felt herself walking in Nio's footsteps. Other men eyed her – she was racking up the boys, look at their drooling, bloody mouths in here. The display she had, her body, her looks, her person, didn't half work, she thought it was the biggest magic wand anyone could have given her.

He moved his coat, settled her in the seat. He touched the choker at her neck and said, 'Told you.' At the same time, without waiting for a reply, he went to buy her a drink. She checked the room for faces she might connect with. When he came back with her Vodka WKD she was excited at *his* clothes, how clean they were, perfect. Even the coat – her hand was resting on top of the soft fabric – seemed as if never worn. For ages she listened to him, he was mumbling so she couldn't understand. All she did was look, she was magnetized by the odd nose, the way the whole of his face cut this way and that; his eyes bored into her, she was disturbed right in the middle part of her stomach, like a spoon had been dipped in and stirred her up. She wondered what he was saying. How chill and blue his eyes were. His dark hair was coarse, plainly set around his ears, across his brow. There was a sense more than anything of bone underneath the skin – his temples, the bridge of his nose, chin. Even his eyes – the cold points of light in the middle of them could have been chips of bone. He stared in a particular way, she thought probably he was waiting for an answer from her about something. She was out of her depth. She shook her head, 'Sorry, I not understood that, you were too fast.' She felt small, weak.

He waited a while, hooked up his drink, took a swig, set it down. Just looked at her.

A bell clanged loudly – it made her heart jump. It came from the kitchen, someone's food was ready. She remembered something and asked, 'Can I come and see your office, where we will work?'

He replied that he wasn't going into the office much at the moment. He went on – she couldn't understand all of it – about how the mobile phone *was* his office, that's all he needed, the phone and the inside of his head, he could do any business he needed like that. But then he suggested, after all, she could come and visit sometime, sure. She asked whereabouts in the West End it was and he said he'd text her the address and put up a time for an appointment – and then he offered to send a car to pick her up and suddenly she was really flying, *a car to pick her up*? A thrill ran through her, it felt like wind in a field of grass, lush. She had to pinch herself but it must be true, yes he would change her life, this was the way, she was travelling now, upwards . . . she could picture the visit, the driver would take her right to the door, Jon would be there to welcome her and show her around. And because she was with him, she'd be treated so, so well.

And she'd have her photographs soon, Jon Rawle would pay for them, he was so generous, she was on the way all right.

There was a lunge, then, in her middle, which was serious, it made her giddy, was it the drink? She told herself not to have any more . . . it was a path she shouldn't go down, she knew that, she'd stopped herself but only just, luckily. He wouldn't like it if she behaved like a bleeding girl. When he asked if she wanted another one, she said no. Instead, excitedly, she talked on.

Nio turned back. Sorrow deadened him. He'd always felt a sense of loss when he and Mila parted, it had always deflated him – yet now it was wrapped in greater importance. It was frightening.

When he arrived back in the Clamp, Charmer had gone. He went upstairs and lay on the bed. Time stood still. It wasn't her birthday!? In the vacuum left behind, the idea of Hallowe'en swept in to take its place. Everyone else was celebrating, not him after all. Nor her – he pictured her alone in the caravan, dressed in her gear. They'd just have to wait longer – that's all. He breathed each moment away, forced them past, reaching for the next one, pushed that behind as well, then the next . . . but how could they possibly do it, clamber over another four weeks? He frowned. There was a change in Mila, over and above the fact that he'd found her out. She hadn't tried to push him around, she hadn't kissed him in the same way. She was different.

Then he told himself, it wasn't worth it, his precious stand, he was tilting at nothing, look, she'd not even kissed him, she'd taken a step back, it meant he was falling into an empty space, he'd lose her if he didn't *do* something. The whole construction in his head, concerning her age, the law, the whole fabric of that honour, which up until now had contained every moment of his behaviour as regards her, disappeared in a trice. If he was going to lose her, then no *way* . . . forget it, his precious stance wasn't worth it, he was going to have her, they'd make love tomorrow; right now – it seemed then as if his life narrowed to an absolute point, he went through it, and came out the other side different – he sat up and made the decision, yes for definite, he was filled with resolve: he'd give her – as Charmer would say – a good boning, before someone else did.

FOUR

Elinor Ginsberg had to stop herself from laughing, this woman had been thrashing around in the birth pool for two hours and her husband wouldn't let her climb out, she was desperate to walk around and scream but every time she stood up he put an arm around her shoulders, pushed her back down, reminded her the water was best, they'd wanted a water birth. His wife begged for anaesthetic when she'd suffered six hours of excruciating pain and was only five centimetres dilated, but he persuaded her to soldier on. Mrs Ginsberg opened the cervix manually before they all died of exhaustion. It caused the poor woman so much pain her teeth nearly fell out. Elinor saw the husband staring at his wife's face in fascination, her lips were stretched to breaking point. Upstairs, the nanny was sick and the other children frightened.

Now they were into the endgame, and the husband was proud and excited. He'd done all this by himself. Elinor allowed herself to be drawn aside. 'Yes?' she asked. She was nearly worn to the limit with having to accept his homoeopathic treatments under her tongue every half hour or so; and also it didn't help that he'd got her name wrong throughout.

'Angela . . . I hope you don't mind.'

'How can I help?'

'I want the colours in the room to be just right, and now we're close, I was wondering if I could ask you to change your shirt?'

'Oh . . . sure. That's OK. Do you have a shirt you wish me to wear?'

'Hold on!' He skipped out of the room, and was soon back with a maroon top from Gap. 'Could you wear this? Is that allowed?'

'That's fine, yes.'

'It's a positive colour . . . all the colours in here are positive colours. We even painted Amy's toenails a positive colour, when she hit thirty-eight weeks!'

Elinor smiled, she really couldn't believe some people, she felt rather sorry for the beloved who was about to arrive. Not too sorry, though. He or she would be looked after, that was for sure, and everyone could escape their parents. She felt a pang of grief at this thought, because her parents had escaped from her, both of them had passed away in the last three years.

'Angela?' The husband was at her side again.

'Mmmm?' She'd quite taken to the name now, it was like being an actress.

'How long to go, would you think?'

'Any time.'

'I'll just go and wake the kids, then.' He laughed. 'The other kids.' And he disappeared.

She checked her watch. Five-thirty a.m.

When he came back he was carrying a frightened girl of around five years old on one arm and a weepy toddler of two or three – Elinor couldn't tell if it was a girl or a boy. He was soothing both of them. Elinor could sense their wonder at such a scene in familiar surroundings, their home. They watched open mouthed as their mother went into another contraction; the experience was written on them for ever.

The beloved arrived, in a slither and underwater. Elinor had her usual sensation of being nudged to one side by the newborn. It was a disturbing feeling: new life pushing at the old, as if she were expelled, her purpose had been served.

As she left the house, a tribe of schoolchildren were running down the street, the postman walked up next door's path, a line of traffic was thrumming, immobile, in the road, a trio of aeroplanes blinked in the dark sky. She breathed in, hard, it seemed like she had to make herself smaller because if she didn't, she might not fit back in. The breeding ground of Muswell Hill was filling up, there wasn't enough room.

She put it down to not having children of her own, that was why there was always this sense of loss at leaving the scene of a birth. She'd been returned to her own life slightly reduced, smaller, divided by a greater number.

Nio shifted up the queue at the Abbey National. The person behind him, the one with the very short hair, was nice, she chatted non-stop, asked him what he needed money for. He told her it was to pay for his girlfriend's photographs – she wanted to be a model and needed a set of ten by eights.

At the cashier's window he withdrew the only bit of money he had in the world, given him by his parents for his twenty-first birthday in an account that he was never meant to take out of, only pay into. Yet, it was nonsense to leave it there if Mila needed it. When he turned to leave, the girl had unaccountably left the queue, but he saw her again, a few minutes later, outside. She and her friends surrounded him, they were excited, she was telling the others what a great guy he was, they all patted him on the back – hey, what a hero for helping out his girlfriend in her career. Like a swarm they passed over, headed further along the Broadway; he waved them goodbye. He felt good about himself as he plonked one foot in front of the other through the dark, wet North London street. This was the thought that kept him: that even without a job, he could help pay for Mila's photographs, they'd get her started on this career with her new manager by any and all means, with the money . . . he patted his pockets, to find the passbook. The cars pressed by urgently. It was 5.30 p.m.; dark sky circled the yellow glow of the city and everyone was hurrying, he was proud to be part of the homeward struggle of London's working population, or nearly part of it, because his girlfriend Mila had her job at Tesco's, and he'd find one soon, he was sure he would. Plus, he was an artist and she was a model. Another step, another . . . they were getting there, wait, hold on. He was splashed by rainwater squeezed from under the wheels of passing vehicles.

Quicker and quicker he searched for the passbook, but then, suddenly, he had to face it – there was nothing in his pockets, it was gone. He realized with dismay that the girls had been pick-pockets, and they'd taken the passbook and the money folded in it. He stopped, blushed with disbelief, and headed back to the spot where it had happened, he ran . . . They'd be long gone, though. Those clever, funny girls, how had they done that? He hadn't felt a thing. Or rather, he'd felt too much, the hand which had taken it had been lost in the petting of the other hands . . . He ran faster.

The next thing he knew, there was a white Ford Escort keeping pace with him. Its front bumper was hanging off and the spoiler on the back was crimped untidily out of line. There was a sharp tapping sound. He glanced sideways and saw the flat of a hand banging against the glass, its white imprint and the rings on the fingers – and he recognized the girl's laughing face, her short hair. She was the one who'd stood next to him in the queue in the Abbey National and the car was packed with all her friends. He dropped to a walk, halted, and the car slowed in line with him, stopped with a jerk. A cacophony of hooting broke out from the line of cars behind it as drivers stamped on their brakes. The girl held up his passbook, waved. A beaming wide-eyed smile, another wave and then there was the sandpaper sound of tyres slipping on wet tarmac as the Escort slithered forward, accelerated hard; it caught up with the back of the queue at the temporary traffic lights and pushed through even when they turned to red.

Nio ran as hard as he could after them. They'd stolen Mila's career. The cars swished by comfortably. He had to run full pelt all the way to the next junction. He was ten yards from the Escort when the lights changed to green and it took off again. He kept going, now it was a further two hundred yards, he saw the Escort's brake lights come on. His chest was bursting but he ignored the searing pressure, he kept running, caught up. He pulled open the passenger door and there was instant shrieking and swearing from the girls inside. He tried to climb into the car. His passbook was thrown at him, he heard the flick of paper and it cut against his neck, fell to the ground. He scrabbled for it, he could see the money wasn't there, so he pushed in, climbed on to the girl's lap. There was more screaming and laughter. Nio asked for the money, he kept up a steady, insistent stream at the top of his voice, 'It's for my girlfriend, I need it for her to have a set of ten by eight . . .'

Suddenly out of all the shouting and general noise his money was pushed at him. He took it and backed out of the vehicle, repeating his thank-yous, smiling to himself, he'd got Mila's money, most of it anyway. The Escort took off, its rear end bucking at each gear change.

But – after all that, when he tried to give it to Mila, she said she didn't want it.

He insisted she took it, he pushed it at her.

'No,' she replied, she smacked his hand away.

He was amazed. 'Why not? It's your career, you can pay me back, or not, it doesn't matter—'

'I'll pay myself!'

'But you haven't any money and that manager guy is waiting, you should do it soon, it's no good just—'

She interrupted, 'Maybe is right, but—'

'And you found the place to do it, take the photographs? You called them?'

'Yes—'

'So you need the money now. Definitely.' He watched the expressions chase across her face. She moaned, rolled her eyes, told him she didn't know if she could take the money off him, or even if it was a good idea at all. 'I don' know,' she complained.

He leaned over to kiss her, but again she turned her cheek. He followed, pulled her closer – she put her hands on his chest, pushed him away. 'Why—' he asked, and she just shook her head. 'Is it the money?' he guessed for her. 'I'm not giving you the money to . . . it's *not* to buy you, only because it's what you want.' She squirmed out of his grip. He felt a blistering panic that everything was going wrong. He had to try harder, win her back. He had to behave differently, be a different man, more assertive. He went after her, wrapped her in his arms. He took the hem of her red top and told her, 'Take this off.' The words sounded wrong, coming from him.

'No—'

'Why not?' He tried to lift it off himself, he tugged hard. She dug in her elbows, stopped him, frowned. He gripped her elbows and lifted them, at the same time he walked her backwards; every step of the way he knew he was doing the wrong thing but maybe he had to. 'Nio—' she complained. Now her arms were above her head and he took both her wrists in one of his hands and held them pinned against the wall. With his spare hand he took the front of her top and pushed it up.

'Nio?!' she called, as if he were far away, 'what are you doing?'

'I want you,' he said, urgently and pushed further, working the lambswool top up around her back until he could see her cleavage, her bra, just like before.

'Don't! Wait!' Mila lifted her knee, hard, just as he bent to kiss between her breasts. 'No!' she said firmly and wrenched her hands free. He coughed, his chest ached from the blow she'd given him. It took them a while to recover. He swore never again to behave in a way that was so wrong, that didn't suit him.

It was so unfair, that the minute he changed his mind, gave up waiting until it was legal and just plain wanted to have her, then she was the one who put him off. He remembered – it seemed like a lifetime ago – how her arms had scissored around her torso, and she'd pulled off her top all by herself, without him even asking, let alone . . . He'd picked it up, given it back to her. He could kick himself. How he wished, with all his heart, he'd just told her to take off the rest of her clothes . . .

'I'm sorry,' began Mila, 'it's just . . . I don' know . . .'

'Doesn't matter,' replied Nio, 'you're right, we . . . everything should be . . . I will get a job. We must get you the photographs you need—' He daren't look at her, he nodded back and forth, to keep himself busy he made the booking for the photographer himself, he used her mobile to dial the Face To Face studio and find out when they could fit her in. Tomorrow at four. She stalked after him, asked him to stop, to listen to her, give her the phone back, but he was ashamed of his effort to seduce her, he'd been rejected. He hung on with all his might to the idea that he was her boyfriend.

When it came to it, the following day, she still refused to take his money to pay for the photographer; she repeated, no, she'd pay for it. He was worried she wouldn't go at all, in that case – and he took her hand and pulled her up to the bus. She was down, unhappy – and he blamed himself. Little Vlad filtered along behind.

Nio stood with them at the bus stop, to prevent her from ducking out. When it arrived and the doors hissed open, his hands were on her rump, he pushed her up to the top deck for the short ride to Highgate tube. No – there wasn't one good reason why she had to wait. He didn't want to hear any more about the money. Call it a loan, if that helped. If she wanted to be a model then that's what would happen. He held her close under his arm on the front seats, the big view from the windows swung wildly from side to side as they weaved around the speed bumps, in and out of bus stops. Five minutes later he marched her off the bus and down the little path to Highgate tube station. He bought return tickets to Covent Garden, only to find that Little Vlad had jumped over already. He pushed the hundred quid into her bag, literally, and aimed her through the electronic barrier. If he hadn't had to attend the gardening agency himself, he'd have gone with them. She had the best photographer they could afford, it was all set up, her whole life depended on it. Go, he said.

Mila hated it so much, taking the money off Nio. God, it was a crime, to use him like that, her best, best friend ever, she could feel his smile, she was walking away from him, it was unfair; she so, so wished Jon Rawle had remembered, it was the manager's job to pay, surely, but he had loads to think about, his own business to run.

A train arrived and she stumbled into a seat, delved into her bag – she loved the way the little silver bells were stitched along the top, all of them silent, but sort of mystical. She took out the CD player, flipped one disc for another and keyed into the music. It was safer because no one could reach her now, she was behind a barrier of sweet sound. She'd learned not to catch any man's eye – if she just once looked at a guy then it was returned tenfold – instead she grazed the advertising panels opposite.

Little Vlad squirmed through the crush of people and quickly disappeared from sight. Some minutes later, he arrived next to her again. She needed him; like the CD player he kept away the pervs, so it really bugged her when they changed to the Piccadilly line and he was all over the place, he went through No Exit signs and took the Hammersmith & City Line indicator for the quickest route to the Piccadilly line platform. He jumped the escalator steps two at a time and then ran back down against the tide to join her, he was a total shame and looked so uncool with his check shirt and corduroy trousers from Oxfam, his face ash grey, his black hair greasy and uncut – God pity her for her younger brother. Mila went her own way and he caught up later, but not until she was on the train and she'd already blanked two guys. The connecting door opened and he slid through.

He had that guilty look because he always was guilty.

At Covent Garden they squeezed into the lift and rose to street level; Mila's mood changed as the glamour of Covent Garden took hold of her. Suddenly it was OK, this was the first step, Jon Rawle was her manager, such a cool guy to do business like he did, from cars and bars, on the mobile, an office maybe somewhere near here, he was the real thing, she was cutting new ground, this was her city now, she was heading for the big time, her English was better, she'd have money, keep her friends right by her, she was going to grow up so fast . . . and yes, she did want to be a model. Was that right, was that what was happening? She felt a pit of fear open in her stomach.

On Long Acre they turned left, looking for Langley Street. She kicked along, but moment by moment both her heart and mind changed direction. She was so nearly sixteen, well on the way, with loads ahead of her now – or was it a waste of time? God, she just didn't know.

In Langley Street she ducked into doorways, looking for the right number. She found the bell marked 'Face To Face' and she and Little Vlad were buzzed through into a narrow corridor. They walked past offices, nothing was happening in there, only the whir of computers. They followed the signs up the stairs at the back, rising two storeys and coming into a big waiting room with plastic chairs arranged around the edge, a million of them. At the far end of the room stood a desk, unattended.

Mila caught her breath for a moment in wonder – what happened in here? The strangeness, the ghosts of people in all these chairs . . .

Little Vlad wandered ahead, fingering a pile of magazines. No boundaries existed for him, the room itself meant nothing compared to his presence in it.

Then a really lush guy came through. She was waiting for a smile, some attention, but not a flicker crossed his face, it was like she was part of the furniture. He found a huge diary scattered behind the desk, leafed through it and without looking up tried to say her name. 'Mila Rosa—'

'Rosapepe, yes.'

He glanced at her and then called over his shoulder, 'Pete, this private?'

An anonymous voice answered, 'What about it?'

'Whose is it?'

'Jimmy M,' came the response and his eyes flicked across to her, briefly. She had her smile ready, but it didn't work. Her mood changed again, swung back the other way. This was a nowhere place – dead, lifeless. With a pang of guilt she took out Nio's hard-earned money and paid the fee. She knew it was wrong, to do this – but when Jon Rawle remembered, she could pay Nio back.

She sat and waited, feeling smaller suddenly, less important, she was too young. The number of chairs . . . Little Vlad circled the room, impatient. She turned the pages of a magazine.

Then a tall gangling man with a case hanging off his shoulder took her into a large room with black walls. He had a crumb of scrambled egg on the corner of his mouth. It moved, dropped on to his chin; she couldn't help looking at it. He set up lights and a camera and tripod, then had her sit in a chair. 'This is just your face,' he explained. Just *your* face, she wanted to say, look, clean up the scrambled egg. Now it was smeared in a yellow streak. He asked her to look away, then turn and meet the eye of the lens when he gave the signal. To look away – good – but how to look back at the camera, when first she'd have to check what had happened to the egg? She tried, back and forth, dozens of times, she really did. The light flashed the instant her gaze met the dead eye of the lens. She felt wooden, all the time on the verge of embarrassed laughter.

Then he posed her against a white backdrop. These were the figure shots. He loosed off more rolls of film, coached her how to hold each stance. She felt stupid, false. Little Vlad watched from the shadows, lounging disconsolately on a huge sofa and stealing from a bowl of chocolate bars which had been left on the low table in front of him, until someone ducked through and asked him to leave them alone.

When the photographer was finished, the fleck of scrambled egg was gone. Where, Mila wanted to know. He seemed in a hurry, he pressed a business card into her hand and asked for her address so he could send her the prints; and here she stumbled, she didn't have the address of Jon's office yet, he had said he'd text it to her, but it hadn't come through. She couldn't bring herself to talk about where she lived, the lack of an address, like this man shouldn't know her personal details. She saved herself by giving Jon's home address, it popped into her head, '15 Queens Avenue, Muswell Hill, London N10.' The photographer scribbled it down and then he was gone.

She was left in the empty waiting room. She heard the sonorous laughter of the men in the darkened booth mix with the electronic score of a video game; it gave the place a sinister air. She coralled Little Vlad, had a brief fight to stop him from tipping the whole bowl of chocolate bars into her bag. Together they went downstairs.

Outside, it was bliss. Mind-numbing. At last she'd escaped. God, if that was what it was like, she didn't want to be a model – pushed around like a doll, smile when she wasn't smiling, like hell did she want that, no way. Creepy job.

Was she sure – was it worse than Tesco's, for instance? It was better paid. She should knuckle down, do it . . .

No. That was her decision, final. No way did she want to be a model.

Then, suddenly, she had no future. Her whole life slipped away. Jon Rawle would cancel the invitation, she was waving everything goodbye. Ilie would no longer sit next to her in that pub, like he'd described. It scared her, please don't take my future away she begged the world. If the rug had been pulled from under her feet this afternoon, she desperately needed someone to put it back.

Three strides later, she had the answer – of course, she was going to be a *singer*. Jon Rawle had told her about a singer he'd found, who'd become a star.

She clutched her throat. Her voice was rusty, though. Suddenly all that nonsense when she was a child, her dad on the spoons and other bits of percussion, the old biscuit tins and other bits of metal he'd so oddly welded together, Little Vlad aged only seven catching on fast with his Hohner squeeze-box, her uncle the real musician, playing everything under the sun, her cousin on the strings, and her own childish voice joining in with her uncle's, all those times made sense, they'd happened for a reason. They'd held Saturday parties on the old river cruiser which was half sunk in the mud, no electricity, the light lowering with the sun behind the horizon, the glint on the drink bottles duller, the temperature cooling fast, and old dustbins burning damp straw to make smoke and keep off the insects. Her own voice repeating again and again those same folk songs she'd churned out a million times, maybe all this was going to pay off. With the excitement came grief, as well, she'd liked her family back then, it seemed they came from somewhere, belonged, however poor, they'd been stronger, whereas now they were still poor but had none of that . . . She shook off the memory, she was going to lead everyone out of this, she alone. . . as a singer.

Hadn't Jon Rawle said he didn't mind what she wanted to do? Even if she'd wanted to be a fashion designer, he'd help her. So now she was going to call – and tell him she was a singer, yes, she wasn't cut out to be a model after all. And he could open any door he wanted. He'd know the right people. They'd talk about it in the office on Tuesday. There'd be the story of that other singer he'd made. Mila was going to follow in her footsteps.

Nio's money had paid for something important: it had told her what she *didn't* want. If half of her life was made up of wanting, the other half was so, so *not* wanting – please, no more scrambled egg guy.

Nio awoke, alone. It was 3 November – twenty-seven days until Mila's real birthday. Darkness poured its black mood into the Clamp through the circular window. If only Mila could be here in this warm bed, maybe she'd dig in and settle for their happiness. They'd joked that it was her turn now to wait until she was sixteen, but the joke had fallen with an unfunny clunk, it wasn't the truth, she was slipping from his grasp and he didn't know why.

Suddenly he was like Alice in Wonderland in his small-size bedroom, he was knocking his head and his elbows, bent double or sitting down while pulling on his clothes in the dark. He crawled downstairs, ignored Charmer in his pile of bedding. He attacked the pot-bellied stove, coaxed some paper and some kindling to take off. There was work he wanted to do here, ready for her. Somehow he thought he could cure whatever was wrong between himself and Mila with furious, sustained, continual hard work. He would earn money, he'd improve this place, he would better himself . . .

When it was daylight he dressed in waterproofs and went outside to carry on digging the soft earth; his rhythm quickened, he attacked like fury, the iron bar was slippery with rain, the mud like glue, his boots heavy and wet through. He grunted, cursed, talked to himself. He pored over every detail of everything that had ever happened between himself and Mila. Charmer watched from indoors; Nio saw his face every now and again, the rain on the glass distorting its already soft shape.

These were the tasks in front of him: work a hole underneath the Clamp, finish off this ditch. In his mind, each drive with the bar was an attempt to break through to the other side of this confusion, his suddenly less requited love, this increasing absence, this lack that spread like a stain on his heart. He used every ounce of his strength and determination. When he swapped from the bar to the spade to enlarge the hole, it was, yes, like he was trying to carve a route back to where he had been. Dig, dig – there was a great hole in his life, because this girl, who meant so much to him, was inch by inch waving goodbye, their conversations paid only lip service to the love that they used to conjure between them. He repeated it to himself, a warning, he was losing her!

His muscles ached, rain dripped from the brim of his hat in a curtain and steadily soaked the back of his neck. The blister on the base of his thumb burst, blood mixed with the salt of sweat and tears. Blow after blow, he wanted to go on, never to stop until he'd dug his way through to her, until she was standing there, and he could take her in his arms. She should come home! What had happened? He didn't know and that was the worst thing – it was like the parents whose children had gone missing and always they said, yes, the same, the worst was not knowing. To be excluded from her life – as he knew he was, now – hurt badly. Or had he made it up, this gentle failing of their love affair, was it instead true, the excuse she gave every time he tried to kiss her, that it was her turn now, to wait for her real birthday?

No . . .

He broke out of his trance, and went inside to take a line on where the trench would come inside the house. At this spot he pulled up the floor and with a hand trowel dug down and sideways until he connected with the rainwater he'd last seen outside. Done. Next – the length of hose lay there: a circle of black. He took it outside and unrolled it, he fought with its ungainly length; it became slippery in his hands, refused to lie down, he had to feed it into the ditch he'd dug, at least eighteen inches deep along its length to save the pipe from the frost, leading to the back of the allotments' water tank. It had taken days of work, and Charmer had refused to help for a single minute.

The next task was to backfill the earth. He drove himself on. Do better. Go faster. Win Mila. Yet, everything he could do, didn't seem to be the answer. Inside the Clamp, he screwed clips to the wall and fixed the tap. Soon enough it was there, he and Mila might use it: a standpipe. All he needed was the cover of night, sometime later this week hopefully, so he could drill into the tank, drain it, hacksaw a hole the correct diameter, and fix the outlet. He wouldn't be seen, and the tank wouldn't be needed in winter, no one would notice. It would refill before a couple of days were up. Meanwhile, he'd be connected to a water supply. But with hand tools only, it would take longer.

He was soaked in mud and water, the tear in his jeans had widened across the knee, the whole place was wrecked, he needed to clean up . . . He was angry at Charmer, always wanted him gone.

Then, he heard a voice – a stranger, closer than ever before. Someone talking to their dogs? His heart jumped. It was three strides to the door, he pushed and went outside. Yes – someone was coming down the path to the Clamp. He went back in, met Charmer's eye; the latter sensed the emergency and his expression was already a question mark. 'Someone coming,' warned Nio.

In two seconds Charmer was gone – up the stairs, out of sight. Nio thought he might follow, he lingered with his foot on the first step, but then he chose not to. Who was it?

The rap of knuckles against the pane of glass was shocking; Nio turned, saw through the glass doors the figure of a man, yes, a total stranger. He felt the invasion right in the middle of him.

Any visitor would have been alarming, after all this place was meant to be a secret, but it was worse, this guy was built like a brick shithouse and escorted by a pair of Rottweilers on short chains.

Ben Parish was self-employed, he mixed up debt-collecting with a bit of security work and now and again dealt with rent arrears. Sometimes it was a domestic dispute – if big corporations didn't want to call the police but nonetheless wanted their man or woman back in the office without too many bruises. This afternoon was unusual, it wasn't debt, nor repo, it wasn't arrears, it wasn't abuse. More like wilful ignorance of planning law. Eco-freaks, he suspected. Whatever, the fixit team at Haringey had earmarked him for the job, they didn't want to pay the legal fees or get involved in any unsightly prosecutions. Quicker and cheaper to send him in, if it would work. As he cut through Coldfall Wood he predicted it would be, yes, a bunch of new-fangled hippies, or the tree protesters, that type of thing. Probably at the sight of him, they'd be off down some tunnel they had ready. What was nice about this morning, though, was that it was a treat for the dogs, a rainy day but nonetheless they were taking a walk in the woods. Nancy and Mary didn't even know they were working, they'd think it was a day off, tramping round the dog-walkers' circuit along with the others. They must be wondering why they weren't let off the leads.

He had a grid reference, but couldn't find a way through the fence. Somehow . . . it took him some ten minutes but then he spotted where they'd sawed through one of the uprights. He unclipped the catch and stepped through. He pushed past the vegetation and there it was, built by someone of ability no doubt, it had a reasonably tight look to it, he was impressed.

It was disturbing to step over these muddy old graves to reach the front door, that would add a gothic touch to your everyday life.

He wound the dogs closer and knocked on the glass door. Experience told him to take a step back, wait for a response some yards away. Anything could come through that door. A little old lady, inviting him in for a cup of tea, or a five pound lump hammer thrown without any warning. Clients came in all shapes of body and mind. And the doors were made of glass – dangerous.

In the event, he was pleased. One skill he'd picked up in his line of work was that of making an accurate judgement on a person quickly, and as soon as he saw this bedraggled young man opening the door he knew he was in the clear. Slow heart beat. Zero aggression, but no cowering or anxiety either. Interested look in his eye. Slight stoop, didn't want his height to dominate. No sign of intoxication. Rain dripping from his hat. 'Ben Parish. For Haringey Council!' said Ben, as if it were good news. He showed his badge.

'Oh,' replied the young man and invited him inside. Good manners for you. In one second flat, he decided he'd give this youngster his best shot. 'How you doing this morning?'

'Hi. Fine thanks.'

'D'you have a name, young man.'

'Er – yes, Nio. Nio Niopolous.'

'No doubt you've been expecting us Nio.'

'Sure, yes.'

Mary and Nancy snooped ahead. Another good sign, the client wasn't afraid of the dogs, held out the back of his hand for them to check, showed natural good sense.

'First off, just so we're reading from the same page, you know this place is illegal, right?'

Nio smiled. 'Ahh . . . I wasn't sure, is it?'

'No planning exists for a dwelling, and no rights are granted to anyone to occupy this land, which is part of St Pancras Cemetery.'

Nio shrugged. 'Well . . . it sort of grew by itself.'

'I was going to say, foremost, congratulations.'

'How d'you mean?'

Ben shrugged. 'If I had your DIY skills my wife would be a happy woman. It's a fantastic place. How long d'you need?'

'Sorry?'

'Look, I could come in here, right, throw the book at you – and have the site bulldozed. Literally. One word from me and this place is in a skip *tomorrow*. But let me tell you something. You've done well, you've built a good place. Plus, you're a good person. I can see that. So, when I make my call back to the ranch, I'm going to instruct them not to do a thing until such and such a day. Within reason obviously. So give me an idea of how much time you need to get out of here with some dignity.' Deliberately he'd put this young man in charge psychologically, made it his decision, given him ownership of this process – it would be his choice, when it was pulled down. Unless he was going to play silly buggers and ask for six months, then it would be the best of a bad job for him.

The young guy shuffled, looked around. Stared out of the window for a considerable time. Tears even – he could have sworn there were tears standing in his eyes, must be the case then, yes, it was a sad day for him, no doubt now.

'How long have you been here?' asked Ben.

'Three years,' came the reply.

He had to stop himself from putting his arm around the youth, like he would his own son. This man had done something impressive and Ben didn't like the taste of what he'd come here to do.

'Can I have a week?'

Silly bugger, thought Ben. It confirmed what he thought, that here was a gentleman, someone he would treat with increasing respect and generosity. 'A week? That's not long enough, is it. You have to find a new place to live, remember. We don't want you on the streets.'

'The end of the year, then?'

That was two months away. Ben made a better offer. 'Beginning of March? That would fit you up better wouldn't it? You wouldn't want to have to move over the Christmas holiday period. Stuff Haringey Council. Gives you four months, more or less, till March the first, OK?' This was such a smooth day's work and he got a nod for that, a half-smile. 'Thanks.' The tears were genuine; Ben wanted to throw in the offer of a free council flat, shame he didn't have the authority for that. Here was a man who'd look after a council property, pay his rent on time, make a good contribution to the life of the borough.

'So this is how it goes from here,' he went on. 'You won't see me again. You won't see the Council. You won't hear from anybody. Nothing happens until March the first. But. On that day – the site is cleared. If they turn up and find you still here, it won't be me they call, it'll be the police and then we'll be into all that nonsense.'

'All right.'

'I'll take my leave. Thank you for the hospitality you've shown to me in your fine home and I wish you the best of luck.'

Nio went back in and told Charmer the news, gave him the dates. Wet through, blistered with work which had just been proved for nothing, Nio undertook to find a new place to live, either to rent somewhere or borrow somewhere – something could be done, if he applied himself to the task. They'd lost the home which Nio had spent three years putting together, but there would be an answer.

A couple of days ago, Nio had had everything he could have dreamed of right in front of him, just an inch from his grasp. Now he was losing Mila, and he'd lost the Clamp. It was only left to him to work even harder, slog his way back . . . He would collect more wood than he'd need for the rest of the month and chop it, ready for the stove. He would clean and paint and decorate the place, her real birthday was in four weeks' time . . .

Lucas slept for an hour, then as usual he died. His heart and lungs slowed, stopped altogether. A nerve ticked in the corner of his mouth. His heart forgot its second-by-second task, it fatally rested. The blood stopped in his veins and immediately began to settle. Then a shot of adrenalin dropped into his system; his heart was frightened into a single leap, skipped twice, then hammered solidly at his ribs; the blood rushed to inflate him. At the same time his eyes flickered, he awoke with a jerk, rising fast from his deathbed. The panic was familiar, he found his rhythm quickly, but it took a while in the pitch black to remember he was in the bed of the mother in Birchwood Avenue. She had an early morning appointment with the telephone, in which he had an interest.

He looked over at her; she was a shadow next to him. He stepped from the bed, dressed and went downstairs. He rifled her fridge, pocketed cash from her purse, listened to the radio, stalked from one room to another behind the drawn curtains. He went back upstairs and watched her for half an hour, he could see the pores in her skin.

At half past seven she stirred, sat up. She was a bit sluggish, first thing in the morning. He walked her to the bathroom, watched her dress, offered a degree of small talk, a few compliments. He was behind her as she went downstairs. At around eight, she sat at the table and beckoned him with a finger. He pretended to have forgotten – oh yes, now was the time. He sat opposite her.

The phone was in front of her, and with a serious look for him, she picked up the receiver and dialled. She spoke to a colleague and asked if she might borrow enough money to save a business investment she'd made from going down – it was worth so much, she'd pay back twice over within a year. He understood from her thumbs up signal that the offer had come through – he was grateful for that, but he did need the money today if possible, rather than next week. He mouthed at her, 'Today?' She tried hard for him, pressed this work colleague into giving way, the money had to be there, she needed it biked over. She asked twice, three times more, she was in tears, there was real grief in her voice, he could hear the guy giving way.

Lucas had scored the full grand. Time to go. He picked up her old man's sheepskin and unhooked the keys to the Audi. Then he was gone.

Anjali watched this boy. He was shaven-headed, of medium weight, dressed in combat pants decorated with a silver chain at the hip and two ragged sweatshirts, one on top of the other. The spider's web tattoo covered one side of his face from the top of his head down to his neck; from that side he looked as though he'd risen from the grave. From the other side, the tattoo wasn't visible. There were studs in his nose and ear.

He twice walked past her spot. He slouched, the heels of his boots scuffed carelessly, yet there was a purposeful light in his eye. He was going somewhere, after something, the lazy attitude was just a display. She saw him kick someone else's foot, and that person sat up sharply, wrapped his arms around his knees and answered the questions with submissive gestures.

When the tattooed boy left, it was a minute or two before his victim moved.

Later, she saw him slope past again. He didn't look at her but she could sense his attention. Anger was evident even in the flick of a finger that sent a cigarette butt spinning crazily from his hand. She watched him linger by the stairs leading out to the street – was he waiting for someone? Then he turned and stared at her; she looked away.

Three days later, she was woken by the same kick to the soles of her feet which she'd seen him deliver to the boy further along. She wasn't frightened. Still struggling free of a dream, she rose and met his cold, predatory stare as if it was something she was waiting for. He was wearing a hooded top which shadowed his expression. The spider's web tattoo was a smoky blue colour over half his face, it looked as if a hole had been poked in its fabric for the one eye to see through. It had been done a while ago: the lines had lost their sharpness, the colour had bled into the skin. She didn't say anything, didn't break with his gaze, just waited, didn't move an inch. It was he who broke the stalemate, lifted the tip of her sleeping bag with his foot, let it drop, moved away a short distance. He lingered, rubbing his nose with the back of his wrist. When he came back, they spoke for half an hour – just the first details of who they were, where they'd come from. The connection was made between them. Then he wandered off without a backward glance.

The next time, it was the other way around. He was asleep. A neatly made square of cardboard was around his head and upper torso, the bag-covered legs stuck out like a mollusc's body. She touched his foot with hers. His head leaped up. In his hand was an ordinary vegetable knife with a black plastic handle. It was roughened, blunt. They looked at each other for some minutes.

It happened two days later in the deep of night. The pedestrian subway was empty of all sound, there was only the possibility of passers-by like a pregnancy, a silence waiting for their return. He held both her ankles tightly. She'd woken with a jerk, on an inhaled breath. He wasn't looking at her but checking in both directions to see that no one was coming. In the yellow plastic light of the underpass, undiluted by daylight, he looked more ghastly than before. She didn't speak, she was locked in silence. A film of wax and dirt – her own grease – contained her in the silent carton of her body. But she touched his forearm because his weight on her ankles hurt – she grimaced and bit her lip. He smelt strongly of beer and sweat and cigarettes. He still didn't look at her, even as he was walking his hands up her legs and then pinning her arms to the ground with his knees, sitting on her middle. She welcomed him silently. She wanted him to have what he wanted, despite the fact that by now she knew he was injecting, she'd seen him use the needle, and that made it dangerous for her.

He started to pull at the button of her trousers. Her arms were free now, but she didn't help him, she closed her eyes. She felt plugged into him through the touch of his hands, she swam into his flesh and blood . . .

A wave of pity overtook her – pity for herself as well as him – as he struggled, trying to clear himself of his clothes, dragged at her. She opened her eyes again to see the tattoo on the top of his head – all its imperfections – only inches away. She understood that both of them were at the end of cruelties visited on them, and now for a moment they'd feel rid of that burden . . . She found herself talking to her parents. If you don't want shame, look away now. This was all they'd need.

He pulled back sharply to squat on his heels. He wasn't seeing her at all. He was racing to the finish, yanking at her clothing. She clung to this experience like she was on a helter-skelter – the rush and panic was the whole point of the ride. He pushed at her legs. She looked sideways to avoid the sight of him and then she was bearing his weight and there was a stab of pain in her groin as he pierced her.

She felt awful kindness for him, it was a desperate and hurried act, unimportant. She held his face in her hands as he thumped, hip to hip. She looked at the grain of his skin, the splits in his lips crusted with thin lines of blood; she felt the grate of his stubbled chin in her palms. Her right thumb dented the spider's web, she wanted him to look at her, but the eye stayed buried in the web, tight shut.

Nio hauled on the rope; it dragged in his hands, this was a Herculean task. Left boot, right boot. Forward, uphill. Every step towards Mila, for her, whether she liked it or not. Some miracle, now, he needed to reach her. Change the position of the rope – the burn on his shoulder. His whole weight thrown into the task. Dragging the horse into the world! Like its birthday. November the fifth.

This was the culmination of half a year of work, it was the end point of that much ambition – and it was all bound up in his desire for her, of course, any enterprise was undertaken with her in mind. He felt like an animal, the lone male who hadn't won his mate; the failure of this, already, was that Mila wasn't here, alongside, as he walked. That would have been glorious, but she was busy, she couldn't come. A car was going to pick her up and take her into the office this morning. She had to wait for the car! He was frightened; she was going so fast, flying so high, she was beyond his reach . . . He wanted to catch hold of her but now she wasn't letting him, it was a cruel twist.

It was cold, dark enough still for the street lights. He had the rope wound around his chest while Nick the photographer pushed from behind. Between them was the four-foot-high horse, a random weave of willow worked on to a hazel frame and finished with honeysuckle, ivy, dogwood and old man's beard, trimmed to shape. At its simplest it was a sculpture he supposed, but he liked to think of it as topiary as well, it could be alive after all; if he thrust the hazel rods into the ground they'd sprout, take root. For the moment, it rolled forwards on sets of wheels hack-sawed off supermarket trolleys.

They drew away from the gates of the derelict Friern Barnet Mental Hospital and towards the North Circular, two men pushing a sculpture of a horse in the pre-dawn quiet.

It's what life's about, thought Nio. He'd built the horse in secret, its basic shape elusive, difficult to conjure out of thin air. He admired Stubbs, Cooper and all the other great horse artists who'd had so much more refined an ability than his own. This was a homage to them. They were artists in their bones and that's how he felt; in the same way he had to make stuff with his hands, do it . . . the only difference was that he didn't go out and sell it, he wanted a different relationship between his art and its audience, he wanted only to interrupt, and for his work to be photographed so it could be remembered. Nio would have to wait for Nick's end-of-year show to see how he'd been portrayed, how his achievements had been validated by the photographer.

Now it was uphill and he heard Nick begin to breathe heavily, he was an overweight youth who looked older than his twenty-two years. He was already balding and had a beer belly. He was for the most part taciturn and unsociable, which Nio felt bound to respect. His own smile, his optimism, he carefully managed in Nick's presence, he didn't want to offend the photographer. He concentrated on their mission.

It was dark and cold, too early for many people to be up. It was a big step, this rolling out of the horse, they would be among the commerce, the to and fro of people tied to work.

Colney Hatch Lane was a struggle. The hill steepened gradually and the rope hardened, burned. When he wound it under his armpit and around his chest, it squeezed him tight. He could hear the photographer swearing at the camera bags which flapped around his neck.

When they reached the Broadway, they paused, took a brief rest.

Muswell Hill was interrupted; the passage of Nio's horse through its centre snagged everyone who saw it. Thousands were a possible audience, either on their way through or at work already. Commuters queued at the bus stops and added line after line of traffic, workers at the shops turned up to unlock and switch off alarms and put out stock, cleaners hoovered and wiped down surfaces and cleared away yesterday's coffee cups ready for today's business; and among these thousands at least a couple of hundred would see the horse, pause, wonder what was going on. All this in the half-dark of a November morning.

The owner of the fruit and veg shop stopped short – what the fuck was that? A horse? She had her four sons around her, they picked up boxes like a set of nodding ducks, the produce was arranged in a spectacular display every morning. She stared. What would that horse be for, then? She could only think it was something to do with the theatre group who'd started putting on shows in St James' church.

The cleaner working in the hairdresser's left off mopping the floor and straightened his back. A strange movement had caught his eye. Through the plate-glass window he saw the model horse being pulled along on a set of wheels and he guessed it was for a shop display; after all, this very hairdressser's, which he cleaned every morning, had a headless torso made out of plaster of paris in its window; find the logic of that, if you can, he thought – a hairdresser's, advertised by a headless torso, some slip of the scissors that must have been.

The bus driver pushed his foot flat to the floor coming up Colney Hatch Lane – the bus lane was his territory and he had to bulldoze out of it the criminals who used it illegally every morning, but today there was a new frustration, not parked vehicles this time nor the commuter bastards blocking his through line but a couple of youths pushing a – what? – a basketware horse up the road. He twisted the massive yellow indicator button on the dash, swung the Routemaster out mercilessly into the other lane and went round it. What mad thing was that, then? Must be those medical students again, on one of the days when they're let out to play jokes.

Elinor Ginsberg was the opposite of all these people, she was just back from work instead of starting out. She was in the large empty home in Methuen Park which she'd inherited from her parents – far too big for her alone – and found herself unable to go to bed. It was always difficult to sleep in the early morning. She had a bath, put on her dressing gown and pottered comfortably upstairs. Then, her routine was interrupted. She happened to look out of the window, and what she saw caused her to open it and lean out, clutching the dressing gown closed at her throat against the cold. This was an odd sight and – good luck for her – if it hadn't been for the beloved who'd been born around five o'clock this morning she'd have left for work already and missed it, so yes, it was maybe the whole line of newborns she'd ever helped birth in her whole life who collectively had positioned her in the here and now, brought her to this moment in this place, and she was grateful. She drew a breath and called out.

Nio paused for breath at the top of Colney Hatch Lane. He wasn't worried about Nick's temper, they'd done enough together for him to be sure of the photographer's support. Then they set off again – Nio pulled, Nick the photographer huffed and puffed behind. The sun was still unrisen, but everyone was up and working. Lines of cars crept along, bumper to bumper, slower than a walking pace. They hauled past Boy, the hairdresser's, moving through a pocket of chill, damp air. The fruit and veg shop was up and running, they felt the stare of the owner, but pressed on without a word. The roundabout was blocked, unmoving, the Routemaster bus swung around them and buried itself in a gap in the traffic, locked solid.

Sweat dampened Nio's back. It was downhill from here, thankfully. They halted to move the rope from the front to the back – downhill mode. Leaning back on their heels, they walked the beast down Dukes Avenue.

He wished Mila was here, it didn't seem right to have gone ahead without her . . . never mind. She would be having her own triumph somewhere else, they'd compare notes at the end of the day. In a day or two he'd have photographs to show her .. then he ticked himself off, he was dreaming, she wasn't his girlfriend any more, he'd lost his chance . . .

They turned into Methuen Park, and stopped. Here they were out of sight of the Broadway where the police hung out. It was a quiet residential road and yet it was a cut-through, so they could hope for some action.

Nick prepared his cameras and erected his tripod for the digivideo. Together they unbound the horse and moved it into the road. Nio tidied up the damage which had occurred during transit. They waited.

It was seven-thirty and the November dark was beginning to thin out. Nio had a halter on the animal's head now, and stood holding it. People would look twice, he hoped.

The first cars spared only a cursory glance before swinging out and passing by.

Nio sat on the kerb, hunched to retain his body heat, holding the rope. Nick guarded his tripod on the other side of the road.

More windows now were lit; the cars increased, the hum of the city was rising. The press of people was seriously applied. The fragile systems of the city would be burst all over the place, but somehow it would cope, stagger on.

Cars passed by and Nio met each driver's stare optimistically. Nick took some video. Nio was uncomfortable with being photographed but accepted its importance, not least to Nick's HND degree course at Middlesex University. Last summer he'd gone to see the end-of-year show. Nick had displayed his work in a booth; he'd captured moments of performance art around the capital. Nio had his own section, titled 'Interruptions by Nio Niopolous'.

To 'interrupt' was his own definition of what he did, he preferred that word to 'installations'. He offered people a moment of irresponsibility, he peeled back a layer of normality to allow a glimpse of the futility of human actions. He picked up the smiles, the laughs, gratefully, but perhaps more important a test were the people who became irritated or took offence. Most of them were men, they were more blind to the absurd, which ironically made them more absurd themselves. Those who couldn't see the emptiness of their own actions were the ones who were most committed to them, however big or small.

Maybe the photographs were more valuable than the events themselves – was it true to say that he was in the service of the photographer, rather than the other way around? It was easy to think so because the photographs were permanent while the events disappeared and were gone for ever. That was prejudice, though – why was a transitory happening less valuable just because it didn't last? With one quick about-turn, Nio could school himself to think the opposite: that an event such as this engraved time passing whereas a photograph merely observed one fraction of a second of it, and at one remove. Yet the events were full of frustration and anxiety and compromise, whereas the chosen photograph distilled a moment of truth, kept it for ever, and made the absurd achievement more glorious than the reality – and perhaps that was art.

Nio's reverie was disturbed by a voice calling him, 'Excuse me?' He rose to his feet. The sweat which had soaked his shirt now touched his skin and drew the heat sharply from his middle and he shivered. He turned and looked for the voice, scanning the windows and doorways of the suburban street. He found her, leaning out of a first-floor bay window, her one hand on the window latch and the other holding a dressing gown closed at her throat. She was middle aged, with a pat of black hair and a thin face. Nio called back, 'Hello?'

'Are you going to be there a minute longer?'

'Hope so, yes.'

'I'll be down in a tick to have a look at your lovely horse, if I may.'

Nio smiled. 'All right.' He wondered if the camera was taping this exchange. 'We're not going anywhere.'

'Don't sell it to anyone else.'

Sell it? Nio leaped at the words. He'd never considered that someone might offer him money for the horse. His idea had been to burn it, tonight being 5 November.

She waved and the window closed.

Something was beginning to happen. She'd take a while to get dressed, he should try and remain calm, but the suggestion – yes, the idea that she might buy it – drove at him with some force. He looked at the horse anew. It looked back at him with eyes made of lumps of coal. They were inclined to slip out of position – if she was going to pay good money, then he ought to fix them.

A woman, a stranger, wanted to *buy* it? In his experience, interesting things happened usually when there was opposition, conflicting interests and beliefs – a traffic official, an irate resident, a gang of disorderly youths, a pair of policemen. Nio had dealt with all these in his time. Now, there might be an affirmative event, a success story.

Cars passed regularly; the smell of exhaust thickened. All these vehicles were starting out on their journeys and were still driving with the engines choked so the fumes made him dizzy. Nick had taken his early pictures – Nio imagined they might be titled 'Nothing Happening' and 'The Enquiry from the Window' – and now he moved his camera to Nio's side of the street. He'd be looking for strong reactions, whether approval or disapproval. Nio felt the event begin to bite.

The horse had effectively narrowed the road to the width of one car and as the traffic increased so a queue built up, both sides jousted to use the gap. A young man in a blinding white collar was the first to throw an angry word as he powered through, but Nio couldn't hear what he said because his window was closed. Then a man stopped, his jeep diving forwards on its front axle at the stamp of his foot on the brakes. He was older, around forty, with a pony tail. The jeep had only a loose cover to protect him against the elements and the window swung open on hinges – as if it were meant for driving across open ground during wartime. In this raw month of November, the driver was wearing sunglasses. The stereo pumped out the sounds: 'Boom boom shack shack, check out the women with the bewww-ty—' The driver asked, 'What is this fucking thing?'

'It's . . . er . . . a horse, which I made in the grounds of the old Friern Barnet Mental Hospital,' began Nio, 'and—'

'Mental hospital is right mate,' the driver interrupted, 'you can go back there and all. Ride your fucking horse back.'

Nio ducked closer to the car and smiled, 'I'm not sure where the horse will end up but there's a woman who's—' He didn't finish because the jeep took off, the driver shaking his head. Nio kept his position. Some passers-by gave incurious looks, others frowned, one or two smiled.

The woman from the upstairs window then appeared, she came over and walked around the horse admiringly. 'But this is magnificent,' she began. Nio glowed with pleasure. Out of the corner of his eye he was aware of Nick filming and he hoped he didn't look stupid, but thankfully most of the photographer's attention was on her. She was fifty-ish, with that healthy clump of black hair and a tanned face. Her eyes were bright currants and she had a jaunty walk as she circled the construction, careless of the camera filming. She wore a heavy brown coat and blue jeans, neatly pressed. She turned to Nio. 'Does he have a name?'

'No,' confessed Nio, 'I hadn't thought of giving it a name.'

'It?' she queried. 'I think it's a him, don't you? Definitely. Shall we be corny and call him Pegasus?'

He nodded. 'If you like.'

'And where are you taking him?'

'We're just . . . showing him.'

'Is he for sale?'

Nio paused. 'I had it in my head that, you know, he should go up in flames, it's bonfire night. Something like that anyway.'

'I'm having a fireworks party,' she replied, 'but there's no way I'm burning *him*. He's far too good. I want to buy him for my garden. Can I?'

'The trouble is, he won't last very long. If he's outside, all winter . . . he's only designed—'

She interrupted, 'In my living room then? I want him in my house. On the landing. Oh, but he's too big.'

Nio swung from foot to foot. 'This is amazing,' he said, '. . . um . . . he'll take up a lot of space.'

'Exactly,' she exclaimed. 'I should hope so.' She glanced at the camera, thumbed in Nick's direction to ask, 'Is he—?'

'He's recording my . . . this . . . for his photography course.'

'Oh.' Now she stood next to Nio, her hands deep in the pockets of the brown coat. Together they stood and watched the cars struggle past. 'I'll give you two hundred pounds for him,' she declared.

'Two *hundred*?' exclaimed Nio.

'That's a *lot,*' she insisted, 'for me, I don't have quite the sort of ready cash like other folk around here . . .'

'No, no,' interrupted Nio, 'I didn't mean that, I meant, it's too much.' He was worried about tricking her, she couldn't have seen how flimsy the horse was.

'Well, how long did it take you to make him?'

'Sort of, bits and pieces, most of the summer.'

'There you are then. If anyone else charged two hundred pounds for a summer's work, they'd die of starvation.'

Nick filmed while they lifted the horse from the road, up the path and through her front door. Nio thoroughly wiped his boots on the mat and stepped into an interior so clean and immaculately fitted that he held his breath. He hardly dared tiptoe across the glossy wood flooring for fear of making a mark. He was amazed, the decor stopped cleanly at every edge, the tuck of each element into the next – floor to skirting, skirting to wall, wall to cornice, cornice to ceiling – was precise and die-straight. Each picture hung on the wall had the same black frame with grey surround. Yet, she didn't mind that the horse left a trail of debris and one of its eyes dropped out and left a black mark on a carpet. They stood the horse behind her sofa and Nio replaced its eye. He also offered to come and make any repairs necessary if the woman's nieces were too rough with it.

She talked unselfconsciously throughout, despite the camera. Nio answered politely. Eventually the subject of her garden came up. Nio showed an interest – told her he worked as a gardener. She wondered, did he know of anyone who might help her, for reasonable rates of pay, hopefully on a regular basis? He answered without hesitation, he'd love to do it. She suggested that he should come through and have a look. He felt his luck building, block after block of it, this was amazing. He asked for the camera to be off; something different was going on now.

Nio and Nick followed the woman through the kitchen, out of

a back door glazed in many colours, into the garden. It sloped gently and then disappeared around a corner – it must have stretched to a hundred foot in all. A red setter gambolled up the lawn towards them, happily assaulting Nio and Nick and tearing off again. Nio exclaimed, 'This is beautiful. How come it goes around the dog-leg, like that?'

The woman led them further and explained, 'There used to be stables here, attached to the dairy, in the early part of the century. The stables were turned into garages, then my parents managed to buy them, when the old fellow who'd converted the dairy died.'

'How long ago was that?'

'Fifteen years?'

'Your family have done all this in fifteen years?' Nio was amazed. It looked like it had been there for ever.

'My father was a keen gardener when he was alive,' she explained.

There was a fountain, a copse of silver birch and a children's playhouse. As they walked past the fountain, the orange gleam of goldfish reduced, shrank to a glimmer in the depths. Nio felt as if he'd stepped into the Garden of Eden.

At the furthest corner, where the six-foot-high partition fencing narrowed to a point, she turned and waited for him. He approached, saying 'Wow', – which was Mila's expression, suddenly she was in his mouth, he liked that, he wished she was here to see this, to hold his hand, do this with him. 'Some garden,' he added.

'What I want,' said the woman, turning to him, 'is a feature. Here.' She stamped her foot. 'Something. I don't know. To fill this corner. To make it, not just the end of the garden. Instead, a special place. The beginning of something.'

'The beginning of something,' repeated Nio, as he looked around. 'OK.' Now he glanced at her and could see that, like Mila, there was a light blazing away inside this woman . . . kindness. He asked, 'A sort of journey, d'you think?'

'All I know is, I don't want a fountain or a statue because I've got those already. I just want something . . . magic. You know about magic, look at your horse.'

He nodded slowly, he was beginning to feel this could be his spot, it felt lucky. 'I could do a drawing, then see if you like it.'

'I don't think you should bother, just do what *you* think is right.'

He could have hugged her, he felt a blistering pain in the end of his nose and his eyes began to water. He'd sold the horse. He had a job! This kind woman liked him and liked his work. It was too much. It was as if a huge crowd were applauding. His smile was so big, and lasted so long, it was embarrassing.

When they started back to the house Nick still trailed them, aimed his viewfinder again; this bit was recorded. Nio ambled alongside her. A steady, undisturbed tranquillity dressed the garden and its creator, this woman, sponsored a family type of contentment, yet she appeared to live alone. Perhaps she was just of that disposition. Or, something had happened to her husband or partner. Was he dead? Maybe her children had left home already. He found himself telling her he was due to lose his own home in four months' time, and she suggested he might like to stay with her for a while if he hadn't found anywhere by then. He rushed to thank her.

They reached the house. She suggested how much he should be paid and gave him a smile of complicity, as if she'd be working alongside him and wanted it to be as much as possible. She took a strand of hair that had escaped on to her forehead and wound it behind her ear.

She was too generous; Nio fumbled, 'Um . . . well, or maybe give me something, I'm quite into bartering, you know – I've got what you want, you can find me a—'

'I want to pay you properly,' she interrupted. 'And first of all, let me give you a cheque for the horse.'

He followed her through to the kitchen. He really didn't want to be paid for the horse. 'No, you don't understand, it won't last, it wasn't for sale—'

She held out the cheque, but he couldn't take money off her for something which wasn't built to a good standard, it probably wouldn't survive beyond a year or two, even indoors. But she put the cheque in his pocket. He took it out and handed it back; she pushed his hand away. 'I'd like it if you started work as soon as possible,' she added briskly, 'there's a lot needs doing. And I should introduce myself, I'm Mrs Ginsberg,' she finished, 'Elinor Ginsberg. And what's your name?'

'Nio.' He shook her hand; it felt strong, warm. 'Nio Niopolous.'

'Can I expect you tomorrow at nine a.m.?'

'Great, that's fine—'

'Good. I'll give you a door key, then. And if you want, come along to my fireworks party tonight. But I won't be burning your horse.'

'Can I bring my girlfriend?'

'Of course. I'd like to meet her.'

It was over, then. He'd got a job!? He said goodbye to Nick and he was free to go, he ran up the road. It was difficult for his feet to touch the pavement, he was so elated. This zooming good luck – how it filled him! And it had been exactly when he *wasn't* trying, when he was attending to something else – when he was being an artist – that suddenly he'd succeeded.

Mila would respond to him now, he was sure, it was just what she needed to hear, everything would go back to how it was before, she'd be proud of him, run her hands around the back of his neck like she used to . . . this would win her.

He told himself to calm down, to slow his footsteps to their habitual loping gait, because he'd done it, he was there, no one was going to take it away. Nonetheless, he had to call her right now, somehow . . . He scoured the street ahead for a payphone. And – an answer to his prayer – there was one. He only had a few coins but still . . . Her voice answered after the first ring. 'Hello?' The sound was like the opening of a window on to that garden.

'Hi, it's Nio.'

'Nio, can—'

'Guess what?' interrupted Nio, he had to be rude because he'd only have a short time.

'What?'

'I've got a job.'

'No!' she was impressed. 'What? *What*? Tell me,' she insisted, 'right now.'

'A woman offered me work. We met because she bought the horse—' The payphone flashed, 'INSERT MORE MONEY'. He hurried to tell her, 'I'm running out of—'

Mila interrupted, 'Someone bought the horse!?' She sounded amazed at the good news. 'Our horse?'

Nio galloped on as fast as he could, 'It's great isn't it, I didn't expect it, I wasn't thinking I'd sell it, but—'

'How much?'

The line went dead. Without her voice, the magic was gone, he was back in the here and now, the sour smell of the phone box returned, it was claustrophobic, he pushed at the door in a slight panic to get out. At the same time he realized he hadn't asked what had happened to *her*, he'd just blurted out his own good news first and she'd have wanted to tell him everything, the car picking her up and all that, maybe she'd even been at the office right at that moment? He could have kicked himself.

Mila was alone at last. Suddenly it was easier, she could breathe OK, didn't have to smile, to try to understand everything the other two girls said, because Jayne and her flatmate had gone to work. Jayne was dead nice, but Mila could stop feeling guilty about borrowing everything now.

Must be dreamy, to live here. A two-bedroom flat in a low-rise block on the corner of Barnard Hill? Mind-numbing. Cold though, at the moment. She shivered, and padded through to the lounge to find a socket for her charger, plug in her phone. It beeped, winked at her. Plenty of signal. So important. The car . . . what sort would it be? She settled down to wait. A limo, maybe, at the front door?! If that happened, she was royalty, she really totally *was*.

She wished Little Vlad had stayed. Where'd he gone? He was like a ghost sometimes. Appearing and disappearing.

For another half an hour she huddled in the lounge. There was a blue two-seater sofa and two matching chairs, an old fashioned TV, a low pine table with two plants on it. The carpet was grey, stained with red wine. The walls were dark blue; here and there were stars and moons. Mila knew, from the times she'd stayed before, that they glowed in the dark. There was also a big mirror above the radiator and Mila courted it for a while. She fanned out the edges of the grunge dress she'd borrowed off Jayne's flatmate, a thin girl called – something odd, she didn't quite get it, but it sounded like 'Hilly' or sometimes just 'Hills'. It was made out of heavy material, mossy green. It had two deep cuts in it through which her legs flashed, neat looking in thick tights for warmth. A pair of big brown boots. The coat hung waiting in the hall, with a fake fur collar. Total new look, she'd never have bought any of it for herself, when had she last worn a dress? Not since she was a little girl. Good though. Or was it? No, maybe not . . . But she'd known for sure, totally, that when the girls were pulling out their wardrobes for her and helping do her hair, they'd thought she might be a famous singer soon and so they'd get to ride along as her friends, she'd liked that feeling, they were working hard for her and yes, she'd take them with her, wouldn't dump them, Jayne was great, really good at work, and she'd always remember Hills for lending her this dress, she'd leave tickets on the door for them and their friends, have them round, even when she was famous.

What time would he call? Maybe she'd have to wait until ten.

Just then, as if the thought itself was torn from her and used to hurry everything, the phone sang its tune, the screen told her it was Jon, loads earlier than she'd dreamed of. It would kick off quickly now, this was it, today was happening. She answered, 'Hello?' and knew she had to be ready, Jon was so fast, she had to catch on . . .

'It's a black Mercedes, and your driver's name is Bill Saunders.'

She leaped ahead, she could play the same trick, be just as fast. 'What time?'

Jon hadn't heard, he was talking through her, 'He's got your mobile number and he'll call when he's outside. What's the address, where are you?'

'Flat 5, Lake's Court, is a building of flats, is where Barnard Hill and Muswell Avenue meet at the corner.'

'He'll be there around ten, he's got to pick up someone else first.'

Someone else? Mila was worried. 'Will I be sharing the—'

'No, no,' he interrupted, his voice was impatient, 'he'll drop off the other person first and then come and fetch you. Sit tight.'

'OK—'

The line had already gone dead. Mila felt a surge of excitement. She couldn't stand still. She paced up and down the flat, literally blowing like a horse, a big smile on her face, this was amazing. A Mercedes! And look how busy he was, from his tone of voice came this impression of everything happening in all directions, and he could have got his personal assistant to call but he'd done it himself. She stamped up and down, in and out of Jayne's bedroom, down the corridor, a circuit of Hills' bedroom, back down to the lounge. Soon she'd have a flat of her own, when she got her first recording contract.

What time was it? Half past nine. Her hair had been washed with Jayne's white plastic shower attachment, blow dried while leaning over her ransacked bed and tied up with pipe cleaners and strips of rag; it was a trick she'd learned from home but over here everyone said how it was unusual, cool. She was so ready to go.

It was unbearable, waiting. She talked to the mirror like a mad woman, her eyes were soft and pleading for her own future. She paced. She looked in the tins in the kitchen to find biscuits.

Waiting, waiting, waiting. Why had Little Vlad left already? He knew she didn't like being alone. She checked her phone repeatedly, anxious that the signal might have . . . it sang in her hand, it was Jon again.

'You on your way?'

'No,' she complained, 'the car hasn't come and—'

'How long did he say?'

'He hasn't called yet.' She heard an impatient noise on the other end of the phone, and a curse. Then he repeated this same phrase, 'Sit tight', and was gone again. She fled to the window for the umpteenth time, to look down Muswell Avenue. Black Mercedes? No. She ran to the other end of the flat, to Hills' bedroom, to check Barnard Hill. Nothing there. Loads of cars, yellow, blue, grey, but no black Mercedes. Maybe the driver was having trouble parking? But he'd have phoned to let her know he was close.

Instead, more waiting. Another half hour. When the phone went again she leaped at it, glanced at the screen, at the strange number that she didn't recognize, she guessed it would be the driver. 'Hello?'

'Hi, it's me . . .'

It was Nio. She had to get rid of him. She drew a breath to tell him to get off the line, 'Nio, can—'

'Guess what?' interrupted Nio.

'What?'

'I've got a job.'

'No!' she had to rush through this as quickly as possible, she was frantic to get him off the line. 'What? *What?* Tell me,' she insisted, 'right now.'

'A woman offered me work. We met because she bought the horse—' Then his voice quickened, 'I'm running out of—'

Mila interrupted, 'Someone bought the horse!?' Had she heard that right? Because if so, it was sad, she loved that horse, he hadn't said he was going to sell it, she felt the ground move beneath her feet, something precious had been taken away. 'Our horse?'

Nio was excited, he was talking fast, 'It's great isn't it, I didn't expect it, I wasn't thinking I'd sell it, but—'

She began to ask how much he'd got for it, but the line went dead, and suddenly she was lonely, abandoned in this flat, none of her favourite people was near, she was dressed in some weird hippie outfit she'd never normally wear. She was meant to be in the car by now, wherever it *effing* was! She felt close to tears. Where was Little Vlad? He'd said he would stay.

Another half-hour passed, she was climbing the walls, then Jon called again. 'You still there?' he asked.

'Yes!' She was trying not to be annoyed, didn't want to burst out crying either. She heard him muttering, 'Fuck up, total fuck up.' His voice was coming as if from underwater, maybe he had his hand over the phone and was talking to someone else. She waited. 'I'm coming to get you,' his voice was suddenly loud again, 'I'm taking a cab right now to pick you up myself. This is a total fucking disaster. Flat 5, Lake's Court, junction of Muswell Avenue and Barnard Hill, right?'

'Yes—'

'I'm coming from the West End. Maybe forty minutes.'

So – she had to watch the clock some more, time dragged unbearably, but at least she knew what was happening, he was on his way to rescue her, something had gone wrong with the car, he was paying a taxi to come all the way, it would cost a fortune, just so she wouldn't be disappointed, mind-numbing. She went to the kitchen and drank a big glass of water, for the sake of doing something. It tasted stony and warm. She wiped her mouth and walked back to the lounge. She could hardly keep away from the windows, watching out for him. She'd go to the office after all. Wait. Sit tight. Perhaps she'd have to be a model first, in order to earn enough money to become a singer, maybe she wouldn't mind that so much . . .

An hour later, he was there. At last, her guardian angel . . . she watched as he climbed out of the taxi, wearing a long heavy coat, shades – cool. From her vantage point above him she watched him pay the driver – she'd expected the taxi to wait, take them back to the office, but it took off. Maybe just to turn at the end of the road. She dashed around the place, she found her phone and remembered the charger, she was ready to go, moved her own clothes in the plastic bag to the front door, pulled on the coat. The buzzer sounded and she opened the flat door, pulling in an icy blast of cold air from the corridor. There he was, God, she could have died, because with that big coat on, he was like, straight out of a war in Russia, the dark glasses against the winter sun freezing his face in this cool, strong expression. He didn't even respond to her greeting, he walked in and asked, 'What's that stuff you're wearing?'

She began to explain, but suddenly her English wasn't so good. She was nervous. He wasn't listening, he'd taken her elbow and walked her back into the flat, whereas she was expecting to leave and pick up the taxi downstairs.

They reached the lounge, so now she was back where she'd started, but he'd taken off the dark glasses and she could see those bright blue eyes, so she felt better.

'Doesn't look like you,' he told her abruptly.

'You don' like them?' She hugged her coat shut across her chest, suddenly it was very cold, she wanted to go.

'Not your style.'

'I borrowed, is why. Does it look bad?' She was hurt.

'Can you change?' he asked.

'OK.' She forced a cheerful tone into her voice but the same tears as before nearly broke through. She hurried out of the room. She went to the front door, fetched the plastic bag with her own clothes in it and took them back to Jayne's bedroom. She unzipped the boots and kicked them off, untied and unclipped the heavy dress, let it drop to the floor.

It was like a bolt of electricity running through her when she realized he'd come into the room, just like her sister would, as if it were something that happened every day, and he was talking about something. She was ready to run, sit down, get into the bed, all at the same time, anything to cover herself, but the shock froze her, immobile, while he bounced on the bed, lying down and crossing his legs, talking about something, 'I have . . . right, a number one . . . and you'd think . . . so I'd be covered, right . . . what happens—' She was half undressed, standing in her knickers and tights, covered in goosebumps, but only for a moment did she have to wonder how to react – thank God for the knickers and tights – because it was all over, he'd kind of rolled it forward anyway, she had to carry on and ignore him, not make any protest, that was all that was left to her, because this was what happened in his world, it was how they all behaved. She hurried into the plastic bag and yanked out her T-shirt, quick, over the head . . . and then her own jeans, she pulled them on, snatched up the mohair jumper she'd bought from Camden Lock Market . . .

Suddenly he was ordering her, 'Hold on.'

'What.'

He sat up, looked at her from top to toe, frowning. She felt stupid, like before – and it was cold. He stood then and walked over to her. He gathered the hem of her T-shirt and rolled it up, taking his time, until her stomach was exposed. Then he took the top button of her jeans, rolled it against his thumb until it came open, the same with the next one. Her heart was in her mouth. He stood back and gave her the same critical look, up and down, impersonal, this was work. Then he pointed at her and – as if he couldn't care less – said, 'Sort of a funky Britney Spears? Maybe that's what we should go for, then.'

She smiled, this was unbelievable, she wanted to tell him off, he was *so* dreaming. 'Oh, right—' She carried on with the jumper, it would make her warm again.

As if by magic, then, he had a square of paper in his hands, it was a miniature envelope, like a letter you'd find in a doll's house. He tore the corner, picking daintily at it, then slit the top open. He took from it a smaller square of intricately folded paper which flashed, turned in the tips of his fingers, it was about the size of a couple of postage stamps. He held it delicately, with reverence, as if it had enormous power. 'You've done coke before?'

'No, never, but—'

'Don't mind if I do?' he interrupted.

She shook her head and watched as he laid out the white powder in two lines on top of the bedside cabinet. Like she'd seen on TV, he rolled a ten pound note and sniffed one line into his nostril. This was nothing like the way her older brother Ilie had taken it. Before their card games, he and his friends would take a pinch of the white powder and put it on the backs of their hands, inhale it from there, then rub the leftovers on their gums. Either way it looked mad, she thought.

He pointed at the other line. 'Try it if you like.'

It was like a shove in the small of her back, the instinct to please him. 'OK. I'll try.' If her brother had, then maybe she should as well . . . then she noticed his twitch, the one she'd come to recognize meant he was annoyed; he threw a leg out, flicked his chin sideways, that tone came into his voice, 'Don't just—'

'What?' She was anxious.

'If I say that, it doesn't mean you have to do it, you can say no.'

She was relieved, she sank back to her normal self. 'All right, no.'

This made him even more annoyed. 'I should tell you something.' He used a flat, tight voice which she hadn't heard before, his blue eyes pinched her. 'There's no model agency, there's no office in the West End. It's all a load of bollocks, I made it all up. I deal this stuff a bit, and some women help me with . . . expenses.' His look challenged her, watched for a reaction.

The shock hit her. There was a moment of disbelief, then it was like falling, terrible vertigo; of course, there was no agency, it was the same bullshit as the guys trying to buy her in the warehouse in Sangatte, just like that, it made her stupid and young and . . . She was crushed, stricken. She went for the door, but he took one step and kicked it shut, stood between her and the only way out. He was dead still, motionless. He only looked away, it seemed, when he was certain of the silence. He dropped his voice, spoke quietly, vaguely, as if he were thinking of something else. 'When we first met, I was talking into my phone. But I wasn't talking to anyone. I was just saying all that stuff, for you, so you'd hear it. We didn't bump into each other. I followed you on purpose.' He took her shoulders. She felt weak. He bent and kissed her on the cheek, then on the other cheek, politely she accepted them. Then he ducked to kiss her on the lips and she was scared suddenly, all alone, she turned away, so he missed . . . but he didn't let her go, instead he pulled her into a tighter embrace. 'We're the same, you and me,' he said. 'We've both got two or three names we use. Both get what we want.' She squeezed a hand between them, pressed it against his chest, ready to push, fight him off, run. She closed her eyes for a moment. This was dangerous now, for real. She needed to get out of here. She opened her eyes again. She pushed harder but he squeezed tighter, so it was the time – she'd known it would come along one day with some guy or other – when she'd have to fight, to kick and scratch and scream and run. As the fear rooted more deeply in her, she began to build up the adrenalin, she'd knee him . . .

Her gaze fell on Jayne's bedroom floor, clothes scattered all over it, and among them, now, she noticed a boy's foot – in the following moment of wonder and disbelief as she realized what it meant she allowed herself to follow up the familiar leg to a face she knew only too well: Little Vlad was sitting behind the bedroom door, looking at her. In his lap was Jayne's gameboy. He blinked, his mouth turned down as if this were an unhappy moment in a film he was watching. Then he smiled at her and waved as if he were at the train station meeting someone. His mouth moved silently, she couldn't lip read what he was saying.

She called out, 'Vlad?!' and almost at the same time he asked loudly and fearlessly, *'Ey, caaat costa?'*

Jon's grip jumped off her; relief and thankfulness literally coursed through Mila's veins, Little Vlad was here after all, he'd saved her.

The sweethearts walked tight against one another, their feet struck the pavement in unison, elbows locked, hands clasped – it was cold that night but more to the point Mila was hanging on for dear life, she'd brushed close against something evil and so she clung to Nio, the fact of his existence, his kindness, his belief in her, the love between them, was saving her, every step. Her other saviour, Little Vlad, followed some distance behind, she'd pushed money at him, she'd allowed him to come to the party, she'd blessed his forehead with strokes and kisses. Nio, meanwhile, was freshly shaved and wore his donkey jacket over a thick fleece, he had his girl on his arm, and this was the miracle he'd asked for, no sooner had he lost everything – no job, no home, no Mila – than it had turned around, he had the job, plus he had the cheque for two hundred pounds in his pocket, but more exhilarating, the true excitement, was that Mila was here, suddenly she was answering him, her breast was jammed against his arm, she wanted him. Something had changed and he didn't care what it was, only that it had happened, his prayer had been heard.

On the doorstep of 9 Methuen Park, Nio started fooling around. Look, they didn't need to push the bell because he had the keys. He folded her in an embrace and she turned to him, squeezed hard, hung on; she thought, save me.

Little Vlad loitered at the end of the path.

Tight in his embrace, Mila could hardly speak from the confusion in her breast, she was trying with all her might to be less stupid, very quickly she wanted to grow beyond this mistake she'd made, she only wanted Nio, any other man was no good to her, without him she'd be afloat, lost, the whole of Great Britain would become shallow soil, she'd have no roots.

The door opened and Elinor Ginsberg was there. 'Ah, my artist,' she said. She was holding a bunch of flowers and Nio suddenly felt ungrateful to have come empty-handed, but he worked for her, it was OK, different rules applied. Nothing could straighten his smile now. He introduced Mila; and she knew this meeting counted for him so she worked hard, she took in the bright inquisitive eyes of the older woman and liked her straightaway; the pile of bricks – this house, its weight and authority – maximum respect as Jayne would say, but Mila quickly felt she might burst into tears because of the older woman's kindness. A sympathetic clasp of hands confirmed it, yes, she pretended it was the cold, making her eyes stream.

They pulled in Little Vlad, who walked in without a word, no respect however big, rich, the place. In the hallway the voices were a loud clamour, it made the language impenetrable for Mila;

like a deaf person swamped by too much sound she'd have difficulty understanding. Nio was brimming, he felt powerful with his horse parked just through there in the sitting room – he was guiding Mila through to see it before anything else – as well as the door keys to here, 9 Methuen Park, his paid job with a start tomorrow, a project in the garden which he could make his own. This was his place, like magic it had found him, and somehow it had brought back Mila to him. Everyone made her the centre of the room. Nio could take all the men, their first glances becoming long, incredulous stares, and he could set them up like skittles and bowl them all over because he was the person to whom she returned.

Mila was still wounded, Jon Rawle's kiss, the whole experience of him, was like a physical injury, it stayed, no one else could see, there were no marks on her but it had destroyed her confidence so she was talking too much and her sentences fell apart. She wanted to tell Nio everything but she was too ashamed. This was the message she sent – threw it as hard as she could – to the back of his head as he cut a path for them both through the party – I love you Nio. Tears brimmed in her eyes.

They swam with the tide to see the horse, and Nio's hands were all over her – on her shoulder, the slope of her hips, waist, they kept her safe from other men's hands, she told herself not to worry, cut it off, what happened, just live this room, this house, this crowd of people, its faces like lanterns lighting her way. They squeezed out of the first sitting room and into the second, their route through the crush of strangers brought them past Nick, the photographer. He was swaying, his belly like a bag he carried, his cameras an affliction, a millstone around his neck. Nio, stopped, brought Mila under his arm. 'This is Mila, remember I was telling you, we had to find a photographer for her?'

'Hello.' Nick was blank, already too drunk, he excommunicated himself from Mila's glamour, that was his official reaction.

'She doesn't want to be a model any more though,' went on Nio. 'She's going to be a singer instead.'

'Oh.'

'Just got herself a manager,' continued Nio, slipping his hand around her waist, 'so maybe, you know—' He came to a halt. Mila wanted to tell him it wasn't true, she kicked herself, really stupid how she'd believed all that rubbish, but look at herself, why didn't she own up, tell Nio what had happened, she'd waited all morning for the car to arrive and then . . . no, she'd lose something, she'd slip a notch, she couldn't afford to do that.

Nick had that look from the alcohol, every thought had a lead weight attached to it, they might try and fly but instead sank, incomprehensible. He nodded, looked over their shoulders. Yet he blocked their path, they couldn't push through without upsetting his position. He raised his eyebrows, and their silence maddened all of them; eventually he squeezed to one side so they could pass; words failed him.

When they reached Pegasus Nio was gratified at the group of people around him, admiring. He stood there with Mila and soaked it up. Everyone had their eyes on him and Mila, they were famous in this room. He was asked for the story of its construction and he might never feel so good, even if Mila was becoming impatient. He had to stay because there was this man, a dentist, wearing glasses, quite a bit shorter than him, Jewish looking, asking if Nio could do another one, how much it would cost. Nio was embarrassed, it made him want to laugh, it was too much success.

Mila was close to tears so she wandered off, feeling lower, more stupid, for every inch higher that Nio was flying. Tears would keep on coming if she wasn't careful – mad, that was. She was pulling looks, some guy tried to talk to her, and all this, what with everything that had happened today, made her see everything differently, she'd always thought life in this country would be, like, she and her family standing outside trying to kick the door down, but now she could see it wasn't like that, no, Great Britain was wide open to her, but it was like a hall of mirrors, each one showing a different reflection of herself – walk too close to any of them and she'd be sucked in, but some were bad news . . . only Nio was good.

In order to save herself and take a dozen breaths away from the party, Mila searched out the bathroom and went in slightly clumsily; there were two women already in there with the door unlocked. They milled about in the small space – one was teasing strings of hair over her eyebrows and the other leaned against the washstand, looking at a mobile. They cheerfully apologized and left, so Mila could take her turn.

Mila washed her face. The tap was a single paddle set in the middle of the basin: she worked out how to press down to switch on, and twist from side to side for hot and cold. She wrung her hands in soap and water, they turned like creatures that didn't belong to her; the nerves tingled to the tips of her fingers and perhaps she was washing away the anxiety, she wasn't used to feeling torn up inside, it was unlike her normal struggles and difficulties, this was right in the heart. She looked at herself in the mirror – and it was as if a stranger had stepped out of the rain in front of her and accused her – how could you have been so stupid? Tears filled her eyes quickly, she smacked them away with the heel of her hand. She answered, OK, she'd learned her lesson. Yes, it was like pinning herself against the wall and bullying that other person – just don't be that stupid again, look at the great man she'd got, whom she loved, Nio, and she'd nearly turned away from him . . . This stranger, the girl in the mirror with the thick brows above the strained, worried face that looked exactly like her, told her it had been the promise of a ride in the Audi car, the future as sort of a funky Britney Spears, going back home to find Ilie, that's what she'd wanted, she'd ached for all that, not for Jon Rawle himself. And all that had been a lie. More fool her.

Then, suddenly, in a flash of petulance, she wanted everything, again – to be funky Britney, a ride in the Audi, to fly back home and find her brother. All that, like jewels threaded on a chain, she wanted still, but she wouldn't go anywhere near Jon Rawle or anyone like him *ever again*. Mila flung the water from her fingers and looked for the towel, couldn't find it, she kicked around the room twice, wiping her palms on her clothes. When she went back downstairs to the party there was so much talking, the voices bounced off the walls, echoed like mad, broke her concentration, the faces around her wore smiles, issued mad laughter now, and she could see teeth, tongues, the bleeding backs of their mouths, it felt like a mad house, but the laughter was human warmth around her, addictive, she was smiling although she didn't understand why, it was over wasn't it, she was out the other side of this and she still had Nio . . . where was he? She had to find him.

Outside, there was a bonfire burning and people's faces around it were moving, it looked like they were underwater, the light a stream flowing over their faces. Around the fringes strode a man setting out fireworks; Mila could see her little brother tagging along. She skirted the heat and went to join them. The man was bearded, long haired, dressed in a tight leather jerkin over a thick jumper; he was in charge, no mistake. She and Little Vlad listened, but didn't understand much. Anxious to find Nio, she turned back. She had a drink in her hand and maybe that would help lift her. Had he finished with that guy yet? Yes, here he was, looking for her. They bumped, she turned her face up to his for a kiss, Jon Rawle's was on her lips still, it stung like the beginning of a cold sore, she so wanted it washed away.

Nio had an idea, he wanted her to see this, he walked her down to the end of the garden to show her where he'd be working. Here – something special, anything he wanted – wasn't it great?

He ran through a couple of ideas – a waterfall, a tower for children to climb, a giant mirror? What did she think? He circled, kept close, shepherded her; and he used the dark, the privacy of this unvisited, fenced-in corner, to turn her to him, hold her tight. She tilted against him, he was surprised because he'd got used to their not touching. Then she had her hand in the hair at the back of his neck again and was pulling at him. Mila wanted him, how bony and strong he was, it was like holding herself against something made of stone or hard wood, but warmth was flooding down her body and she clung tight to him, their long, deep kiss wiped away everything, who knew where the time would go, where it would take them, but this was her ride, Nio was like the men from home, his hands under her clothes now were holding her up, she wanted to fall, this was where she'd escaped to, she took his hand and laid it over her breast, she squirmed against him, she peeled the coat off his shoulders, took off her own and threw it down as well. She went limp in his arms so he had to lower her to the ground; he pulled the coats under her. The ground was chill and harsh on the back of her head; Nio tore off the fleece he was wearing and folded it under her neck, this was it, somehow it was going right, he knew better than to think about anything, he didn't care, he'd reached her somehow again and that was all that mattered. She put her hands on his shoulders, stroked him, held him; he opened her coat, pushed her T-shirt and vest up from her waistband, he breathed feverishly against her stomach, her scent was magic to him. She lifted her hips to help him pull down her jeans, a deep excitement and carelessness uncoiled in her loins, she wanted him at any cost; he hung over her, poised ready, and then carelessly he went for it and she felt him inside her and she squealed, this was it, go. She locked her arms around him and started crying freely, she kept her head lifted from the ground, buried in his shoulder as it moved against her. The small of her back hurt, there was only the coats between her and the hard, cold ground. The pain was mixed with loads of other things, the flow of pleasure, the fear of the party not so far away, the heartache of life going wrong, not being easy, but all of that lost in the here and now. The cold air was full of their breath and the sound of the revelry around the fire further up the garden. Nothing else mattered but their rhythm against one another. By the time it was done, over, she'd rubbed her back raw, he'd scraped his knees, there hadn't been anything like the kind of mad pleasure she could give herself, but she was saved wasn't she, no need to tell him anything, what they'd done here and now was what counted. She held his head in her hands and even in this dark corner she saw his wonder, he looked shocked, tearful. 'God,' he said, 'I thought—' He couldn't believe what had just happened.

'Shhh—' Mila stopped him, soothed him. 'Don't say . . . don't say . . .' She was up and running with Nio.

Later they grasped hands tightly and walked back towards the bonfire which crackled, flamed languorously, lifting its insect-like cloud of glowing embers into the night sky, the blackened silhouettes of figures circling. Through her grip, her hands on him, he could feel her attachment grow, to match his own. They joined the circle around the bonfire. The heat baked their faces, hands. In the firelight her skin was glossy, as if the light was coming from inside her, golden. They were given plastic cups of warm mulled wine. No one else around this fire had done what they'd just done, this was happiness.

They saw that Little Vlad had found a group of other children, they were pushing a banger into a potato.

When it was time for the fireworks, they were among the chosen few invited to watch from Elinor Ginsberg's bedroom. Nick muttered something about 'completion' and carried his cameras outside to take the most powerful image distilled from the event, which would go on to help win the photographer a first in his end-of-year exam. It was a black-and-white shot of Nio looking out at the fireworks from the upstairs window, amazed and impressed, while Mrs Ginsberg, renowned local midwife and chief of the Haringey Home Birth Team, admired his profile, and on the other side of him Mila's open, pretty features smiled up at him also. The women's faces and Nio's wonder and the reflection of the fireworks exploding in the glass made for a narrative, said the examiner, which encapsulated beginning, middle and end dynamics of Nio Niopolous' interruption.

FIVE

Muswell Hill itself observed the exodus of the caravans from the slip road – maybe, even, expelled them, using a slow massage of its population, because Muswell Hill was stretched to breaking point and couldn't take these people. It already accommodated many times more than it was designed for, but now accepted residents only of a particular type and class. The good state schools were pulling in clever, concerned and populous families, the house prices were rising at above the national average so as each property changed hands the streets became richer, the cars newer, more exciting and numerous, the youth increasingly well bred and spending like mad, and so, hour on hour, Muswell Hill chopped away at the poorer end of humanity, it lost to the cheaper parishes on its borders those who couldn't afford to hang on while sucking in the better off and breeding their two, three or four children as fast as the women's bodies could stand it. The mound of the hill itself, topped with its square mile of boutiques on the Broadway, bristled with Christmas shoppers who fought their way in and out of doorways and squeezed past each other down the narrow aisles to wait at the overheated tills. None had found car parking space, they all resented each others' vehicles, they didn't want to have to carry their shopping home. But the street decorations were beautiful, the whole place gleamed in this Christmas month of December, its position as the highest point in North London gave it an airy happiness and the amount of children meant it was filled with innocence and laughter.

So, thousands glanced at the expulsion of the caravans or even paused to watch – pedestrians criss-crossing from one pavement to the other in front of the slow moving vehicles, the occupants of the cars jammed solid at the various junctions, those who were working harder than ever during the Christmas period. The sweetshop boy noticed it as he walked up Colney Hatch Lane, taking a break from lifting chocolate bars, newspapers, magazines and cigarettes. His hands were blackened by silver passing back through them and his arms felt like they'd drop off, he barely had time to do his homework. The fruit and veg shop owner registered the caravans as they slid past her shop on the Broadway; her thumbs and forefingers were chafed from her cold mornings of handling damp vegetables, she used the same heavy duty moisturizing cream every year. Her sons lifted and carried, their minds on the Christmas TV and video, Premiership football, music, girls, local fame, fights. The cleaner at Boy, the hairdresser's, was having a haircut himself, for free; it was a friendly gesture by the owner and so he was wrapped in a thin black cloak to keep the hair from dropping on his clothes as he watched someone else sweep up his offcuts. The sight of the soft broom moving silently back and forth made him feel unbearably sad, he didn't know why, and he looked up, and saw – over the shoulder of the headless mannequin in the window – the swinging orange lights of the Haringey Council tractor which towed the first trailer. The bus driver, as usual, ploughed his bus lane, inch-perfect in his careless throwing of the big Routemaster through the gaps in the heavy traffic, and ended up drawing alongside it, glancing in through its windows.

The Rosapepe caravans were towed to a new site in Camden offered by an evangelist Christian group which owned an empty lot on Royal College Street where their church had formerly stood. The Rosapepe family were used to these religious nuts, they cropped up wherever there was poverty and suffering with their orphanages, halfway houses, legal and immigration help – all this was a continuing recruitment drive, it was the Adventists who'd donated one of the trailers in the first place.

As for the abandoned, ex-Highways Department Cherokee used for a while by Lucas Tooth, it was scooped up and pushed into the breaker's yard on the other side of the fence, once the CCTV monitor had been disconnected and removed. It was as if it had backed up there itself, ready to die.

The Rosapepe family made their new home on this site surrounded by a chain-link fence with concrete feet – it guarded the compound against outsiders but it made those within look and feel like prisoners. There were fifteen caravans in neat rows. One or two looked as if they'd been there for years, they had around their skirts well constructed gardens made out of pot plants along with additional storage boxes. Some had handrails fitted to help with the steps up to the front doors. The Rosapepe troupe were at the other end, where the square of tarmac gave way to rough ground on which the church had stood. The bricks that had made the building now formed a low barrier, like a wave, around the perimeter of their section of the site. The trailers were parked in a line, backs against the wall of the neighbouring building which had been sheeted up to prevent the weather infiltrating. For a couple of days the family laboured, levelling the ground, heaving at the ends of the caravans, two lifting while a third pushed in or removed bricks underneath. Their breath clouded the air around them as they worked. Mila often picked her way over the rubble, her hand would rise to signal the men that she'd brought out tea. For a while she'd stand canted over on one leg, talking to them. Her breath vapourized; her hands were gloved in heavy mittens.

The Christmas holiday offered Mrs Ginsberg no respite, she worked just as hard, planting Muswell Hill's streets with perfect newborns, and she passed Christmas day itself listening to the cries of a family whose first child was unwrapped while their possessions, furniture and gifts were still in their boxes.

Charmer squatted in the Clamp. He refused to go home, burned all the wood that Nio collected and ate Christmas pudding alone, straight from the wrapper, uncooked.

Ahmed did well for himself in the New Year sales, he moved a lot of furniture. He was confident enough to take all the Searsons invoices with the false VAT number printed along the bottom and dump them in a skip, he wouldn't need to engage in any fraudulent trading ever again. Then he lost confidence and went back to rescue just a handful in case of any unforeseen downturn in business. He patted his jacket pockets, found the Camel Lights, and fired one up. Good stuff. Well done Ahmed.

Mila's actual, real birthday had come and gone with the lovers hardly noticing; they were ahead of that crisis, now. His gift to her – at last she'd got her hands on it – had been a set of miniature arrows he'd made, no more than six inches long, complete with a quiver made out of shoe leather. The arrows were tailed with flights made out of peacock feathers and tipped with chips of coloured glass. The quiver was decorated with a picture of Cupid cut from a magazine and chased into the leather. He'd thought of doing this because she'd told him about this Cupid in the church near her village, carved out of wood and painted in bright colours which had faded now, and how much she'd liked its inscription, 'My Heart's Desire', although she'd always felt sorry for the Cupid because it was all alone, there was none other. Mila held Nio tight, she loved her gift, she'd keep it always. Near to Christmas she went to meet Nio's parents for the first time, she struggled through a whole tea. She admired the house, looked at photographs, ate Greek pastries, deciphered what the two of them were saying, with Nio as interpreter. He claimed they'd only learned the English words for different types of ice cream in all the years they'd been here. Nio's mother smiled and nodded a lot, she appeared and disappeared through the coloured streamers hung in the doorway between the kitchen and the dining room. His father looked stiff, he sat for most of the time in a high wooden chair as if he'd damaged his back and was in pain, but he had a kind, dark face, she liked him. They stayed on into the evening and took advantage of the bathroom. Nio's mother fetched towels and ran the hot water for her; Mila realized she was being chaperoned, Nio was expected to keep away. It was more hard work, to accept kindnesses from this strange Greek woman with the sallow skin and orange hair, but Mila was determined to do well. Once she was alone and naked in the bath, she felt lonely, estranged. The lock on the door sealed her away in this unfamiliar place, with its old-people smell of soap and toilet cleaner. When she got out she called downstairs, the bathroom was free, and his mother was first up the stairs, quick as anything, she immediately showed Mila to a bedroom where she could change back into her clothes and the door was gently closed behind her. She heard Nio's voice as he spoke to his mother, then she was gone. Silence. Mila crept out and knocked softly on the bathroom door; Nio hurried her away, he didn't want to upset his parents. She started to laugh and to shut her up he put his hand over her mouth, but he was laughing, too. She dropped the towel from around her, she was naked and damp in his arms. He bundled her back into the bedroom, scooped up the towel and threw it in after her, but she bounced straight back out, by which time he was a few strides down the corridor. She ran at him, jumped, she had the feeling she might go through him, over the banisters, but he was there, he braced to take her weight, she wrapped her legs around his waist, found his mouth and kissed it. She hung off him, there was a real fear in her breast that she might fall. She clung to him, kissed him some more, for all her life's worth, they went and fucked in the bathroom, quiet as mice, it was intense.

On the return visit to *her* home two days later she didn't bother to commandeer the best caravan, Social Services, instead she took him straightaway into the Kingdom of God, no pretences to her family that she was doing anything different but fucking him. She drew the curtains along the plastic wires, undressed and climbed on top, she rode him as fast as she could, looking for the sensation, coursing towards pleasure, working hard. The rhythm of their coupled bodies set the trailer moving, she imagined those spindly aluminium struts might give way, they must be moving inch by inch off the bricks, the whole lot would come loose and they'd roll on to the broken ground, the trailer would snap in half.

Soon, also, they had the confidence to ignore Charmer playing gooseberry in the Clamp, they didn't care what he overheard, they christened it again and again, and when Nio saw Mila naked in the light thrown by the circular window, aglow with colour, then all the effort he'd put into this place over the last three years was given its true reason – it was work done towards this one end and who cared if it was knocked down, now. The mournful Charmer persisted; he didn't want them to have the privacy of the Clamp, so he was forced to listen, sulkily, to the sound of their happiness.

Other than that, they swerved crazily from place to place for their sex life. She dragged Nio to the grounds of the abandoned Friern Barnet Mental Hospital like countless teenagers before them. It was uncomfortable, funny, cold, but she clung on. In the tangled depths of St Pancras Cemetery she leaned on the top of a worn, old stone tablet and arched her back to display for him; halfway through she realized there was faint lettering on this side, so she was standing on the grave rather than behind it as she'd thought, therefore she was hanging over the abyss, this was life and death all right, except she had contraception now from the doctor at the Centre for the Homeless near Oxford

Circus. They made love in Coldfall Wood, Coppetts Wood, Highgate Wood, in St Pancras Cemetery, around the back of Tesco's, in Mrs Ginsberg's garden. Their indoor places included Social Services, The Home Office, The Kingdom of God, in the bedroom Mrs Ginsberg offered them and which they agreed to use only if it was very cold, in Jayne from work's bathroom and the bedroom they borrowed from Hilly while she was in America, and also more than just the once – always just as quietly, secretly – in the bathroom of Nio's parents' house in Curzon Road; they never knew that in total ecstatic silence Mila fucked their son, Nio. She stared intently at his body, they were getting good at this, it was love, for real, she found the pleasure in it now, she was with him, she'd chosen him, was riding with this man for ever, she really was.

Mila gave Nio a mobile phone for Christmas so she could keep him right by her, all the time. It was a pay-as-you-go Motorola from Tesco's. She entered his number into the memory of her own phone, and, on her speed dial facility, she put him at number one. Nio was drop-dead pleased with this, he was part of the cast of her phone now, he was among that intense scramble, the signalling that followed Mila around, he could compete. Wasn't he number one, after all? He kept the charger for the phone at Mrs Ginsberg's. On his part, with the money from his job he could buy Mila jewellery and music CDs for Christmas.

So Muswell Hill, plum like, a pregnant belly itself, moved satisfyingly into the New Year.

Lucas Tooth clawed back the sheepskin coat, unclipped the phone from his belt and pulled up the menu. He chose the phone book: the list of names stacked in alphabetic order. He liked how the phone worked for him, made life neat. He scrolled down – Alice, Angela, Anjali, Anna, Beattie, Carol, Caroline – and then back up again. With each name came pictures. Alice – that strand of hair that always caught in her mouth. Angela – a way of blinking when she talked. Anna – a position she liked when sitting down. Beattie – the glint of the rings on her fingers. Caroline walking fast in long skirts always made of wool or fleecy material. Which one should he call?

He was stuck in a traffic jam in the Audi. The sound system kept him sane. The music gave some power and drama to the occasion. He turned it right up. The beat concussed his lungs, made his heart vibrate, skip.

As he nudged through the hundred or so names, the pictures of the girls disappeared, they just became a jumble of letters; the music was more important. He carried on. He put a lot of work into this list, maybe eleven years of full-time concentration had gone into making it and he worked the roster of mothers and sisters every day, but in the end they became more or less the same, the edges between them blurred, they became merely a map of his past, scrambled, busy, lost in the story of the song.

He closed his eyes – and so even the names disappeared, there was just the music calling, the pressure of his thumb on the button on the phone, the to and fro of the breath in his nose. He was in a black, empty place, only the music measured him, his heart skidding dangerously. Who was the lucky one going to be? He didn't care. He wanted by some magic to create a new girl, a composite of all the others . . . or all the Tesco girls together in a Jacuzzi. He stopped scrolling and still with his eyes shut he moved his thumb on to 'call' and pressed the tit.

Only then did he open his eyes, switch off the music and see whom he'd chosen. From the little window on the phone he read her name – Mila. Call connecting.

He was faintly annoyed, he'd bust her wide open, she'd only say no. In any case, there weren't either of the two essential ingredients with her because she wasn't sad and she wasn't innocent. She went along too easily – he pushed her and she fell.

There was not enough of what he found most compelling, plus she had no money, no house, no car. She was a looker, but she was a foreigner, he didn't like the sound of her accent. He lifted the phone to his ear, listened to the ring tone. It crossed his mind not to bother, but he imagined her – she would stop in her tracks, take off a glove, paddle in her bag, hold up the phone to see who was calling. She would read his name; unless she'd deleted him from her directory. She knew the truth about him now – and had had long enough to get over the shock. So what would she do? He was curious. He chewed at his cuff, waiting for her to answer. His sharp nose, his brilliant eyes were aimed at her, his concentration willed her to answer quickly because otherwise he'd . . .

The call signal stopped abruptly and diverted him to the answering service. The line between them went slack. For it to have happened like that, after a few ringing tones, meant she'd cut him off.

Lucas Tooth was snagged by that. For the rest of the day he thought about it, smiled to himself. Of course she'd cut him off, what else could she do? He laughed – this was more like it. He phoned her twice more – and again, she blocked his calls. He enjoyed the thought of her worry – she'd panic that he was stalking her. Then he became angry, a slow fuse burned in him.

It was another two days before he had time to take it a step further: he waited for her to leave work and then followed her from Tesco's all the way to Royal College Street, in Camden. So . . .

The next morning he was up early, the cold was numbing. He crouched in the darkness to unlock the Audi. Then he drove the short distance to join the usual queue for the main road. He sat there for fifteen minutes, moving a few feet at a time, the heater blasting away, jerking in fits and starts towards the traffic lights, Mila in his sights. How dare she just walk away? In the dark shadows of the Audi's interior, he felt more interested in her, fiercer, keen. He pictured her on the way up from Camden, her face a white ghost showing through the window of the bus. He moved forward another few feet. Three more turns of the lights and he'd be through. He lifted his sleeve to his mouth and found the comfort of gnawing at the ragged cuff there, working his incisors steadily, feeling the cotton separate into finer threads, working until pieces littered his tongue.

He blasted down the North Circular for a couple of miles, cutting up the traffic, making use of the hard shoulder and then hiving off for the Tesco supermarket. He parked in a distant corner and began his wait. He shunted the seat back, tilted it, to sit in comfort. Around him, the car park filled up, holding him at its outer edge. Meanwhile he had a trap to set. He took out his phone, changed the set-up so his number was blocked, she wouldn't know who was calling.

When he saw her arrive for work, he took down the window halfway so he could see her better. He hefted his mobile as if he might be about to throw it at her, pulled up her number and pressed to connect, same as before.

She stopped in her tracks, dug in that bag for her phone, looked at the screen. It wouldn't be his name on there, instead it would read, 'Anonymous'.

Her voice sounded tired. 'Hello?'

He cast his line straight off. 'Bad news. It's me.'

There was a pause. He watched her turn half around, staring at the ground. Then he heard her voice. 'Jon? I don' want—' began Mila.

'I know you don't want.'

'Ohhh!' He saw her stamp her foot. He sat dead still in the Audi, looking over at her from his side window, blinking.

'Tell me why not.'

'I don' care, is because—'

'Listen,' he broke in, 'it's OK, let's say goodbye.'

'I have to—' He could see the way she leaned into the phone. He heard her breathing, for a while. 'You know what?' She paused. He listened intently to her tone of voice, while he watched her body language, her staring at the ground, her hand to her face, as she went on, 'I don' want to talk with you again, is that OK?'

Lucas Tooth felt his heart tip and swallow its load of blood the wrong way. For three seconds he thought he was going to laugh. His knee was jigging fast. 'I won't call you again.' He kept the smile out of his voice, he was even, deliberate, 'But, it's like I told you, right? We have a talent for being . . . the same as each other. We both—'

'I'm late for work,' she interrupted, 'is so far to come up here now, and I'm so, so always late, I have to go.'

Now he was angry. 'You'll always listen to me – and you know why? Because I don't give a shit how good looking you are, it means nothing to me. You could be a donkey for all I care, I'd still take you upstairs and fuck you. And that's why you'll want me.' He closed down the call without saying goodbye. Then he watched as she stared at her phone for a moment, dropped it into her bag. She walked – quicker – then ran into the superstore. He wondered, would that work, was she on the hook? Maybe not.

He chewed on the cotton threads from his cuff, then took a pinch of his own skin between his teeth; and for one acute instant the thought of Mila's rejection made him bite through. The pain was sharp; he felt his teeth meet, tasted the saltiness of his blood, its metallic flavour rinsed his mouth. He worked at the clip of flesh with the tip of his tongue. There was no doubt he'd have her, if she was going to try to fight him off then all it did was put a handle on her, give him something he could get a grip on, so he could twist it. He was going to do well with her, he could smell that now. Suddenly she was staying with him, living in his head, it was a good sign, just what he needed to get serious, sharper, quicker.

He climbed from the vehicle. It was freezing, his fingertips burned with cold when he touched the car door to close it. The scent of petrol and plastics was flattened by the chill.

Keep on telling me no, he advised her, and it means yes, bring it on; she would be the path ahead whether she liked it or not, he was nosing down it, now, as surely as if it were attached to him by a line. As he walked, his breath clouded in front of him and his feet were cold as earth. He went quickly to the superstore, shaking out the blood to his fingers and toes, trying to warm up. He slipped inside like a ghost; the electronic doors barely had to part an inch and he was through, off their radar. He swung into the café at the side of the store and heat folded over him, it was warm as life itself in here. He shivered and his wrist was at his mouth again. His tongue found the little tag of skin and he bit, flattened it, chewing.

There was already a queue moving drearily along at the supermarket café but he ignored everyone, moved straight to the coffee machine and punched the buttons to fill his cup. Then he found a table and kicked the chair to set it square. The girls' backs would be towards him as they sat at their checkouts, he'd glimpse their faces now and then, but they wouldn't see him. Jayne, Maria, Lynne, Emma. And Mila, with her fake name tag.

Warmth seeped into him; he jigged his knee and blew on the coffee. He felt the resentful stare of the woman in charge of the cafe – he hadn't paid. Would she dare confront him, ask for the money? He thought not. Furthermore, now he went and lifted the plastic flap guarding the pastries and scooped up an apricot Danish with the tongs and loaded it on to a side plate. He strolled back to his table unconcerned. Once before, in the early days of his coming here to watch the Tesco girls, the manageress had complained. He'd been the soul of politeness, paid up, but later he'd returned and threatened to feed her on her own cakes until she burst. Now there was no grief from her.

The warmth set Lucas up and his well-being increased when the sound system kicked in with a classic Supertramp number. The music and his courageous abuse of the café told Lucas that yes, he was driving this superstore, he could have any number of its young sisters, they were all here for him and he could swing the place anyway he chose. Staff in their uniforms scurried like ants, customers in their grubby clothes, safe in their families, eked out their weekly shopping allowances; Lucas Tooth could bring the place to a halt by stealing a coffee and a pastry . . . he could turn the place upside down and shake the money from the tills.

Then, as he watched, Mila rose from her position and fled. She was literally picking up her bag, her coat, and running out of the store. He rose to his feet briefly to shake out a spasm in his knee, and to watch her go. The music soared, lifted him with it, suddenly it was like a revelation, it lifted him so high . . . and on top of that it turned him around – look at Mila, running for dear life across the car park. He'd done that, he'd set her going. In his throat Lucas felt the first hundred of his crimes revisit, like a sickness.

Mila tore the loop on her coat as she yanked it off the hook, then she ran out of Tesco's, she fled. The phone call had frightened her, he was turning into a nightmare, she just had to find Nio; he must be at work. She felt the eyes of everyone on checkout. Her supervisor called out, 'Donna—' but she ignored her. She had to wait for the sliding doors to open; the cold air rushed to her lungs, made her breathless with shock. The speed bumps in the car park broke up her stride but she kept going, dragging out the phone, she texted Nio, 'where r u?' and she was the other side of the bridge before she got the reply, sure enough, 'at wrk'. She bounced back, 'coming to c u'.

If she changed her phone number, maybe Jon Rawle wouldn't get to her. He might turn up at work – so she'd give up the Tesco job, she was going to do that anyway, a new job would be easy to find – she could walk around Camden Lock Market and work on any stall she wanted, she knew that now, from having trawled the place; every time people came up to her, talked, she was always saying no to stuff because it was obviously guys just hitting on her. But, she could turn around and say yes to one of them . . . So, she could get rid of Jon Rawle, she knew she could, eventually. She had her family to protect her, and Nio, he was solid as a rock, hers, number one, the strong arms would save her. He was working now and he had a new commission for another horse to make for the dentist. He was putting in loads of hours, he said Mrs Ginsberg might lend him the money to buy a van.

Methuen Park – here it was, she knew her way without thinking, she'd come here loads of times in the three months that Nio had worked here – on very cold nights to stay in the bedroom that Elinor offered them, or to pick up Nio from work, or walk with him to work, and sometimes at weekends – so, it was so familiar now, number nine – the white-painted gate, the rich, mansion-quality front door. Elinor, the woman, Nio's boss, had from that first night of the party, ten weeks ago, made her feel welcome and it hadn't stopped, she felt the same as Nio, that she was their guardian angel. She knocked, rang the bell as well. She danced on the step. Come *on*.

When Nio answered she saw immediately the worry on his face, he was begging for knowledge, what had happened? She had to fob him off, told him it was work. She wanted to splurge and tell him everything that had happened but there was so much, it was like it was all stuck at the top of her throat, she couldn't. Instead she just reached up and hung off his neck. 'Nio—' was all she managed. This was life and death.

'What is it? What happened?'

'Nothing, is nothing, just had to see you, didn't want that work.'

They stayed like that for a while. She drew a breath, thought she might cry. That guy was so scary. Then he brought her in and shut the door behind her. He was staring at her, he wore that frown because he knew something was up, tears were standing in her eyes, he held on tight to both her hands. She was so ready to tell him . . . but it had to be everything, he had to understand. She couldn't begin, though, so he got there first, 'Come with me a minute . . . want to show you something.'

She let out her breath, felt a wave of disappointment because she hadn't been brave enough to leap in and tell him what had happened, she'd have to save it for later, everything was still OK, he just wanted to show her something; she allowed herself to be led through the house and into the garden, he was burbling away incomprehensibly; all the million things she'd been about to say she swallowed, they'd have to wait until it was her turn.

The earth was iron hard under her boots, the grass crisp with cold, a grey-green expanse of lawn. The red setter – what was its name – snooped around her. They went down to the bottom and around the dog-leg. 'Not quite ready, but it sort of works, what I've been up to,' said Nio as they skirted the fish pond. 'See?'

The last time she'd been this far down the garden – well, there'd been fireworks all right. But now, where it narrowed to a point, and where before there'd been nothing but a pile of old rubbish, some broken tools, rotten fencing panels and an old plastic water-butt, there stood an octagonal wooden hut like you might see in a children's picture book. It was amazing that he'd built it this quickly. It looked like it had been there a long time already because it was made of old stuff, and the branches of trees, not like wood that you'd buy to build a house. Its roof was made of wooden slats and rose to a single point from which projected a flagpole. Nio was explaining it to her, but she didn't understand everything. She nodded and walked closer. He strolled ahead and opened a door – she didn't quite see how it worked, she wouldn't even have guessed the door was there, it looked just like one of the other sides that swung on hinges. 'Come in,' Nio was saying, 'have a look.'

She stepped in and felt the gritty surface of a concrete floor underfoot. There was a strong smell of resin and pine and cement. Nio shut the door behind them and the dark closed in; she could see a little more as her sight adjusted, there were chinks of light let in through the woodwork. Each of the eight sides of the hut was identical; they stood in the middle.

'OK,' began Nio, taking her by the shoulders. 'Now, close your eyes.' She did as she was told. Nio twisted her shoulders. 'Turn around. And around.' She allowed herself to be turned in a circle three times. 'Abracadabra,' intoned Nio, 'keep your eyes shut.' The pressure on her shoulders changed, he spun her back the other way twice more. Then he stopped her. 'OK. Open.' She could see better now. He was standing in front of her, smiling, he was excited. 'Now I'm going to open the door again.' He leaned forwards, pulled on the latch . . .

The garden had disappeared. Instead, there was an illuminated picture: slivers of golden light, a sea shimmering, a bird sharply cut against the sky – she blinked – it was a sunset, amazing, the shape of the land was a black silhouette against the sea and sky. She noticed more – a tiny cutout figure walking on the horizon, birds wheeled in the bay, a silvery beach, a boat rested peacefully. 'Wow.' It was beautiful, the way the light came from the other side, like the stained glass window in the Clamp.

'You like it?' asked Nio

'How . . . did you . . .' She walked closer. 'Is a different door!' she exclaimed.

'One at the front and one at the back,' explained Nio, opening the door into the garden as well so she could see. She turned back and forth, looking at the two identical doors. He was going on, 'I haven't finished ni— no point at all . . . corner of the garden . . . a box onto this side . . . make like a . . . you know, back-light—?' She shook her head, when he explained things too fast she couldn't follow. 'It's light coming from behind the picture, shining through coloured perspex . . . what d'you think?'

'I love it,' she replied truthfully. Nio closed both doors and darkness closed in again. She tilted; he caught her, held her close. Here was the very spot where it had first happened and now to reinforce it, to lay down another layer of the feeling between them, to protect her, she wished for them to do the same again . . .

Anjali had a violent dream, that women and girls were jumbled up together like chickens thrown in the back of a truck, there was only the sense of their limbs, she saw an ankle bracelet, a wedding ring, a painted toenail, the instep, a shoe hanging off, a thumb, and all these girls were alive but motionless. To save them she had to eat, didn't matter what, but there was nothing to hand. In a frantic hurry she knelt on the ground and scooped up handfuls of dust and lifted it to her lips, but there was nothing there. She scrabbled, lifted countless handfuls, but her mouth remained empty. A short time later there was half a banana, she could eat that and save them, but in the same instant she knew written into the banana was a name, in the way lettering is written into a stick of seaside rock. She couldn't eat that name, she would rather see the women and girls . . .

She woke suddenly, in a panic. Close around her was the card-board house that she and Spider had built. It felt dead cold, like a coffin.

The dream unsettled her for hours, she tried to calm her nerves. She walked, listened to music, talked. She began to think of having a cigarette – although a voice inside told her that cigarettes weren't an anaesthetic, not like drink. She counted them – there were eight left. Not too bad a habit, given it was the same packet. She stared at the name and telephone number written there by the policeman who'd given it to her. PC Tony Glover. She drew one and lit it, waited for the nicotine to hit.

She saw Spider loitering where the plane of daylight fell from the steps and illuminated the blue and orange tiles running along the wall of the underpass. At his feet a pool of something – urine or beer – congealed and the mashed pages of a tabloid newspaper stirred like the wings of a butterfly stuck to the concrete.

He swung around, came back slowly, started tinkering with the heavy grilles which protected the exit ducts from the tube's ventilation system. He clung to one, pulled himself off the ground. He hung in a loop underneath the grille and somehow still had the strength to kick at the very structure which was supporting him, trying to break it – but its rigorous square shape wasn't dented by his efforts.

A lone passenger from the tube clicked through the tunnel, her heels echoing. She was a heavy young woman clutching her bag close to her front. At the sight of the cardboard house made by Spider and Anjali, which took up half the width of the underpass, she faltered, the rhythm of her heels was broken for a moment, then continued, a slower beat. She kept one eye on Spider hanging from the grille and the other eye on the cardboard house. Spider now dropped to his feet and walked out to meet her. She halted, drew a breath, her face white, she stared at him for two moments then sidestepped and angrily continued, her heels brittle on the hard surface. Spider sidestepped also, bringing her up short. Anjali knew it was for her benefit, it was part of the display, but she didn't want this anonymous woman to suffer on her account, it seemed to tie in with the dream she'd had. She struggled to her feet and found herself talking, it was still unusual, the words broke from the back of her throat, sounding incompetent, badly formed. 'He's not going to hurt you.' The girl was breathing heavily and wouldn't take her eyes off Spider, who nonchalantly kicked at the shoulder of concrete buttressing the wall of the underpass. Anjali linked arms with the girl and escorted her past the cardboard house and down the slope to the exit. Together they climbed the steps up to Charing Cross Road, blinking in the thin February sunlight. The girl shrugged off Anjali's arm and headed into the traffic without a word. Anjali watched as she threaded through the moving cars and gained the pavement, heading downhill, out of sight.

Anjali then turned back and descended to the underpass. She made a decision – to go back to Muswell Hill and visit the police station. Immediately.

Spider was squatting now outside the door of the cardboard house they'd made, elbows on his knees, it was so cold he kept his gloves on, making the roll-up. Anjali ducked past him, inside, closed her book and squashed it in a pocket, folded her sleeping bag over so it was out of the way. She glimpsed a syringe – Spider's. It was half drawn back, new looking. The sinister liquid was colourless.

When she was ready to go, with courage which surprised herself even, she ignored him. He ignored her back. She headed off, walked up the slope towards the tube station. Before she rounded the corner she stopped and gave him a chance to come with her. She watched his head tilt as he brought the flame to the tip of the cigarette. Then he inhaled, stared between his feet, holding his breath. A funnel of smoke expressed from his nostrils. No, he wasn't going to.

Hunger gnawed at her, but as she walked down to the tube platform she nonetheless greeted the looks of strangers with her usual half-smile. All these people, with their jobs, friends, places to live, no sooner had put in place such desirable things than they were brought back to where she was, the same place – a flesh-and-blood carrier of a human conscience that could only be concerned with its own happiness and satisfaction. . . She imagined telling her Dad that, look, all our fancy clothes, our nice houses and new cars deliver happiness only for a moment, they are transitory, after which the conscience is left again only with itself and those of its closest comrades or family and somehow, rich or poor, it is the same, it is the engineering of the human conscience towards justice, and happiness, that is the task set for everyone.

Without the money for a Travelcard, she hopped on to the steel barrier, then swung her legs across. She took the Northern line to Highgate, where again she performed the same feat, but in the face of a ticket inspector. She ran like crazy up the steps and fled across the road into Highgate Wood. From there, she walked to Muswell Hill. She didn't turn left at the Broadway, which would have taken her down to the police station, but continued down Colney Hatch Lane, heading for the North Circular Road. It was like an itch she had to scratch. She would go to the police station immediately afterwards, on the way back. As before, the bridge stretched ahead of her; she halted at the junction just before it, where the slip road drew off the westbound traffic, and looked left.

This time, there were *no* caravans at all. Not one. She stared for a while, then walked slowly down there, the cars accelerating at her side. No – nothing. Bare road. She might have imagined the whole thing, except she could identify where his caravan had stood: there was the ridge of debris which had built up against the tyre. She poked it with her foot; it easily dissolved, lost its shape – a smear of litter and silt, some organic matter. She was standing in the exact spot . . . She cast further around and in the mud at the side of the road found more tyre tracks, where the other caravans had been. Something else was different – next to the wrecker's yard a section of fence was torn down and a site cleared – they were going to build something.

She felt a terrible guilt: other women would be betrayed, maybe attacked, because she hadn't been brave enough to confront him, nor tell the police. She turned back uphill, angry, tears burned her. Yes, it was about revenge, but it was also about not letting it happen again. Not to anyone.

There was a shout, then, and a movement on the bridge caught her eye. A young man was in an altercation. Someone pushed his chest and he staggered back, only to face up to the other man again. He had his coat hanging off one shoulder, one arm free. Both had aggressive postures. Her first thought was that this must be her attacker, but she was shocked to recognize even from this distance that the bald, younger one with his coat hanging off was *Spider*. He must have followed her. It gave her a lift of pride; at the same time she immediately, without a decision necessary, moved towards him, worried.

The confrontation worsened by a degree. Spider was holding his arms out and blocking the other man's way. His head was angled back. He appeared to be inviting the other man to push him again – which he did. The bridge was like a stage slung in front of her, Spider was like a puppet, his exaggerated movements comical.

By the time she'd reached them, the fight had tumbled into the road. The other man, realizing he wasn't going to win, had stepped into the traffic to try to cross, escape. Spider was fearless, he didn't heed the danger from cars. His arms were still held out, his coat dragged on the ground, and she could hear coming from his throat, opened wide by the tilt of his head, a harsh, tuneless song. She also noticed, now she was closer, that dangling from his arm like an insect feeding from his blood was the syringe. The tie around his upper arm fluttered as he pursued the other man among the cars. Anjali felt dismay. She increased her pace to a run and shouted, 'Spider!'

The two men by some miracle reached the other side of the bridge. The victim was hurrying onward and Spider walked behind and imitated him: adopted the same prissy, angry gait and mimed the bag he carried, repeated the look backwards over his shoulder. Anjali had seen clowning like this performed in Covent Garden and in front of the Pompidou Centre in Paris. Spider could take on someone else's physical character – she wondered if he possessed other skills – was he a circus performer?

They were off the bridge and by now she'd caught up – just a dozen paces separated them. She called out, 'Spider!' He didn't appear to take any notice, but he gave up, with a sniff, then pressed one finger to his nostril, aimed the other one at the man in front and fired an oyster-sized dollop of snot. Then he veered away, tweaking the syringe from his arm and spinning it towards the railway sleepers containing the wrecker's yard. He ignored Anjali's calls, pulled on his coat and carried on back the way they'd come, towards Muswell Hill.

Anjali stopped at the place where he'd ejected the syringe and gazed after him. Who would have thought now, as he stumbled uncoordinatedly, out of place in this crowded breeding ground, that this was her boyfriend? Her parents would be furious.

She should find the syringe, it might injure someone – a child might find it. After several minutes' grubbing about she saw it, picked it up self-consciously between finger and thumb. She knew it should be disposed of professionally, not just chucked in a bin.

Another thought occurred to her: if she took it to a hospital and explained the situation, they might be able to test what was in it. If she knew for sure it was heroin, she could get him on a treatment programme.

There was a hospital in Highgate, whatever it was called. She walked back the way she'd come, up Colney Hatch Lane, through Muswell Hill and onwards, losing another hour in idle thoughts on the way, the syringe held unobtrusively at her side. It was made of clear plastic, it looked new, the needle was pristine. She was careful not to touch it – and she would wash her hands in the hospital toilets.

It was called the Whittington Hospital and she'd come here with her various injuries when she was a child and the name had been associated with the fairy tale. She wandered into the reception area. Everyone – even the staff, even the *building* – had a sickly pallor. She supposed she looked ill, too. She walked calmly up to the reception desk and put the syringe down on the counter and then explained what she wanted. Could they do that? Apart from the reception clerk, she was overheard by an elderly couple, a young dad with a pram and a porter. She felt their eyes on her, it was like they expected a lot from her: that she should change, grow up, wash – and the irony was, she felt herself to be more changed for the better, more grown up, cleaner in spirit, more ready to go, than ever before.

For some hours she waited, she had to speak to two or three more people. Eventually they came back and surprised her: they told her it was insulin, her boyfriend was a diabetic.

She was thinking so hard about Spider and his diabetes that she didn't know what to do with her hands, she smoked three of the cigarettes, one after the other, on the way back to Archway tube.

Ahmed climbed in, sighed, squirmed in his seat. He hitched his trousers, made himself more comfortable, slung the driver's seat back on its rail to make more room between his stomach and the steering wheel. He started the beast, then he was off. He tossed a mental coin, trying to guess Mila's shift. If she wasn't there, he had to give up now, admit he wasn't going to find her. She'd gone for ever. So, where was she now? Easier if the caravans had been still in the Retail Park, he could have kept an eye. How he'd built her into a tender dream! Ridiculous. Ahmed felt absolute 100 per cent fucking embarrassment. What was this, he was making a fool of himself over a schoolgirl he'd never even met properly. He was a married man. Yes, all of forty-seven years old – she could have been his daughter. Why did she live in his memory like this? He reached into his pocket and withdrew the flask. Ouzo swept into his throat, its thin heat flaming on his tongue and gums. More later.

He was in a long queue, inching towards home. Radio on. Business as usual. Waiting. Thick ropes of traffic. Endless brake lights – streamers of red, miles long. Weird, how many people. Making their way.

As always, he glanced at the slip road on the opposite side as he drove past the Muswell Hill exit off the North Circular. But – no caravans – it still looked odd. He half expected them all to come back and settle there again, like a flock of birds.

He sat back in his seat, rested. Stared. She was somewhere, after all – had to be.

An Audi veered across the bows of the Shogun; its engine tone rose and fell sharply as the unknown driver cheated in front of him, stole the use of the hard shoulder. Its certainty of purpose and youthful vigour – what did that make him? Middle-aged. Slow. Creeping back and forth between home to work. He watched the Audi disappear ahead of him.

One hour passed. Journey nearly over.

At the next exit he spun off, gave the power-steering a beating on the mini roundabout and high-tailed it for the dual carriageway. The power and authority of the grand vehicle buoyed him up. Another day of work done. Alcohol unbalanced his head, dulled his hands on the steering wheel.

He hit the dual carriageway for two seconds, triumphed over every other vehicle, busted the 50 m.p.h. limit wide open – he knew where the speedtraps were. For some reason the image of the Audi popped up in his mind – the way it had just used the hard shoulder, carelessly. He turned up towards Hendon and weaved his way through the lines of homes until he found his own. Still drunk.

As soon as he opened the door he started shouting in Turkish. His wife, familiar as an old coat, hurried out. She asked, 'What happened?'

He blamed the people behind him in the queue in Tesco's, they had taken his shopping bag. Why were people so *stupid*?! 'Idiots can't even take their own shopping!' He staggered, bumped against the kitchen chairs. 'Look!' He pulled out the gift box of champagne. 'And they have our milk and bread and chocolate cereal!'

She frowned, 'Ooof.'

'We've done better, though,' shouted Ahmed, tearing one bottle free of the cardboard wrapping. 'This is an OK champagne, man, very expensive.' He rummaged in the kitchen cupboard for glasses. 'They can keep the fucking bread and milk.'

Then Ahmed sat down and worked on his wife, he built up a bit of a row between them, eventually got it going. She admitted that yes, she did look at young men sometimes. 'See!?' he cried. 'You women are all the same.'

Nio and Mila, on the twenty-ninth of February, were shuffled sideways three steps by Nick the photographer. Nio's arm stayed across Mila's shoulders, hers was around his waist. They took up their new position, gave each other a self-conscious smile. Charmer malingered somewhere out of the way, in the background. In front of Nio and Mila were the few metres of jumbled graves, the camera on the tripod with Nick retreating now to lean over the viewfinder, while beyond, the giant beech showed its black fingers against the winter sky. The sycamore had already started growing its leaves, while beneath these sturdy giants a confusion of undergrowth lingered, waiting for the urgent competition of spring. Nio stood straighter, his chest was deeper, his heart more full, his arm stronger, he had his courage and Mila's as well it seemed in both hands. She had used the traditional prerogative given by the leap year to ask him to marry her – and he'd been proud to say yes. For an engagement ring, Nio's father had given him the gold band cut from his own father's little finger during the war, minutes after he'd died, and now it had been pinched to the right size and soldered with silver to fit Mila's hand. Nio's smile was easy, broad, confident. To have Mila, now, meant he'd climbed his mountain, taken command of his ship; he was twice the man he used to be, no, ten times, a hundred times . . . it made all the difference. She was here, under his arm. He cared about nothing else. It was as if yards and yards of love were unspooling in his breast and he could hardly cope, it was a kind of endless freedom. It had to show up in the photograph, he couldn't believe it wouldn't.

Nick loosed off half a dozen shots including a close-up of the ring, then walked the happy couple a yard backwards and directed them to stand either side of the notice pinned to the wooden shack and laminated in clear plastic against the weather; on it was printed a succinctly worded message that Haringey Council considered this structure to be in contravention of planning laws and so the order had been given for it to be demolished.

Stop smiling so much, instructed Nick, this was a different story now, not their engagement but the tearing down of their home. Look directly into the camera and point at the notice. He took some frames, but then paused. Not quite right, he suggested. They looked too happy. He proposed they should try and wear the same expression as might kidnap victims asked to hold up that day's newspaper as proof they were still alive. Think of it as a witness statement, not a holiday snap; this photograph was evidence.

Click – the camera's eye opened for a fraction of a second, took the image.

For the next shot, Nio was positioned in the ditch he'd dug to the allotments' water tank, the pick and the spade leaning against his hip. Mila was taller than him now, as she was standing on the edge of the ditch. Again – proof.

The next photograph was inside: Nio was on one knee in front of the pot-bellied stove, its hatch open. Nick requested movement, he wanted the blur of Nio's hand as he threw in a chunk of wood. This took several goes; Nio had to reach into the hot stove and take out the log, throw it in four or five times at different speeds. Nick wanted to see that there were flames burning in the stove. He asked for Mila to be in this photograph as well – but just her legs, her feet – an anonymous presence.

After that, they went upstairs: the window, the bed. They didn't pose much; he asked them to forget he was there.

Before it was over, Nio went and found Charmer, actually had to lay hands on him, it was the only way he could get him to come and be recorded for posterity.

Nick the photographer left, then, carrying his gear with him. Nio and Mila wandered, a bit mournful and sorry the place would be gone the following day. Mila told him he had to take the stove with him, he could ask Mrs Ginsberg to store it for him, or he could leave it in his parents' shed – in either case for however long it took to find a new home. And the window as well – she had the idea that the pot-bellied stove was the heart of this place, the window was its soul. If he could pull out those two things and save them, he'd have rescued the Clamp. Nio looked into the future, he could use the stove and the window somewhere else, in years to come – when he and Mila moved into a house next to the golf course, when they were having children. He'd dismantle them this afternoon, stash them somewhere nearby, in the undergrowth of the graveyard, until he'd arranged for transport.

They climbed the unguarded steps to the bedroom, Nio waved at Charmer below and thought that this slightly heavy, troubled youth was becoming smaller, Nio was travelling away from him fast, leaving him behind.

*

Charmer tried a song or two, made sure it was out of tune, but as usual nowadays, it didn't work. When their noises started up – strange animal snuffling, sighs and whispers, he couldn't bear it, he left.

He skulked along the fence which divided the playing fields from the cemetery. During the winter months, the cut flowers on the graves had appeared brighter than ever, they were dots of unlikely colour, this crop of grief thrown up more remarkably next to the various shades of grey – roads, overcast sky, leafless trees. Even now though, not even March yet, there were some changes. Buds were appearing, tightly wrapped, and grass grew underfoot. The flowers on the graves looked like they might have grown there. Global warming, must be.

A figure or two, he noticed, walked the neat paths. He wondered who they were, what dead person was it that they were coming to see? Charmer was alive and no one was visiting him. He was just in the way. He trudged on.

He stopped by the rusting skeletons of two of his scooters. All the plastic and paint had burned off; the heat had welded the metal components together. He kicked them. The wheel rims were sinking into the earth. He talked to them, 'Hey, stick around a bit longer.' He gave the carcass of the saddle an affectionate pat. 'Spread the word. Charmer's the guy with the scooters.' Then it was as if he were looking down on himself from a great height – a mop-headed, slightly overweight lad, morose expression, talking to a burned-out scooter?! Sad case, that was.

He wandered up to the Broadway, the busy commercial centre of Muswell Hill. Here it was worse, he found himself talking to a man who'd set up a stall with all the literature – fun pack and everything – selling subscriptions to the RSPB. Charmer stood and listened, but didn't take much of it in. He watched the guy carefully and felt a strange surrogacy, like this was his dad trying to look after him, bring him into the fold, include him. Birds in

Britain were losing their habitat. Your ordinary domestic cat was a villain. Charmer nodded, asked a few questions, but then he had to duck out when it came down to it; he didn't have the money to join the RSPB.

Back at the Clamp, there was no sign of Nio and Mila, not even a note. The pot-bellied stove had gone out and there was no kindling left. He tried to light it with a plastic bag, some bits of cardboard and a big log on top, but it didn't work. In the old days, Nio had always come home with a dozen branches under his arm, fuel for the stove and a surplus to dry out. Now there was nothing.

Charmer felt the waxy abrasion of dirt on his skin. Hunger and cold combined, he was having to wear all his clothes at once and the duvet he used felt damp and chill to the touch.

The following day Charmer was still in the Clamp, slowly going mad waiting for the bulldozers, when he heard a scratching sound, it freaked him a bit. He pulled open the door and there as if by magic was a cat, grey and silky, half climbing up the wall, sharpening its claws on the woodwork. It looked at him quickly, gave him this stare. He remembered the RSPB guy and called out to it, 'You're the villain.' Without hesitation the cat trotted over, searched the hand he lowered, bumped the side of its jaw along his knuckles. He went inside and found something it might eat: crisps and a crust of bread which curled at the bottom of the plastic wrapper. The cat showed a brief interest, then refused, but Charmer kept it nearby by stroking it until it was brave enough to come indoors. Later on that evening it patrolled the doorway constantly, it wanted to be let out. He kept it in until morning, but the minute he opened the door to leave himself, it shot out and was gone from sight in a few moments.

The next night, Charmer took the lantern torch and climbed the steps to Nio's bedroom. The window was a gaping hole; it was freezing. He lay under the covers, all his clothes on. He found a small silver radio and switched it on. A cheerful voice came into the room, filled it with talk about a folk festival. There was music, and then a conversation with a guest about line-dancing.

He fell asleep and woke to find the torch dimmer by half – the batteries were running out. As he switched it off his hands brushed the bare wooden floor, gritty and unvarnished. It was cruel, comfortless, in the dark. The radio spoke on, bringing its different world. He went back to sleep. It was a refuge. There were other people in his dream, he knew them, but when he woke it was empty again, he couldn't remember one person. He was stiff, cold. Another morning. Would the bulldozers come today? He took the radio downstairs. Someone to talk to.

He had to find somewhere else to go. Anywhere.

Little Vlad circled the girls – he was like an outrider; they were a herd of horses, trotting along, their legs flashing white in the dark. Peals of laughter rang out. Several of them carried alcopops, his sister Mila had a pocketful of Schnapps samplers she'd got from somewhere. It was automatic for Little Vlad to follow. Any amount of stuff could happen, the fish and chips girls were always good fun. Besides that he liked to see his sister drunk, she lit the place up, literally there were hands clawing at her as she moved among London's nightlife, she was a glittering plaything drawn through the crowd, everyone wanted her. He was her satellite, he kept her safe.

At the moment there was a gang of jewelled youths following them. Shouts between the two groups broke the night. Then, as they skittered along Charing Cross Road they crossed with an Asian girl, rough appearance, round faced, carrying a plastic bag, trousers scuffed and frayed at the hem, stained with road dirt who turned quick as a hound on a scent and tailed the group, a few yards behind. When they spilled off this side of the pavement to cross the road, Little Vlad clocked her, still with them.

The jewelled youth were harmless, but this girl wasn't part of the surface fun-mongering of tonight, she was for real, she might have accomplices, he knew the trick would be turned soon. Little Vlad carried on, scouted this left-hand side of the road, balancing on the edge of the pavement and wondering at the awesome night club queues. There were millions of people throwing themselves around carelessly, is what it felt like – exciting.

The youths hived off after their shouts and calls weren't answered. The Asian girl, though, stuck close to the group all the way to Centre Point. Little Vlad drifted to one side, watching for signs of whoever she was working with.

In a huddle the girls waited for the night bus back to Camden and Muswell Hill. They stamped their feet and sang. Little Vlad would make the same journey, but he hung back. Mila wouldn't include him, she'd know he didn't want to be mauled, breathed on, petted or laughed at by her friends. The Asian girl was still hanging around but it wasn't like she was waiting for the bus as well, there was definitely some business she had with the group. Little Vlad felt a professional interest. What was the game? The Asian girl began to speak to his sister Mila, and the rest of the group veered away, didn't fancy the homeless asking them for money, but Little Vlad shifted closer, he wanted to listen.

He took in the girl's appearance: a sheen on her face obscuring the brown skin like a mask, the chocolate eyes dead friendly so was she about to ask for money? Mila in her silver puffa jacket and jeans looked richly dressed.

'This?' Mila put her hand on the striped woollen bag hung from her shoulder.

'Hope you don't mind my asking, but I'm curious to know where you got it?'

Little Vlad knew this trick – pretend it's all about something else, not begging for money but just putting yourself nice and polite in the way, have some really generous conversation, give a lot, which somehow would swing around to taking something – it was a good play. Or – the girl would look at the bag closely and then snatch it and run off. The kindness in the girl's voice told him everything – she was a pro.

Mila nodded in his direction. 'My brother find it and I hand it for the police but no one says it's to them, so they gave it me—' She added, 'Why, is yours?'

'No,' replied the girl, smiling. 'But I recognize it. Enjoy the bag, it's a nice bag.' She gave a wave and began to wander away.

Little Vlad couldn't help admiring this – she knew how to light a slow burn, all right. He dawdled after her and called out, 'Hey!'

The girl turned and waited.

'You take the bag, then? Yeh?' suggested Little Vlad. 'Come back and steal it, is that your idea?'

As if it were a difficult question, she was frowning. Then she replied, 'No . . . It's just that I made it.'

'You made it?!' Mila was drunk, she was emphasizing everything.

The Asian girl nodded, 'I used to carry that bag with me all the time, I made it myself, so it must be the same one.'

'God!' Mila's face filled with pity and concern. 'You have it back with you—' She unhooked it from her shoulder. Little Vlad was amazed, Mila dipped in, handed him the A–Z, her make-up roll, her mobile, and . . .

'No, it's your bag now,' the girl said firmly, 'you must keep it.'

Little Vlad thought it wasn't possible – please don't believe that, he told his sister; it was the girl who'd made the bag, not likely. Mila was banging on, her voice twice as loud as normal, 'Is so mind-numbing, that you see it, you must have it back with you, so is yours.' Little Vlad saw what was like a change of weather in the girl's eyes, as if clouds were passing by fast and suddenly obscured her. The girl looked at the bag and then at his sister. 'I don't need it any more,' she insisted. 'It looks nice on you and it is a better home for it. It's just . . . good to know where it ended up.'

And now the girl was walking away . . .

Mila was chasing after her; Little Vlad followed, keeping his distance, looking for anyone she might be working with and keeping one eye on his sister who was walking alongside the other girl as they talked. His sister looked so young, in her clean clothes and in her fresh, new skin, her stride fluid. Suddenly Little Vlad felt older than Mila, more streetwise, she could so easily walk into something, it was a good job he was here.

'I don't need anything,' he heard the girl reply. Mila came to a stop; Little Vlad drew closer and together they watched the beggar girl walk on, diluted by the flow of people. Then a young guy with an ugly tattoo on his face suddenly appeared and tagged along with her – this was the danger sign Little Vlad had been waiting for. He took hold of Mila's sleeve, stopped her from following. She was talking non-stop, she took all the items back from Little Vlad and refilled the bag while explaining to him in an excited voice what had happened. 'Incredible, amazing,' she exclaimed. He didn't mind, he just needed to stop her from following, springing the trap. When she'd finished telling the story again Little Vlad shrugged – there was no magic in it for him, it was just a stunt that hadn't gone off.

'Amazing,' repeated Mila, 'that was the girl who made this bag.'

'So she says,' muttered Little Vlad.

'She wasn't lying,' replied Mila.

By now they were back with Mila's friends, the bus doors were opening and the crowd swirled towards the gap like water down a drain, but Mila caught hold of him – she took a pinch of cloth at his shoulder and swung him around.

'Whaaa—' asked Little Vlad, but he could have guessed, she wanted to give the girl some money for the bag, it wasn't charity then was it, just a fair trade, because the girl was poor, and they knew what it was like, what did everyone need, just a bit of kindness . . . He let this drift over him, it was part of the climate when you were around Mila. Things happened, this kind of nonsense had to be gone through. Now they were following this girl, again.

It was a fight to break out of the crowd around the bus and make their way towards the tube station. Little Vlad stared at the drunken men, looked right into their greedy eyes, returned their looks on behalf of his sister, keeping her safe. Among the thousands of fun-seekers there were the usual hustlers and drifters around the entrance to the tube – illegal cab drivers touted for fares, foreign students earned part of their own fees by handing out leaflets for the English language schools, the beggars held out against others to keep their pitches. Little Vlad knew some of these people; already he'd tapped into a hooded youth for a few minutes, but he kept one eye on Mila as she went down the steps to the underpass and wandered around, looking for the Asian girl. He caught up with Mila when she ducked into the foyer of the tube station itself, she was a grain of sand followed by a million other grains of sand, that was what it looked like to Little Vlad, he didn't want to lose her, it felt dangerous. There was shouting, music from somewhere . . .

It was difficult to prevent himself from being carried through the turnstiles by the drunken crowd. He swam sideways, followed her around and out the other side to the underpass that let out at Centre Point; this was where the homeless laid out their bags to take advantage of the warm air issuing from the tube's ventilation shafts.

When he caught up with Mila she was approaching a square box-like construction made out of cardboard packaging which blocked two thirds of the width of the walkway, forcing people to squeeze around. The panels were taped together and covered an area around three yards square, reaching to chest height. The top was draped with blankets of varying colours, neatly turned at the corners and sealed with brown tape.

Mila swayed in his grip – drunk. Trance was playing on a boom-box inside the cardboard house. They walked past but there was no door that they could see – it appeared closed off on all sides. They turned back and approached from the other direction. Who was in there? God knows.

There was a noise – made them jump – and now they could see the entrance: a cardboard flap stood ajar. Little Vlad caught sight of a flutter of movement through the angle of the door – it was something white which had flashed in the gloom. His sister was straining against his grip, she wanted to look inside, check whether or not the Asian girl was in there, pay something for the bag . . . No way was Little Vlad allowing that. He hauled her away.

Mila closed down her phone, she really didn't like that tune any more, she'd have to download another one off Steve at work, something cool this time, not funny, it was different when you had to listen to it twenty times a day, she got that many calls she needed something she could live with. A joke's a joke.

She broke into a trot, each footfall carrying her closer to Royal College Street, which was more of a home already than the car park and the slip road, if they could put up with the Adventists. Especially, if *she* could put up with one particular Adventist. Straight up, it was mad, if it wasn't the junior housing officer from Haringey it was this skanky priest or whatever he was from the church, seven days or something they believed in, she didn't want any of this, didn't want to deal with any of this *ever again*, he was really in her hair now, pure solid nuisance factor. She jogged back to the wire-fenced compound, unlocked the gate and walked down through the gap in the first row of caravans, and there were her lot, Social Services, The Home Office and The Kingdom of God, picturesque against the black plastic sheeting on the side of the neighbouring building but looking more battered than ever when you compared them to these other mobile homes which had been parked here for years and had practically taken root, turned into little houses with gardens around them and everything. Had that priest guy seduced all the women in these caravans, was that the deal? Is that how you got to stay here so long? She could believe it. She stood on the concrete block which served as a step and pulled open the door.

A greeting came at her in her own language, '*Buna ziua*, darling—' She was cross because although it was Little Vlad who'd said these words, she knew what it must mean – another bunch of flowers had arrived from her stalker, Jon Rawle, who'd trailed her here somehow – and sure enough, she pushed past her brother who was pursing his lips, trailing his new gameboy in one hand and pretending to kiss her, and there at the end of the trailer were sitting her mum and her cousin and on the fold-up table was a spray of flowers.

'*Nu!*' She stamped her foot, cursed, she so *didn't* want to be stuck with Jon Rawle, how had he found out where she lived?

'I love you,' mocked Little Vlad. 'These flowers are a sign of my great love for your ruby lips—'

She smacked the top of his head; everyone laughed.

'Your beautiful eyes,' went on Little Vlad, ducking away, 'your lovely hair, your touch on my skin—'

Again she went for him but he was ready, he climbed on to the seat, hid behind their mother. 'You are my love,' he crooned. 'Never leave me, please, until the end of the earth I will—'

'Shut up, idiot!' She picked up the flowers; the first thing she noticed was that there wasn't the usual little envelope. Did he know she was throwing them away? She asked everyone, 'Did you see him?' Her mother shook her head, no, the usual, the flowers were delivered. Mila picked them up, went to the window, wrestled with the stupid aluminium catch, pushed it up – it took all her strength – then dropped them out to join the rest. She peered out to see the pile, she couldn't bear to look at all those flowers, she shouted at them, 'Fuck off!' and then came back, pulled the plastic window shut.

Inside everyone was laughing. She grinned, cupped her hands to her mouth and shouted at the closed window, 'Fuck off you mad dog!!'

She chucked on a CD. She texted Nio, they made plans. If she could escape now, ride out of here on the sound of this music, live with Nio, get married, her residents' visa, she'd grow up massively this year, way ahead, in one leap . . .

Charmer went home. His parents were pleased, they even gave him money to encourage him to stay for a while longer. So he found himself back in this, like, *house*, with bath and toilet and central heating, it was a culture shock. His dad was a teacher and his mum a travel agent, they got up at the same time every day and left the Edwardian semi to go to work together, even on this first day of his return. It was a traditional Muswell Hill house, albeit too close to the North Circular for comfort. There was the usual stained glass in the front door and as it closed behind his parents Charmer was reminded of Nio's bedroom before the window had been removed, how the coloured light pitched through and gave the hallway, like, a druggy calm . . . it was strange that although he'd been brought up here, he was weirdly disconnected from it now.

There were good things – the dressing gown sat lightly on his shoulders, his whole frame felt brand new after a bath and a night's dreaming on a soft bed. The tiled floor of the hallway was cool on his bare feet. Just like the old days.

Now, a shadow swam in the pattern of coloured glass. He knew who it must be. He pulled the door open and sure enough, the postman stood there, bang on time, grinning and holding out a parcel which wouldn't fit through the letter box – Charmer felt like he was in the middle of a film of his own life and someone was about to be murdered and a little old lady would come and solve everything . . . It didn't matter, there'd been a result in it, for playing this part suddenly, because his parents had given him money. He couldn't help being cheerful, at the prospect of spending it. He went upstairs and climbed into clean clothes – bizarre, rich, he felt like he was eleven again.

He went downstairs. The blondwood flooring squeaked underfoot. Look at the chairs in here! Everything looked different to him now. Who was going to sit in all these chairs? There wasn't a speck of dirt in the place, curtains like from some big manor house, held back with gold ties – all that stuff. Charmer couldn't believe how much he'd just taken for granted, no wonder he'd wanted to escape all this.

The wedge of cash felt unfamiliar in his back pocket, but he loved it, that here he was with a bundle in his pocket. He stumbled on the phrase – pocket money – of course.

He let himself out of the house – not a nail to pull, but a five lever Chubb deadlock, this was what it was like to live on the OK side of the tracks. He went down to the newsagent's and bought a newspaper. He stopped off for a full breakfast, he was tight as a drum with all the food. He couldn't stop himself from thinking about a Panasonic widescreen TV and a Nokia 3311 mobile. Retail, those two would add up to more than a grand, so he wasn't up to that level yet. He shouldn't blow this money they'd given him, because it was meant to help him find a place to live. A dreary idea, never mind that – the only thing to do was to go shopping. Straight off, he bought Tommy Hilfiger strides and shirt. It felt good to drop cash like that – he wore the new clothes and stuffed the old ones in the bag. Then he trawled the Broadway, drinking a can of Special Brew as he went along, the other three cans dangling from his fingers. As he passed a bike or two he judged whether or not he could take them – but there wasn't the hunger to do it, with near enough a ton in his back pocket, still.

When he was back at home, Charmer went upstairs and stood in front of the mirror. He was there, the same as ever, with the same black eyes and the heavy flesh on his cheeks and the flop of hair and the same solid body – but dressed neat as a new pin in Tommy Hilfiger. It looked wrong. That was something else he'd always done as a boy – bought ridiculously bad clothes. He tore off the brightly coloured trousers, the top as well. How naff, to have that gay boy's name across his front! Who was Tommy Hilfiger anyway? Who cared?! He felt annoyed with himself. He emptied the carrier bag to get his old clothes back, then hung around, tried to get his feelings under control. It took a long time. Then he felt dead, and slow. And worried. That had been a mistake – wrong costume. How crap was that, to buy someone else's name for the front of his chest? Did he know who he really was? It was serious, this was his life going wrong, not hitting the right note. He told himself, from now on he wasn't going to pretend to be anyone else, not for Nio, nor for anyone, not for one minute. He was hurting badly. He walked into his old bedroom where he'd slept last night clean as a baby. Its lifeless calm was stirred up by the whirlwind of designer clothing and shopping bags. Bedding also was strewn around the room. He snatched up the Tommy Hilfiger's and pulled the cash from the pocket where he'd left it, tucked it back in his familiar jeans. He kicked his way back through the litter and went downstairs. He slammed the door on the way out, he was hoping the fancy glass would shatter and fall out but it stayed put. He walked, shaking his head vigorously to kick free of the fucking *dream world* he'd just strayed into, what was he thinking?

Yet, if he looked on the bright side he'd come out of it a clear sixty ahead overall. And there'd be more where that came from. His pace quickened. Run, get away from all this stuff in his head, these thoughts. Steer himself in another direction, away from Nio, away from his parents, quick. How about a *job*? That was what people did to get a life, find themselves, stand on their own two feet – why couldn't he do that? But what kind of job, what could he do, that anyone would pay him for? Once he had a job, he could leave home for good.

'Bike Mechanic,' he murmured. It was the only answer, look, he already knew how to smash the ignition, break the steering lock and drive away; putting it back together shouldn't be difficult. 'Get your arse in gear,' he told himself, 'come on Tommy Hilfiger, or what?' He burned off the half mile to Crouch End in no time. He ducked into one step of the gangsta, 'Do it man', then reminded himself no, stop that. He felt like some army guy, beating himself along like this. He had a plan: he'd walk into every sodding garage he could find. Wouldn't someone give him a start?

Lucas Tooth strolled around the outside of the wire-fenced enclosure in Royal College Street. The links in the fence blurred his view of the trailers, threw his sense of balance. He stopped, shook his head, waited for the synapses to connect in the right order. Sometimes the continual lack of sleep stacked up, then it was like a cloud of anaesthetic in his brain, he was softened, slow.

People passed by, either overtaking him or coming the other way, in both cases he was conscious of being observed, he stood out, he could smell their curiosity, even if they didn't directly look at him. He crouched, then, and delicately, with the backs of his fingers, he swept the pavement clear of grains of dirt, and into it he dropped one knee, clothed in immaculate white denim, it shouldn't be marked. Then he untied his shoelace, so he could tie it again. The glare of interest from passers-by subsided.

He glanced sideways; the caravans stood the same as before, in a row against the sheeted wall. Three of them. They weren't quite straight, the middle one was at an angle. Between the first two ran a rope, from which was suspended the dog's chain. The old Cortina was there, its lazy mouth propped open a couple of inches with a block of wood, the electrical cable looped into the window of the nearest trailer. He recognized the dull orange of the Calor Gaz canisters attending each one. Around them was an area of bare earth littered with small stones, from where the site had been cleared. The mound of rubble at the outskirts was like a defensive barrier in addition to the fence; both excluded Lucas Tooth. For a moment he hallucinated; the wave of broken bricks was coming towards him, knocked him over, its harsh, aggressive weight would bury him . . .

Silently, from this distance away, he advised Mila what everyone walking this earth should know – in any attempt to defeat him, there would only be a more sure guarantee of his winning.

Slowly he tied the first shoelace, then dusted clean another square of pavement – and for a moment he was on his knees, oddly. Not a customary position for Lucas Tooth; it was almost funny. He couldn't think of a prayer, but the idea of one came to mind, briefly, before he brought the second shoe up, untied that shoelace, tied it again. The sound of people moved around him, he was inconspicuous among the clicking of a woman's heels, the murmuring of rubber soles, the hum of traffic. Even without the heat of their suspicion, he wanted everyone else gone, it was difficult to concentrate on this one sister when there were so many coming from all directions, interfering, no wonder his brain was muddled, not focused enough. He wanted to sweep everyone else away, as if with one movement of his arm across a cluttered table, just so Mila could be attended to and her resistance . . . answered. Yet, to be effective right now, spying on her, he had to become smaller, disappear among the clump, the mass of people, be insignificant.

This time, as he looked over, he directed his gaze at only one thing. He sucked up the meaning, he fed off the insult. His flowers, the ones he'd bought, paid to have delivered, complete with tempting envelopes, wilted in an untidy pile under the window of the middle trailer, the one branded 'Musketeer', the trade name written in slanted mock-handwriting across its rear. He knew, from previous stalkings of this site, that the flowers had been thrown out fresh, as soon as they were delivered. Yet, the envelopes had always, without exception, been taken off.

That was callous.

The sweethearts lay naked under a duck-down duvet in Elinor Ginsberg's guest room. Nio was awake, propped on an elbow, watching Mila asleep. He'd wanted a photograph of her just like this, if a camera could read such a tentative light. Her face was tilted, her mouth open just a fraction, as if she was sipping at the magic night air. Her shoulder blade held a pocket of shadow. The duvet was a luxurious covering for his treasure.

He watched her mouth work, as if someone had put a drop of liquid to her lips. Her closed eyes fluttered. She was dreaming.

Mila was approaching the cliff's edge, there it was, steadily nearer. The grass ended in a jagged line drawn with white chalk; beyond was the blue void of sky and sea. She walked too confidently – a panic gripped her – the cliff might crumble beneath her feet but she stood at the very lip, her body fearless, separate from the panic in her mind. The cliff was a jumble of outcrops: grey and white rock dropped two hundred feet to a beach, where a figure lay. She knew the figure was herself. It was curled like a shrimp, the white shirt a flag, her head neatly resting on her hands – was she asleep or injured? Had she fallen from the cliff? As if to answer the question she stepped over the edge and felt a surge of gravity, there was nothing to hold her up and then fright segued into relief and amazement, because she was flying.

Beneath, a figure approached, walking this long and flexible stride, and stood over her where she lay. She could see the top of his head, the black curly hair moved by the breeze, which also tugged at his shirt. She recognized Nio and felt glad. His shoulders were a broad plank she might alight on, if she chose. She called to him, although there was no sound. As she watched, he crouched next to her on the sand and touched her cheek with the back of his hand. There was no reaction from her figure. Then she watched as he scooped her up. She lay prone in his arms. High above, she felt the return of gravity, the air squalled around her noisily, vertigo was an electric current suddenly plugged into her, there was nothing that would save her. Then, as abruptly as it had started, it was over, she was safe in his arms, enclosed . . .

Nio followed the tic of blood pulsing in her eyelid. She was in a dead sleep. Her blonde hair was scruffy, tied in places, decorated with coloured beads. Her thick brows were relaxed, the gap between them gave her face its open look.

He stayed awake, listened to the birds start their first, shy calls. He was waiting for the first rays of the sun to brighten the curtains. Then it came, this dawn tide, and at the same time his love for her lifted him with absolute certainty to a place that he now knew existed – here it was – heaven on earth. He woke her with kisses to her eyelids and forehead. He planted kiss after kiss; she stirred in his hands and spoke incomprehensibly, in her own language.

Sleep fell away from Mila and she felt his lips on her face, neck. As she came out of her dream she knew she was perfectly OK, sorted, on the right track. She straightened out in the bed so Nio could lie along the whole length of her; she loved his weight. She opened her eyes and saw him an inch away . . . magic.

Nio kissed her on the lips, put a hand to her breast. His smell filled her. When she put a hand on his shoulder it felt smooth and hard as iron, except warm. He was naked, he gleamed marble-white but patterned with light. On his chest was a fan of hair.

He cupped her face, looked at her.

She kissed the palm of his hand, watched him just like he watched her, before she pulled his shoulders. He turned her on her side, lifted her knee on to the crook of his elbow. Her voice came to him almost as disembodied from where she lay, a white shadow printed by the early spring light. He knelt, poised, and when they moved it was with all the ease of lovers who've made it in different places, they found their way quickly to where they wanted to be, the edge of their greatest pleasure and running fast for the boundaries. He watched closely for the blood to rise to the surface of her skin; she made sure she caught the look in his eyes when he came, the leap into the distance when she captured him. She wanted to arrive at a great truth she knew was there, waiting to be owned and understood, about love.

They stayed, curled up. This was home, his body was her territory, she was falling further and further into Nio.

SIX

Anjali leaned on the parapet of Blackfriars Bridge and looked down on the River Thames, grey and heavy as oil. She tried to work out which way the river was going – upstream or down? The tide ebbed and flowed twice a day, so maybe the same piece of water constantly ran back and forth past the same spot for ever. It couldn't be true – the water made its way to the sea eventually, only hindered by the backflow – yet she clung to the idea of this river acting like a pendulum, swinging to and fro while history unfurled from the Palace of Westminster, visible from here, pale gold in the sunlight, straight out of a fairy tale. And perhaps, she thought, time itself was like that, it wasn't a straight line which started at the big bang to continue unbroken until it ended with a whimper, but rather it was a rubbing away at the same spot, back and forth, it was like a polishing of our understanding of the world, so it brightened, became sharper, but also smaller and less mysterious. Somewhere ahead of her, she knew, lay God, or a God-like idea. Maybe there was a gravity pulling everyone in that direction, a small, constant undertow which couldn't be ignored, it would win in the end . . .

She walked along the bank of the river towards the Palace and crossed Westminster Bridge. She stopped in the middle and leaned over the rail, blotting out the race of traffic behind her and putting herself among the swirls and rivulets of the water. The ironwork felt hard against her ribs – she had lost weight. City grime had added an extra tone of darkness to the skin of her hands, she noticed, as she stretched them towards the river. She stayed on the bridge for some minutes, watching the sunlight gild the tops of the wavelets as they marched the surface, her fingers a sillhouette against this pattern . . . She pulled out the packet of Camel Lights. Two left. She took one and lit it, then turned the packet in her hands. She couldn't quite read the surname any more, the ink had smeared too much.

She begged all afternoon from the tourists who had started to visit now it was the end of March and the schools had broken up for the Easter holidays. Slowly she meandered back through Trafalgar Square, up Charing Cross Road and into Soho.

As the evening wore on, London began to sink into the usual vortex of energy and danger. The noise of people was heightened, drunken. Chaos threatened. She went looking for Spider. When she caught up with him, two men had his arms in the air like posts, twisting them to bring his head low, to meet the bigger man's knee as he lifted it two, three times. Without thinking she ran and jumped at the closest one, she wrapped her legs around his waist and wound her hands in his hair and pulled. 'Leave him alone, get off him—' The man spun, he unlocked her feet from around his waist and then she was flung from his shoulders like a sack of corn. She was aware of an audience growing, people were shouting. She screamed, 'Leave him alone, I'll call the police—' She could see now that he was a heavy-set man, he looked angry and bewildered. He pointed at her, 'You are fucking crazy.' Then he turned and walked to Spider who was on the ground, the other man's knee in his back. Anjali heard them talking, then they left him alone, walked off. The bigger one turned and thumbed his chest, 'We are the police, all right?'

Anjali shouted after them, 'He's a better man than either of you! He's a *better man*!' She was hoarse with anger, tears burned her.

Spider was on his feet now, careless of the blood flushing his nose. He was staring at her, didn't spare even a glance for the two men walking away. She asked, 'Are you all right?' She was frightened by the sight of the blood which looked black in this dark street, it occasionally glinted red as light strayed from overhead.

For some minutes she stood and watched Spider wander around. The blood reached his shirt. He mooched in the gutter, bending once or twice to pick at something. He pulled at the handle of a long-closed bar-restaurant, idly, to see if it would open. Then he ambled over to her. She kept up a stream of suggestions, 'Shall we go home? D'you want to go to Casualty? Let me clean it up?' Then he came and stood opposite her. The cobweb crawled over half his face, one eye poked through. Beneath his nose was an apron of blood. He stared unblinking.

She returned to their cardboard house in the underpass – from time to time Spider would appear in front or beside her but never for long, mostly he tailed behind. When they reached their home they had to turf out a drunk who didn't know the scene. Spider made short work of him; then they were alone. Anjali clawed into Spider's clothes, unbuttoning, unzipping, she wanted to get hold of him. Then his weight banged into her, merciless. His hands were claws fixed on her shoulders. She stared at his eyes tightly closed in his face as he worked at her, his mouth heavy with blood and set in a grimace, saliva hissing as he panted through clenched teeth. She wanted to know where his mind was, she didn't know if this was pleasure or not, for him. Quickly, repeatedly, she stroked his back, held him close, and gave him the words 'I love you' again and again, the words lost their meaning as her gaze wandered over his punctured skin stained with the cobweb, she watched his closed eyes and once or twice touched them. The pain carried her off, her repeating of the words became a broken rhythm crudely set by his hips. He gained momentum; as he finished there was a moment of animal joy in her, buried deep underneath the pain and distress: she had won a piece of him that was incorruptible and innocent, she loved it, it was a treasure tossed to her. It was only brief, then she waited, there was silence except for his blowing.

After a while their breathing settled, then he softened, fell asleep.

Anjali remained awake; she kept stroking his back. How far she had come, such a long way . . .

Mila wore flared jeans, tyre-bottomed trainers with a three inch stack, a crop-top and the baby-blue short fur jacket for warmth. Her loins were a flat cut of muscle, she moved quickly, she was well in charge of herself, she was totally and utterly sorted, she had the man, the job – and the place to live was about to happen . . .

Through the station concourse Little Vlad was a satyr around her, omnipresent, he was the familiar to the witchcraft of her good looks. She turned right out of the station, headed for the underpass. As she began the gentle descent along the concrete tunnel, a block of daylight was let in via the steps up to New Oxford Street and she paused to take advantage of a signal to return her texts. The daylight caught her bowed over her mobile, her thumb moving on the keypad, the dozen ribbons tied into her hair threads of colour in the drab underpass, the headphones delivering the Toploader CD, her stance perfectly balanced; she was herself an indrawn breath, a moment of promise, and even as she stood there she knew, for certain, yes, message, she was a love-thought in Nio's head some miles away, she knocked back a reply to him, *message sent*, she wanted the future they held out for one another.

When she'd finished with her phone she moved on and the sunlight split like cracked ice and freed her to the underpass.

She walked towards the square cardboard house. A further

wing had been added to it since she last was here; the side of this development was printed with the word 'Indesit'.

She drew closer. Little Vlad appeared at her side, overtook her and was first at the entrance. He crouched to look inside. She lifted a foot to his shoulder and pushed. He didn't fall but wheeled away; she ducked and peered in, 'Hello?' She smelled incense – and sure enough a candle burned dangerously in this house of card.

She heard the reply from within, 'Hello?' – and she smiled, she marked this moment, wanted to fix it in her memory because she hoped it would be the start of her career in fashion design, it was the story she'd tell when she was famous, it all started here . . .

Anjali, her name was. Mila explained what she wanted – she had this new job working part time on a retro seventies clothing stall in Camden and she could sell a dozen of these bags every week, just like the one Anjali had made. She reckoned she could get so much for them, which meant she could pay half of that to Anjali for the manufacture.

Anjali didn't want to knit bags, but told Mila she could copy the pattern, get someone else to do it on a machine, then just stitch on the little bells by hand. It would be more profitable. Mila said she'd do that and give Anjali a royalty for every bag she sold. They shook hands on it.

During the following weeks Mila went down there loads of times to discuss what else they could design together, often she visited before or after her nights out with friends, and she would huddle under a blanket with Anjali. She liked to watch the older girl smile, she liked her music, everything she said, the way she thought about life and translated her thoughts into actions. Mila felt a lurch of pity at Anjali's face which was always a bit dirty with no make-up, but if she asked what had happened, why she was here, where she'd come from, Anjali avoided the question.

Often Spider's boots stuck out from the cardboard extension

they'd built, it was like a dead man lying in a drawer in a mortuary. They'd talk more quietly, not to disturb him.

There were usually some minutes of silence between them; and Mila liked that about coming here – it was a secret world where nothing needed to be said. This cardboard building, the smell of incense, serious Zen and Radiohead . . .

Mila compared herself to Anjali. Mila was taller, yet Anjali was older, twenty, she must have dealt with quite a few guys already. She'd been to college and Mila sucked up the older girl's experience, she wanted to find her way ahead, go to study fashion, perhaps at Middlesex just like her – because if she and Nio were married then she could get residency, he was born in this country so it would be all right. Plus, she could get the free English lessons the government gave in Leicester Square, as well. She also told Anjali they thought they'd found a place to live together up in Barnet, because it was close to Nio's work and it was cheaper than Camden. They had to do something quick, they only had Hilly's room for a couple more weeks and the Clamp was over, it should have been demolished by the council already but for some reason hadn't been, yet, but they couldn't go back there in any case and she didn't want to go back home. She was full of plans, Anjali helped her identify what to do next, what bits of paper she'd need, which numbers, what qualifications, assets. They exhausted her future, put her, yes, at the same college as Anjali, if they could get in somewhere together. Anjali often read a book. Mila would feel the magic of their friendship steal over her – how instantly it had happened, that she could lie here next to this girl without a word passing between them and both of them remain in their skins, so comfortable. There was no one else that Mila could think of, like that. She wanted to be the same.

Once, Mila even fell asleep. When she awoke, the atmosphere had changed: There were many more feet going past – it was noisy. Spider was awake, bent over his knees, both hands testing for stubble on his shaven head. Mila glanced at Anjali, who was reading. Mila liked Spider but only because Anjali did.

Her friend then put down her book and took out a battered-looking packet of cigarettes. There was only one left. She picked it out, Mila noticed it was bent out of shape. The older girl stared at it for a while, then put it back in the packet.

Spider's hand stopped checking the surface of his skull and he reached into his breast pocket for tobacco and papers. His head stayed low, the unhealthy tattoo spanned one side of his bare skull. His fingers, Mila noticed, moved deftly to encase the tobacco. He put it to his lips; like a reptile he swept his tongue along the gummed edge of the paper and then sealed it. When he looked up, Mila looked elsewhere. In the gloom of the cardboard house he was a powerful, violent presence. Mila didn't like to feel chicken, she knew she had to like him because Anjali loved him.

Anjali was rummaging to find some more music.

The cigarette hung in Spider's fingers, a perfectly tight stick of tobacco. That stillness, Mila thought, was like a tiger's, he was ready to strike. She wanted Little Vlad to come back; she and Anjali needed someone else to dilute the place – Little Vlad would take the charge out of the air.

A glance at Anjali told her she was right, they were both waiting for him to go off. She reached for the cider bottle, unscrewed the plastic cap. She needed to be doing something. Maybe it was time to go, soon.

The cigarette moved; as if on its own accord it walked through Spider's fingers, appearing and disappearing; it should have been crushed and broken but it remained slim, straight. Then it walked back between his knuckles and arrived at his thumb and forefinger again. She and Anjali watched, entranced.

Without looking up, he held the cigarette out to Anjali. For a moment, she did nothing. Spider drew it back, offered it again, this time with a definite push of impatience.

'Thanks—' Anjali took the cigarette as gently as one might have withdrawn the Sword from the Stone. She pegged it in her lips and that prompted another offering from Spider, he snapped open the body of his lighter, then with a wipe of his palm against the flint wheel a small fire burned in the top. Anjali swayed towards the flame. 'Thanks,' she said again. She turned to Mila and said, 'I only have one every now and again.' Then she added, 'I never smoked or drank, before.' Mila felt tears suddenly, at those few words, because she guessed there was so much behind them, the whole story of why Anjali was here . . . No one would believe it, the bag had brought them together but, over these last few weeks, it was as if a thick, densely woven rope had sneaked around them, pulled them tight. She wound an arm around her new best friend's shoulders, they both knew how life was, they were dealing with guys, just sliding through as best they could, and they were going to get qualified, whatever, they both had rich, rich lives, yes, that was it, they were totally sorted.

Lucas Tooth was trying on new clothes when someone tried to barge into his changing room; the guy called sorry through the cubicle door and backed off quickly but it was enough to drive Lucas Tooth mad, he checked the bolt was still across OK and then leaned back, knocked his head against the padded wall of Charli's for Men, rolled sideways, his feet caught in the new clobber on the floor – a couple of white shirts, some chinos – that he could steal easily because of the sales girl he'd turned in here last year, but he wasn't thinking of clothes, or the sales girl, or the scrum of people in the cubicles on either side, he was going fucking mad over just that one person too many breaking into his personal space . . . who was it, who'd tried to burst in on him? He leaned his shoulder, forehead against the furred material of the partition between cubicles, swaying from side to side, kicking the gear out from underfoot, cursing and looking down at his hands. The blade was locked open, held against his wrist, and where the sharp edge pressed into the skin he could sense underneath the tough, gristly sheath that carried the arteries to his hand. One hard swipe and he'd redecorate these four walls. 'Do it!' he told himself. Not enough sleep, that's what made him hanker for a final, unending darkness.

He leaned back, spreadeagled, knees bent, he stuck the blade in the wall, stared up at the ceiling. There were too many people, it was maddening. He had flashes of the sisters dancing in his mind's eye, Mila lifting her hand to protect her eyes against the sun, the face of that girl turning sideways, the nose stud glinting, the shame of the mother on the phone in Birchwood Avenue, the anonymous bodies of the Tesco sisters as they tilted to sit on the bog. Too many sisters, too many mothers . . .

From the cubicle on one side of him there was laughter, while from the other side there came a sound as if furniture was being lifted, and then in front of him he heard the sales girl's voice, 'Are you OK in there?' He didn't answer, just pulled on the flimsy half-door hard enough to shear the pencil bolt clear off and he walked, ignored everyone, his eye on the exit. He was out of there, on the street. He caught his shoulders twice against passers-by, he was walking fast, straight, unforgiving, everyone else had to get out of his way. As he went he folded the blade shut and threw it hard into a skip. None of that.

He kept walking. The hot afternoon pressed on him. Traffic fumes thickened, constricted his breathing. In his head he trawled his list, there were around eight mothers and sisters he had under control, he should have one of them right now. He turned down Coniston Road, and immediately there was the sense of an invasion, a school was letting out its pupils and the cars picking them up were jammed solid, the pavements thick with a swirl of parents, nannies, children. He had to sidestep, then pause for half a second . . .

Muswell Hill thickened to a critical density in Coniston Road now, the school opening its doors caused a sudden increase in the population which meant that for one moment everyone had to halt, or step sideways. The cleaner on his way to work was blocked by the stream of children pouring across the pavement, while the children themselves came up against the edge of the road and so their line bunched, jammed solid, plus the bus driver on diversion around the roadworks on the Broadway was going too quickly and nearly hit the back of the Range Rover belonging to the woman who ran the fruit and veg shop, she was picking up her youngest son from the school and was reversing into a parking space but had to jam on her brakes because the bus was right up her arse, and then Tony the Sweetshop Boy was walking back from the Broadway, nodding along without paying attention, staring at the ground, so he came up against some guy who'd stopped short and he had to dance quickly around him, just catching him with his arm . . . it was a tangle.

Lucas Tooth hated being thrown off his stride, his balance interfered with, it infuriated him, not only that but some idiot behind him wasn't looking where he was going and jogged his arm as he went around; and it was a crazy coincidence but on top of that, here – right here – lived the sister he'd turned over all those months ago, the one with black curly hair and the stud in her nose, he'd forgotten her, never visited again, she didn't have anything he needed, but as he passed the door it flew open and this middle-aged woman came out of nowhere and bumped him, like he wasn't there, she didn't see him at all, and for these two crimes against his person a fury rose in Lucas Tooth, it just tipped the balance, it really was the sorry end of the world as it should be, thc apology she gave him didn't count, he wasn't going to be treated like this. He kept going, didn't acknowledge anything, anyone, the street, the cars, the sky, the people, he stripped them all away, there was only the inside of his head and its sleepless hunger.

Elinor Ginsberg and her deputy gave each other a look – they both dreaded what was coming. You're not a member of Haringey's Home Birth Team without having to deal with stuff like this.

The poor girl huffed and puffed, moaned, squirmed, then she drew a big breath, held it. She was leaning forward against the tiny kitchen counter, head flung up, there was hardly room for her to wave her hips from side to side, the centre of the pain was right in the middle of her, Elinor did sympathize. Then she let it go, she really *screamed*, it was wall-blasting quality, for a full thirty seconds, four or five breaths' worth. Elinor's teeth were set on edge, the hairs prickled on the back of her neck, the pain was a knife in her head. The cheap wine glasses in the cabinet rang, gently. The stereo speakers answered back.

They had a screamer.

A muffled voice came through from the other side of the wall, 'Shut the fuck up!!'

Elinor went to her bag and took out earplugs; it was dangerous to be in close quarters with that kind of volume. Her deputy, she noticed, had not only put cotton wool in her ears but now placed a pair of Walkman headphones over the top as well. She tucked the trailing wire into the neck of her midwife's uniform.

The contraction passed. The girl sobbed, her mouth turned down, her eyes were shocked. She moaned, turned away and waddled into the other room. It was the only place to go in this first floor flat in Coniston Road. No one was going to escape.

Elinor followed. The flatmate was there, holding on to her pregnant friend, a leaning post, bringing her down on to the sofa.

The girl knelt on all fours, rested her head on the sofa. Two or three other friends looked on anxiously, she wanted all of them to witness this, it seemed, lacking a mate. It hadn't been part of the birth plan, they'd have to go, except for the one nominated as birth partner.

First things first; Elinor was trying to attach the monitoring belt around the girl's middle when she gave that same warning: the moan, the big lungful of breath held for a while, the eyes opening in terror, the diamond stud in her nose a glittering point behind the tumbling black hair as her head nodded forwards. Then she let it go, several long screams, like she was being killed. The windows vibrated, Elinor's temples were tweaked with pain.

Elinor remembered the police at the same time as she heard the siren. She had the monitoring belt on the girl now, so she could spare a minute to dial the Muswell Hill station. The siren was closer as they answered. She quickly explained they'd be receiving calls about a girl screaming in Coniston Road, but no one was having a hot skewer stuck in them, it was only a young single mother, who'd got pregnant by a man she'd met in a bar whose last name she didn't even know, having her baby now. By the time she'd finished the call, the police car was outside, slewed to a halt.

The girl's screams tailed off. The sirens stopped. The flatmate and the other birth partners all looked shocked, white. Elinor needed to clear this place, it was too cluttered with girls, there were too many conversations, too much fear, not enough peace. And the room wasn't warm enough.

However, no sooner had she got rid of most of them than a gang of boys turned up. They carried cans of beer and the first scream had their eyes popping, they were laughing, sitting in a line on the sofa, rocking back and forth in disbelief. Elinor was holding the girl's forehead as she lay in the bath. At her elbow was the other wall of the bathroom, it was that small. She asked the birth partner to push the boys out.

By the time the baby was born, tidied up and warmly wrapped, Elinor felt more than ever before like a bar of soap being squeezed out of a pair of hands, even with the carrying of her bag she shot out of the front door so fast she bumped into someone in the street, a man, there was the blur of his aftershave on her senses, she apologized but he said nothing, and he kept going as if she weren't there, like his head was somewhere else and no one else existed, which increased her sense of having been divided. Could it be true that the more people there were, the less value each person had, like each individual was diluted, became . . . smaller? And there was that expression, the madness of crowds – for instance, during football matches, the crowd itself became a person, an ugly person. Her life's work at a stroke became sinister, like she was in a science fiction story, seeding more and more of these creatures, people, until they took over the earth . . .

Nio turned up alone on the doorstep of 17 Newton Avenue, Barnet, at 9.15 in the morning. Mila couldn't come because of the part time job working on the clothing stall in Camden Market, she didn't want to upset her new employer by asking for the morning off, it was only her fourth week.

He had a bag of spare clothes with him, he was that confident everything would be all right. The money was a solid lump in his pocket – Mila's contribution plus his own made it more than any amount of cash he'd ever carried. He'd been instructed to have it with him, otherwise he'd lose the place.

A man and a woman with two small children waited at the gate also. Nio nodded a greeting to both of them.

The man asked, 'You on social?'

Nio smiled. 'No . . . you?'

The man shrugged, but didn't say any more. Nio tried to think of something with which to carry on the conversation, but – nothing. Instead they waited in silence.

Seventeen Newton Avenue was a newly appointed 'Dinglis' – there were hundreds of them named after a notorious landlord, but he wasn't the only one to make a fortune out of buying cheap London town houses and converting them into multi-occupancy dwellings and then letting them to as many large families as possible on income support and housing benefit. Nio and Mila were paying over the odds, therefore, because they had to match the money available from the local council to house displaced families, but it was all they could find, given the deadline of Hilly's return from America and the Clamp about to be pulled down at any time. They'd get into this place, then try and find somewhere cheaper and better, as soon as possible.

At 9.30 sharp, a young man in a burgundy suit jumped smartly out of a Vauxhall Astra and came to them, manipulating a string of keys, all with differently coloured tags. 'Morning Gentlemen.'

Nio returned the greeting; no one else did.

They followed him into the house. The hallway had been blocked in and divided into four entrances. The young man unlocked three of the doors and glanced inside each room – one was the shared bathroom, the other two were self-contained living quarters. His examination took in the fabric of the interior, he didn't say a word to the occupants. The sound of TV flared and then became muted. Nio and the others were crowded in the hallway and could glimpse the faces of people, sullen at being disturbed, and piles of stuff – children, bedding, clothes – before the doors were closed again. The young man then unlocked the fourth door, which opened on to the staircase. They followed him up to the first-floor landing. From here, identical doors led on to a shared bathroom and three more self-contained units.

'Who's in D?'

The other guy raised his hand.

'This is you in here.' The young man held the door open. 'If you go in and wait, I'll come and deal with you one by one.' Then he added with heavy irony, 'In the privacy of your own homes.' He moved to the next door and unlocked it. 'E?'

Nio raised his hand and gave a polite smile. 'That's us.'

'Here you go.'

He was let into a room facing on to the front of the property, which would have been a bedroom in its former life. A breakfast bar had been built in one back corner, enclosing a gas cooker, a sink and kitchen units. In the window bay was a sofa bed and fixed against the side wall was a folding table.

Nio put down his bag, and waited alone in the room. He took in the radiator: there was central heating, he remembered. A proper cooker, yes. The shared bathroom – he and Mila were looking forward to having a bath in their own place. He was frightened at how blank and charmless it was but he and Mila would bring some magic to it, make it OK.

He went and stood behind the breakfast bar – proper units with doors. He opened one and smelled the newly cut chipboard. Everything was in pristine condition. He turned a tap – there was hot and cold running water. He twisted the knobs on the cooker and there was a hiss of gas, it must have been switched on at the mains, good. He could heat up some dinner for them. The next cupboard revealed the miniature Potterton boiler for the water and central heating.

Here, he and Mila would live. They'd sleep on that bed, draw open the curtains, cook their meals here, it was their first home, even if only for a few months. He noticed that the sealant around the edge of the sink had come adrift: he took the white tail of polymer and pressed it home.

Then, the suited man came in and interrupted his reverie. He was checking his list. 'Neeo, Neeop—'

'Niopolous, yes,' said Nio.

'And Mila Rose—'

'Rosapepe.'

'Blimey. Couple of tongue twisters, you are.' The man hitched his trousers and parked himself halfway on to a stool. He sheafed through his paperwork and teased out two sets of pages stapled together. 'Nighpolous and Rosypeppy,' he repeated. 'Here we go. Double occupancy, where is she?'

'Err . . . my girlfriend, she's working.'

'That's cool, just write her name down as well. You're both of you severally responsible for the whole of the rent, whatever. The contract is pretty simple, you only have to understand a couple of things. A month's rent in advance. A month's deposit. You're up for any damage of course, and for maintenance of the property and the goods and chattels.'

Nio nodded. 'OK.'

'The deposit is non-refundable,' he added, 'we hold that against wear and tear on the decor, which always, always comes to more than that but it helps us, you know, towards the cost of running the place.'

'Right.'

'So, you've got some money for me then?'

'Yes, sure.' Nio withdrew the folded notes from his shirt pocket. He had earlier counted the exact amount and now he watched the other man check it. Suddenly he had a picture of Mila, how hard she worked, she just went at it, ate it up.

'That's fine. Now I just need your paw print.' He turned the papers until he reached the end page of both copies of the contract and positioned them in front of Nio.

As he signed, Nio was handing over two thirds of his working week to renting this place, but it wouldn't be for long, they'd find somewhere cheaper, better, given time. Still, there was the sense of excitement, their first home together. He signed his name on both copies of the contract and then stopped, the pen held over the paper, as he saw his future – they were getting married, she was going to sixth form college or the London School of Fashion, he was working, they . . .

The man was tugging at the contracts and talking – Nio hadn't been listening. He leaned back. The pen was being taken from between his fingers. He almost had to shake his head to clear the vision of Mila. The man was saying goodbye. There came a grating sound – two sets of keys were lying on the kitchen surface. Nio picked them up. He was standing in a studio flat in Barnet, North London, belonging to himself and Mila.

Once the landlord had gone, he patrolled the boundary of their quarters. The folding table worked. He sat on the sofa bed and thought about where to get sheets and a duvet. Maybe they should be new?

There wouldn't be enough room in here, to store the pot-bellied stove and the circular window from the Clamp, they'd take up too much space, get in the way. When he'd organized the transport, he'd take them from their hiding place and store them somewhere safe, in his parents' garden shed or at work . . .

His phone called him – message. He thumbed his way to it. He was headshakingly admiring of how fast Mila's fingers moved over the keypad, how fiercely came her thoughts and feelings, this message took up two slots, she'd just pressed the send button when she'd run out of space, sent another one straight on the heels of the first. 'I really luv u number 1 and want u pls cum n meet me off the bus if u can we shll go mad togethr n I will really giv to u I wnt to deal with u, nio don try n stop me I hav—' Then came the hiccup, he scrolled to the next message where it continued, '. . . a so full heart 4 u and frever I am urs.'

An insane grin took him over, he couldn't stop it spreading. What would Mila say, when she arrived, walked in here? She'd love it. Yet, against the palette of this room – white, clean, new – he himself appeared clumsy, tired and dirty and it occurred to him that he could just make his way right now to the shared bathroom, turn on the taps and have a bath – the mad luxury of this made him laugh. Their own bath! Of course. He took his keys, unlatched the door which he could feel was light as a feather, barely heavier than the air it pushed aside, so they weren't firedoors. On the upstairs landing he felt exposed. Any of the occupants of 'D' or 'F' could suddenly appear. He quickly unlocked the bathroom door and went inside. There was a small aluminium bolt and he drew it across. In the utter silence, he was glad to twist the hot tap and hear the boiler ignite. A thin column of water found the drain. He put in the plug and felt the water steadily heat.

The bathroom suffered the impersonal coldness of the rest of the house yet it was his and Mila's to use, any time they wanted, he'd never have to take her around to his parents' house again. No more would he have to undress beside a bucket filled with cold water stolen from the allotments' supply and use a flannel and a sticky bar of soap.

While he waited for the bath to fill he took off his clothes. His body was waxy from layers of dried sweat. It had been hard work, the planting season; now they were about to enter a sunny time. The light broke into this white-tiled room and bounced off the surface of the water to create a sense of movement; Nio was transported with happiness and success – he never thought this would happen, the links in the chain were holding up: the lucky break given him by Mrs Ginsberg had grown into something he now dared hope was a full-time job, which in turn had given him the money to pay for this room, where he and Mila could make a start in life. He'd need to go out shopping, buy some food, put the place together a bit . . . He realized he didn't have a towel with him. He'd have to dry himself on his shirt.

He turned off the tap. The boiler fell quiet; silence returned. He climbed into the bath and sank in hot water. It didn't cover his body; he'd been too impatient.

The silence grew; without his knowing how or why, suddenly it built in him a bubble of apprehension as delicate as the surface tension of the water which clung to his limbs. To break the spell he splashed his fingers, sat up sharply. It was as if a presence had passed through the room.

Mila hurried, the cobbles twisted her ankles, on all sides were the old railway buildings which had been converted into Camden Market, every corner was tenanted by stallholders; the bigger spaces housed furniture, bargain finds, repro items of chic, every table flew rails of clothing like flags, a lot of it stuff she herself might buy; it was great here, she was at home among all this junk and youth and the crowded alleyways, she wanted to know every one, it would take loads of time to explore, there was always a new bit which she hadn't seen yet. She loved this job, genuine retro clothing was somehow more romantic than modern gear. As she squeezed out of the market she added up sums in her head: another two shifts per week and she'd equal the same money it took her a whole week to earn at Tesco's, and without the night work. But for the first time – this was totally amazing – she had to think about rent.

She crossed the road and headed over the bridge, dabbing the keypad on her mobile. She waited for the voicemail to pitch her any messages – but she could count on hearing Nio's voice. Had he got their place together? And there he was, stumbling through, the soft heart. She melted to hear him, 'Er . . . Hullo Mila. It's me. Nio.' There was a break. 'Ummm . . . yuh. Flat E, 17 Newton Avenue, London N10 4YU. Good post code eh – 4 y-u – for you?' Then she could *hear* him trying to think of something to say. 'Guess what, I had a bath!' Another pause. 'But you should have been here, should have waited for you, never mind. I'll have another one when you get here.' There came another long pause. Mila could just see him, walking towards her, against the flow of people, to smile, lean over in his slow way and tell her, Mila . . . 'Anyway,' continued his voice, 'call me if you can't find it on the A–Z, really, really hurry and come up here. Bye for now.' Mila waited, listening to him like a ghost in her phone as he made up his mind to finish in his usual way, here it was, '*Love you.*' She felt her heart lurch, the affection for him was like a bird struggling to escape.

Mila moved on to his second message, a more excited voice, 'Where are you, come on . . . *so happy* because we've got this place to live and we've both got jobs and we've got . . . everything. Hurry up! Bye.'

Mila kicked along fast, on her way to Camden tube, she'd head up on the Northern line to Highgate from where she'd catch the bus to Barnet. She scrolled through text messages next. The phone was a slim tablet, encased in a leopard skin fascia. The numbers sat with their accompanying codes of letters. The menu button stood muscular, proud, in control of the keypad. The screen was an illuminated square, the on–off button was small, shy, at the bottom left-hand corner. How it walked by her side, now, it was a stream of connectedness, she trotted around the lines drawn by this phone, many of them scribbled between friends, mostly free of charge. The space in their caravan, the air around Camden, the sky itself – and she imagined this was *true* – carried millions of voices, in all languages; in her imagination they didn't travel in straight lines but blew madly like clouds of bees, all of them having a joint purpose – to arrive – but different, individual destinations. Everyone had a crowd of voices swarming around them, some of them were fantastic and large, they had friends, a business, big family, then there were the people with smaller amounts of conversations, but vigorous and loyal – she might be one of those – and perhaps some people only had one or two voices . . . and she supposed there might be an unlucky few with none but their own voice, a form of solitary confinement, but it was difficult to imagine.

Then – it made her *jump* – the phone sang in her hand, it uttered its call too loud, she didn't want that comedy tune any more. And the square panel lit up, showed 'Anonymous'. She'd come to know it probably meant Jon Rawle was calling her, it was like a knife inserted under her ribcage and twisted, she must change her number, just swallow the cost of doing it, it would be worth it. The tune sang again, insisting loudly. Guilt – he'd know if she switched him off. She should wait until the message service kicked in, then he wouldn't be offended. But it was embarrassing to sit here with the phone going off. Maybe she should answer?

Why was she being so polite? She didn't owe him *anything* . . . She killed the signal, kept going.

Just as she was ducking into Camden tube station, her phone chirruped – a text message. Who from? Whether this was from Jon Rawle, or Nio, or Jayne, or Petru, or Steve or whomever – she couldn't know. She pressed OK to read it now, and stared at the bright green square.

Everyone noticed Mila.

The drunk saw her walking back and forth. For half a minute she stood still, frowning at her phone, so he held up his thumb, blotted out the view of her, cursed. She was blinding, he wanted nothing to do with it.

The architect on his way home noted her perfectly engineered shape: legs straight, the flare of her hips, the neat tuck to the waist, her shoulders a plinth for a beautiful head. He loved the way she turned so neatly. She looked worried, though – his guess was, she must be waiting for someone who hadn't turned up. The way she looked around, searched in the distance for faces, walked back and forth. She really moved so well, that was an unbeatable piece of work. Classy.

The youth waiting for his own girlfriend kicked his heels outside the station and saw in Mila a better score than the one he'd made, he wondered who had her, who was running with her, lucky guy, girl like that would create havoc. She probably had loads of guys on the go. She was waiting for someone, more than once she went past, she was worried, scanning everything, someone was keeping her keen.

The stallholder checked her out for some minutes, her hands buried deep in the capacious pockets of the money belt slung around her waist. There were countless young girls around here, they always looked odd next to all the tramps and winos. She watched as this one stopped her search and abruptly disappeared into the tube station. The street darkened, she felt the gentlest disappointment.

Mila hurried into the tube, down the escalator. She pushed the message forward, looked at the phone number it had come from, she clung to the hope it was a mistake but it told her what she already knew – anonymous – it was Jon's. She held her breath. Was it for real? She read it again. 'I can c u.' She looked behind her, counting each person carefully up to the top of the escalator, including those who were walking down past her. No sign of him. On the platform she paced up and down, sought out every face to make sure he wasn't there. No, it was a trick he'd played, he was trying to scare her, he was bluffing.

She entered her phone's address book and pulled up Jon Rawle; his number stared at her from the illuminated square of the phone. In smaller letters underneath the phone asked the question – Call? Her thumb sat lightly on the OK button . . . but there was no signal down here. As the sound of the approaching train grew in the tunnel mouth, she stamped her foot in anger and disbelief and pain, this stalking of her was so *unfair.*

Charmer was lost without Nio, he was like a dog bereaved of its owner.

When he told them he was going out, the eyes of his parents were blank as stones in a stream, so obvious was their thought that he must be going out to commit some crime or other. The dark playing fields outside the window beckoned mournfully, this whole creepy house was like from a past life, but he was stuck in it for a while. He kicked the door out of his way and walked.

The dusk was a grey miasma; he steered northwards along the edge of Coldfall Wood. The glare of street lights reflected off the leaves of the oak trees. Once he'd gained the main road he turned left and within a few streets he'd crossed the boundary between Haringey and Barnet. Newton Avenue was quarter of a mile into the cheaper borough.

When he reached number seventeen, he didn't know which flat Nio was in so he pushed all the bells at once. A whole bunch of towel-heads appeared at the door, at the windows and from around the back: it was like a nest of them, comical. He was repeating, 'Nio? I'm looking for Nio', but no one understood. Then a sash window was lifted on the upstairs left-hand side and Nio's head was there, poking out, draped in a net curtain like an old Islamic lady, and there was a thousand watt smile on his face, which fell at the sight of Charmer. What little confidence he had summoned now rushed from him, disappeared, but he managed to call up, 'Come on, open up.'

Nio replied, 'Hold on, I'll come down.' His head disappeared; the net curtain was a cushion of air merely, proud of the window. Charmer diverted his attention to the front door, he felt, yes, again, like a dog, waiting for it to open. When it did, his first thought was that Nio was scrubbed clean and dressed up and looking a bit wild around the eyes. He dug deep to find any last ounce of courage, because no doubt he'd have to face up to Nio's skanky gypsy girlfriend, he'd have to take that hurt, but he, Charmer, was lonely enough and broke enough and pissed off enough, to suffer all this because he wanted to drop all pretences, no more showing off, he was a lonely fucked up youth with a bad hairstyle. He didn't even want to talk because the voice he used for his own self sat in his mouth all wrong, it was like listening to his so called mates – where were they now, good question.

He walked with Nio into the house. The place smelled of curry. Or was it incense? Whatever. He saw the door to the stairs and went on up. He called back to Nio, 'Is she ready for me? Are we sharing?' No answer. He glanced behind him, saw the top of Nio's head, the latter was checking his mobile phone, not listening.

On the landing, he headed for the open door – the geography told him this was the room from which Nio's head had appeared. He braced himself for the sight of her, perhaps she'd be in bed with the covers pulled up to her chin, nipples showing through the sheets . . . but there was no one here.

It was odd but he felt the loss, he was expecting to have to face up to this person who'd stolen Nio, yet . . .

Nio closed the door, asking, 'So, how are you?' in a distracted, polite voice. Charmer answered, 'All right.' He looked around. The table was laid out like in an Indian restaurant, it had a cloth on it and knives and forks and a couple of coloured candles. The bed was there, all trim and shipshape, but laid out in squares on the duvet were *pieces of fruit*. . . Charmer commented, 'Looks nice.' He pointed at the lines of grapes, apples, pears. 'Where is she?'

Nio mumbled, frowning. 'She's meant to be here by now.'

Charmer shuffled, limped heavily to the breakfast bar. He opened his mouth, 'What's her name again, Mila was it?' He opened a kitchen cupboard and shouted into it, 'Come on out of there!' He opened other cupboards, calling her, 'Come on, show yourself.' He caught sight of Nio's face and stopped. Silence was better, boredom was OK.

'Meant to be here?' asked Charmer after a while. He looked at his watch. It was nearly ten o'clock. 'Where's she coming from?'

'She was at work,' said Nio. 'But . . . she hasn't called to say why she's late and she's not answering her phone.'

Charmer kicked shut the cupboard doors and wandered across the room. The fruit laid out on the bed – that was something she'd go for, she'd find a kick in that, the ripe grape knocking against her lips, the flesh of a pear torn open and run against her skin.

Both men waited. Nio was forever checking to see if his phone held a message. Charmer made up his mind, he would leave when and if she arrived. He moseyed around, picking at the fixtures and fittings. 'Sure she's coming?' he asked suddenly.

'Yes,' nodded Nio. 'Course.'

'When d'you last speak to her?'

'Few hours ago.' Nio sat on one of the chairs facing up to the gaudily decorated table, hauled one ankle on to the other knee and now rested his head on his hand, kneading at his temple, the phone at the ready. 'Normally she'd phone.'

'Perhaps no signal where she is,' suggested Charmer, 'or her battery's flat.' Then after a pause he added, 'Nice place, room or whatever. You've done well. Wouldn't mind this room, myself.' There was no response from Nio, who continued to draw his forefinger across his brow. 'Just a corner, mind. I could bed down here, couldn't I?' He tapped the skirting with the tip of his toe. There was no answer from Nio. 'I mean, where else am I going to go?' Charmer wandered over to the bed. 'And I like the fruit, good turn that. I'd go for it.' He glanced at Nio – it was sad the way his shoulders were canted over, the numb drawing of his fingertips across his brow. Charmer loved that face. He drew up the stool and sat opposite, so now the two of them were as if waiting to be served at an Indian restaurant. 'Well, I'm here anyway,' he said cheerfully. 'And I'm prettier than her.' He picked up his knife and fork and planted his closed fists on the table. 'Let's see what we've got.' He forked a little dish of sliced tomatoes and something that was sitting there in the middle. 'What's this?'

Nio answered, 'Um . . . tomato and feta cheese in olive oil.'

'Tomato and what?'

'Feta cheese.'

'Fetter cheese, what's that then?'

'Goat's cheese.'

'You're joking.'

'No.'

'Where d'you get the idea to eat that?'

'From a cook book,' said Nio wearily. 'Ummm – Mila was brought up with goats—'

'Brought up with goats?' He was ready to laugh but his gaze wandered over Nio and he couldn't, it was too sad. He pondered then, 'Cheese from a goat. All right, what's good enough for her is good enough for me.'

After a while he asked, 'Do we just spoon it in from there, or what?'

'You eat it with crusty bread.'

'Why all the cooking oil?'

'It's olive oil.'

'Oil from olives, logic tells me.'

Nio nodded. 'Yes.'

Charmer twiddled the condiments. 'Salt and pepper, always nice.' He turned the plate. 'And a nice clean plate. Not like we're used to, eh?' There was no reply from Nio. 'Candles with "love" written on them. Very nice, no complaints. Come on then, I'll start if you will.'

Nio was still downcast, but now the finger stopped wearing at his brow. A stillness took hold of him. The breath passed over his bottom lip – this was all Charmer could see underneath the hand held protectively over Nio's eyes.

'Shall we?' asked Charmer. 'I could eat the actual goat, let alone the, er, whatshisname cheese—' He stumbled to a halt. 'She can join in later, can't she, when she turns up,' he added. He pronged a piece of tomato and lifted it to his mouth. The oil escaped down his chin. It felt cold, slimy, but it tasted good. 'Lovely, ' he said. 'And look, the old napkin.' He wiped his chin.

Nio was staring at the ground. Then he stood. 'There's bread to go with it.'

Charmer put down his fork obediently and watched as Nio opened the oven door, put in a french stick and closed the door again. He twiddled the knob on the oven and said absently, 'Just a couple of minutes.'

'Good service in here,' commented Charmer. His words hung in the air, he could see they didn't reach Nio. Nonetheless, he didn't want this silence, he wanted to cheer him up. 'Not what you might say I'm used to,' he burbled on, 'but with your new money and that, your success, it's your due, isn't it, to go a bit upmarket with your cookbook. Go for it. But don't forget the old working man's café. What I like about a working man's café, right, is it's a cheerful place. They don't have to wash their hands all the time, the people serving you in those places, and none of that boring washing up, the egg can stay on the plate from the last man. They don't have to make a *pot* of tea, do they, all they have to do is wave a tea bag in the water and hand it over. And that makes the workers happy. There's none of this milarky, is there, of trying to find the right stuff from some far flung nation. Your cheapest egg from your battery hen down the road is the idea. And that makes for your happy staff, and your satisfied customers. No effort. Look at you, you're the prime example. You're running a posh gaff here now, and look at the hours you're having to put in, the amount of work what with having to buy your oils and your goat's cheese and your stick of bread. Therefore – look at you. A bit miserable.'

Nio didn't reply, but opened the oven door and took out the bread. He didn't bring it over, but instead threw it. It skidded across the table. Charmer trapped it with his hand. 'That's more like it,' he said.

'D'you want a drink?' asked Nio.

'Drink? You mean real drink, not your sparkling mineral water, real drink?'

'Real drink,' confirmed Nio.

'What is going on? Tell me it's Special Brew.'

'Carling.'

'That's all right. Hand it over.'

Nio unhooked a can from the pack and threw it, also. Charmer caught it. 'Score.'

Nio came back to sit opposite him.

'What *you* having?' The can fizzed in his hand, he sucked the foam from the rim.

'I've got to go and find Mila.' Nio went for his phone, dialled. Nothing doing, he threw it down.

Charmer chewed on the bread and sipped the beer. 'She's coming soon, no worries.'

'She would have phoned,' said Nio. 'Something's happened.'

'Tell you what, I'll be your girlfriend.' Charmer tipped his stool over. 'I'm good looking enough. I can do everything she can do. Let me be your girlfriend, go on. Why not.' He picked up his stool and sat down again. He had to suffer, then, Nio's stony, blank expression, the frown. He didn't want this slow, uneven despair in the room. He wanted to pick Nio up, hurry him along, beyond the girl, get him somewhere else.

Then of all things, Nio asked him, 'D'you think you've ever been in love?' This was such a shock, the answer ran at Charmer, leaped to his mouth, but he didn't say it – yes, with you Nio, you must know that by now. His eyes smoked, his face burned. His answer, 'No', came out all wrong. He was chewed up, so in love. Nio was everything.

'It hurts in here,' Nio continued, banging his fist against his chest. Then he asked, begged, 'Where is she?'

For a while there was silence again, before Nio burst out, 'I am only alive, only *alive*, so that I can be with her for ever, and if she's not *safe*—'

Charmer was close to tears. Watch out, said a voice inside, he must not allow Nio to see one glimpse of the storm, it was fatal, it was weak, it would have him down and out cold if Nio saw one inch of the feeling he had for him. He broke off a chunk of bread, chewed automatically.

Nio stood abruptly; Charmer could see that he was beginning to panic, he looked stricken. 'Where is she?' He picked up his phone again, stared at it, pressed to call. He paced the room, staring at Charmer. 'No reply, something's happened to her.'

'She's got stuck with this friend.'

'It *can't* be that. She'd call if she was delayed. It's something else. Her father has taken her away. She's been hurt. Or—'

The bread was impossible to eat, Charmer's mouth was so dry. He couldn't swallow so had to go on chewing. He took another sip of lager. 'She'll turn up. No news is good news.'

'What if she's lying in hospital unconscious after a road accident?' Nio fell silent. He stared at the floor, hands on hips. His tears were running freely now, he stood limply, wiping his face with the back of a sleeve. 'Something's happened—' He breathed heavily. 'What?' he questioned, breathing twice more. 'I need to know she's all right, I can't just . . . she might have been—' He began to look for his door keys. 'Sorry, but—'

Finally Charmer managed to swallow that bread and he could take a decent mouthful of the lager. He got the message – it was time to leave. Nio wanted to go and look for her. Charmer would be out on his ear again. He'd get drunk. He took another can – no, two more cans – and walked out, there wasn't anything else he could say or do. Nio pulled the door shut behind them and trotted downstairs quickly. Charmer fought his way past the lightweight doors and the plastic locks and the manky concrete path and through the stupid pointless little gate at the end of the path and then he was out of there. Nio was distracted, he apologized and said goodbye, ran for the bus stop. Charmer waved, said it was all right, don't worry, let him know what had happened. Then he plodded down the road in the opposite direction, stinging in the chill night air. He took another suck of the Carling as he walked. Really drunk, he'd get. His eyes were still smoking with emotion, tears stood on his cheeks, but it was no good, nothing would ever come back to him from Nio. It had always been hopeless.

Lucas Tooth steered the Audi into a side road opposite the Southend Green car park and tucked it into a resident's parking slot. The traffic up the side of the Heath was slight; it was one o'clock in the morning.

He waited for a second, just to let the moment sink in. He glanced at Mila, hunched in the seat next to him. This would be his biggest crime.

Then he got out, went around to the passenger side and opened the door for her. He took her by the elbow and guided her across the road and on to Hampstead Heath. He put his arm around her shoulders and tilted her head on to his shoulder; they walked as lovers do. He'd won her co-operation because for some hours previous to this he had embedded, deep in her, a threat, not made against her, but against her little brother. Lucas Tooth had shown her the green plastic container of petrol. He'd opened it; the smell had filled their nostrils. He'd described in detail where her family lived, on Royal College Street. He informed her that Little Vlad was stealing the little envelopes off the flowers, that he'd been selling the contents – so he could have Little Vlad arrested. Or, he might pour petrol all over those brand new clothes he'd bought with the money, and set him alight. All these things he could do. And if, for any reason, he himself was unable to perform these tasks – any reason whatsoever – then his own brother would shoulder the responsibility instead.

So now he escorted her across the Heath, easily.

It was as dark as it ever was in the city, but darker still here. He didn't hurry, kept it to a languorous stroll, because people might be watching from their cars on the road behind, or from the insides of the houses – concerned citizens with phones nearby.

The area of open ground narrowed, then, to a track which became muddy. He quickened and became rougher, because the vegetation closed in and hid them. He was taking her into the depths. She lost a shoe but he didn't want to stop. Further on, he stopped and kneeled at her feet. He ran his hands up her legs, his touch light as air. She turned, tried to run. He tripped her, removed the other shoe. 'Walk barefoot,' he suggested. He stood and pulled her on, reminded her of the threat to Little Vlad, to keep her compliant. He was near his destination and the fear he could conjure in her was his only weapon. When the phone went off in her bag – yet again – he yanked it off her shoulder and flung it in the undergrowth, screwed her arm behind her back, wound it tight, and used it to push her along.

They skirted the entrance to the men's swimming pool and struck uphill. Damp foliage wiped their legs, it would be chill on her bare skin. The note of anxiety grew in Mila's throat; Lucas listened for it.

They struggled a further hundred yards. A light rain drifted across their faces. He heard a warning tone from her, she was helpless, it didn't matter. He swung her around and drew her to him, squeezed her tight, held both her wrists behind her back. He ran his other hand over her face, wiping the moisture over her neck before holding both sides of her shirt and pulling it apart. She beat and clawed at him; he walked through the pain as if it weren't there. As the rain thickened he kneeled and like a man at prayer pushed his nose into her navel while he lifted her long skirt over the circle of her hips. She fought harder, he had to use all his strength to push a finger under one seam of her panties and bunch the flimsy triangle of fabric to one side so he could find her; against his chest he felt her knees and her tone of voice, whatever she was saying, was furious, shocked, dreadful, pleading. He concentrated on holding the bunch of cloth in one hand. His upturned face accepted more rain, the sharpness of her nails against his skin, then with an involuntary shudder he wiped his face against her loins, mixing the cloudburst with his own saliva and the blood from the scratches on his face to paint a wet slick on her skin. She was straining against him and hitting out but he carried on, he worked until his cock was free and then he stood, the fist bunched to hold her panties, at the same time lifted her leg off the ground and for a moment he thought it would be one perfect movement: he would stand, lift and pierce her in a single upward flow – but they fell. She gave a cry and landed heavily on her back, her one knee over his elbow, winded. With his spare hand he was holding his cock ready to sink into her. She was crying now, it was different, jumpy breaths in her chest, rain and tears running down her face.

He murmured, 'What, what—' and stopped dead still. Her breath was jagged, uneven. With one push of his hips he'd be done, but he enjoyed this last flutter of her willpower. He let his weight relax on her, yet kept his cock up to the mark. 'No,' he echoed, 'OK, I won't.' He felt her soften, at the same time he touched her forehead, wetted with rain. 'I'm sorry,' he whispered. She'd be thinking she'd stopped him.

Then he peeled her shoulders and slavered, pushing the rainwater over her skin. He found the cups of her bra and pulled them beneath her breasts. She was crying hard again. The sodden earth was under them, he could feel the tear of brambles against his knees and his elbows were pointed in mud. He kissed her neck delicately and felt her fingers tighten in his hair, pulling as hard as she could. He took an inch of her skin between his teeth and bit, he clamped his teeth shut. Her hands spread on his forehead and her thumbs pushed into his eyes; he rode the pain, shook his head to clear her grip. Her hand moved to his hip – keeping him away. He nudged, to test her strength, and felt the heel of that hand push him away; he pressed harder. She struggled, which aroused him. He was going to have her now. She gave a scream when her heat enclosed him; he found his stroke and immediately she didn't matter, she was his meal and he consumed her, and she was young, a peach, so within a minute he found himself steering for the orgasm and he rowed carelessly hard for it. Then he was there, tipped into it and the pressure in him built; he let it go without a change to his stroke nor a sound from his throat, his blood banged in his head and his lungs emptied and filled quicker but he succeeded – emptied inside her, worked out the last residue of feeling.

Afterwards he stood up. She scrambled to her feet and ran, flailing. He trapped her, pushed her to the ground, held her down. Her back was soaked and muddy, there were last year's leaves in her hair, she was incomprehensible.

Her body stiffened as he leaned closer to her ear – he really wanted to plant this warning deep. 'Now you listen – I know your little brother's name, where he lives, what he's done with my little envelopes. I know the names of all your family. I can go and find Ilie by myself, if I should feel it was necessary, God help him, wherever he is, if I'm ever shut in prison. God help your little brother if my head is cut off by your relatives, because my own brother has a gallon of petrol in his car, also.' He took slow steps backwards, then stood motionless for a while, he could only see the shadows and white planes of her face. He announced, 'I'm going to leave you here by yourself. You'll find your way out. Beware of asking for help, you might easily be attacked again. I think it's best just to go home. And let me repeat, if you ever say anything about this, about me, to anyone, your little brother will suffer for it.' Then he turned and walked down the hill. Within ten yards he was out of sight. He ducked sideways, off the path, and waited. He thought, someone should tell her that love was scary.

He heard her stumbling, snagged by undergrowth. The fear caught in her voice as she cried uncontrollably. There were more footsteps as she found the path. Then she was gone. It was silent.

Minutes later, Lucas Tooth was standing in the same spot. His short dark hair was jewelled with rain, his shirt clung to his skin. He wasn't thinking of much. Nothing moved him. This was a dry place he'd found. He had the enforced stillness of an animal with many predators nearby, yet the truth was he had none except his own kind. After a quarter of an hour the rain stopped and he emerged, picked his way back the way they'd come. The dark was a tunnel he moved down, as big or as small as he cared to make it. His walk was quick, single-minded. He searched for the spot where he'd taken the bag off her. When he found it, he felt for the purse, took it out, dropped the bag. He unzipped the purse and removed the notes, didn't bother with the coins. Then he heard her phone ringing, again. He dug in the bag and took it out, looked at the screen. As before, its illuminated screen read, 'Nio.' This time he answered it, 'Hello?' A man's voice asked anxiously if Mila was there. No, he replied, she'd just left. Then he killed the signal, took off the back of the phone, levered out the Sim card and pocketed it. He murmured, 'Very sorry', and walked on. The carcass of the phone slipped from his fingers and fell to the path, the spoor of his most serious crime, so far.

Two hours later he jumped over a garden fence and lay low in a paved area at the end of someone's garden. He examined the house. He'd chosen it because a downstairs toilet window offered a small section pegged open. There were lights showing from the downstairs windows, but ten minutes' observation told him the occupants were watching television. No movement interrupted the light. There was no other sound.

He squeezed through the impossibly small aperture and found himself in the bathroom. He washed carefully, silently; she'd scratched his hands and face. When he was finished he rinsed the basin of blood. He checked himself in the mirror and patted his skin dry and replaced the towel exactly in the position in which he'd found it. He trod silently past the room where they were watching TV and went upstairs. He looked in on the children sleeping in their beds, then found the parents' room. He rifled through a wardrobe and selected a pair of jeans, a pristine ironed shirt and a jacket made by Yves St Laurent. While he shrugged into these, the sound of canned laughter came from the TV downstairs. He transferred his own clothing to a designer shopping bag and left the room. Downstairs, he unhooked a slim, fashionable overcoat from the peg and left – quietly, during a loud burst of applause on the TV – via the front door. He dropped the soiled clothes in a refuse skip skewed in the alley between the gardens.

SEVEN

Anjali heard the usual thunder made by trains passing over the concrete causeways above them, they carried the mass of working population to work or brought ticket-holders to cultural journeys available in the South Bank arts complex.

It was a bit early in the morning for her, but she withdrew the last Camel Light cigarette from the pack and lit it. She liked this new spot, although it was a shame to have lost their cardboard mansion – it had been quickly destroyed to prevent others occupying it when London Tranport Police had moved herself and Spider on from the Tottenham Court Road underpass. They'd only managed to carry off the blankets and other possessions. Here, under the South Bank arts complex, tight against the River Thames, they were constructing something bigger still, but had so far only taped together part of the floor and one wall.

Just as she finished the cigarette, she looked up to see a figure coming towards her. It was Mila, yes, but her gait was different, her head was bowed, there was no bounce in her stride. Her hair had no clips or ties in it. She wasn't dressed as usual, but instead her shape was covered by a bulky fleece. When she was closer still, Anjali could see her eyes were red.

She stood, frowned, watched as Mila picked her way through the heavy stares of the youth, the concrete beams framing her in grey and black shadow. Down here lingered the skaters, waiting their turns to roll the slopes and clatter down the steps, and other youth who took to skidding along the handrails, while the homeless contingent occupied the corner out of sight from the riverfront parade. They all watched as Mila threaded past.

Anjali now hurried to draw Mila behind the one cardboard wall that was built, to find out what was wrong. She whispered, 'What happened?' and Mila's face crumpled, she replied, 'I lost your bag, and my phone, and . . . everything.' Anjali sat Mila down and held on, just wrapped both arms around her, and felt her, then, shake with crying; such unhappiness caused a vibration of sympathy in Anjali also; something worse than that had happened, the crying wouldn't be stopped, Anjali could tell, it came despite Mila's efforts to hold it back and made her helpless, lost. Anjali squeezed harder, for a long time, her cheek on Mila's head as the younger girl suffered – the squall of tears carrying her through Anjali's silence. Anjali's hands strayed over her friend's head, holding her. During a lull, she planted kisses on Mila's brow, on the top of her hair, the girl was messy, unruly with grief. The crying returned and Anjali cast around for soft clothing to make a pillow and she lay Mila's head down, and then she lay as well, hauled the duvet right over their heads so they were deep, dark in privacy. She squirmed so that every inch of her body was pressed to Mila's, and threaded her arm under Mila's head so that she could contain the hot centre of the girl's wretchedness, hold it against her heart. The suffering infected her also, it rose in tears which rolled down Anjali's cheeks because she thought she knew what must have happened, although not a word had passed between them, and in their communion now was a tangled sense of rightness – here was the only place to be, this was the only thing to be done, it wasn't a cure and nor could anything be put right but it was the only way to bear the carrying of this, the trudge across a barren, remote and heartless place.

An hour later they were in the same position, but Mila had stopped crying. Anjali's arm was numbed by the weight of her friend but she remained motionless. The edge to Mila's breathing softened, sleep rescued her and carried her off. Under the duvet Anjali could feel Mila's hair, fibrous, gritty under her hands, and a shoulder which rose and fell gently, a knoll of a womanly shape, all socket and bone compared to a man's muscle. Anjali stayed on, she let the familiar hunger gnaw at her centre. From outside the duvet, beyond the wall, came the cries of the skaters and the other residents of this cardboard city, some aggressive voices veered close by, sometimes a scattering of laughter carried off the anger or it petered out. Whichever, she monitored the sounds only for the danger they might present to this immediate square of privacy occupied by herself and Mila. She heard the near-silent tread of trainers close by; that was Spider. She didn't move and he didn't interrupt. In the silence that followed she knew Spider was protecting them – no one would disturb them now.

Then, perhaps because this place of safety had been granted her, Anjali herself was asleep and she dreamed she was walking across the side of a hill sprung with gorse, it was a golden morning, the land was wet, a dewy mist like a grey shift – the water droplets were sequins – covered everything. A spider's web was strung between the thorny points of a gorse bush and at its centre was the spider, waiting. She walked on and saw another. Then, yet another, just inches away, on the same gorse bush. Then, for each fraction that she moved her eyes, they alit on another spider's web. She realized that the entire landscape was thickly covered with them, each holding its host. The grey shift wasn't made up of mist, it was the fantastic work of countless spiders weaving a blanket of thinnest silk to cover every bit of flora – every one of them waiting to catch their prey.

Mila stirred in her arms. The physical movement called Anjali from sleep and it took a moment to forget her own journey and concentrate instead on her friend. The only thing to do was to give information, as if she'd been in an accident and had just recovered consciousness. 'You're here with me, it's Anjali, you've been asleep—' Mila looked at her for the first time and Anjali was shocked at how much depth had opened in her eyes.

They walked together along the bank of the river. Anjali held Mila tightly around the shoulders. She guided her into the café which she and Spider sometimes used, near Waterloo. She bought a cup of sweet tea and watched her drink it. She took her into the railway station and begged for pound coins so she could pass through the barrier, down the steps and take a hot shower. She held her clothes and waited.

Later in the afternoon, Mila started talking, but it was about other people: her family, mostly. Yesterday her cousin had bought a rent book and a set of keys from a man in a pub. The rent book was in someone else's name, but it had allowed them to move immediately out of the trailers and into a newbuild housing association property in Camden, the only drawback being that they had to pretend to be this Turkish family and if their true identities were known, they'd be thrown out. She loved her new job in Camden Market, and she was going to give up all her shifts at Tesco's once she was earning enough commission, or once she'd found a second job, better paid, in the market.

That night, Mila slept on the square of cardboard with Anjali. Spider came and went wordlessly. A fire was lit by a group nearby; the blades of light gave off smoke which drifted outwards and dispersed in a grey fug. A hundred yards away, people exited, blinking, from the late night showings at the National Film Theatre. On the other side, cars trailed each other along the south bank of the Thames.

The next morning Mila left to go back to her family's new housing association flat and change her clothes. Anjali waited, only making routine sorties to scavenge for food. She begged enough to buy a packet of batteries and some tobacco for Spider.

Mila came back again the next evening and together they listened to music. They watched Spider take his craft knife and dissect a cardboard box, which had previously contained a large screen TV. He fashioned it to brace the first corner – they'd learned that for a structure of any size, the corners had to be at least three times as strong. They also were planning to make a double skin for warmth.

It was late on the second night before Mila told them what had happened. Spider was on the edge of their cardboard square, separate from the intimacy shared by the two girls, cleaning his fingernails with the point of the craft knife. His hair had grown a quarter of an inch, so the cobweb was blurred as it entered the hairline. Anjali could feel the invisible line that went from him to her. Mila herself was folded into the corner which had been braced by Spider with the cardboard box the previous day. Behind it, the concrete upright held her weight as she leaned sideways, her shoulders hunched. She pinned her hands between her knees. The fleece stood in thick, unlikely waves around her, made her soft, shapeless.

Anjali waited. She saw anxiety disturb the expression on Mila's face – it creased, then after an effort straightened again.

'You don't have to tell me,' said Anjali.

But Mila did – she told her how she'd met this man on a train . . . it was as if she were talking only to herself. She described the facts – things she could rely on: for instance, the way he'd taken a polaroid picture of her in the pub. Anjali recognized this precise handling of the memories, Mila was trying to find out what she'd missed, why she hadn't seen that this man . . . her tone of voice was as if she were working it out for herself, describing the facts in order to fit them together, because they were so unbelievable.

Then there was a long silence. Mila was clouded with anxiety; Anjali waited, dreading that this was the same man, who'd . . .

'I was meant to go up to our new place,' began Mila, 'but then comes a text message—' She pinched her lip and gave a cry of distress. She held her hand over her mouth and tears jumped from her eyes.

'What happened?' asked Anjali and felt her heart break as she listened to how he had – for hours – driven her around and threatened Little Vlad, but how Mila, when the man had got out of the car to take a leak, had managed to send a text message to Little Vlad, to warn him . . . and then . . .

Anjali held both Mila's hands, tightly, as she was given the whole story, but she knew for certain, now, that her own life was entwined with Mila's. This was the same man, without doubt. There was too much evidence – Muswell Hill, for a start – and the way in which he had gained her confidence, the biting, what he looked like, his clothes . . . She didn't interrupt, but yes, the man who'd dragged Mila across Hampstead Heath was the same man who'd gained *her* confidence, whom she'd run from. Her guilt, fear and anger tied a knot of iron, of dreadful iron, in her stomach. It was the same man, it must be. She felt strength and wonder, also, that she and this girl were now the same; it seemed God-given, there was an impossible, fearful symmetry to it. What was it – what force of life, of fate – that had wrought their experiences into a similar shape, to give them sisterhood? The attachment between them was impossible to break, life itself had led them both to this same spot. They *had* to do something.

Nio went to the bus stop, but then couldn't wait, he ran to the police station to report Mila missing. It took ages, he had to fill in forms. From time to time he phoned her, but she didn't answer. Once he'd finished at the police station he went to the nearest hospital, the Whittington, to ask if she'd been admitted. There was no record of her.

By now it was nearly two o'clock in the morning. He tried to phone her again for the umpteenth time and this time someone answered, optimism flared in Nio, but when he heard a man's voice say, 'Hello?' it was the opposite, the sudden dread at what had happened chilled him, it was a blank, unfriendly voice. He asked quickly, 'Is Mila there?' The stranger answered, 'No, she's just left', and the line went dead. When he tried to call again, the phone had been switched off.

This hint of wrongdoing tortured him – the knowledge of Mila's fate was held by that voice, it drove Nio mad with anxiety and fear. He went straight to the wire-fenced enclosure in Royal College Street, Camden. It was often padlocked, especially at night, but on this occasion the aluminium-framed gates stood open, and also, it was unusual to see three cars canted over on the pavement where they breached the parking regulations, plus there was a flare of light around the trailers, and torches, and voices, so something was wrong, this was where he'd discover what had happened. It was three o'clock in the morning.

He loped through the gates and hit the gap in the first row of more established caravans. Then, as he moved across the more open space where the church had been demolished, his mouth hung open with dismay because Social Services had a chorus of people attending its doorstep, their torchlights cut the dark this way and that. From within came the sound of shouts and crying and the swords of light moved continuously. Nio thought his worst fears were about to be confirmed – for hours and hours he'd imagined she'd been mown down by a car or she'd been held prisoner by her father or the family had been moved on and she had no way of getting in touch because she'd dropped her phone as she was thrown into the police van . . . something had gone wrong and Nio was going to find out what it was, so now he ran towards Social Services, what would it be, the car accident, she'd been badly hurt by a vehicle mounting the pavement or even killed, given the number of plain clothes policemen, or whatever they were, grouped around the doorway. Maybe he'd learn of a scene of domestic violence – she'd killed her father or vice versa . . . these imaginings he'd rehearsed one after the other, continuously.

Three men and a woman were gathered around the concrete blocks stacked against the caravan door. They all had their backs to Nio – they were looking inside, at whatever was happening. Nio was running – one of their number held out an arm to stop him – perhaps it had been this one, who'd answered her phone an hour ago? A torch was shone in his face.

'What's happened?' he begged.

'Who are you?'

'I'm a friend . . . of the daughter's—'

'What daughter?'

'Mila Rosapepe, the daughter.'

'I suggest you stop right there for a moment.'

He heard a raised voice from inside the caravan, a question asked over and over again, a woman crying. 'What's happened?' he repeated.

'Immigration.'

'Immigration, what d'you mean?'

'What I say. Immigration. Removal of absconded asylum applicants, as approved and paid for by you and me, the taxpayers.'

'*Removal?*'

'Correct.'

Nio couldn't believe what he was hearing. Were they going to take away Mila's entire family? Where did they remove them *to*? 'Can I talk to her?'

'Who?'

'The daughter, Mila Rosapepe.'

'There's no daughter. There's an infant son . . . Not much use to you.'

Nio was speechless. He didn't know if he ought to press the point, that there *was* a daughter, because if he did then maybe he'd spoil some plan they'd had, to pretend she was someone else so she at least would get to stay in the country. He had to know who was inside – specifically, was Mila inside the caravan? Or had she been *removed* already? Because if so, then maybe that's what the voice had meant, '*She's just left . . .*'

'Can I go in?' he asked.

The men looked at each other. 'I'd stay out, if I were you.'

'Are you the police?' asked Nio.

'No, Immigration. But we have powers of removal.'

'Remove where to?'

'On the plane mate, we send them back home. Straight to the airport.'

'Can I go in and see if my friend is inside?' persisted Nio.

The three men glanced at each other. Nio sensed they didn't know the answer to this. One of them repeated, 'I'd stay out, if I were you.'

Nio waited for a moment, uncomfortable in their circle, as they no doubt were with him. Then he explained, 'I just have to step inside and see if my friend is there. Is that OK?'

The man repeated again, very slowly, 'I'd stay out, if I were you.' The flashlight crossed his face, left him in the dark for a moment.

Nio obeyed, he waited some more. The atmosphere was hostile. Then he put one foot on a concrete block. 'I'll only be one second.' He walked up the steps sideways, expecting them to haul him back, but in the event none of them moved and he stepped into the caravan. His eyes adjusted and he immediately checked each person to find Mila. There were only two people in here carrying torches, and he needed to see for himself . . . he knew he had to be quick, at any moment he'd be pulled out. The light crossed a woman, much older than Mila, maybe in her thirties, and she was packing clothes into a holdall. At her feet sat a baby, a dummy stopping its mouth, it was watching the pools of light from the torches cross the ceiling, walls, floor. The woman trod around the baby to pick up clothes from the floor and stuff them into the bag. She was watched by two men dressed similarly to those standing at the door: anoraks and jeans, but also collars and ties. Nio guessed they must be immigration officers also. At the end of the caravan, in the kitchen area, stood a man with cropped blond hair wearing a fleece and khakis, who was staring insolently at a female immigration officer, but not saying a word.

There was no one here that he recognized, not one member of Mila's family. Nor was there any evidence of the family's possessions. The TV with its fringe of lace was gone. Nio was slow with disbelief, it was like he was in a dream. Was this the right caravan, even? Undoubtedly, yes it was. He remembered sitting there, doing tricks for the toddler. He remembered the fight with Mila's father. Mila had lit candles, here, there. She'd run to that window, clawed back the curtain, when the guy from the furniture shop had banged against the window. The flowers . . .

That man's voice was a ghost in his head – *'No, she's just left.'* Who'd said those words and why?

The woman officer was talking in a loud voice, holding the torch on the man and waving a square of paper in his face. 'You say you're Polish, OK, say something in Polish. Say "it's a nice day" in Polish.' The man remained silent. 'Say "I live here" in Polish,' the officer went on, 'if you're Polish that shouldn't be a problem for you at all should it. Say "this is my caravan and I live here with my wife and child", *in Polish*, and I'll believe you. And what's more we'll go away and leave you alone. Mmm?'

The young woman started shouting now in a language Nio didn't understand. She stepped over the baby and stamped over to the man with the cropped hair. She gesticulated angrily and swore at him. He blinked, but maintained his silence. Then she stomped back and sat the baby on her right hip and picked up the bag she'd stuffed with clothes. Her face was crossed with anger and worry and the pattern looked familiar, her face was worn with it. She kicked her way through the rest of the stuff that littered the floor and headed out. She was followed by the two officers who'd been standing over her.

The female officer at the end of the caravan faced up to the younger man again. 'Say, "my wife has left me", in Polish, then. Say "she's taken my child and she's really, really pissed off at the way I'm behaving." *In Polish.*' She waved the document. 'You're not Polish, you never have been Polish and never will be. We know exactly who you are and you're out of here, mate. No more fun and games.'

The man with the cropped hair was now looking at Nio, and the immigration officer picked up his presence, also. She shone her torch at him and called, 'Who are you?'

Nio blinked and replied, 'No, er, I was looking for my girlfriend, Mila Rosapepe.'

The immigration officer pointed her torch to the left, right, up and down. She called sarcastically, 'Is she anywhere around, then?' She stared at Nio. 'D'you see her anywhere, at all?'

'No,' answered Nio, 'but I was wondering—'

'So is that all right then? Are you done, we're in the middle of a removal here and I want to get it over with, it's not particularly pleasant for anyone, so if you'd like to be on your way?'

Nio couldn't think what to do next, he was wrong-footed. He waited.

'I'd be obliged.'

'OK,' replied Nio. 'Thank you very much.' He felt like he ought to help the Polish man who was obviously too frightened to speak, but he couldn't decide what was the right thing to do. He stepped towards the door, and the purposeful voice of the immigration officer faded behind him, 'Now, I'm going to walk out of here and you're going to come with me. If you don't, you'll be picked up and carried out like a stick of furniture, OK? It's your choice—' Nio descended the concrete blocks, and moved through the circle of men who eyed him warily. Fifty yards away, under the streetlights, he could see two of their number walking alongside the woman who was struggling with the baby on her hip and the bag hitched on her other shoulder. Right there, behind that other caravan, was where he and Mila had . . ..

Nio stumbled through the dark to the fenced gateway. There he stopped. He couldn't believe what had just happened. If Mila's family had been moved on, why hadn't she called him? Maybe she had, but she'd dialled incorrectly and left a message with a stranger . . . was that possible? But she'd have called again, they talked to each other all the time, it would have been the first night in their own place, there was no way she wouldn't have called. It felt like he'd gone to sleep and missed out a whole bit of her life.

As he waited, the woman unholstered the baby from her hip and tossed it unceremoniously onto the back seat of one of the cars. It looked callous but Nio could see that the seat was deeply upholstered and the infant would probably have been OK. An immigration officer had opened the car door for her, but it was demeaning to put his hand on her head and press down as if to squeeze her into the vehicle, although maybe he was trying to save her from bumping her head.

Nio was frantic. Mila was a gap torn out of his side, she'd been taken away by someone or something unknown and he didn't know how he was going to find her.

As he waited, the blond-haired young man came out, escorted by two officers who held him by the arms. He looked sullen. He was placed in the same car, and Nio suddenly believed it might be this man who'd answered her phone and he shouted, 'D'you know where Mila is?' just as the doors were shut and there was no answer, the cars were driven off, he was left with nothing.

He wondered what he could do next – how to be organized,

effective? He'd done the police and hospitals. He was meant to go to work this morning, but instead he should check Camden Market, where her new job was, he should perhaps visit the police station again, just to persuade them it was important, they should put some manpower into searching for her now, instead of just filling in a couple of forms, she wasn't a non-person. He should try Tesco's – all this ground had to be covered. Other hospitals might have news of her, try the local council maybe . . . these avenues seemed bleak, unlikely. Yet, it had to be done.

First he caught the night bus up to Muswell Hill and walked to Tesco's, because it was open twenty-four hours and she might have gone there. Next he came back down to Camden, to check the stall as it opened up, but they were missing her too. Again and again he called her mobile, but the voicemail always cut in straightaway, which told him that wherever her phone was, it had been switched off by the man who'd answered it.

Since he was in Camden, he checked back at the site in Royal College Street, to see if last night had been just a dream – or maybe she'd come back. No – all three caravans were deserted. No sign.

As he left the compound, Nio became aware of the sound of the fence stinging under an assault of some kind. Someone was throwing something. He took a step and glanced sideways; he was in time to see Little Vlad, dressed from head to foot in skate-boarder-type gear, accelerate towards the fence, run halfway up it in two quick strides, then flip over and land on his feet. He turned to square up for another run.

This was the piece of luck he needed: Little Vlad would have all the answers. Nio stumbled forwards and called out. When he heard his name Little Vlad looked at Nio, but then quickly accelerated, quicker if anything. Nio kept going, he was expecting to reach Little Vlad just as he flipped off the fence and back on to his feet, but then Little Vlad reached up with his hands and ran all the way up, hooked on to the wire at the top and pulled himself over. The fence swung outwards under his weight, then he partly climbed down the other side, jumped and ran off.

Nio couldn't think why he'd run – he dashed for the gate, headed after him; and as he gained the other side of the road he saw Little Vlad swing himself around the corner at the end, then he was gone from sight. Nio ran, shouted his name. As he gained the corner himself, cars poured towards him down three lanes of this one-way red route into London. Ahead of him pedestrians walked amiably; there was no sign of Little Vlad. He kept running, but spared glances down the side streets and across to the other side of the road. He doubted whether even Little Vlad could have jaywalked so quickly and not been flattened by the thick onrush of traffic. At the junction with Camden High Road he stopped, breathless. He could see clearly in each of the four directions giving off this major junction and he stood on tiptoe and peered through the pedestrians to see as far as possible. He was begging for a view of that small male figure, either running or walking, or lurking in a doorway . . .

More slowly he combed his gaze up and down the pavements, searching. What would he, Nio, have done in Little Vlad's place? He came to the conclusion he'd probably have run into Sainsburys and out the other side, through the car park and towards the canal. If only to hold on to one last slender hope of catching him, Nio started to follow, see if that was right . . .

Before he set off, he gave one quick last look in each direction. He sidestepped a clump of pedestrians to check the way he'd come, and Little Vlad appeared out of nowhere and ran straight into him. Nio fumbled, held on. Little Vlad squirmed to escape but in a lucky accident Nio's little finger caught at the armpit of Little Vlad's spanking new FireTrap jacket. It gave him the split second necessary to grab hold with his other hand, but in a trice Little Vlad had slipped his arms out leaving it empty in Nio's hand, but then Nio grabbed again and this time he held Little Vlad's wrist, flesh and bone.

Little Vlad immediately started up a plaintive crying and pleading, 'Let go, help, don't hit me, don't—' at the same time as he picked up the jacket.

'What happened, where's Mila?'

'Help,' repeated Little Vlad. He was focused on a middle-aged woman who'd paused, concerned at what was happening 'He's hurting me, help—' The woman looked from Little Vlad to Nio and back again, hesitant.

'I'm not actually hurting him, he's the younger brother of my girlfriend,' Nio explained.

'He's hurting me,' moaned Little Vlad.

Real tears were springing from Little Vlad – how did he do that? 'I'm not hurting him,' explained Nio to the woman, but he could see it looked bad, he felt sorry for the woman who'd stopped and who wanted to help – she wasn't to know that Little Vlad was pretending. The woman believed Little Vlad. She was becoming frightened. Nio let go of Little Vlad's arm; at the same time an idea came to him, just as Little Vlad squirmed away and threaded through the crowd Nio called out, 'I'll pay you!' He saw the break in Little Vlad's stride, the sudden slowing of his escape. Nio followed, ignoring the people around them. He repeated, 'I'll *pay you*, I'll pay you to tell me what happened.'

Little Vlad had broken away from the junction where people thronged to cross the road and now he was in clearer, less populated space. He dawdled, shrugging into his jacket again and looking back at Nio, making up his mind.

Nio walked towards him, reached into his pocket and pulled out some coins and other bits and pieces. That wouldn't be enough. He fished in his back pockets and found the notes he'd thought were there and pulled them out. As he looked at what he had, he became aware that Little Vlad was close by, counting also.

Nio didn't bother to finish, he thrust the notes at Little Vlad and said, 'If you tell me, OK?' Little Vlad wiped his palms against the sides of his trousers and nodded. Nio repeated, 'If you tell me where she is? What happened to her?'

When Little Vlad put his hand on the money, his touch was light as a feather. Nio let go and the notes disappeared as if by magic. Little Vlad looked to the sky, it appeared as if he was working out what to say. Nio could examine him now more closely than ever before: he took in the boy's dark eyes, the black pupils unfathomable, the surrounding irises brown flecked with lighter tones, the eyebrows stitched across the bridge of his nose, the white expanse of skin ingrained with city dirt, the untidy swipe of black hair across the forehead, the broad nose and the childish, uncomplicated mouth. He asked, 'Where is she?'

'I thought she is with you.'

'I wasn't with her!' exclaimed Nio. 'We were meant to meet but she never showed up. I came back and I found she . . . you weren't, none of you, in the caravan any more, and . . . where is she? Why did you run away?'

Little Vlad paused and looked down at his hands. The money was there again, it had reappeared and he was counting the notes. He shrugged. 'She send me a text message . . . er, half a text message, it said, run, just that, run.' He went on, shifting uncomfortably. 'So I run.'

'A text message? Do you still have it, on your phone?' Nio felt as if this boy was looking through him, or seeing parts of him that others couldn't see, it was uncomfortable.

'Don' know,' murmured Little Vlad and flipped open a brand new Motorola. He found the message and held it out for Nio to read but Nio couldn't understand it. Little Vlad translated, 'Is something like, "*Run, you must and if*" but that's all, it ends in half, just stops.' Nio asked Little Vlad to scroll down, find out what time the message had been sent. He read off the screen, 11.28 pm.

Nio's mouth hung open. Tears were in his eyes, his throat was dry, he felt sick and shocked. Something terrible had happened last night. This message, and the man's voice answering her phone two hours later . . . He was trying to win any little clue he could from it, as Little Vlad teased the phone out of his grip and pocketed it. He watched, then, as the figure of Mila's brother tilted from side to side, down the street, faster and faster, breaking into a trot as he passed the bus stop, then fled around the corner to the pedestrian crossing, running away on a sparkling white pair of trainers.

Mila couldn't have done this alone. At her side, as they made their way towards Queens Avenue, was Anjali, step for step, their arms were locked together. Spider was somewhere but she couldn't see him. Anjali had coached her to trust him, he knew what he was doing, he was streetwise enough. As long as Little Vlad was safe, no longer at the compound in Royal College Street, they could do this and the threat to Little Vlad would not only be met, it would be extinguished.

They passed by the pub – he could easily be in there. On the corner was the stall selling flowers – a figure of a similar height stood under its green striped awning . . . To Mila's fearful imagination he was everywhere. Each footfall was his – until she knew otherwise. She was in trouble, she could only thank God Anjali was here, and Spider.

Yet, she longed for Nio, as well. Her heart was broken, because she didn't know if she could face him, her beloved, steady and kind-hearted Nio. She was a victim now; it was like a serious punishment which she'd visited on Nio as well. He would be in agony now, she knew that, and he was the only person who could hold her up, keep her from falling into the abyss, yet he was the one person she couldn't bear telling, she was certain he wouldn't want her any more if he knew. She didn't want to find that out . . . held it off, like the biggest danger of all.

When she turned into Queens Avenue she was so heavy with nerves, but also she was hurting with anger and the injustice of what had happened; they were going to doorstep Jon Rawle and she wanted to throw something in his face, see him hurt. She knew she'd scratched him, she wanted to see her fury written on his face, add more revenge.

They reached number fifteen and walked slowly back and forth three times before they stopped. Out of the corner of her eye Mila saw Spider saunter down a pathway that cut between the detached houses, around the back.

She stared at the windows. Was he in there? The Edwardian façade looked harmless enough, yet it was his fortress. Her fists were bunched, she was ready to really, really, fight. Anjali and Mila crossed the road together, climbed the steps.

This front door – it's where he'd previously sat drinking his morning coffee . . . Anjali pushed the bell for a solid five seconds. They waited. There weren't any cars on the paved area in front of the house. No one stood at any of the windows. There was no sign of life; the place blanked her. Most of all, she wanted his wife to answer. If he was married, she'd so blow him out of the water.

She almost ran, or fell, her knees gave way with the shock when the door opened and an older man stood there, smiled at them, puzzled. 'Yes?' Anjali turned and looked at her, they both knew this wasn't him. After a beat Anjali asked the old guy, 'Can we talk to Jon Rawle?'

'Who?'

'Jon Rawle? Or his wife?' added Mila quickly, 'Or . . . some-one?'

The man had a foreign accent. 'I'm sorry, there's no one of that name living here.'

Mila felt, like, a stone dropping in her middle. The old guy was looking at her in a curious way. 'Can I help at all?' he began, 'because—'

With a flurry of apologies they interrupted, made it sound as if they'd made a mistake, got the wrong house. They didn't stay to listen to what he was saying, they were taking the steps two at a time down to street level, nerves still running high. 'Doesn't live there,' said Mila, sure of it now.

'But you—' began Anjali.

'I know, but I never *saw* him go in, he was just drinking a cup of coffee on the steps, he was *pretending* he lived there.'

For a while they milled about, thinking what to do. Anjali took her arm and walked her up the road, talking hard. Spider reappeared from around the back, the scaffold bar hidden under his jacket.

'Sure it was number fifteen?' asked Anjali.

All the houses in Queens Avenue were similar in design and construction, they had the same steps up to the same front doors, the parking areas out the front, the galleried upper storeys, the Edwardian residential design, the crumbling orange bricks, yet the others meant nothing to her – even the number was engraved on her memory – and she couldn't have made a mistake. 'No, definitely it was that house. But he doesn't live there.' She so wanted to kick him, hurt him . . . through the blur of tears standing on her lashes, her and Anjali's knees popped back and forth, their booted feet measured the squares of pavement before they pushed them behind. She took Anjali's hand, wound it tight.

She'd agreed with them both eventually – find him, face up to him, don't let him get away with it, save others from this happening to them. A name, a description . . . if she could have gone to the police, that would have done the trick, the British police were kind and good, they'd have helped her – but neither she nor her family had a visa, she'd borrowed a National Insurance number to steal work, she was illegal . . . her whole family . . .

She found herself standing stock still, mouth hanging open. She pinched her cuff between her fingers and the heel of her hand and used it to wipe the tears from her eyes. Anjali hung on to her arm. 'Maybe,' she suggested, 'he was hiding behind that old man, who is his father, who is protecting him?'

'I don' think is likely . . . No.' Mila knew it, instinctively – he'd never lived at number fifteen, it was another trick. She remembered – he'd climbed the steps, left his cup at the top, there'd been a set of keys in his hand, yes, but he'd never used them.

They turned back to walk towards the Broadway. Ahead of them, Spider kicked a low brick wall idly. As they walked past he ignored them.

On the apex of the curve, the house came into view again and her heart hammered in its cage. The façade was as uncommunicative as before. As they drew closer they slowed, and stared more openly. Anjali wound her arm tightly in hers. The house returned her view with closed eyes, holding its secrets. She felt Anjali trying to draw her on, but then she was stuck, because a movement in one of the windows caught her attention. 'Look, someone.'

They watched intently – and there it was again. An image floated in the glass, moved through the static layer of the reflection. Was it the old man?

As they watched, the figure drew closer to the glass and materialized; Mila held her breath and it was an effort to stop her knees from giving away. Moments later it disappeared. Then the front door opened and there was the old guy standing at the top of the steps. He signalled, urgently. Then he started towards them.

They waited, hesitant. 'What does he want?' asked Anjali.

'Don' know.'

'Maybe he saw something.'

The old man descended the steps with a stiff, one-sided gait. He checked the road for speeding cars before hurrying across.

'Shall we stay or go?'

'Where's Spider?' Anjali found him – he was close enough.

'Let's stay.' Mila's pulse was racing and the conflicting

instincts – to run or find out what he wanted – held her static, in stalemate.

The old man wore a beret and a sturdy suit and his lace-up shoes were shined. His skin was nut brown. Between his lips was perched a black cheroot, which he occasionally waved at them.

They were on the point of running off. Yet, he was a benign character, there was no sense of threat coming from him, rather the opposite – Mila could see that he wore a keen, interested look. And Spider was close by.

As he approached, he called out, 'Are you Mila? You are Mila Rosapepe, yes?'

He knew her name!? Immediately she had a different picture of Jon Rawle: he was a sick conman who lived alone with his parents, this was his dad, who'd fathered the monster. Her mouth was dry with anxiety.

'Forgive me,' the old man was saying, 'but I think it might be important that I talk to you.' His voice wore a French accent which explained his beret and the strong complexion. 'My name is François.'

She could read his face now, it was sympathetic and kind. His limping gait meant they could run, escape easily. 'It's very important,' he repeated, 'because it's odd, but,' – and here he paused as he thought how to phrase it – 'we've had a little mystery, in our house, over the last, well, few months I would say—' He was close to them now and leaned towards her, his eyes peered intently into hers. 'We received an envelope, you see,' he went on, 'and it was in your name. So we opened it, but it didn't contain a return address, nothing at all, except a set of photographs. But now I think we can return the photographs to the correct owner, yes? Is that why you were looking at the house?'

No, this man wasn't Jon Rawle's dad. He became harmless. She didn't mind if he loomed too close; he was sharing out his beaky look between her and Anjali.

'I suggested to my wife,' the Frenchman continued, 'that the person who'd written the wrong address on the envelope would soon realize what they had done, and if it was important, they would turn up and ask for the photographs. You see? So I put them on my table in the hallway. And, of course, being an old man, and having not much to do, I have, I admit, been looking for you; in fact, such was the impact of your photographs that I have been, well, you might say I have been scouring the streets for you. We have both, my wife and I, been hoping that you would come here and ask for them, but I . . . I have been hoping rather more than she has. In fact, I can admit to you, that your pictures have been the cause of some little disharmony in our tranquil household, such has been my, ah, concentration on the task of reuniting you with your missing envelope. So you see, I am at the same time pleased but a little sad also that you've come. It is the end of an era. A small era, I grant you, but my life is made up of small things, and not many of them are as attractive and—'

Mila knew that tears were streaming from her eyes, she found either the sky to look at, or the pavement. His hand arrived on her shoulder and gave her a little shake of encouragement, optimism. 'So you see?' he persisted. 'The pictures have been waiting for you, and now you have been very clever, in working out what happened, and so come, yes, and fetch them yourself, it will be my privilege . . . will you come?'

Anjali and Mila were escorted back across the road. The old man was on one side, Anjali on the other, as Mila climbed the steps which previously she'd seen Jon Rawle sitting on – the ghost of him was malevolent, incredible. The key was found to unlock the door; meanwhile she stared at the spot where the cup had been placed on the step, she stared until her vision swam. Then the door was open and they were inside. The old man walked to the bottom of the stairs and barked, 'Puis, les photos!' After a while came a woman's voice, faint. He called again, more crossly,

'Oui, tu plait, les photos! Est ici. La trouvé!' Then he turned to them. 'My wife will bring them down. Come, come in.'

They passed through to the front room, plumply furnished in hues of green and lined with columns of black and white portrait photographs. He steered them to a sofa and she felt herself sink into an unbelievable softness, Anjali next to her. 'My wife will bring the photos,' he repeated, peering at her anxiously. She was drying her eyes and feeling stupid, young. She didn't want the photographs. She wanted to go. But she realized he was being kind to her and she should make it all right for him. The old man was murmuring, 'I count myself very lucky indeed to meet the beautiful young girl who has so filled my imagination and . . . in whom I can't believe . . . there can be . . . should be . . . any reason for sadness—' Mila heard his voice through her tears, 'My dear, whatever's happened I hope can be put right, but if I can help in any small way . . . I hope you'll tell me.'

Yet, she couldn't say anything. She sat there, holding hands with Anjali. They had to get out of here. This was ridiculous. She was aware that he was moving around behind the sofa: she heard footsteps, the click of a latch, a soft fumbling of objects being moved.

Maybe she could just say, keep the sodding photographs? Then they could go. She met Anjali's eye. They had to get out of here.

Now Mila could hear his breathing – it had the difficult, uneven edge of old people, which she was familiar with from her father and uncles.

She was just about to say she wanted to leave, but he spoke first. She swallowed her words, let him go on. His tone was gentle, undemanding. 'When I was a young man, there was a singer known as Hutch.' She heard a slight squeak, and looked around to find he was bringing a stringed instrument, something like a guitar but smaller and bowl-shaped, across his knee. His fingers were on the strings. He wasn't looking at her, but instead at his instrument, that same affection crossed his expression. He went on, 'And he wasn't French, as I was, but he was brought up on a Caribbean island, a French colony, so we could pretend he was French, and he'd come out of New York, so we could assume he'd seen it all, and was right there, you know, at the birth of jazz. And he was beautiful to look at, so he had many lovers, both men and women. Among them, was your Noel Coward. He was just the sort of person, who can cheer anyone up. It will be a pale imitation of the great man's voice, but I hope you will receive . . . er . . . the spirit . . . I hope it will make you happy and cure all your ills.'

The old man now took up his position in front of the sofa. His shoes gleamed. He straightened his shoulders. 'It's a song by the Gershwins, called "High Hat". It actually tells you how to treat women, but I think it works better the other way around. It's how girls should treat boys . . . very definitely, high hat. With a certain carelessness, you know?' He was smiling at them. 'This is how it goes—' He neatly picked out one note, and began to sing: 'When a fellow feels, he has to win a girl . . . he will send them loads of flowers, tons of candy . . . no use stepping out that way, you can't win by treating her as if she wore a halo . . . what is my solution . . . you've got to treat them high *hat* . . . you'll win them like that—'

Mila really, really didn't want to hold his eye any longer, but she was trapped. What was going on? This old guy was singing to them, in his suit and shiny shoes, in this strange house in this foreign city where he'd been poring over her photographs for weeks? How weird was that? She was going to laugh, she really, really was going to laugh. Or cry even more. She nudged Anjali; they stood up and he immediately stopped singing. They stumbled through saying 'Sorry' and headed for the door, Mila pushed and pulled at the handle. Anjali stepped in and did it, they were out of the room and into the hall. It was cruel but they couldn't just sit there and be sang to . . . no way, that was too much. They fled.

She paused on the front step, glanced back, he was following, saying something. An old woman – his wife – was coming down the stairs carrying a large envelope. Vehemently the passion shot through Mila – she never wanted to see those pictures. The worst of it was, Nio had paid for them. She slammed the door shut and these two flights of thought, one attached to Nio and the other attached to Jon Rawle, one good, one bad, were complicated ropes of feeling that wound her, practically tripped her down the half dozen steps, away from the house. Anjali took her hand, she was grateful for that. Behind her, she heard the door open, and the old guy called out to her, 'Good luck!'

Nio walked the familiar route to work; it was the first time he'd gone back since he'd lost Mila. Yet, he might just see her among the people on this street. He counted faces one by one, so he wouldn't miss her. The occupants of the cars that sluiced past were checked also, the mums and their children travelling to school, the executives in their fleet cars, the working men and women in their trade vehicles, the buses which were now sophisticated enough to curtsy at the bus stops to allow older passengers an easier step – all these people Nio grazed conscientiously, the anguish and panic had solidified now, he made this a solid march through as many people as possible. She was somewhere and he only had to look at every person in the world to find her.

He reached the Broadway. From here he followed the same route as when he and Nick, the photographer, had hauled Pegasus up Colney Hatch Lane, all those months ago. To walk, now, was different. In both knees lived a dense ache. A blister had grown under his big toe and so each step on that side was squeezed with pain. He'd put in so many miles in the last couple of days. He'd walked to the Middlesex Hospital, to the Royal Free, to the Hackney General. He'd walked to police stations in Bounds Green, Barnet, Muswell Hill, Camden, Hampstead, Golders

Green, East Finchley, Wood Green, Tottenham. He'd criss-crossed the common ground in Highgate Wood, Hampstead Heath, Regents Park, Coldfall Wood, Golders Green Cemetery and he'd walked the Camden canal network as far as Hackney in the east and Edgware Road in the west. Nothing doing. Now it was important to carry on working, he had to pay for their flat, keep that dream going, number seventeen, make it a lucky number, and he had to set himself up for the long haul, stabilize his finances so he could afford to carry on looking for her.

As he passed the doctor's surgery he could see the backs of the patients seated there, waiting for treatment, their figures diffused through the net curtains. His eye ran along them and there was one who, possibly . . . He ducked sideways and sloped up the wheelchair entrance which turned back and forth, incongruous in front of the converted Edwardian mansion house. He queued at the receptionist's desk and when his turn came he received the same puzzled smile as before. 'I was wondering, if—'

The receptionist's expression broke, she remembered who he was, why he'd come here several times before. She leaped to answer his question. 'No, no sign of her, I'm afraid.' She was always sympathetic but thought he was mad, she was just trying to get rid of him. Maybe she hadn't noticed . . . He nodded his thanks and turned to go, but then couldn't give up, he took advantage of the amount of people, the goings on here at the receptionist's desk, to slip past their guard and into the waiting room. Now, from the front he could view the same people he'd seen from the street – he could tick them off – none of them was Mila.

He left and took up his walk to work. His former happiness haunted him. There was the phone box from which he'd called to tell her about his new job. How untroubled he'd been, not long ago. The freshness of his success had been rubbed off him in just a few hours by this disaster, and by the constant work, the task of finding her.

Mrs Ginsberg's house stood as confident as ever among this row of senior residences. Here – this was where Mila had turned up, this was the door she'd knocked on, the bell she'd rung so many times, they'd made love for the first time here, and subsequently, again and again. The glass in the windows was clean and glossy, the white-painted door fresh and inviting. Mrs Ginsberg's kindness and appreciation of his work brought a lump to his throat suddenly, the acceptance – no, more than that, the value she put on him – was now so much more needed, maybe with it he might kick free of the exhaustion, find the energy to keep going . . .

Ahmed drove fast down the tunnel of light shot by his own headlights. The road was a grey floor described by white lines which slashed past. The engine noise was no louder than a sigh in this protected, high vehicle. Beside him the verge stretched wide to protect the privacy of the houses set alongside the main arterial route, but with no other traffic it felt to him that the extra width was granted to allow him through, it was a measure of his importance. The steering wheel was fat, confident in his hand. The seat was up to his weight. He veered left from the A1 to the A406 North Circular Road and climbed fast through the brickwork tunnel where the speed cameras often lay in wait. At the crest of the hill he cranked some more fuel to the intake and the acceleration caught him in the back, he poured down the slope to enjoy the sway of the corner, how it carried him, tested the grip of the Shogun on the damp surface. His finger sought the stubby volume control for the CD player mounted on the steering column and he prodded up the music until his head was lifted off. The strange romance of the road took him over, he felt the trance beckon, he could drive for ever. As if by magic the fuel would keep loading in, the tyres stay freshly cut, the oil at the precise level, he would never be tired. The music carried him further into the idea and he felt his eyes smoking with wanting it. What was he running from, that was so terrible? He had his own business, his wife and children that he loved, the motor of his dreams, some money in his pocket, yet if he could pull back on this steering wheel and the whole thing lift off, he would do it . . . he put his foot down further and felt the engine bite into another chunk of power. The high vehicle rolled but kept solid on its line as it swooped past Tesco's, under the bridge, towards the Retail Park. He gave his H-frame steel warehouse barely a glance as he pushed for the tunnel, the engine noise suddenly bouncing off the walls as the green eye of the traffic light drew him on. He crossed the junction in a satisfying rush, blowing past slower vehicles and rolling eastwards. There was no destination, no end game, he would just continue. He was impatient through the surfeit of junctions that littered the North Circular at this point and only regained his trance when he was out the other side, with four lanes almost empty of traffic, so he could try out every one just for the sake of it. Then he shifted leftwards to catch the M11 slip road which lifted him a clear 50 yards off the ground so he flew towards the motorway. He descended, tracked the opening left hand corner at speed and then settled into a steady 110 m.p.h. zoom up the M11, he stuck it right there with the cruise control. He thumbed the volume button again to lift the music above the rush of noise. Where was he going? Somewhere beautiful, it felt like. There was the strongest sense of purpose in him, but no destination. It was the journey itself, that was the point. The flight, to be carried along . . . He reached the M25 and swung left. He felt like a powerful bird, a raptor capitalist type of bird, circling his nest with his two children and wife asleep, while he kept guard.

On the M25 the magic of his flight was slowly diluted by the presence of too many other cars. He began to come down to earth. He was not any type of bird, he was a Turkish man well over halfway through his life, his family was the same as anyone else's, part of the crush of citizens – all numbered, tabulated and well-organized souls so densely packed in London. His car was the same as everyone's, the paths he trod were well trammelled, apparently devoid of choices. He could do nothing but take the A1 south, his mood descending, a cloud that would envelop him. It was this he'd been driving to escape from and for a while it had worked, he'd had anything he wanted.

As the familiar log of exit roads unwound towards his own, he felt his strength wind down. His girth was a mound in front of him, on which sat, almost, the steering wheel and he felt all his desires weakened by his old, overweight body. He slowed for his exit, but then pictured his house, the front door, everything inside in its proper place. He couldn't go back now, without anything to show as a reason for having taken such a ridiculous journey. He could feel the sense of loss waiting for him there . . .

No, he decided he wouldn't go home, instead he'd go to the warehouse and work, for a while. So he didn't take the familiar exit; instead he started the same circle again, this time slower on the North Circular, punctuating his speed according to the lights, the speed traps, the energy conserved just to arrive. He checked the time as he passed through the new brickwork tunnel and it wasn't too late, he screwed back around the slip road to greet East Finchley and visit the off-licence for a bottle to take in with him. Then, he'd settle to his inventory and achieve something, so he might return home with some progress around the loop of tasks that came back to him again and again, month after month . . .

Here were pedestrians, traffic lights every hundred yards, shops . . . suddenly there was a figure standing in the road right in front of him and he cursed, gripped the wheel hard, stood on the brake with all his might, gritted his teeth. He could feel the ABS thudding under his foot, the brake pads grabbing all four discs and then letting them go a hundred times a second. The weight of the car, his weight, every loose particle, was thrown towards this figure which he saw with disbelief was standing there, watching him and not making any effort to get out of the way. He couldn't veer right because there was an oncoming car, he couldn't go left because the row of parked vehicles would catch him and throw him sideways, out of control, and he'd swipe this mad pedestrian. He banked on keeping straight and boiled the hydraulic oil in his brakes.

He came to a halt with the stranger taking an audacious step towards him, even, steady as a rock. Ahmed stared. It was a young man, in a disgusting state. A cowl covered his head, which gave him the air of a Hallowe'en ghoul. His face was white and insolent and unshaven in Ahmed's headlights, half of it covered with a tattooed spider's web. The trousers hung shambolic and torn from his hips.

Ahmed elbowed the door and jumped from his seat. The shock had wrung him out like a sponge; he was sweating copiously. 'Hey!' he called as he walked around to the front of the vehicle. 'You, what an idiot, what you doing, you can kill yourself, go ahead an' kill yourself any way you want, man, but don't do it on my time, not with my car, you understand, go kill yourself by yourself, instead of trying to take a load of other people with you, I could have had my family with me, I could have gone into another person and boom—' – Ahmed clapped his hands violently – 'I'm dead too. And I have the wife and kids, you know. So fuck off.' He waved his hands at the young man, who remained motionless. Then he climbed back into the vehicle. By the time he'd buckled himself in, the youth was still there, maintaining his stance. Ahmed cursed and waved, 'Get out of the way, you wanker, you mad or what?' He glared from behind the windscreen. Was this going to be an auto-theft, was the guy after his car? What sort of person was it, who could paint a spider's web across half their face? And then stand in front of moving vehicles? It was drugs, wasn't it? This was an addict. Ahmed unclicked the handbrake, pulled the stick back into reverse and rolled the heavy vehicle backwards as far as he could until stopped by the car behind him. He was already spinning the steering wheel to drive around the addict when he turned to look forwards again and discovered that the man was now standing even closer, an inch in front. The difference was, Ahmed had no room left to manouevre. He shouted, 'You fucking wanker!' and pulled the stick into gear. He lifted his foot off the brake just a fraction, enough to push the youth, show him who was boss. These fucking addicts . . .

There came a bang at his side window and he recoiled. He saw another face, an angry girl, another druggy type, she was slapping the window with the palm of her hand, must be a friend of the addict. He lifted his foot another fraction. He had to barge his way out of here. There was a chance his vehicle would be damaged and he didn't want to lose the no claims bonus on his insurance policy. The car crept forwards, with the tattooed youth pushing against the front and the angry girl banging at the side. As he picked up speed to a walking pace Ahmed saw someone else, it was *her*: that girl, the gypsy or whatever, she was standing on the pavement watching, her arms folded tightly against the chill night. Her face was a glare of white in the headlights from the car behind him and her eyes were bright, anxious, as she looked at him, inching forwards every time the vehicle moved; then she called to her friend, warning her to come back to the safety of the pavement. Ahmed braked, stared at her. What was happening – his blood chilled – was this an attack on him to exact revenge for Ahmed's having helped tow her family off the site? Or was it just a coincidence? He felt a crazy need to escape. Everything was at risk. He set the vehicle forwards again, pushing the youth with the spider's web mask. As he slid past there was a shout, a curse, then he was given one last glimpse of the girl on the pavement – her strained white face didn't look like a child's any longer, it was pinched, angry – before he was gone.

Adrenalin sweated from his body as he bowled the heavy Shogun eastwards along the North Circular and peeled off at the Retail Park slip road. He veered hard left at the roundabout, charging 100 yards before wheeling the vehicle around the hairpin and into the car park. He thumped the speed bumps as usual, his headlights bouncing upwards at each hit, and then he lifted his foot from the accelerator to idle along the bottom edge of the vast, empty concrete square. He had the pick of any parking space he wanted. Outside the warehouse he came to a halt, switched off the engine and sat quietly in the silence. The interior lights came on automatically for a minute or two, but then went out. The engine of the Shogun ticked, cooling. The odd spate of cars raced past on the North Circular, unleashed by the traffic lights on the other side of the hill. He waited for a minute, then went inside.

For some hours he worked like a dog crunching numbers on the Excel spreadsheet, adding up, taking away. Inventory, sales, turnover, profit. So – as it happened – he was there, when they came first thing in the morning and invaded the building. Ahmed was pinned in a corner and told what was happening: he was being raided by Customs and Excise. He swore blind, waved his arms, but there was nothing he could do, there were too many to thump them all. They carried out boxes and boxes and loaded them into the back of the white Transit van which was parked outside. The dreaded VAT! It was those fake Searsons invoices, someone had squealed on him, there'd be fines to pay. It was the frigging Customs and Excise, he was done for.

Lucas Tooth was a shadow moving through the sodium-yellow cast of night-time Muswell Hill. This street – packed with young families – was asleep. His footsteps were silent. As he moved, the houses' radar picked him up and porch lights sprung to life, to defend themselves against him. Minutes after he'd passed by they switched off, the state of alert was over; the cars safely ensconced in off-street parking were returned to the dark. There was a slight gradient through an S-bend; unseen Lucas unwound from the side of the street, his figure a romantic spectacle in the middle of the road. He halted because suddenly a fox trotted ahead of him, mangy and lopsided in its gait. Lucas followed; he was a different animal, but of similar inclinations. Both tracked up the middle of the road, forbidden territory during daylight hours. He gained the pavement on the other side, ready to join Alexandra Park Road which carried steady traffic all night. The fox had disappeared. A profusion of ivy overhung a slatted wooden fence; he broke the pattern of its shadow as he moved alongside.

Then he stopped, because ahead of him there was a figure, watching for him. He didn't feel threatened immediately because it was a girl. She was a darker shadow than he was, she was coloured . . . Lucas took another pace or two and now he could see her face, he recognized the Asian sister, the one who'd talked so much that he'd become bored and . . . she'd run away.

She must have friends with her, to be this confident. Sometimes the mothers and the sisters could turn on him, however good the threats he made, the visits to their homes. She might have recruited men to come with her; it had been known, when his power over them was slipping . . . He could do without a revenge attack. He turned and walked back the way he'd come, casting left and right, ready for someone to run at him. He could hear the soft pad of her footsteps following him down the street. What made her so confident, brave enough? Maybe she had a gun. He knew how to shake her off, in this particular section of street, but it entailed some risk. Yet, to run full pelt might draw attention to him. Instinctively, he mapped the area – the hidden paths through gardens, down alleys, through fences . . . and not least the other mothers, the other sisters whom he controlled, who'd let him in . . .

Another figure was standing in the road – in front of him. He couldn't see who it was but he recognized the trap – one behind, one in front. No wonder her confidence. He was being chased into a hole, needed a way out. He swerved, trotted across the road and without hesitation walked through the glare of the porch light up to number 109, threw his foot against it where the cross bar met the jamb and burst the lock. He walked in, closed the tattered door behind him. He searched for bolts, for chains – anything to close it. There was a bunch of keys on the hall table; he snatched them up and tried one key in the Chubb lock, but it didn't work. Then the next key . . . no. With his other hand he fiddled the chain on.

When the Chubb slid across, he knew he was safe for a while. He checked the bunch of keys – ycs, there was a car key. He turned it in his hand, looking for the marque printed in the plastic key fob: Renault.

He trotted upstairs. The staircase turned back on itself. He gained the uppermost landing and turned left, walked into a bedroom. He had to float through a greater depth of darkness in here, trusting to find his way to the timid fluorescence showing around the edges of the curtains. As he went his pupils dilated, he could see. He inched aside a curtain and looked down on the street below. Two girls were there, heads together, talking. He looked for a Renault – there was a green Clio, three cars down.

Behind him, he heard a gasp and the sudden snap of bedclothes. He turned around and in two strides caught the sister's wrist at the bedside lamp. He cautioned her, put a hand over her mouth to stop her scream. He murmured instructions. He pointed two fingers at her forehead, pushing gently until her head lowered to the pillow. Then he put her arm down. She lay as if hypnotized.

He moved to the wardrobe and started pulling out clothes. He chose a dark rollneck pullover and swapped his jacket for it. The sleeves were too short, but otherwise the wool stretched enough to fit. He pocketed her car keys and left the room, trotted downstairs and scouted the double doors which led to the garden. He found the key on the ledge and wound the locks open. The garden stretched for forty feet – there was a children's playhouse hidden at the bottom by a screen of foliage. Lucas made for this screen and used it to climb over the fence. He dropped into a tangled, dense wilderness; the garden this side hadn't seen any work for years. He crouched low, and for a moment kept still, listening. When he was satisfied there was no threat, he ducked through the vegetation, clawing a path. A short distance before the cover disappeared he stopped again. Ahead of him was an oblong of rough, hummocky ground – untended garden. From here he would run across, climb the flat roof over the back extension and cross to another property, before dropping into an alley and filtering on to Colney Hatch Lane. He might or might not double back and borrow the Renault.

There was neither sight nor sound of anyone in the back extension. He inched forwards and waited on his hands and knees at the edge of the clearing, utterly still. There was a danger that wakeful neighbours might look from their upstairs windows and see him walking across the garden and climbing the roof. Yet – even so – there was not much risk, he wasn't breaking in, he'd be gone before any of them managed to call the police. He got to his feet and walked calmly. He'd taken one step before he was aware of a blur of movement from his left and he was already hiving off fast when the blow hit him across the shoulder. A bolt of pain slotted in his right side and he was on the ground. He moved quickly, he was up and accelerating when the second blow caught him on the back of his head, there was no pain this time just the internal shock of concussion, a thud he heard – a vibration – and his eyesight blurred. The ground flew towards him, every instinct was telling him to run, but it was as if he'd forgotten how his limbs worked. He lay on his back. Red hot pain burned in his skull suddenly and he couldn't turn his eyes to look anywhere else, so he was stuck with this someone appearing and standing over him, it was a man wearing a mask, or half a mask covering his face, a length of scaffold pole held like a sword in both hands and as he watched it lifted again, he knew it would come down on him and he wanted to close his eyes but couldn't, not even a blink, he'd lost contact with his body. There was a grunt as the man brought the sword down, it was a line coming towards him, straight down, very fast, the sword would kill him . . .

Adrenalin surged through his body, the same as when his heart alarmed itself, and he turned just in time, it was so close he felt the air swirl against his skin as the pole hit, thud, next to him, but he was already up, running the course. He wouldn't be caught.

Nio walked from Newton Avenue to the Clamp. Ordinary pedestrians seemed graceful, stately in their slow progress on this sunny, casual afternoon. Nio's disappointment – that none of them was Mila – was heavy, familiar, an old enemy . . .

As he pushed through Coldfall Wood, he wondered if the Clamp would still be there. Each time he went to check on it, he expected it to have been dismantled. So it was always with some trepidation that he unsnagged the wire, stepped through the fence. As he wriggled along the path he told himself to think it would be gone, this time. He rounded the last screen of vegetation and saw – it was still there. He stepped over the graves and tugged on the nail. The notice of demolition still warned him of what was meant to have happened, but the date had come and gone, he had no idea when they'd actually get around to doing it.

His first action as always was to check that the note he'd left for Mila – in case of her return – was undisturbed.

This place was like a ghost of their past, it stayed here, as if waiting for her. He went upstairs and crawled over the bed. For some minutes he lay with his hands behind his head, his phone on his chest, thinking about what he could possibly do next. The circular window was gone, a hole torn out of the building. From time to time the sun burned a fierce heat on his body as he lay there. He fell asleep for an hour and woke with the certain knowledge that something was wrong. A moment later he remembered what it was – he'd lost Mila. He didn't know which would bring a quicker result – go out and look for her, wait at number seventeen, or wait here . . .

He crawled to the hole in the wall and looked out over the thicket of vegetation which surrounded the Clamp. He listened hard – but there was neither sight nor sound of her.

He removed his boots, then his socks as well – they stuck to his skin at two or three points where sores had developed. On his right foot, the sharp corner of a toenail had chafed through the skin of the neighbouring toe and a tide of blood, dirt and sweat had flooded the area. At his heel, a column of broken skin showed raw and seeped clear fluid. The ball of his left foot, now, was growing a blister as well as the one under his toe. Both feet were hot, the arteries stood out, overworked. Unfamiliar lines were printed and the hairs pressed flat; his feet were strangers to him. They had to work so hard, to take his sorrowful weight and lift it forwards . . .and it was always the same questions that bore him along: *where* was she, *who* was that man who'd answered her phone, *what* had happened, *why* . . .?

Mila imagined phoning Nio a million times a day, but couldn't remember his number because when she'd called him before, on the phone she'd lost, she'd always speed dialled, number one, so she'd never learned it. He wouldn't be in any directory because he was pay-as-you-go. She remembered 17 Newton Avenue, it was only left to her to go up there and find him, if she could bear it. Several times she changed her mind, she was frightened of his reaction.

One tube and bus ride later, she stood at the door. Which flat was it? She tried to remember the message he'd left – had he said E? For a while she lacked the confidence to try, she even left and started walking back up the road but then she told herself to go back. There was no answer, anyway. She waited for a while, hoping that someone else would come to the house, or leave it, so she could ask them if Nio lived here.

Maybe it had been flat B. She plucked up the courage and pressed that button. The door was opened by a young guy, an Arab type with chocolate looks, whose eyebrows popped when he saw her and he grinned, showed massively white teeth.

She asked, 'Nio – I was looking for Nio Niopolous, who lives here, but maybe at . . .' – she pointed at the row of bell-pushes –'in flat E, or—'

'Who?'

'Nio Niopolous.'

'Yes,' said the boy, suddenly flinging up his hands, 'he lives there', and he pointed wildly to the whole house. 'Nio, yes.' His grin was pasted on his face, he was pleased with her.

'OK, thanks. I need to check, you know, but if he's not in, so I'll come back—'

'No, no,' said the boy quickly, 'come in with me, come and wait for him in my flat, we make you comfortable, you can wait, have coffee, wait until he come in comfort, promise, promise.'

'Is all right—'

'No, come in and wait for him, why go back? Why?'

'It's all right, no thank you,' she smiled at his efforts.

'Don' leave me,' he begged her, 'wait for him with me. We

both wait for him, we are both his friends, he wants us to wait for him—' He was smiling madly.

She shook her head, began to walk away.

He followed her. 'OK, then I tell you, is OK, you can wait in his place, inside his room, not with me, but I can let you in, all the keys are the same, you can wait for him anywhere you like, I promise . . .' He persisted, he followed her up the road, repeating over and over that all the keys opened any of the doors in that place, he could let her in to Nio's room.

He was so young and harmless and enjoying himself, Mila felt careworn and so, so tired, really exhausted – she wanted just to stop, to be in one place, and to be found by Nio. She accepted his offer – she'd wait in . . . which one was it? He'd show her.

They went back and she followed him up the stairs. When he unlocked the door to flat D, someone was already in it. They tried flat E and she saw immediately that this was it. The Arab guy thought his luck was in but Mila shooed him away and closed the door. She leaned back against it – and checked the room.

She walked forwards, staring. Yes – the bed was decorated with *fruit*. She walked over and looked more closely. She picked up a pear – and it slid from her hand, it was softened by the sun. A stain marked the sheet where it had sat. The grapes were wrinkled, shrunken. They'd been here for a week. She wandered to the clothes rack and was amazed to see some of her clothes. She couldn't believe it, how life had changed.

There was a knock at the door and her heart was in her mouth – was this him? – before she remembered he would have keys, he wouldn't knock. Sure enough it was the young guy again, who'd come to make sure she was all right. He came four or five times more during the next half hour, to offer her refreshments, conversation, anything. Eventually, maybe she'd put him off. She found the bathroom, and waited for ages for the bath to fill – and that was the best thing.

She was so, so tired. After her bath she went to the bed and lifted off the entire cover, fruit and all. She lay down and felt the blissful cool of the pillow. The spring sunshine baked her through the window and quickly sleep began to steal over her.

Her last thoughts were, Nio come home.

No, don't.

Yes, please come home . . .

Muswell Hill was under a cloudy London sky, that night.

Mila slept through until early next morning at 17 Newton Avenue. This house – fractured, divided to increase its capacity – squeezed her in. She was an exact fit in the lucky gap which had opened up in the space allowed to people in this city. Her shape while she slept was a foetal curve, her fingers grouped close to her mouth, eyelids shuttered and still, the brow smooth.

Anjali and Spider slept rough in Highgate Wood, a sudden switch from town to country living, they'd swapped their cardboard house in the concrete chamber underneath the South Bank arts complex for a children's den they found in these five acres or so of woodland much crawled over by families and dog-walkers in the daytime but at night deserted, a dangerous catchment area for lunatics, drug takers and the dispossessed.

Charmer snored carelessly in his old room at home, his feet sticking out the end of the child-sized single bed, the headboard decorated with the Pokemon stickers which had been his juvenile passion. His old stomping ground of the playing fields and Coldfall Wood and St Pancras Cemetery was a triptych of ground, moonlit, outside the window. Tomorrow he'd point the other way for once, away from his usual trails and into the urban sprawl on the other side of his parents' home, towards Alexandra Palace Road and the motorbike sales and repair shop – his first job.

Little Vlad found his corner at one end of the southbound Bakerloo line platform at Oxford Circus. His back against the wall, he used the protruding iron door which guarded the tube's electrical supply unit to avoid the platform's closed circuit TV camera, so he wasn't thrown out when the staff slid the barriers across the multiple entrances and exits at 2.22 a.m. Then he slid down the wall to a sitting position. Half an hour later he dozed with his head on his knees.

Ahmed was at home in Barnet, in a bed he'd bought from his own retail warehouse, floating in dreams, his wife moored alongside. He slept on his back, head canted back and to one side – the air moved in and out of his body easier that way. His arms lay outside the duvet, which held his body like a jelly in a mould.

Nio was in the Clamp, hands clasped behind his head, staring at the low ceiling. Each of those nails he'd hammered in himself. He could see their points wink in the moonlight. It occurred to him to count them, maybe it would break this spell of eternal wakefulness. But his visions of Mila were too dense, prevented him from sleep. Every ten minutes, he looked at his phone. Nothing.

When Anjali woke, the first thing she saw was the roof structure of the children's den in which they'd made their shelter for the night. Boughs of trees broken off in recent storms had been leaned on either side of the horizontal trunk of a fallen beech tree and closely woven with smaller branches. She'd woken because Spider was tugging at her clothes; she helped him. She heard birdsong – the dawn chorus. Underneath her, the ground was soft as a sponge, fibrous and damp from the countless years of accrued leaf litter. She was cold; a chill crawled on her legs as her naked skin met the air. Then Spider was hanging over her. She looked over his shoulder – early sunlight that had filtered through the trees already was split a second time by their rustic structure. She observed that the tendrils still attached to the displaced boughs were drooping, dried leaves clung on, they saddened her, so unvigorous, without life, when above them was a dense green canopy, new growth in which the birds sang. The death of those withered branches had been a slow thirst and Anjali felt sharply the answering need – she herself wanted a glass of cold, clean, fresh water . . . She remembered there was a tap by the children's playground, they'd used it last night.

Spider's movement against her was familiar now, she was shunted, his rhythm was like a jog as he ran towards his orgasm. Her clothes were rucked, the discarded trousers hung on one ankle, it was enough to make her laugh, like a childhood dressing up game had gone wrong and she was trying to escape, her brothers were there . . . with a lunge she felt the old affection for their games. The ground beneath her was on a slant and Spider's movement edged her downhill an inch at a time; just now it put her in the way of a spray of sunlight and she squinted to catch sight of the spores of some plant bouyant, their movement as if mite-sized moths were entranced in the beams. The warmth was a blade across her brow, she wanted its caress over her whole body. She closed her eyes. On this slope, her head was filling with blood, she could feel her own pulse in the nerves in her teeth, her body was rubbed by the movement, the ground was naked under her hands as she clung on. Then she opened her eyes again, took his head and lifted it from her shoulder to check. No – he was concentrating on his journey. *Eyes Wide Shut* – she remembered the title of the film. She didn't mind that much, she just wanted to make the journey with him . . .

She wrapped her arms around his neck and her legs around his body and clung on, she squeezed tight, she whispered 'Shhh—' over and over, as much to herself as to him, she wanted to stop all her thoughts, to quieten to a perfect silence, to have peace arrive on a breath of air, and sunlight draw its lines over them, hold them fast . . .

Spider's movement slowed, stopped. His breathing was shallow. She stroked the back of his head. His chin, gritty with stubble, was buried in her neck. Everywhere there was abrasion – against the ground, against their clothes, the still comic interference of her trousers hanging off one ankle; only at the joint where they were coupled was it smooth, the science-fiction act of sex . . .

His breath was heating her shoulder, his weight increased, pressed her into the earth. She felt for his head, gripped hard and again lifted it from her shoulder until it was square between her and the sun. His eyes were closed, yes. Inside this bony carapace of his skull was the machinery of his brain, she wanted to live his thoughts, not only know what they were but feel their genesis, where they'd come from, the individual kernel of truth he'd built for himself at his very core, that would control his chemistry, determine his actions and reactions. She checked the details of his face: the softened edge of the tattoo over his brow, between his eyes, down his nose and dividing his mouth, chin and neck, the crop of stubble on his jaw, the skin pitted with imperfections and grained with dirt. She wondered if he was holding his breath. She took her hands away.

There was a clatter of wings from a tree overhead, suddenly, but then the birdsong dropped to nothing, a mysterious silence followed. She stared so hard at Spider, she was tripped into asking something of him for the first time, she had to demand, 'Open your eyes? Mmm? Go on . . . you ugly old brute.' She slapped him lightly on the side of his head.

The silence held; then as if a switch had been thrown, he did open his eyes. She saw into the grey-blue irises, muddy and aggrieved, and felt love quicken inside her, there was the sense of a door opening. He started to move again, but held her gaze, frowning . . .

She would invite him to meet her parents – they would really, really hate him. Her smile broadened as Spider moved her over the ground . . . inch by inch . . . eyes open, looking at her. She felt delirious, she went with him.

When Mila awoke, at 4 a.m that same morning, she saw

shadows. A ceiling, painted white. The bed was strange – square and firm underneath her. The window was huge, a pane of glass clear as water. Outside, the street lights cast their orange, fuzzy light. She'd slept through the previous afternoon and nearly all night. At first she didn't know where she was; then she remembered. Nio had been here. He'd prepared for her arrival, this was meant to be their new place, but she'd never come. Now it was deserted. The fruit on the bed . . . In this room he'd left his love for her behind. It had gone stale, like a past way of life laid out for display in a museum. When she stood, she realized she was still in the same clothes. The recent past – her ascent back to Muswell Hill with Anjali and Spider – came back to her and she pored through the events – the old man singing, the near accident with Spider, their revenge, finding this place, the young guy who kept on trying to help, she'd had a bath, then she'd fallen asleep, a total wreck – and woken up not much better. She smeared her hair back. God – she was hungry, she was sad, she didn't know where anyone else was, she had no phone. Nio hadn't come back – where was he? She wandered, touching where Nio had touched. She felt the want in her worse than hunger, to turn back the clock. It was sick-making.

Without her phone, she couldn't think what to do next. It was the calls she had with people that controlled her toing and froing. Her pockets felt light, empty, without the mobile. Any time it had been on the charger, her whole life had had to wait, she'd closed down and recharged, herself.

She wandered the room, made and discarded several plans. See if Nio was at the Clamp? No. It must have been knocked down by now. Wait here. She didn't know what was best. She wished she'd learned Nio's number, instead of having it on speed dial. He would have his phone ready for her, she knew that. The next moment she wanted to run, she was ashamed and scared to tell him, or show her face, he wouldn't want her.

Where was Little Vlad? She needed to put a finger on everyone, friends and everyone, wind herself back into her life if possible. The city was lonely, its crowdedness made her smaller with each person less she could touch on . . . She remembered when her group had first arrived in this country, it was on Christmas Day, they'd been dropped off at a garage forecourt on the M2, and after waiting for some hours they'd been offered a police escort back to Dover, but then after all, it seemed they were too many, so they were requested to make their own way back and report to the authorities there. The disappointment tasted bitter. If there had only been a few of them, they would have got a lift. That's what she wanted again now, a police escort to take her to her life. A British policeman would be able to put her back on the rails.

There came a soft knock at the door. She stopped pacing and stared. For one crazy moment she thought this must be the policeman, come to fetch her. Then she checked her watch – it was five in the morning. Could it be Nio? But he had keys, he wouldn't knock. She stepped forwards to open the door.

A few miles from Mila, Ahmed awoke in his Barnet semi-detached home. The first thing he saw was the back of his wife's head. A swatch of her dense, curly back hair – as if seeded and growing from the crack between pillow and duvet – looked dusty and lifeless, now that she was older and turning grey. A thought occured to him – her hair wasn't attached to a body, his wife had disappeared and left it behind. He could pick it up and fling it to the other side of the room . . .

As he lay there, he tried to guess the fine he'd receive for evading VAT. How did they compute the fine, over and above the amount he'd avoided paying? Would he have to pay their legal costs? He'd been making good progress, now he was about to be carried way back. He wasn't going anywhere, not now. Not even in a circle. Merely slipping. He visited that sharp, sour area of his mind where his lies were harboured, always available to pick over.

Oof! He'd like to have them all sink without trace, but they never would be gone.

An alarm bell woke Charmer. His eyes opened on his childhood bedroom, cheap as a cardboard box. For a second, he asked himself some urgent questions about the alarm – his reflex was to think it was his mum trying to get him to go to school, then he remembered he had a start, that was the answer, his mum had played the same trick today as she tried back then, coming into his room like Father Christmas except to leave an alarm clock, but now for this work ethic, not the school ethic. Charmer, a job? Impossible thought. He felt the usual twinge in his guts when he sat up. He'd always told himself before that it was nausea, after all wasn't it a sick world, no wonder the yawning pit in his belly, it was only rational, but now, as he sat here on his childhood bed, half dressed in yesterday's clothes, confused with sleep and the alarm pip-pipping away, it came to him, that wasn't what it was, at all. The sickness was his own fear, he was generally afraid. And he couldn't be doing with that, Charmer couldn't be afraid surely, it went against the grain, he was going to lift out of it, he was.

Little Vlad had woken but hardly noticed the difference, it was possible that he slept with his eyes open. In any case, now he wandered back up the southbound platform and made his way up the first set of steps signed 'No Exit'. He turned left at the top of the stairs and level with his ankles he could see through the ironwork grille the roof of the train streaked with dirt sliding past and the rumble of its weighty labours shook the brickwork, reverberated in his chest. He went and found her, she was standing in her usual corner where the streams of people divided at the bottom of the escalators. She had the guitar around her neck, her chin cocked in the air, swaying from side to side as she sang, the usual long dress awash around her ankles. Little Vlad sat nearby and listened. He watched the coins fly in like a flock of exhausted birds to inhabit the dark, mossy landscape of the old coat which lay folded in front of her. Often she'd given him some of those coins, or something to eat, when she'd finished; now it was his turn to pay her back, because he still had some money left over.

Nio couldn't sleep. In the dead of night, he was visited by his worst fear – that Mila might be dead . . . killed by that voice, *'she's just left—'* The thought of it sent a spasm of energy through his frame. He crawled to the hatch and let himself downstairs. It was almost pitch dark. Silence hung about. He switched on the lantern torch and set it on the table, he was on the edge of its eerie circle of light. He wished Charmer was here – it felt lonely in the woods, like in the middle of a fairy tale. The graveyard was a stone's throw away and as always, since her disappearance, its huge acreage, its thousands of dead and forgotten, mockingly signalled everyone's mortality. Yes, she was dead . . . in the darkness he could feel the truth of that, but knew he should ignore it. He found a piece of paper – the back of a letter sent to him from some assurance society, they were arriving at Mrs Ginsberg's, now he had a credit card. On it he wrote to Mila, it was just idle stuff, what he'd been doing. It occurred to him that he'd buy a diary and write to her every day, as if he were talking to her. It would give her a place in his life, a time. When he found her, there wouldn't have been such a break, he'd just hand her the diary. Maybe she was doing one for him, somewhere. He filled the page, then stored it carefully in his pocket. He wanted the thread unbroken.

Once again he called her number. There was always a slight hope alive in him that she might answer, but as before the system switched him to her message service. He listened to the timbre of her voice, its thick accent, wondering what had happened and who the man was, who'd answered instead of her. He left another message – told her this was what he was doing – just letting his voice sink into her, wherever she was, it gave him life, hope, kept his love safe . . .

An hour later Nio felt tired again, he was slow with disappointment. He climbed back up to the bedroom and into bed. Sleep circled closer, he was drawn in eventually. It was a downward spiral, he fell to the very depths. There in his ragged and disconnected dreams he'd found a house named after her, its doorplate a cut of slate engraved with a jaunty, italicized '*Mila*'. Someone unseen called out the name and a dog stopped, one paw up, its head sharply swung around to answer. A gaudy bird printed flat on the pages of a textbook had a phonetic description printed alongside – Mee-lah. A mauve flower bloomed with impossible profusion within its host of dark greenery – named after her. Nio was dragged through these namesakes; he had to follow whether he liked it or not.

Mila, yes, decided to answer the knock and pulled open the door. She found the boy from downstairs standing there – again. 'Sorry,' he said, 'I heard your footsteps and I was worried because it is the middle of the night and—' He smiled.

She interrupted, fought him off, pushed him. So many boys – they were always in the way. The smiling and friendly ones were the worst. Such an intrusion when it was so early in the morning was sinister, it made up her mind – she couldn't stay here. She wouldn't bother to find out if there was any food – she just took a crust of bread that was lying on the table and left. Downstairs she dreaded that she might be locked in, but there was only a Yale, she let herself out. The night was empty and quiet. It would still be dark for some time. The cold made her shiver. She walked from Barnet to Muswell Hill, light as air, no phone, no bag. Yet she was heavy, she felt an extra weight transfer through her heels to the pavement below. She wouldn't slow down, she had momentum, a sort of emotional gravity pulled her. The darkness began to lift.

*

Nio was held by his sleep, gently. He was in an empty and deep space, each thought was a bright star, useful and interesting but too far away. He floated in this emptiness, the sensation was like being in the middle of a yawn. He desired those distant thoughts, wanted to travel and arrive at them, but it was impossible – how would he get back? He just had to live with the hope of their coming to him . . .

The sweethearts found each other, early that morning.

Mila expected the Clamp to be gone but found it still there – as if it were waiting for her, she thought – and it gave her a sudden burst of hope. She stumbled hurriedly over the graves. Then she wasted a full minute just standing with her hand on the nail, plucking up the courage to pull open the door. Tears streamed down her face. She couldn't do it. She walked away, then came back – she had to switch off that voice inside her head and simply go in; pushing away all thoughts she did just that, and climbed the steps, crawled over the bed calling his name, took his shoulders; Nio heard it, the voice insisted in his dream world. He looked around but no image was there, it was just black around him, but the sound of his name wound him upwards like he was riding the groove of a screw, he came out of his tiresome sleep and still heard his name, a figure was leaning over and calling him, there was a scent, and at his shoulders hands were tugging him. When all these sensations joined up he knew it was her; Mila had come back. A cry rose from his belly, it seemed like the noise issued without air passing through his throat, it was a ghost of itself – as she might yet prove to be a ghost, but he felt the solid, recognizable girl, her body was like a slender blade in his hands. He pulled her close and wrapped her in his arms; her feminine grace and youth were an instant blessing.

She was crying silently, telling herself over and over that he wouldn't want her any more if she told him what had happened, she was so stupid and ashamed, all it would do was push him away, kill his love for her, she had to be ready for that.

There was the sound of their conjoined breath as they embraced each other, neither could trust themselves to speak. Inch by inch there sank into Nio's very core the one thing he'd so missed since her disappearance, the raw element which refuelled his desire and told him over and again that his love for her was rational and true, and which was so intoxicating – his ecstatic belief in her. Yet, there was this terrible panic which poured through him as he asked, 'What happened?' He sounded angry, he didn't mean to but knew his fright and impatience made it come out like that.

Mila took his face in her hands. 'If I tell you, you will not want me,' she insisted.

'I want you now, I don't care—'

She could guess from his voice that he must have guessed, more or less. 'You will not want me,' repeated Mila, 'but promise you come and find me, one day. Do you promise?' She burst into tears, she tore free of him, pulled back. 'One day soon?!' she cried.

He called back, 'It won't—' but she fled. Lighter and quicker than him, she'd left the Clamp by the time he'd got to the stairs; while he was still calling her name he heard the door banging. He pulled on clothes, hurried after her, but clambered too fast through the hatch and so lost his footing, and because there was no banister he fell off the side of the steps and was forced to jump, he landed awkwardly, his ankle folded, he was in agony. He held his foot, literally watched it swell in his shoe.

Mila weaved through the graves as fast as she could, not quite sure now which was the right path but knowing that if he cared enough he would come after her, for sure. The first rays of sun were clipping the tops of the trees, lifting them into brilliance. When she didn't find the railing after half a minute, then she knew somehow she'd taken a wrong turn, she was confused. She turned in every direction, listening to Nio's voice calling her name. Cold dread filled her. Why hadn't he run after her? Tears blurred her vision. She pressed deeper into the thicket; the graves loomed on either side, overgrown with ivy. Brambles spiked her path. She thought, maybe there was only a certain amount of love in the world, and she remembered as a child how she'd always stared at the solemn Cupid in the little painted wooden church which was like a dot on the slope of the hill outside the village – but maybe there was only one Cupid, whose duty it was to bring love to the whole world, and the poor exhausted thing had to visit so many, it could only alight on each heart for a shorter and shorter time, before moving on . . . and because Anjali and Spider had found their love, it meant hers and Nio's had suddenly faltered.

She kept going.

Three months later than the date advised by Haringey Council, over a two day period, Nio helped dismantle the Clamp, so there were four men in all on the job. With sledges and jemmies and five pound hammers they broke apart the roof, the walls and the floor and with gloved hands carried the timber and the broken glass out to a trailer parked the other side of the fence. By this time Nio had gained their confidence, so when they were done, on the last load, he retrieved the stove and the window – heat and light, heart and soul of himself and Mila – from their hiding place nearby. He carried them both to the trailer, and the Haringey contractors gave him a lift to 9 Methuen Park, where he stored them.